MALICE

MALICE

A NOVEL

L M SHAKESPEARE

HOPCYN PRESS

ACKNOWLEDGMENTS

My warmest thanks to Jonathan Pegg, my agent at Curtis Brown, for inspiration and detailed invaluable editing. Thanks are also due to Peter Day, whose idea it originally was to use the letters of Liselotte of the Palatine as the basis of a novel, and to my friend Lauro Martines, the distinguished historian and writer, for reading through my manuscript and for his encouragement and discriminating comments. My friend Verena Boggis Rolfe had a copy of a rare book on provincial France in the seventeenth and eighteenth century which she let me borrow for an inordinately long time, for which I am still grateful. My thanks are always due to my husband, David Evers, for his patient reading, inspired comments and enthusiasm. Roger Barnes, of Church Green Books in Witney, kindly slipped a copy of d'Auvergne's Famous Castles and Palaces of Italy into my bag without even telling me. It has been invaluable for the architectural detail of buildings encountered in this tale. Many thanks to all my friends who have given me advice and help, and to Hopkin for hours of companionship when I was writing.

For Peter Day
Distinguished bookman and indefatigable ally

HOPCYN PRESS
42 Russell Rd
London W14 8HT
Tel: +44 (0) 20 7371 6488
www.hopcynpress.com
Email: info@hopcynpress.com

ISBN 978-0-9570820-0-7

Printed in England
By MPG Biddles Ltd.
www.mpg-biddles.com

From *L'Indiscret* (I, i) by Voltaire

...à la cour, mon fils, l'art le plus nécessaire
N'est pas de bien parler, mais de savoir se taire...

Vous ne connaissez pas ce dangereux séjour;
Sur un nouveau venu le courtisan perfide

Avec malignité jette un regard avide,
Pénètre ses défauts, et, dès le premier jour,

Sans pitié le condamne, et même sans retour.
Craignz de ces messieurs la malice profonde.

· · ·

...at court, my son, the most important skill
Is not that of talking well, but knowing how to keep silent...

You are not familiar with this dangerous place,
And towards a newcomer the perfidious courtier

Mischievously casts a hungry eye,
To spot his weaknesses, and, from the very first day,

Without pity, and without a second thought, condemns him.
Expect the most intense malice from these gentlemen.

Translated L M S

CHAPTER ONE

The King said to me once, "It would not be appropriate for someone of your condition, Monsieur de Brisse, to have expectations." So I followed his advice. I lived unobtrusively in the seething magnificence of the court, not like a dog, because dogs were sometimes loved. More like a rat or a spider.

When I was still a child I lived in the country. It was a part of France where the chestnut trees are prolific, and my memory of it is overlaid with their enormous leaves, as if they had fallen in Autumn and buried that life, as they might cover the rotting body of a dog. It is not the sort of memory that one relishes the thought of disturbing, but I must do it.

To someone clean and well fed, destitution and misery, an empty stomach and a body abraded with sores and running with lice is outside the scope of serious, and certainly of fashionable, attention. And so I will not mention these details. I need only say that in a small family of peasants so poor and ignorant that it might seem that no human being could rank below them, I occupied the position of servant.

In addition, at the age of five I had three pigs to look after. If they ate, I ate, and I certainly never hoped to have better food than theirs. When I was cold in Winter I could get some warmth at night from sleeping among them. I remember the smell of their straw, their filth, and their rough warm hides that they would push against each other and against me for greater comfort.

In Winter my foster mother and her children and husband moved their quarters into the cow byre and slept at the far end to keep warm, but they wouldn't put up with the presence of the pigs, or of myself. They also had a field mattress filled with oats, but I had none.

This woman had been my wet nurse. I had no means of knowing at the time that she had expected me to be taken away after I was weaned, and that it was only their extreme poverty that persuaded her family to keep me. They were paid for it by my father, as I later discovered; a courtier in attendance on the King Louis XIV. What they were paid came with an exemption from taxes, so that it was worth double the amount it would have been if the collectors for the *Tailles* and the *Aides* had taken their share. But even so, every time they set eyes on me they cursed me, and crossed themselves. I understood that the reason for this was that I was exceptionally ugly.

At the age of six, without any explanation or warning, I was handed over at noon one day to the driver of a rough carriage which had been brought a league across country from the road. There was some discussion about whether to put me inside, or tie me to the outside, and because my rags were soaked in urine from the pigs they decided on the latter. My foster father demanded money, but at first he got none. He and my foster mother ran after the horses, and in the end the driver threw down a few coins.

They picked them up without responding to my cries, and my last view of them was with their heads bent together turning over what was in the palm of their hands.

It rained after an hour, and I was cleaned a little by the time we reached Paris. But at that point if I hadn't been tied down, I would certainly have leapt off the tumbril out of sheer terror at the sight of so many and such massive houses. Having lived in the country and seen nothing but mud hovels, I didn't even realise that these were houses built by men. I can just still catch, on occasion, the receding memory of how I first perceived them, with their fearful colossal fronts pierced with great orifices that I could not recognise as windows and doors.

The carriage crashed about in this maze of stone until it eventually came to rest and a woman who I had not known was travelling inside, got out and ran off. She returned with two other women and a man. They were all wrapped up in dark shawls and cloaks, but from inside these coverings their clothes made an extraordinary noise that I could not account for. I was not familiar with the loud rustle of silk and it added to my terror.

By this time it was getting dark again. The cords that had tied me to the box were cut and I fell to the ground partly because I was numb with the cold and from being bound so tightly, but also because, my legs being twisted and uneven, I could not get my balance. I cried out, and the driver hit me across the shoulders. I think one of the women was sorry, because she made as if to touch me, but plucked back her fingers in the air before actually laying them on my rags in a manner that was more expressive of how repulsive I was than if she had had no pity at all. So they all stared down at me in silence until I was able to stand, and then urged me across a paved yard, through a door into a passage way, and from thence to another and another.

At the time I could not understand how, while being indoors, a person could walk so far. And the staircases! For someone who had only once seen a ladder they were conjuring tricks and besides, in my condition I could not climb them at all well. My companions looked on with revulsion as I struggled upwards. No one made any move to touch or help me again, but I was too terrified not to do what they apparently expected.

Eventually I was thrust into a room and the door behind me was shut. I say a room now, but then I could not have identified it as such. It was not the sort of room that I had ever seen or heard of. It was more like another piece of appalling enchantment. Huge as a field, the glitter and colour made me sick, and moreover it was full of people; men and women who I could hardly recognise as being human when I compared them to what I was used to. Their clothes shone with gold and coloured silks, and their heads were decorated as if they were gods or demons.

At the sight of me there was a sudden silence. The nearest women drew back sharply, snatching at their skirts. And then they all, every one of them, either came from far away to look, or, being too close in their opinion, trod on the toes of those behind them in an effort to get away. I was left standing alone in the midst of them.

I was small, even for my age, and dressed in filthy rags that must have smelt and certainly were alive with vermin. I had a hunch back – and of course I still have – as well as a hare lip and legs which had grown, and continued to grow, unevenly. In a word, I was hideous. Even later, when I became familiar with the court and realised that there were many malformed in one way or another, I never came across anyone as ugly as myself. The second Dauphin was a hunch back. The Duc de Luxembourg had two. Almost all the King's children by Madame de Montespan were marked with some deformity or other from birth or small pox or that other disease that we called the anvil because of the way it refashions the shape of any person unlucky enough to survive it. But I was unique in combining so many deformities in one stunted, disfigured body.

As I stood there, twisted, filthy and alone, there was a sudden ripple of sound followed by renewed silence and the attention of all those around me was abruptly transferred to a man who entered the room from the far side. He said something and the people between myself and him drew back deliberately to expose me to his view. My gorge rose in terror and the next moment I think I would have thrown myself on the ground if something about the manner of this man had not stopped me.

I watched him – Louis XIV, the King of France – walk into the centre of the room until he could see me well. He was tall and handsome, and the majesty of his presence was remarkable. He came within a few paces until at last I found myself looking up at that magnificent being for the first time.

His face was composed in an expression of benevolence which did not leave it even when he saw me at close range. I was fully aware of how filthy I was, and how the wet from my nose and my eyes had blurred my vision and dripped into my mouth through my hare lip, and yet His Majesty looked neither angry nor contemptuous at the sight of me. This may seem a small matter to a normal person, but I assure you if it is the first time in your life that you have not aroused fear or indignation in a stranger merely by existing, you do not forget it.

Then he turned away; but in that moment he had given me courage. I stifled my sobs. I tried to wipe the slime off my mouth and chin with the palm of my hand, but cautiously, and listening meanwhile to try to catch the drift of what was being said.

The discussion that was going on was almost incomprehensible to me because the words and accent I was accustomed to bore almost no resemblance to the language used at court. But I now know that the lady who had me fetched from the country was a discarded mistress of my father, the Chevalier de Brisse, and her motive was to embarrass him; to be revenged on him by making him a laughing stock for having rejected her, only to father a monstrosity such as me with his legitimate wife, who had then died. That he had subsequently attempted to hide me away in the country, disowning his duty as a father and lying to his friends, was considered shocking.

Throughout the explanation that went on over my head I stood there silently looking up at the King. I found that if I looked at him I was less afraid.

Eventually he turned back to me. I paid eager attention, but this time I could not catch his eye. He looked at my rags and said that I must be made clean, and dressed in a way suitable to my rank as the son of a nobleman. He said that from then on I should live at court, as it was my right, by birth, to do. He later provided a small pension for my maintenance, as he did for those who came to court but had limited means. My father, it transpired, was not rich.

I never saw my foster family again, or my three pigs, or the kitten I was keeping near the well cover. Years later when I had to travel through that country I went leagues out of my way to avoid going near the particular piece of land.

And yet, the physical change in my circumstances did not satisfy me. As soon as my body was well fed my heart began to cry out for nourishment. I became aware, in a way that I had not been before, of the starvation of my affections. I felt my loneliness as I had never done in the country. In this country – 'ce pays ci' as those who lived there called the court – the apartments and passages thronged with people day and night, but no one except the gentleman the King appointed as my governor, ever spoke to me. And he very rarely. Everyone else, as soon as they got used to seeing me, ignored me. Often they seemed not even to see me. They spoke in front of me as if I were deaf, and even the gentleman who was apparently my father forgot eventually that I was anything to do with him, and would no longer blush if I was near by.

But my heart was not by any means always sad. I consoled myself with beauty and learning. There were books in the King's library that I taught myself to read. There were exquisite paintings and objects all about me, and conversations of wit, learning, or scandal to be overheard. Although it is not my intention to dwell at length on the years of transition when I became accustomed to court life, I did, of course, change. I was not befriended, but neither was I particularly tormented. I think I was simply too ugly. I learned to tolerate this really very well, and I became knowledgeable about the life at court and sometimes useful in ways peculiar to myself. It was thanks to this that about six years after my arrival, the most wonderful and fatal encounter of my life took place. You might say that I had already drained the cup of marvels for any mortal, in that having lived in squalor as a child, fortune had weaned me of that portion of my misery in such a spectacular way. But this was as nothing compared to what followed.

CHAPTER TWO

About a hundred years ago a Spanish adventurer called Niños de Cabaja wrote letters home to the King of Spain from a far country and I read a copy of one of them in the King's library. As a result of his experience Cabaja concluded that the moment when two strangers meet face to face for the first time epitomises the greatest drama of human life. I was very struck with this remark at the time, but remembered it when one meeting that transcended all others, and exactly confirmed the truth of what he said, changed my life.

It happened in Winter.

The Court then was at St. Germain. I was about twelve. The King had ordered the most magnificent celebrations to mark the marriage of his brother, Philippe Duc d'Orléans, to a German princess. I had as little knowledge of this German princess during the first days of her marriage celebrations as I had had of the Duc d'Orléans' first wife. This first wife had been the Princess Henriette – called Minette – who had died. It did not come naturally into the way of a mere child living at court, and certainly not one like me, to be in attendance on so great a lady, and so I scarcely knew her even by sight. The same would have been true of the second wife, but for the most extraordinary circumstance which I will relate to you.

The name of Philippe's second wife was Elizabeth Charlotte of the Palatine, and she was known by those who loved her best as Liselotte. She was nineteen at the time of this marriage. When I first saw her I was merely a spectator among the several thousand members of the court, and therefore it did not qualify as an encounter by the rules of our Spanish adventurer. In fact my memory scarcely differentiates between her and her attendant women, and I have a far more vivid recollection of the magnificence of Louis XIV and his brother that day.

The King and the Duc d'Orléans led the procession through the huge gates which were flanked with massive wrought iron braziers full of fire. The King wore the costume of the Rôi Soleil, with a golden oriole fixed around his head, while Monsieur, his brother, wore a jerkin of plum velvet embroidered with gold and silver thread, and under the jerkin a knee length coat of gold brocade fastened with gold braid inlaid with rubies.

I had heard the Duc d'Orléans – called Monsieur at court – argue for a day and a half on the subject of whether his knee breeches of fine wool should be of a sable colour and his stockings vermilion or the other way around: because Monsieur's interest in dress was of the very most refined and intense nature, and certainly outweighed his interest in his wife. He looked handsome; beautiful one might almost say, with his large black lashed eyes, and his dark hair tied with two wide vermilion ribbons matching the plumes in his hat. As the wedding procession approached the gates fireworks cascaded out of the wrought iron braziers. These fireworks pitched stars into the sky that swelled and burst and reformed in the initials of Monsieur and his bride. The princess herself followed behind, and was so closely attended I don't think I even saw her.

The crush was immense. If I had not been so small I would never have succeeded in seeing as much as I did. There were several thousand courtiers more or less permanently present at court, and when this procession was over there was a grand presentation and a ball; and the next day a dinner for the whole court, music, games and a ballet. The celebrations went on in this way for two weeks, Most of the children of the Court saw only the drawings of the great set pieces for the wedding celebrations executed by such men as Le Vau who had only just started on the rebuilding of Versailles, but did not despise these smaller displays of magnificence. But I, because in effect I belonged to no one, heard and saw everything.

I had one half sister at the court who was seventeen when I was twelve. But although she – Climène de la Tour de Brisse – sometimes spoke to me, I was under a strict rule from her never to approach unless unobserved by others, and only then if she asked me. On about the fourth day of the wedding celebrations, in the afternoon, I was walking along one of the upper floors when I heard a rustling sound come from a cupboard, and I opened it. In common with almost everyone at court Climène adored playing at hide and seek, and during these *jours de fête* the intervals between one entertainment and the next were invariably filled in that way. I found her now crammed into the small space so that the crisp silk of her gown was crumpled into a nest trimmed with lace and blue ribbons out of which peeped her lovely face. But she certainly did not want to be found by me, or indeed anyone else except the Chevalier de Lorraine, since in common with so many other ladies at court she fancied herself in love with him. It was only when I offered to

7

fetch that gentleman that she became quiet, like a trapped kitten that suddenly pulls in its claws; and before sending me off, her eyes sparkling with anticipation and excitement, she said, "Oh, I do pity anyone who does not live at court!"

To find the Chevalier de Lorraine and send him to Climène's hiding place, the best strategy was to look for the Duc d'Orléans, who we at court called Monsieur. He and the Chevalier were always together. Monsieur, although naturally admired and courted by everyone, was bewitched by the Chevalier de Lorraine, who he adored. He could not live one day without him, and he never had to try because the Chevalier, with the help of Madame Gordon, Elizabeth de Grancy and the Marquis d'Effiat, tended their Prince with more care than Naboth did his vineyard.

I found them all now in Monsieur's apartment. As I slipped between the skirts and the legs of those who were in the ante chamber I could hear the sound of muffled sobbing, and once inside the door that was being kept ajar to exclude other members of the court I saw the Duc d'Orléans with his head on the Chevalier's shoulder and that gentleman's arms around him, while a common person kneeling on the floor in an attitude of anguish held in his hand a bunch of ribbons. Apparently they were of the wrong colour.

Madame de Grancy, dressed as the Spirit of Fidelity for the procession of the fête – a joke which the court considered to be in bad taste – was also attempting to comfort the Prince by holding a piece of silk soaked in perfume before his face, and stroking his brow with a damp cloth. Mme. Gordon, although not actively engaged, stood aside with an expression of anguished concern. The fourth member of this little band of friends who habitually surrounded the Prince, the Marquis d'Effiat, was missing.

I ventured to slip in close to the Chevalier. No one saw me. Monsieur's desperate sobs gradually quietened under the influence of his friends, and at last the Chevalier was able to explain that more ribbons could be fetched in good time, and that the precise shade which Monsieur had been so inspired as to choose could be found in the shop next to À La Perle des Mouches in the Rue St. Denis. The individual who was on his knees seized his opportunity and withdrew.

Incredible though it sounds, I can bear witness to the fact, as told me by an old soldier once, that this same Prince was as brave as a lion on the field of battle and led his men with such magnificence and courage under fire that he was greatly admired. His talent as a soldier was outstanding. And yet here, over something as absurd as the colour of a ribbon he made more fuss than he would have if he lost a leg on the field. He wept and apparently trembled with emotion until at last, with a gesture of self conscious bravery that he would have scorned to make whilst storming, under fire, the ramparts of a foreign castle, he drew himself upright. He turned to view himself in the glass. He was calm again. Madame de Grancy, with a tender smile, wiped away the trace of a last tear. "I dislike these scenes," he said, as if they were made by someone else.

Conscious of the fact that Climène, in her cupboard, would be beginning to tire, I took the opportunity to give the hem of the Chevalier's jerkin a discreet pull. He looked down with contempt and would have spurned me, but I had developed the trick of looking straight back into another's eye if I had something useful to impart.

As the Chevalier looked down at me Mme. Gordon, with a look of disgust in my direction, nevertheless distracted Monsieur with a question about the lie of his collar so that the Chevalier could attend to what I had to say, and indeed he followed me out of the room while the prince was still engaged on the problem newly presented to him.

Perhaps the Chevalier despised himself for making use of me at the same time as being unable to resist the convenience, or perhaps it was just a normal expression of his habitually spiteful nature, but he paused just before reaching the cupboard to tell me something. I knew it would be unpleasant. I felt the fluttering of fear in my veins.

"Thing!" he said, as a way of addressing me. Lorraine wouldn't bend, of course, to come nearer to me. He stood thrown back on his heels, looking down through the almost closed lids of his eyes. He had diamond buckles on his shoes, and rose and purple enamel decorative pieces on the belt which hung across his body, weighted down on the left by his sword. When a truly handsome man is young it hardly matters how evil he is, he can still look beautiful. The Chevalier looked beautiful then. Much later his spirit began to trace marks on his face and body, but not yet.

"Thing," he said. "Did you know de Montespan has killed your birds?"

What a question! It stuck straight into my soul, like a knife. He saw it, and he looked satisfied. My lip began to tremble. If I am upset the ruptured muscle tends to flap and it can't be stopped. I could say nothing. I forced myself to stand my ground for long enough to point out the cupboard to him, and to turn away with a pretence of courage even if the frightful flapping of my skin betrayed me.

But as soon as I was out of his sight I rushed with all my strength towards the tower steps that led onto the roof. I had some birds that I had tamed and kept there. I thought that no one knew about these creatures, which were my own particular treasure. I thought that no one at court knew about my birds. When I took morsels of cake and bread up onto the leads I was careful not to be seen. I had tamed five pigeons. I could sit against the stone and watch them preen, and peck at crumbs. They would be quite calm, crooning and circling close to my feet, responding to their names or spreading those beautiful wings to leap into the sky. Often they would fly back to the hand, and you could swear that wisps of heaven trailed from their pinions.

Stumbling over my own feet and hobbling to try to go faster I came at last out into the open. Two of my favourite white birds were missing. Because of what the Chevalier had said, I knew they were not just foraging in some other field or garden. They had been caught, perhaps more easily because of their trusting friendship with myself, and as for what unkindness or cruelty might have been inflicted on them in being killed I could not bear to think of it. But I did.

There was a thin layer of ice on some parts of the roof. I could have easily slipped. I could have let my miserable body fall onto the ground, and escaped that way. I thought of it.

Eventually I came back down into the upper rooms and from there went to the most unfrequented series of apartments. At the western extremity of the building at that level there was a passage off which four rooms opened one into the other, each one being a small cube intricately panelled with carved wood like a jewel box. They were empty at that time and when I needed to escape this was where I came. That afternoon I crouched behind a screen although the room was bare and this the only piece of furniture in it. And then I wept. Even today I remember the bitterness of the tears I shed. The incident unpacked afresh the foul burden to my spirit that was my deformed body, and I wept for that too as if it was being visited upon me for the first time.

If some explanation is needed for the fact that the Montespan had these two birds killed, I can quote now from the records of de la Reynie, the Lieutenant of Police in Paris at the time, who was such a painstaking and conscientious man. He investigated charges against Madame de

Montespan and some others for sorcery, and some years later than the day on which it happened this incident was included in his indictment. The following is a copy, or partial copy, from his report. He writes:

The purpose of the spell was to obtain the good graces of the King and to make Mademoiselle de la Vallière die, although Mariette says it was only to make her go away from court. Montespan then gave them two pigeon hearts for which they had asked; these two hearts were given to Mariette so that he could say Mass over them and pass them under the chalice. This Mass on the two hearts was said by Mariette in a chapel of the church of St. Severin, and Madame de Montespan was present. Lesage said that the pigeons' hearts were put under the chalice, while Mariette denied this and claimed that he had merely put them in his pocket while saying Mass.

As I crouched there, suddenly the door of the room I was in burst open with a crash. I was terrified of being caught. I drew into the middle of the screen and then peered through the crack between the panels, and was appalled to see a young woman whom I recognised as the new Duchesse d'Orléans. She was making a great deal of noise, although she was alone. She had been running, and she was out of breath and laughing in a suppressed whisper at the same time. No doubt the game of hide and seek combined with her unfamiliarity with all of the palace of St. Germain, had prompted her to run into these unfrequented rooms.

Her dress, which was very elaborate and sewn with layers and layers of pale blue silk, made an immense noise that reminded me of that dark night when I first arrived in Paris. She stood there moving from foot to foot, clasping her hands, radiant with excitement and looking for somewhere to hide.

I tried to hold my breath. I was in despair. I could not, at that moment, bear to be exposed before a new face and one so exalted. At the very instant when only silence might have saved me, an involuntary hiccup of sobs broke from my chest. In dismay I put my head in my lap and wept.

There was a sudden rush from the direction of the window, as footsteps crossed the floor. I tried to brace myself. She came to the edge of the screen. There was the sound of her dress crumpling as she bent down. I raised my face to warn her, giving her a chance to avoid too close a shock. But, to my absolute astonishment, she did not draw back. She put out her arms, and catching hold of me she actually embraced me, and I heard her say, with a strong German accent, "Don't cry, little goblin. What's the matter?"

CHAPTER THREE

I find it impossible to describe calmly, even now, how overwhelming that moment was for me. Until then not one single person had ever embraced me, unless perhaps my mother did before she went wherever she went. I doubt it.

Madame was plump. She had red lips and the prettiness of youth, but – or so the word was at court at the time – not much more. I never agreed with this. To me, who felt the softness of her arms wrapped around my famished heart and heard the kindness in her voice, she was beautiful beyond anything or anybody that I had ever seen, whether painted in a picture or adorning the greatest court in Europe. I took in what was happening with the panic stricken blindness of a man suddenly embraced by an angel, But ever afterwards more and yet more details of the smallest imprint of that moment – the blue of her gown, a terrified glimpse of her soft skin, the scent of it, the touch of a strand of her hair – made their way, and continued to make their way all my life, down the half strangled passageways of my affections. Although, as it turns out, I have lived a long time, this is the one moment in my life which never recedes; which has always only just taken place. If I turn my mind in its direction, the eyes of my soul grow wide again with love and gratitude, and I feel the incredulity and bliss of the encounter as if it were happening once more.

The gesture was not repeated. When for a moment or two she had listened to my story, the Princess asked me to guide her back to the main gallery. Subsequently she showed herself my friend, but in ways which were in keeping with her position. She tolerated my presence. She never spurned me.

But as for me, what would you expect? From that day onwards I worshipped her. I was her slave.

This event was the turning point in my life. This is the meeting between two strangers that I referred to. From then onwards I began to frequent her surroundings in my own fashion, slipping unnoticed through a door masked by the comings and goings of others, and then remaining still for hours in the shelter of some hangings or an unlit corner. My one desire was to contribute to her happiness, and to be near her.

Of course, it goes without saying that everyone else also came to pay court to the new Duchess. They were all ambitious to be noticed by her. Her apartment was usually crowded, and very frequently attended by her husband the King's brother, and his particular friends. Although from her very first days she would sit and write long letters to her family and the friends of her youth, she would often do it while surrounded with conversation and laughter.

Monsieur was pleased with this. However fond he was of young men and boys, he was not ill disposed towards his new wife. If there was an obstacle to his affection it lay less with his sexual proclivities than with his friends. He had this particular group of favourites whom I have already mentioned, led by the Chevalier de Lorraine and including Madame Gordon, who had come to court as a lady of honour attached to the first Madame, Minette, until she died. Then there were also Elizabeth de Grancy and the Marquis d'Effiat. These four were fanatically jealous of their privilege as Monsieur's favourites. They were determined not to cede the pre-eminence of their status, as would happen should Monsieur develop too warm a liking for his new wife. In their estimation Monsieur's marriage was to be a formality that would leave their own influence undiminished, and they looked with venomous suspicion, from the very first, on any development which augured otherwise.

Madame Gordon, particularly, from the first would have a wry expression on her face when some slight event or exchange of words made it clear that the new Madame had every intention of pleasing her husband, and could become a rival for his real affection.

The court noticed this just as I did. Madame de la Fayette, unaware of that little tick in her lip that betrayed her excitement and most especially when she vied for the attention of the Duc de la Rochefoucauld, her most especial friend, began to mention it often. But at first I thought that it was not important, or that it would not continue. I was drunk with the delight of my new life, and with Madame's tacit permission to be in attendance, although unobserved, for many hours each day. It seemed as if unkindness could not come near her, and for a while happiness simply blinded me.

I paid little attention to how extremely closely Lorraine and his band of friends continued to attach themselves to Monsieur, without a sign of being willing to cede position to his new wife. Or to the fact that

Lorraine was a ruthlessly cruel man capable of seducing the very heart out of the body of almost anyone alive and then eating it.

In an attempt to diminish Madame's appeal in Monsieur's eyes, from the very beginning he and his friends eyed each other at every remark that Madame made, looking out for any opportunity to wound her, or to debase the coinage of this new association that threatened to reduce their own influence with Monsieur. But I did not, at first, pay much attention to them. Like anyone who had lived at court for long enough to hear the intimate conversations of friends who traduced each other and ambitious enemies who competed for advantage, jealousy and mischief made up a familiar diet which I was used to. Only when these qualities for the first time threaten the happiness of a person one loves is the effect altogether different.

The first real hint of this was aroused by a scene I witnessed two or even three months after the wedding. There was to be a performance of a new play by Molière called *Les Fourberies de Scapin*. While Madame was in her bedchamber being dressed by her ladies, Monsieur was attended by that particularly intimate little group of friends to whom he was so much attached. They were in the ante room and Monsieur, turning carefully so that the light from a full branch of candles could fall on the shoe he held out, wanted their opinion upon it.

"Oh!" said the Grancy – and you could tell from the little barb of a smile that she directed sideways that she had something spiteful in mind to say – "shall I run and find out what Madame is wearing this time? She may have another gown of pale blue silk. Quantities of it were bought specially I am told."

This was a reference to the pale blue silk gown Madame had worn in the beginning of the wedding festivities – the one that I had felt against my cheek warmed by her skin and soft with a softness never to be repeated. It was, one must admit, rather oddly fashioned. In France we are inclined to think our own way of dressing superior to that of every one else, and this blue silk was commented upon with a good deal of sarcasm at court. Madame de Grancy, whose own clothes were dirty even if they were stylish, was bound to take every opportunity she could find to say something spiteful.

Monsieur d'Effiat let out a laugh, catching the Prince's eye with a look of complicity at the same time so that there was no risk that Monsieur might consider himself excluded from the winning side in this repartee. Then the Chevalier, putting his hand around Monsieur's neck as if mirth rendered him incapable of standing without the support of his friend, laughed until he coughed.

I felt my skin grow hot. I realised that it was their intention to hurt Madame if they could; to humiliate her. The room was full of other courtiers who could overhear this little scene, and witness Monsieur's complicity in the ridicule of his wife. Madame had already shown herself, to the whole court, as kind and good natured, and simple and straight forward as well as dignified, and I had imagined that this was an advantage. But all it did was to feed the envy of these jealous satellites of Monsieur and give them cause to fear her. They must also have noticed how the King, her brother in law, showed a decided preference for Madame's company and how all of this made Monsieur proud of her and inclined to like his wife. I suppose they thought that to lose preferment to someone who deserves it better is as bad a being robbed.

I realised all this in the very moment Monsieur joined with the muted sneers of his friends, and then I could not believe that I had been such a fool, even at the age of twelve and even for a week, to forget the treachery of court life. As if to make up for my previous innocence it now could not have shocked me more if they had been talking of killing Madame rather than just mocking her clothes.

Into this poisoned atmosphere, where the tinkle of spiteful laughter had been abruptly hushed, the Duchesse herself came from the adjoining room with a smiling face. It was impossible to tell whether or not she was aware of any unkindness. She was wearing cream damask, not blue silk at all. The collective company turned to her with varying expressions, reflecting more the skill of concealment or lack of it, than anything. In contrast, an observer couldn't fail to be struck by the pleasant simplicity of Madame's demeanour compared with all these. Her lively expression, her graceful step, the sweet scent of her clothes. She showed only pleasure at meeting her husband and at the prospect of the play, and it seemed that such innocence combined with such eminence – because she was after all the second lady in the whole of France at the time – must disarm envy and bring everyone into the charmed circle of her admirers. But a courtier knows that it will not.

After the play that evening there was a supper, and the following evening a ball. Each phase of each event could only be followed through a crush of fine silks and damask skirts and ribbons which often cut off the view of what was going on. At one moment Madame de Chevreuse said to Monsieur that she thought that Madame looked very handsome;

but he didn't agree. Madame was dancing, partnered by the King. She moved delightfully. No one could criticise her for that. She held herself very straight but without stiffness, and with each movement the impact of her feet on the ground had the same effect as when a ball of dandelion seed lightly dips and bounces across the turf. But although his comment was made in his usual pleasant style, Monsieur, having looked at her again across the room, simply replied that he did not find her at all pretty.

He moved off after that, shadowed by d'Effiat, to talk to the Duc de la Rochefoucault. Madame de Chevreuse turned aside with a little *moue* of displeasure concealed by turning her face towards another friend.

"I never thought Minette a great beauty," she said, "but clearly Monsieur thinks this second wife is plain. Perhaps I can persuade Lorraine to let Monsieur find her eyes and lips pretty as long as she puts on weight and does not make him laugh."

The two ladies were immensely pleased with this witticism. And in talking of the first Duchesse d'Orléans, they followed the general fashion, as the arrival of Monsieur's second wife had somewhat revived the memory of the fate of his first. It was a tragic history and I will recount it here.

Henriette, the sister of the King of England and Monsieur's first wife, was known as Minette. Madame de Chevreuse continued to talk about her, now that she had begun. She made out as if she was looking through some gap in the air and actually seeing the murdered Duchesse as she began to talk about her. Madame de Choin was rather small and Madame de Chevreuse pointed her face downwards but without, needless to say, noticing me.

"Do you remember," she said, "how charming Minette was? I liked her. I did. I can see her now."

"You'll become like the Clerembault," said Choin.

"My dear, I don't imply that I can see ghosts. But you must admit yourself that almost the only enemies she had were Lorraine and his friends. She charmed everyone except them. I was her slave myself, I really was."

"Madame de Soissons…"

"I was more intimate with Monsieur and Madame then than Madame de Soissons was, for all her boastful talk. But even she agrees that Madame was very forbearing towards her husband's friends. It's a pity that they could not be satisfied with taking precedence in Monsieur's affections immediately after his wife, and not before. But they'll do it again. You wait and see."

There was a long pause. There was something both wanted the other to know, but neither was prepared to say. Eventually they both started at once.

"The King..." said Madame de Chevreuse.

"The K..." After another pause Madame de Choin decided to continue. "His Majesty was *so* upset," she remarked. "But he was satisfied that she had not been poisoned."

The King's preference, then, had not saved his sister in law. Would not, perhaps, save this one. I was becoming such a bundle of anxiety that I came close to treading on the Choin's skirt. The near accident distracted me and I missed something.

You will think that I must have heard this rumour before, and I had. But the court was always full of rumour and intrigue, and I had not paid particular attention before. I had been too young during the time when Minette was alive and had no such reason, as that which had brought me close to Monsieur's second wife, to attempt any sort of intimacy with her fate. Now here I was, straining after every word, and I stood for nearly half an hour behind the skirts of Madame de Chevreuse that evening while she discussed the matter.

It gave me a different view of Madame's success with her husband when I heard that only the other day d'Effiat had cursed her when she had spent one whole afternoon helping Monsieur to make patterns for a new collar and pocket. And he swore, in private, to poison this wife as he had the first. "What a boast!" Madame de Chevreuse exclaimed.

She laughed. Was it a joke to her, or was she merely ridiculing a far-fetched rumour to which she paid no real attention? Whichever it was, she found it so amusing that she did a little backwards and forwards shuffle with her feet almost like a dance and I had to get out of her way.

The next day, as a result of these cares, I fell asleep in my corner where Madame's lady in waiting, Theobon, had her permission to let me stay. I awoke to see Madame and Monsieur together and it was his laughter – a triumphant shout – that woke me. Madame had apparently just succeeded in working out the correct way to tie a garter as shown in a drawing over which Monsieur and his valet had been puzzling for two days and he was so delighted that he took her hand and kissed it. When he laughed, with his teeth so perfectly even and white, and those long thick black eyelashes for which he was famous, shading his eyes, then he certainly was a handsome man. And an amiable one. He half turned in his chair, still smiling broadly, to wave the drawing at the Chevalier who was, as usual, not far away.

Madame laughed too. Her laughter was frequent and pretty – except when occasionally she laughed so much that she snorted.

She did no such thing just now, but Elizabeth de Grancy, pretending to an exaggerated outburst of sympathetic delight, did. She got the timing and the tone of it so exactly right that, taken by surprise though everyone was, they laughed again where normally they would have been disgusted. Amid the general laughter it was no longer possible to tell who was laughing at what, but Madame had not missed the rudeness. There was an extra touch of pink in her cheek, but she did not know how to respond. Then she leaned over to take the drawing from Monsieur and whispered something that made him laugh again. She succeeded in making the interchange appear intimate, and glanced up at Madame de Grancy in mid sentence as if she might be the subject of it.

When some time later Monsieur and his friends had gone Madame said to Theobon, her lady of honour, speaking of the Grancy, "I would not bear her near me if Monsieur had not especially requested a place for her."

Theobon frowned. She was folding a fan that had become rumpled and perhaps she also saw how each little prize of friendship that Madame won from her husband was gall to his friends.

"I wish them all to the devil!" she muttered.

Madame had not yet understood the lengths to which jealousy and ambition could prompt certain people to go, and she said there was no need for them to venture that far. She said, "They can stay here if they will just understand that I intend to be the best of friends with my husband. If they can be content with that, all the better. I think I could like the Chevalier well enough. And the Marquis d'Effiat spoke to me yesterday about the medals which I mentioned to you, and he spoke so well that I have decided to start a collection."

As time went by, these scenes accumulated and in their recollection now I review the progress of those early years like someone watching the approach of wolves. There was another occasion when Monsieur came to Madame's drawing room to ask her what gown she would wear for the play that evening. They had a discussion about it, the explanation being that he wanted to paint her face for her. This was a thing she loathed. Other ladies used a great deal of paint, and Monsieur himself used rouge and dyes and pencils. But Madame hadn't got the patience for it, and she said it only made her ridiculous

However she could see that he was set on it. She could not bear to cross him, and as soon as he looked a tiny bit displeased she agreed to let him have his way. She retired to dress, and promised that she would sit still afterwards for as long as he liked.

Monsieur was so impatient that he returned before Madame was dressed. He brought a quantity of paints with him, and made Theobon send a page for more candles because the light was fading. He was very fond of paint, and used it himself rather well; that is, not too much. But he seemed to have got hold of the idea that his wife needed a lot.

When at last she appeared he made Madame sit down in the window. Immediately she screwed up her face as soon as Monsieur began with the rouge. He rested his little finger on her chin to steady his hand, and brushed the colour on with all the concentration of a great artist, commanding her to relax her lips and her eyes. She could only twist her face up more, until the Prince became impatient, and then she made a great effort and was still for about ten whole minutes.

Meanwhile Monsieur d'Effiat and Madame Gordon had come to the door and wanted to be allowed in, but Madame's maids of honour sent them away. There was a glass fronted cabinet standing against the wall at right angles to the door, and reflected in it I caught sight of the shadowy figures of Monsieur's special friends, who would not go away but waited just outside. Lorraine had joined them now. D'Effiat at one point kicked the hem of Madame Gordon's skirt as a sign of something. Only the lower parts of their dress were visible in the glass, the colours muted by the overlay of space, as happens with mirrors. And not dissimilar, either, from what happens according to sailors who tell these stories on the Pont Neuf in Paris, of how sharks may be seen lying in wait and shifting in deep waters.

The folds of what was probably the Grancy's skirt were pressed against those of another, and the Chevalier, who was wearing blue stockings that day, stepped into and out of the frame.

Monsieur stood back from his work at last, and looked at his wife with his eyes narrowed and his lips braced firmly in an expression of determined consideration. Madame would have jumped out of her chair but he commanded her to wait.

"I have had enough," she said in a pleading tone. But he absolutely insisted on adding a little of something or other. She sighed. The bosom of her dress heaved under the little garment which she called a zibeline, and for which Monsieur's envious satellites pretended to feel such contempt that they talked about it at court as if it was a vice to wear a sable tippet. That is all it was, although I must admit it had an odd shape.

When at last he had done, Monsieur invited Madame to look at herself in the glass. She was mortified. She let out a little shriek of dismay, but then she laughed, and said "This time, Monsieur, I will wear it for your sake. I only hope it pleases you."

"I think it looks very well!" he said indignantly.

Madame could see that she was trapped, and would have to either praise her own appearance – which she never did, because she was convinced that she was very plain – or else offend him. So she took a step back and put her head on one side and said, "I am not used to seeing myself looking so well, Monsieur. Your friends will be quite jealous of me."

He smiled placidly. Madame's wit passed her husband by, He continued to scrutinise his handiwork with an air of satisfaction while Theobon removed the zibeline, and then Monsieur and Madame left together. The reflections in the glass parted to admit the pale glimmer of Madame's silk damask skirt, and Theobon, who had forgotten me, began to speak to one of the maids of honour.

I went back to my own apartment, and I think it was on this occasion that, once alone, I had a long and painful meditation on the subject of Madame's dangerous position at Court, the details of which I yet remember. I fell so deep in thought that the scenes conjured up still remain like paintings hung in the spaces of my mind whose colours have scarcely faded.

My servant then was the disgraced valet of a former courtier who had been saved from outright exile by the offer of serving me, and I often ate, and always slept, alone. My room was at the furthest end of the passage where my father's room had been, but by this time he had been moved, and his connection with myself so much forgotten that I had been left where I was.

On that evening the palace was brightly lit even in some of the passages, but the rest were in darkness as usual. I made my way along without finding a servant to light me. Since I was hungry, on reaching my room I sent Bonhomme, as he was called, to fetch me something to eat, and sat down to wait for him, and to reflect.

Perhaps two years, three, had already passed since my first encounter with Madame. It had been long before my satisfaction and delight at being able to spend so many hours in her presence began to be seriously tempered with anxiety. The innocence of extreme youth rests so much upon acceptance of the established world into whose jaws the newborn child is dropped that even I took time to lose it. I had always observed acutely. But little by little the ruthless ambition and jealousy of the Chevalier de Lorraine and his three friends aroused my indignation, and with it the seed of opposition was planted in my mind.

If it were true that he had engineered the murder of the first Madame, Lorraine would be capable of manipulating the same, or similar, events again. The thought terrified me, as only those fears based on reality have the power to do. I could not wean my mind from a morbid preoccupation with the predatory images that I had seen mirrored in the glass of the cabinet just now, as they waited outside her door; their restrained shifting and circling in anticipation of an opportunity to get more close, like creatures hungry for their prey.

My speculations fed new images into the frame as if that glass had the power to hold and reflect once more events which were long gone. I could have sworn I saw there the hand of the Chevalier holding something. I don't know at what point I later realised that the Chevalier himself did not administer the poison of which Minette died, because he was still in exile then. But he it was who managed it all, who procured the poison, whose hatred inspired his friends, even though it was d'Effiat who did it.

The Chevalier's hand looked strong and well made. Even his fingers were elegant, and many others besides his best friend Monsieur, the King's only brother, desired to be stroked by them. It is hard to believe that God himself could have bestowed such grace on a man at the same time as giving him the heart of a leper and the spirit of a famished wolf.

But even the King loved him. And the three friends who clung to him most closely after Monsieur – that is, the Marquis d'Effiat and Mesdames de Grancy and Gordon – scarcely ever left him alone.

When the Duc d'Orléans married his first wife, Minette, the very idea of someone else being closer to Monsieur than he was, drove the Chevalier mad. It was a political rage, not a *crise d'amour*. He simply defied anyone, even Monsieur's wife, to relegate him to second place. He would be first with Monsieur, or burn in hell, or both.

Consider. The closeness of that bond made him what he was at court. Was it at all likely that even the sweetest and most attractive lady – and Minette was considered to be both these – would be other than hated by him if circumstances made her his rival in the affection and authority of Monsieur? And so it was only logical that he should be suspected of having murdered her. His heart was quite black enough for it. He was spiteful towards her from the very beginning; but then one event went against him and roused the most vicious side of his nature.

Minette was the sister of theKing of England. Louis XIV made use of this connection in secret, and through the interest of his sister-in-law who spoke privately to her brother, he was able to put forward views which were advantageous to France.

Somehow the Chevalier managed to ferret out details of this business that didn't concern him at all. He thought he saw a chance to make mischief by telling Monsieur that it damaged his reputation at court when the King preferred to use Madame rather than his own brother, when it came to influential diplomacy. As a result Monsieur was angry with his wife. Minette informed the King, and for once His Majesty resisted the magnetism of this extraordinary man, and sent the Chevalier into exile for two years.

A day may come – who knows? – when a man may be sent from court, or even prefer to go, and not feel any the worse for it. But certainly such times are distant. In our day unless a rich and honourable appointment entices a man elsewhere, and for a limited time, life at court is simply irreplaceable. Many would sooner be dead than leave. And Lorraine was one of them.

Having said that, the death of someone else would always be a tempting alternative to a man like him, assuming he had the strength and ingenuity to effect the exchange. In this case he could not avoid going into exile first, but he sent home the means to avenge himself, and forestall any further disadvantages.

His shadow moving deep within that glass showed him to me when several years of scheming against her marriage had apparently ripened the fruit of his hatred for his friend's wife until people standing close to talk to him could almost smell it. He dissembled. He had such charm. But however skilfully he simulated, the Chevalier could never overlook the injury done himself by the very existence of Minette. And once she had procured his exile her days were numbered. I became quite sure of that. Madame de Soissons later told Mme. de Coetquen that the Chevalier once spoke to her openly of his hatred and then immediately afterwards assuming a gracious manner, smiled at Madame so convincingly that de Soissons said she experienced a sense of unreality as if she had dreamed the conversation she had with him five minutes before.

From the point of view of Minette it must be very strange to be smiled at so much by a man who hated her bitterly. No doubt she had her suspicions. But as for thinking him capable of murder, its very unlikely she had even a hint of it. She must have stepped in and out of his shadow day by day without being remotely aware of how each passage brought her closer to a moment of complete eclipse; I mean that of death.

I myself had seen, and I watched now in this phantom image of the past, how Lorraine could put on such a show, conjuring up an admiring softness in response Madame's words, and fashioning the glass of his face so that it is silvered over with deceit like the back of a mirror. Not a flicker lets slip how he really feels, unless he chooses. Even to Monsieur, his tender friend, who pets him, he keeps the secret of his hatred. With Elizabeth de Grancy, Madame Gordon and the Marquis d'Effiat he confides his real feelings and makes sure that they share them, but to others he dissembles.

I had always heard that Madame Minette was considered to be very kind, and pretty. I do remember that I saw her once when she was walking in the garden and she held one shoulder very slightly higher than the other; not at all an ugly singularity. In my mind's reflection I now created the picture as she walked in the garden on the last morning of her life, with Monsieur, Mmes de Grancy and Gordon and Monsieur d'Effiat. Others were present, such as, for example, Mme. de Soissons. I could swear that I was watching a scene take place in real life as I sat there, immersed in the activity of my shadows. There went M. d'Effiat, leaving the garden on some pretext to go ahead of them to Madame's apartment where they will all take chocolate together later. A footman comes in and finds him with Madame's chocolate cup in his hand, but he only wipes it with paper and says that he had noticed that it wasn't clean. Ten minutes later the royal couple, accompanied by Mesdames Gordon and Elizabeth de Grancy and others, come into Minette's apartment, as arranged.

Apparently Madame is as light hearted as if she was destined to live for years. And here is Monsieur, who is as ignorant as his wife of what is about to happen, talking only about the rules of a new game of chance that they are in the middle of inventing, and looking just as I saw him this afternoon. Minette takes her cup from the footman, and continues to make jokes that the name of a little greyhound puppy that Monsieur has given her should be adopted for the new game. If her hand shakes as she holds the cup and the chocolate is poured into it, it is only with laughter. A moment later, I watch the shadow of what she once was raise the cup to her lips. My own are dry. I am watching hell.

And there is d'Effiat standing in an attitude of relaxed and courteous attention. His rather sallow face even looks unusually relaxed, and certainly he can't be the first to flinch, above all not before she falters. He lowers his eyes, as if about to take a sip himself. A blemish on the skin near his mouth twitches. I have watched this man with such concern lately that my mind draws his phantom shape with supernatural accuracy. He is thinking of the Chevalier de Lorraine, and the pleasure he is about to give his absent friend.

The Princess begins to drink from her cup. D'Effiat feels his eyes drawn to her neck. He wants to see her swallow, and although he denies himself because he is nothing if not a disciplined assassin, he swore afterwards when whispering to his particular friends that he had watched the smooth skin of her throat undulate. Her lip, moist and soft, rests against the rim of the cup. That's what he watched most of all. She drinks again.

So does he. So do they all.

Minette's cup is Sèvres, patterned with gold. The painted shadow of it takes a special place in the picture I am so mesmerised by. I see her put it down, and Madame de Soissons bends forward and catches it before it falls because Madame has misjudged the edge of the table. At this point d'Effiat still pretends to have noticed nothing. Elizabeth de Grancy can't manage to be quite so discreet but fortunately all eyes are elsewhere.

"I don't feel well," Minette says. "I must go and lie down."

She has risen to her feet, but her skin has already changed colour and from saying one moment that she needs no help to walk next door to her bedchamber, the next she is almost carried there.

And then the panic of the courtiers, who are so frightened in these sort of circumstances. The ugliness of sickness or death is thrown into sharp relief when it strikes those who are our protectors, our source of comfort, entertainment, preferment. All those who are in that room, except for those who killed her, (if indeed they did) are suffering.

Of course the three friends – the three enemies of Madame – keep pace with everyone else, the dismay, the sudden pallor, the hands clasped. D'Effiat assumes an expression of such anxiety that Monsieur says to him, "Come, come! She is just a little sick."

The assassin is only too ready to correct himself. He is about to say something when the terrible sound of Madame's first shriek of agony from the next room puts an end to all talk. Everyone is shocked almost out of their wits. A footman is sent tearing off at a run to fetch the doctors, and Monsieur himself goes into the bedroom and stands at the end of the bed, his skin almost as livid in colour as his wife's, gripping the garland of flowers carved around one of the bed posts so tightly that he snaps off a leaf as he watches her die.

D'Effiat probably counts himself secure now that all eyes are fixed on his enemy. Here is his image in the glass again. He appears to be resting in an interval of amazing stillness by the door; of perfect satisfaction. Later on he produced as much in the way of tears and sighs as anyone could expect. But for now he is very quiet. He has served his friend Lorraine, and his own interests, very well. And besides, he likes danger. And also the two women will be coming to him soon with their triumph. What enemies to fear, should anyone cross their path again. A second wife, for example?

I emerged from this contemplation like a man from a very deep sleep in which his dreams have not been good. After the death of Minette it is known that the corpse stank so that people talked of poison straight away, but the Chevalier had been absent, and his friends had all drunk of the same chocolate as Madame. Neither the King nor Monsieur believed that Philippe's favourites had anything to do with the death of his wife. But because it is not clear how a thing was done, that is no reason to assume that it was not done at all. Although they were really only phantoms of my own imagining, and not real images of the past one could be sure of two things; the new object of Lorraine's malice was Monsieur's second wife, and Lorraine himself, and d'Effiat and the two women were enemies to be afraid of.

Bonhomme took his time fetching my supper, and my morose reflections were not cut short. I had not forgotten that the new Duchess, my own most precious and loved protector, was unlikely to be any more robust and skilful at dealing with enemies at court than the first had been. Her character was too simple and straight forward to survive if the '*cabale*', as she came to call Lorraine and his three friends, decided to destroy her. This was a lady who was fond of recounting how much she used to enjoy walking on the hills outside Heidelberg at dawn, and sitting on the ground for a breakfast of cherries and dry bread. The sort of person who enjoys such simple, almost peasant pleasures, is not one who is likely to thrive among sophisticated and dangerous enemies at a French court. She might have a robust, even coarse, sense of humour at times, and in fact the King reproached her for it once when she spoke too graphically in front of the Dauphin; but the sort of depravities enjoyed by the *cabale* – and for which no one reproached them – disgusted her.

As well as his numerous affairs with women Lorraine, in company with his friend d'Effiat, frequented the exercise schools where the sons of noblemen received instruction in the skills appropriate to their position. The boys there were familiar with the Chevalier's tastes. The fact that he was loved by Monsieur with a devotion which never faltered until the day of his death did not deter the Chevalier from pursuing not only numerous women, but also various boys to whom he took a fancy. Lissieux, the defenceless orphaned son of the former sword master was debauched by him, and there were many others. And one among them called d'Effiat the most wicked man on earth. To be so named by a French courtier was a distinction that he must have earned by depravities more complicated even than those of Lorraine.

Then consider Madame Gordon. She had been the Scottish waiting woman of the first Madame, and she had certainly not defended her mistress from the malice of her husband's friends, but joined in herself. Here she still was, flourishing in the sunshine of royal favour, long after her poor mistress was in her grave. These were the individuals who Madame would have to consort with every day unless she alienated her husband by opposing them.

Bonhomme had at last returned, and at his feet trotted a little dog. He prepared my table, and as he did so the animal came over to me and put her nose in my hand. The hair stood up round her neck in a ruff and she had pointed ears and small eyes.

"Is this your dog?" I said.

"Yes, Monsieur," he answered.

I couldn't make friends with this man. I never had.

"Will you part with her?"

He named a sum of money. I would go in the morning to Monsieur

Chambrette who was nominally my governor, and I could be sure of securing that amount. I gave Bonhomme my promise and kept the dog.

The next day I begged a ribbon from Climène, tied it round the neck of my little dog, and went to Madame's apartment. When one of the maids of honour approached I gained entrance, and handed her a note which I had written. She took it quite kindly. I had purchased some snuff for her recently when her mother was ill. Madame d'Orléans hated snuff and would have been annoyed if a young member of her household had bought it. The lady placed the note before Madame, who was writing at her table. I waited.

However, although I hid myself discreetly in my usual place, the little dog that I had with me was less cautious. As long as I kept my finger looped around her ribbon she remained fairly quiet and only changed position from time to time to curl her body round the other way and resettle with her head against my leg. But when in a careless moment I let go, she scampered out. Her claws rattled against the parquet floor and Madame, who had not ceased writing for one moment since I came in, gave a startled cry and looked down. Charmille – that was the name I had given the dog – had reached her chair, and standing on her back legs put her front paws on Madame's skirts as if begging to be lifted up.

Madame put down her pen, and said, "Who is this? What a dear little dog. Who has brought her?"

Trembling, I stepped out a pace, but without being observed because Madame was too engaged with Charmille. She had her in her arms, and the little creature was half hidden in the folds of her court dress, but very excited and trying to lick the face that was bent over her. Eventually the maid of honour who I mentioned before bent down and whispered in Madame's ear. My letter was opened out, and Madame turned at last to me.

I was profoundly afraid that she would consider my attempt to make a gift to her of this little dog presumptuous. And certainly the thought crossed her mind, because I saw a fleeting coldness in her face which perhaps my own obvious and desperate anxiety may have done something to dispel. She took a deep breath before saying anything more, and stroked Charmille.

I managed to execute a bow. It was always very difficult for me to balance if I put one foot too much forward, because the right leg was the one which was so much shorter and my left foot was the one which was twisted. A smile which really belonged, I think, to Charmille was shared with me as Madame looked down, and the expression in her eyes changed to one of kindness. A small dimple appeared in her cheek that I had not seen before. She said something affectionate in German, and kissed the little pointed ears and then said to Theobon,

"You may tell the young gentleman, Madame de Beauvron," (Theobon had the title of Countess de Beauvron in addition to the name of Madame Theobon favoured by Madame) – "that the Duchesse d'Orléans accepts his gift, and thanks him."

Her accent in speaking French was tinged with German just enough to give a delicious flavour to commonplace words; a charm she never lost. When I heard what she said I felt as if my heart would burst with happiness. I would have danced if it had been appropriate; or possible. All fear and melancholy left me. For several days the noise of my own spirit singing made me deaf to the spiteful words and innuendoes of her enemies. And as if her capacity to arouse such devotion made her immune to mortal dangers I assumed that if she were threatened she would merely extinguish her detractors like an angel who in a clap of golden feathers could tip the air under the feet of evil men so that they would fall off the edge of the world.

CHAPTER FOUR

Another element in life at that time also restored my confidence and stifled the anxiety that my observation of Monsieur's friends had aroused. I mentioned before that the King loved his new sister in law, but his friendship continued and strengthened until it lifted her above the petty jealousies and schemes of her husband's acolytes. The King's favour was as vital to her, although in a different way, as it had been to me. He had the power to breathe life into any individual or idea or enterprise that he chose to patronise, and the arrival of a new Princess at court was an event that others would judge according to his opinion. The King said that I was to be tolerated, and I was tolerated. He said that Madame was to be admired and loved and the court began to admire and love her.

I began to take comfort in the thought that Monsieur's envious satellites would in time, recognise the convenience of being Madame's friends rather than her enemies. But of course, His Majesty had been extremely fond of the first Madame too.

An example of his affection for the new Duchesse was that, seeing how happy Madame was to have one little dog, the King gave her two more. He was very fond of dogs himself, especially spaniels. It clearly delighted him to see his sister in law share his pleasure in them. She shared other characteristics with him as well, because he had a great appreciation of the open air – he was always throwing wide the windows in rooms where the more outspoken of the courtiers ran away shivering afterwards – and did not use paint like his brother, or lack enthusiasm for hunting and other outside activities. Like her, his natural temper was open, but more acutely observant of those around him than she was. A natural sympathy developed between them, which was a serious obstacle to those who would have liked to harm her.

In the beginning when she was new to the French court, and might have been embarrassed by not knowing what to do on ceremonial occasions, the King took care of her as if he had indeed been born her brother. During the presentations that took place during her early days he would whisper aside to her when she should stand, or sit, and he would even give a little prod to her elbow if she was in danger of missing her cue. Once I had had a view of her face when she did not know what she was meant to do or say next, and being much shorter than the King, who was, as you know, tall, she looked up with a questioning air, and the very rounded shape of her chin and rosy cheek, and the ball of her eye turned up, looked momentarily childlike. I was just reflecting that she was only seven years older than myself when the chamberlain noticed me, and I had to go. He did not actually bend down to speak to me, but he kicked in the corner where I was hiding and I left. It was my age at that time, not my status, which debarred me from ceremonial occasions at Court. But I usually avoided being seen.

If there was one more thing to cement the King's friendship for his sister in law, it was the discovery of how much Madame loved to walk. The first time after her arrival that the court went to Versailles in the morning, he and she walked for more than an hour. His Majesty was amazed and delighted. Except for Madame de Chevreuse he had never had a companion who liked to walk any distance. The rest of the court were exactly as Madame herself described them. They behaved like lame geese if they had to traverse as much as an acre of level green sward, puffing and panting and looking desperately for somewhere to sit down. But she herself walked like a country woman. The courtiers, who would have sneered at her on that account, refrained when it brought her into such favour with the King. The warmth of his friendship changed their attitude, and by the time she had been a year in France she was loved and flattered by the whole court. Except her husband's special friends.

From the point of view of my own undistinguished person, as I grew older I was still, at the age of fourteen, scarcely taller than a well grown child of seven, and still entirely solitary except for this great boon of being allowed to wait upon Madam.

If this memoir is ever read at all, I would not like my reader to think that I grieved over this very much. I had never known anything different. I had never been led to expect otherwise, and my unusual physical condition accustomed me from the very beginning to the notion that I was different. I felt no need to take offence at not being included, or handled with affection, since no one had ever promised me otherwise and nature herself seemed to have made a special provision. Those flowers which grow in a man's heart in response to love and kindness were not destroyed in me; they only remained like seeds in ground too cold for germination. But in time this changed, and notably in the following fashion.

One evening, I made a friend of a little page who was sent over from Holland to be brought up at Madame's court. His name was Eberhardt Ernst Franz, and he was six. Madame took great trouble about him because he was the son of her former governess, Frau von Harling; – his room, his bed, and who should have care of him was all settled by her. He was taught at once to wait at table for the Maids of Honour, who petted and kissed him as he went about his tasks partly because he was in Madame's special charge and partly because he was so pretty.

He was courageous too; but nevertheless one evening soon after his arrival, as I was making my way quietly along a corridor, I heard him crying in his bedroom for the sister that he had left behind in Holland. As it happened, I was carrying with me a little wooden horse that I had made, with a leather saddle, and legs that moved. I was adept at such things. My arms were strong and my hands quite neat, in direct contrast to the rest of me. I enjoyed making toys, and working out novel ways of getting them to move or even make sounds.

I decided to give this horse to the child, and so I slipped quietly into his room where, as I suspected, he was alone. If I had found his governess in there I would have withdrawn so quietly and fast that no attention would have been given to the opening door.

I approached the bed. I was afraid to speak to him in case the boy was frightened by my mouth, though it was almost dark in his room at the time. So I simply sat myself down nearby and pushed the horse into his hands.

I heard him catch his breath. I moved the candle, which was on a table, nearer to him, so that he could see the horse better. There was a sudden scrape of a chair in the adjoining room just at that moment, and the voice of his governess said something in a tone that was both hushed and sharp to someone else. Another door opened and a man's voice said "Marthe!" A draught momentarily drew the candle flame to one side, but then they went off into another room.

Ernst had not taken any notice of all this. He was entranced, holding the horse, with his mouth hanging open and his fat cheek rounded with a great smile, moving one of the legs up and down. I showed him how, if the horse was gently dragged against a hard smooth surface, all the legs were activated in the proper sequence. He nearly laughed out loud as he looked up at me. I was so pleased that I forgot to turn my face away. He must have been looking at me for several seconds before I remembered, but as he seemed not to be afraid of what he saw in my face and it was too late anyway, I did not try to hide my features. He asked me if I could make a carriage to go with the horse, and I told him that the horse's name was Joyeuse.

It is amazing how someone who had been completely friendless can suddenly find that those days are over. I now had not only the interest of Madame and the tacit acceptance of her household, but also the friendship of this boy. Admittedly he was very young, but he was clever, and he seemed not to care about my deformities. He would even put his hand in mine.

All this made me wish to improve myself if I possibly could, and this is why I went to the King to request that my allowance should be increased in accordance with my age. He would either tell my father to do it, or give it himself. My idea was to have some new clothes. I had always kept myself clean since I came to Court, but it had seemed pointless to attempt to dress my wretched body with any art. Now, however, it began to occur to me that there were ways by which my ugliness could be lessened if my clothes were carefully put together. This was the occasion of the King making those remarks to me which I quoted; but he did also see to it that I received six hundred livres a year from then on.

The improvements I was able to achieve were limited. I could not do anything about my face; but to take one example among many, the Duc de Luxembourg with his great humps before and behind managed to be considered a very attractive man in his way and he had many mistresses. As there were so many at court who were deformed by crippling illnesses in childhood, small pox or malformations at birth, our tailors were expert in the use of horsehair and panniers to construct clothes so that regardless of a misshapen body they would lie straight. And as for height, shoes and wigs could make all the difference. For example, in later years the Duc de Saint Simon wore the highest heels in court, but for a while I had that honour.

However, I kept this finery for special occasions. I had learned to value my invisibility too much to abandon it entirely, especially as after a period of time the malevolence of Madame's enemies began to resurface in a new guise, and all my initial fears sprang back to life. To protect her from harm became my absolute obsession. The fables of La Fontaine were very fashionable just then, and I thought I recognised in myself the Rat who returned the kindness of the king of beasts by saving his life.

MALICE

CHAPTER FIVE

The state of siege in which Madame lived under the watchful but frustrated eye of her husband's jealous acolytes lasted for three, or even four years. During that time, although I could see that Monsieur's friends remained unconverted from the stance in which I had first detected their enmity, yet they were so thwarted that their attacks were limited to the mixture of ingratiating and malicious behaviour quite familiar at court. I watched constantly for signs of more dangerous schemes, but there were none.

Theobon, the Countess de Beauvron, was as watchful as I. This lady had become as much my friend as any ill-favoured boy could expect a noble woman to be. And as she was never one to mince her words I had become a convenient confidant when her feelings got the better of her. But the fact was that despite Philippe's inclination towards young men and boys, he fathered three children by Madame, and the delight which this brought to his wife and those of her household eclipsed other matters. And I had often watched how, with ceaseless good humour in their daily life at court Madame cultivated the good natured friendship of her husband, and with such success that if only her enemies could have been taken elsewhere by their friend the Devil, Monsieur would have adored her.

But just as sailors describe changes of weather at sea, when calm water suddenly heaps itself up and crashes down on the helpless men, one unforgettable afternoon a certain event marked a catastrophic change in the life of Madame.

It happened when the Duc de Valois, Madame's first son, was three years old. He was a delightful child, born without a single defect, as was his brother the Duc de Chârtres a year later. Neither of them showed any tendency toward the hazards that so often mar a child and develop, through infancy, into the humps and hunch backs and other blemishes which feature so noticeably at Court.

Madame adored babies, and she would have spent most of the day playing with them if she had been allowed. Monsieur, since he was so handsome himself, took all the credit for their good looks, and said that their robust health was the gift of his wife. Perhaps that was why what happened happened. Madame's enemies would have liked to destroy all coinage that had her image stamped on it. Only the limits set by her being so much in fashion had temporarily masked their cruelty.

One week when the Maréchale de Clerembault, the children's governess, brought the little Duc de Valois and his brother, de Châtres, to Madame's apartment after the *levée*, the Duc de Valois had a cold. Madame took them one by one in her arms as usual. Vienne had not yet arrived to do her hair, nor had she put on her court dress. Whatever anyone said about her plainness, the truth, regardless of any predisposition on my part, was that she had many moments of beauty. She didn't need rouge on her cheeks in the morning. They were pink and made her eyes sparkle, and her entire body looked full of sweetness.

As she held the Duc de Valois, the rumpled fine linen fell back from her sleeve and shoulder. Any church painter could, if he had had the sense to do it, have used her as a model for an image of the Virgin.

"It is only a cold," the Maréchale said.

Madame held the little face against her cheek. She made a remark in German that sounded like something between the purr of a cat and a snatch of song. His baby brother, the Duc de Châtres, had been put down by his nurse where he could hold onto Madame's knees, whereupon she planted a kiss on his upturned face with such vigour that he fell over. At once three pairs of hands reached to lift him up and Madame, laughing, made the child laugh too. But the Duc de Valois started to cry.

I thought perhaps Madame had squeezed him when she reached down for his brother.

"I think he's ill," Madame said anxiously. She felt his forehead with one hand, and with words of endearment in German questioned him, and held her face against his cheek again.

"He's very hot!" she said. But then caught herself up and said to the nurse, "I forbid you to mention it."

This was because she feared the practise of French doctors who might come and bleed the infant to death – or so she thought – before she could stop them and if they could find a pretext to do it.

The Maréchale looked sternly at the little child, and said over her shoulder to the nurse,

"How many times were you woken in the night?"

"Twice, Madame la Maréchale."

"And he was sick?" asked Madame.

"Infants are so often sick, Madame."

In the end Madame let him go, but as he was carried off she followed after him, leading his younger brother by the hand. When they were gone she said to Theobon, "I wish I had a German nurse, but Monsieur won't allow it. He thinks the French management of infants is the best, but as I said to him, 'Why then do they die? They don't die like that in my country. We don't bleed them, and bind them, and feed them the wrong food.'"

Theobon's lips were sewn together. Even with her reputation for tart remarks and straight talking, she knew when to hold her tongue. And besides, she loved Madame.

Later in the morning Madame vented her anxiety in a letter to her aunt, and complained in full of French doctors and their care of children. The Duc de Chârtres had been wrapped in a poultice at eleven months that blistered his arm, and she was still furious about it.

Madame didn't regain her good humour until her friend Dou Dou came to talk to her about a new play by Molière. Also the King had arranged for the performance of a new ballet at Marly, and Monsieur had a visit from an Italian silk merchant. The pace of the day quickened, and although she still sent to the Duc de Valois' apartment for news every hour, Madame became engrossed again in the business of court life. By evening the talk was all of Marly, and there seemed to be no doubt that she and Monsieur would go as usual.

Of course, I did not go to Marly. I still have never been there, and there is no reason why His Majesty should ever do me the honour of inviting me. The King had invested the energy, wealth and genius typical of him in the creation of this country retreat. Regularly those courtiers who were invited to accompany him would go there for the weekend. The gardens and the water and fountains were described as wonders to those who hadn't seen them. And the King prided himself on entertainments that surpassed those in any court in Europe.

Monsieur and Madame had their own apartment permanently set aside for them at Marly, and those courtiers who stepped up to the King on the eve with the question, "Marly, Sire?" were triumphant if they received a nod of consent, and bitterly disappointed if it was a denial.

Naturally Madame could not be rid of the Chevalier de Lorraine even there. He always went, together with the other three favourites. But this time I was surprised to discover that Mesdames Gordon and de Grancy were not going; and then Mme. de Grancy let slip that the Gordon was unwell and she, Elizabeth, was staying behind to comfort her.

If Elizabeth de Grancy was suddenly going to indulge in acts of self-sacrifice, it was time to keep an eye on the sun in case it rose at midnight. But people pay little attention to uncommon details when they are busy with enjoyment and fashion. Even I hardly noticed it. In the evening the Duc de Valois was reported to be still sick, and Madame thought of not going to Marly. But on the morrow he seemed better, so she went.

Life for those left behind in the Palace of St. Germain was dull. Courtiers not invited to Marly tried not to show their faces in the hope that it might be thought that they had gone. And then it was extremely quiet without Madame, not to mention the King himself and his mistresses, and the Queen. I, who liked to read, shut myself up in the King's library, or spent my time looking at paintings, and studying them.

At about five o'clock I decided to go to see if the Duc de Valois was well again. I knew my way, of course, to the children's apartment. I knew my way everywhere. I approached very quietly. The door of the ante room was open. The curtains were half drawn in the room, and all was in shadow, so that as I slipped noiselessly in it was easy to be unobserved. That said, it was unpleasantly silent. The Duc de Chârtres was still playing in the garden with his nurse, where I had just seen him from a window, and in the hush of the bedchamber even my footfall would have attracted the attention of the nurse if she had not been just at that moment walking with her back to me out of the room. I decided to stay a little while. There was a screen conveniently placed near the child's bed behind which I could hide if his attendants should return too soon.

The Duc de Valois was in a heavy sleep. I could hear his breathing, and very soon the swish of skirts as the same, or another, lady returned. She eventually seated herself between where I was hidden and the bed. There was also a curtain behind the screen and in an alcove, the window. I looked cautiously out into the room. My methods for remaining unobserved when I wished were very thorough. For example, I looked for any glass in which I might be accidentally reflected and discovered. In this case there was none. The woman sitting beside the sleeping child was a familiar figure among the Duc's attendants, but in a humble capacity and under the charge of Mademoiselle Héloise, a niece of the Maréchale de Clerembault. After a few moments she got up and resettled the pillow and the linen on the bed. I looked and saw that the child did not wake from his heavy sleep. Then she walked over to the middle of the room to fetch something that was there and I could have made my escape without being seen, but I did not.

Why I took such pains to remain in hiding I never knew. I have wondered since what instinct may have prompted me, because just then who should come tip toe into the room with their fingers on their lips and unfamiliar expressions of motherly concern on their faces, but Elizabeth de Grancy and Madame Gordon. I felt the hackles on my neck rise. The nurse stood, and made a deep curtsey.

"How is the little darling Duc de Valois?" whispered the Grancy. The two of them approached close to the bed.

"Isn't he adorable," whispered the Gordon.

Elizabeth de Grancy had something in her pocket. When she took it out it was only a little kerchief of brown silk.

"Where is Mademoiselle Héloise? Fetch her. We will watch over the child for you."

It was at this point that my heart, previously beating at four times its normal rate, stopped. The nurse looked from one to the other of them. The attendants on the royal children are not allowed to leave them in the company of any one not appointed by His Majesty, even for a moment. The two evil wretches who were now standing there knew this well, but they were in luck because this nurse was no more than a humble servant and unlikely to assert herself in opposition to their will. There were exceptions to this rule. The old woman who had been King Louis' wet nurse still woke His Majesty every morning with a kiss. But not all such servants were raised above their station. To take a very humble example, look at mine.

This one looked over towards the door from which Mademoiselle Héloise might reappear without being called, or someone else. But no one came. And so she made another deep curtsey, and in spite of knowing that she should not do so, she went out, leaving the two visitors alone with the sleeping child.

At once Elizabeth de Grancy took her finger out from that piece of brown silk in which she had been rummaging. Then she bent over the bed while Madame Gordon kept watch over the door opposite, and put her finger between the lips of the Duc de Valois.

I could see her through a join in the screen, as I had once seen Madame in such a different place. I wonder what the expression on the

Grancy's lowered face may have been, as very gently, like a dirty maid testing the surface of cream being settled in a pan, she dipped her poisoned finger into his mouth. Instinctively the child, still sleeping, sucked.

Although I saw everything, I was also bewildered. I could not believe what was happening. I should have shouted and leapt out and seized the woman by the throat, and in my imagination, for the rest of my life, I tormented myself with vivid reconstructions of the scene in which I flew through the air like a cat and grappled her neck and shoulders with my nails and teeth until she bled to death. But at the time, I did nothing. I simply witnessed it, frozen in horror at what I saw. I have since read of the dreadful crime of Charles de Navarre who poisoned the infant daughters of the Dauphin with arsenic, but that's another matter.

In the next minute Mademoiselle Héloise came back into the room. Madame Gordon was very astute, the way she stood between the door and her friend. By the time the Lady in attendance on the child could see both her visitors, Elizabeth de Grancy had taken a step back.

The three of them exchanged a few remarks, and then the intruders left. Mademoiselle was joined by another of the ladies attached to the royal children. From that moment the room was never empty and because of the precise place where I had hidden myself, I could not move without being discovered. So I stayed where I was.

It must have been half an hour later that one of the ladies made an exclamation of alarm and concern. I heard another go running, and then Mademoiselle Héloise was in the room again.

Apparently the child had opened his eyes, but appeared not to be seeing anything, and his complexion was livid and sweating. The next thing I heard was that he began to scream. It was a terrible sound. It was like the scream of a cat being crushed under a door.

In my hiding place I was at my wits end. If I was discovered I would certainly be suspected of having harmed the child myself. Elizabeth de Grancy would deny it if I said what she had done. Even now I doubted the evidence of my own eyes, and there was nothing more certain but that I, and not she, would seem to be the criminal in the case if I revealed myself and attempted to accuse her. The thought turned me to stone. I hardly dared to breathe.

I heard the doctors arrive. The child's pulse was very weak. It stopped screaming, and one of them said, hopefully, that the crisis was over, and the child would sleep now and wake well.

But then he vomited. In the silence after the screaming, and in the watchful pause of all around him, it was an awful quiet noise. A lady said, in a voice of horror, "Look!" And then I had the impression that she fainted, because there was more commotion than can be made with a small body.

I was trapped in my hiding place for two hours, and I remember with shame that I wet myself and not just with tears. Word was sent to Marly to fetch Madame. The doctors meanwhile decided to bleed the child. I knew how angry Madame would be, but again of course I could do nothing. If I had ever imagined I could be to the Princess as the Rat had been to the Lion, and save her life, the vanity of my fancy was bitterly brought home to me, because I was useless. All I did manage to do was to hide myself effectively for as long as I had to, and escape eventually without being seen. The Duc de Valois died during the night.

Madame had set out from Marly, with the King and Monsieur when the child was still alive, and arrived before dawn not knowing whether the child was dead or not. It was raining, and the King's doctors stood near the gates. Although the coachmen leapt down while the wheels were still turning they could not be in time to open the carriage door before Madame herself threw it wide. But she remained seated, with her hand held to her mouth, and her eyes fixed with terror on the Doctors – Monsieur Tissot and his colleagues. They would have hurried forward if the child had been well again. They held back with their faces bowed.

The rain soaked a large swatch of her gown where her cloak had fallen open. Her attendants in the following carriage seemed equally frozen with fear as if they dared not come near her, and the sudden silence underpinned with the deceitful drip of water, the dark night, and stillness of the horses was, to my guilty consciousness, unforgettably menacing. In the end it was the King himself who came forward and stood beside Madame in the rain, with his hat in his hand.

His Majesty was renowned for the exact distinction with which he would acknowledge every living person in his realm. Even for a washerwoman he would touch the brim of his hat, and with all the gradations in between, for a Prince he would briefly raise it. But before a mother who had just learned that her child was dead I think he might have stood bare headed in the rain whether she had been his sister in law or not.

Madame bowed her head where she sat, and wept in silence. No one moved. A wraith of daylight, like a ghost, crept along the margins of the gates, but still the only sound was the falling of the rain and the movement of the horses. At last the King said, in a low voice, "Madame," and held out his hand to help her from the carriage.

Monsieur descended from the other side, and while he was walking round to join his wife, she stepped out and took the arm of the King. The futility of little cares in the face of mortality meant that neither Madame herself, nor those around her, noticed if she was soaked to the skin or not. She turned her face up to the King and said, "Can I see him?" as if she thought perhaps the answer might be no, and she would not be allowed to see the body of her dead child. She looked, as she asked the question, in an unforgettable manner at the King. I had noticed before how Madame could suddenly change, and the form of a simple young woman emerge from the chrysalis of majesty, but it never happened in a manner more likely to break the hearts of everyone around her than on this dark and wretched dawn.

When the King reassured her, the idea of holding even the dead body of her child filled her with a desperate anxiety to have him at once, and she moved with such haste that she tripped and nearly fell.

When at last she found herself looking down on the little figure of her child she felt – as she said later when writing to her aunt in Hanover – as if her heart simply left her body. Worse still, for an instant she thought she saw a movement. She gave a gasp and crammed her fist against her mouth. But she was mistaken. Then she leaned down, and with mouse like care, as if afraid to wake him, began to lift him up. But she couldn't do it. Unwieldy with the stiffness of death, he could not fold himself into his mother's embrace as he had before and his body resisted the softness of her arms like a log of wood. With a little moan of despair she put him down. She held her skin against his face, but his cheek felt like a tea cup, or an apple in Winter. In the end she let herself be led away to her apartment.

When next I saw her all the formalities to do with the death of the little Duc de Valois were over. He had been laid to rest, as the saying is, but knowing what I knew I could not believe he rested at his ease. The very sight of Madame herself was excruciating to me. She began to take part in court life again, but I knew the deep sadness that she felt and I simply could not bear the knowledge that she had been so wounded deliberately, by an enemy.

Knowing myself to be the only one alive with the knowledge of the murder, with the exception of those two unspeakable women who had killed him, the deed was lodged in my own heart. Even now I can hardly describe my state. It always pained me to some extent to sit or walk or stand, but now it was as if I had swallowed something terrible which weighed heavily inside me and crushed my vitals every time I moved. I was weary to death. I felt like another assassin.

Madame herself hid her grief. It was not the part of a royal princess to be weaker than other women, and so she bore herself in the way that she had been taught to do. But the very fact that she showed such courage increased the anguish of anyone who observed and loved her.

One day Theobon, who often spoke to me, planted herself within a foot or so of my corner and said, without actually turning her head toward me, but out of the corner of that thin mouth of hers,

"Well, Monsieur de Brisse," (she called me Berthon usually,) "I begin to wonder whether it is you or Madame who has recently lost a child!"

"What do you mean?" I said.

"Why," turning round squarely on me like a hen defending a patch of grain, "Madame has her own suffering to take care of, and yours, I can tell you, being added to it is too much."

"Madame la Comtesse," I said to her, "What have I done wrong?"

"I will tell you what you have done wrong!" she said predictably enough, since she was known for being very generous with her opinions at any time; "You have become even thinner than usual. Your colour is all gone. And you sigh."

"I do not sigh!" I said, aghast.

She just clenched her lips together. There was a silence between us, and in that silence I heard the silvery laugh – the tinny laugh – of Madame Gordon, followed at once by a giggle from Monsieur and a loud guffaw from Lorraine. Taken in conjunction with what Theobon had just been saying I could hardly have been expected to bear the presence of Mme. Gordon at that moment. And for an instant I contemplated taking Theobon at least into my confidence and telling her my awful secret. But she pre-empted me. I think my skin must have flushed and I certainly dug my nails into the palms of my hands because she made a point of noticing both these in a very tart fashion and was about to say something when Monsieur Tiladet suddenly appeared and she was called away. But she did not forget me.

It was as a consequence of this conversation that later in the afternoon, when she was writing her letters, Madame ended a page and then laid down her pen and looked around the room until she detected me in my usual place. She looked at me for a little while without saying anything, holding her head on one side and with her tongue between her teeth. The corner of her lips lifted in what was not quite a smile and she shook her head,

"Come here, Monsieur de Brisse," she said.

I bowed deeply and came forward. Charmille, seeing that I was to approach within her reach, half stood on Madame's lap, lost her footing on a fold of silk between Madame's knees, and was pressed back into position, which she accepted with a number of small squeaks and flurries.

"I have been writing to Madame Harling," the Princess said. "She was my governess, you know. And I had not had time to tell her yet about the death of my dear child."

She spoke with great composure. It was her intention to set me right because Theobon had complained about me. I said,

"I am so sorry Madame. Words cannot express how much I grieve for you."

She raised her eyes brows gently and looked at me down her nose.

"Too much, I think," she said.

I braced myself. I could hardly look at her. Her expression was all kindness, although I think she intended to be stern. And I stood there knowing that I had watched her child being murdered, and done nothing.

"It is natural," she said, choosing the very worst word. There had been nothing natural in this case. "Children do die, you know. I have spoken sharply about the doctors, but the fact of the matter is that they had no hand in this. No one knows why children become ill sometimes, and that was the case with him. I must bear it. And so must my friends."

I felt my heart would burst. It was almost as bad as having killed the child myself that I should know, and not inform against, his murderers, but be consoled by his mother in this way. I made a supreme effort and remained standing and silent, but my eyes poured out tears as if I had water in my veins in place of blood, and this is not permitted in court. Instead of becoming angry with me, Madame pointed at the cushion at her feet, so that I could sit down.

"Theobon told me that I must forbid you to grieve any longer," she said, "but now I must confess that it comforts me to see that your sadness is almost like my own. You never had a mother, did you?"

"No, Madame," I said.

"Poor Goblin," she sighed. "Because mothers love their children. They love them in a way, you know, which is not often spoken of in this country. But that's not to say they don't feel it. A lady who lost a child last spring never said a word and laughed and played as ever, but I happen to know that she wept bitterly in private." She paused, and then added with a small, sad smile, "and so do I."

I could see that I would have to keep my secret for the rest of my life. If Madame ever discovered that Gordon and Grancy had poisoned her son, it would drive her mad. I said, "Madame, the Duc de Valois was an adorable child with such pretty ways that if he had been born in some humble place instead of as the son of a great princess he would still have been admired."

"He was very pretty!" she said. If it had been her plan to scold me for melancholy, she had forgotten about it.

"Do you remember when he kissed Charmille on the nose and she sneezed so hard in his face that he fell over backwards."

"And laughed," I said. "He laughed."

She was pleased that I remembered that. She had a way of holding her arms across her body and then at times, when amused, lifting her shoulders and she did it now, looking full at me.

"You know that little dog you gave him, with legs that moved? He had it in his bed."

With her mind upon that, Madame paused a long while. The expression on her face lost all its warmth. When the thought of the little boy was most present in her mind and then the fact that he was dead, it shocked her again and again. I think she decided, "If I can unburden my feelings occasionally to this strange little creature who seems to love me, I may have some help from it, and it can do me no harm. He can't use my confidence like an ordinary courtier."

Even so she had had enough of this conversation now. She dismissed me, saying, "I may talk to you again, Monsieur de Brisse. And in the meantime you have my permission to be my secret companion in these feelings. Which means that you must not be too sad, because I have my duties, you know. It will not do for me to be too sad, and therefore you can set me an example. And from time to time you may recount your memories to me, and that will be as good as having his portrait, which of course I have had painted but it is only a picture, and does not give me as much comfort."

I got up from the ground, and bowed deeply to her. The interview was over. And from then onwards I tried to do as she had told me.

CHAPTER SIX

I like to think that the heart of man is essentially courteous; that we recognise our mutual helplessness in the ragged puzzle of mortality and pay the respect we owe to each other's suffering. But where I got such a notion and why I keep it when I live here at court is as great a puzzle as birth and death itself. Take the tragic history of the little Duc de Valois as I just told you. There were those among Madame's friends who did feel for her, but among those who did not there was apparently no compunction in causing her further suffering.

It was now a matter of weeks since that event, and as I said Madame bore herself and had resumed the pattern of her normal days so bravely that life went on in her drawing room as before. One afternoon I was in attendance as usual but hidden from view by the folds of a curtain that fell heavily in that corner of the room, when the quiet of the apartment – never long maintained, because of the continuous attention of those who came to pay court to Madame – was shattered by the arrival of Monsieur with ten or a dozen others to sit and play Bassett. As usual Madame was perfectly content to continue writing if she happened to be engaged on a letter, but this time Monsieur's companions made such a tremendous noise with their game that eventually she laid down her pen and put her hands over her ears. Her husband was shouting, and everyone else competing to shout louder, and first, the words *Albiura et la face!* They were so rowdy that Motte began to bark. Madame, laughing, put down her pen and positively shouted over the *melée*.

"You are making more noise than the hounds made this morning," she said, "when my horse started a hare out hunting with the King."

I was glad to hear her say this. The affection of the King, and the general awareness of it by others, should provide some measure of protection for Madame against the dangerous schemes of her enemies, and it did them good to be reminded that she was, in hunting as in walking, a favourite companion of His Majesty. At this time, Madame herself was the height of fashion at court. Even her style of dress had been imitated. Félicité de Blonde, who was sitting at this very moment beside d'Effiat, had had a zibeline made, and many of the ladies had rushed to get little sables in one form or another. It was a laughable form of flattery. Worthy of devotion though Madame was, it was not for her taste in clothes that one admired her. It was her sense of humour; her regal presence; her kindness; her way of gently pulling Charmille's ears when at a loss for the right word; the lightness of her step; her wit and lively intelligence when talking of Racine, Molière, Lully and so forth. Her dress sense would have always struck any sensible person as flawed.

But to return to the scene at cards when all this hung in the balance, in response to Madame's remark about hunting the gratified smiles of others showed their pleasure at the preference the King demonstrated for her, but d'Effiat bit his lip. A female foot under the table shod in violet snake skin with an enamelled buckle in the shape of a letter G, gave his ankle a nudge. It must have been Elizabeth de Grancy's foot because such small and stylish slippers would not have fit on the great Scottish hoof of Madame Gordon. Having tapped d'Effiat's ankle this little shoe slithered around to the other side of his foot and as if still worn by the snake that must have given it substance in the first place, gave three strokes to the inside of his leg.

Meanwhile the Chevalier de Lorraine, who had come into the room as if on cue, was looking at Monsieur's cards over his shoulder with one hand resting on his master's neck. There was a moment's pause during which, if the eye had been trained to it, one might have detected the preliminary swelling of a treacherous wind. Lorraine must have planned carefully with his friends to create this moment of opportunity. They must have deliberated and plotted precisely the current that should be stirred up, to agitate the waters sufficiently and capsize the little boat of Madame's happiness. He cast a measured glance at her from the sideways corner of his eye, and said.

"Did the Chevalier de Sinsanet catch the bridle of your horse so that you might not be carried away again, Madame?"

On the face of it, this was only a remark; and yet instinct warned all who were there to pay particular attention. A frisson went through the room. A courtier can always recognise an attack.

Madame looked up. When all was said and done she had been raised at court herself, and she knew the Chevalier was not her friend. With the smile of a moment ago half suppressed but still turning the corner of her lip, she said,

"Not on this occasion. There was no need. I ride behind the Guards, you know." She glanced down and folded a sheet of paper. "They only help me when I want it."

She proceeded to write again as if unaware of the heightened atmosphere around her, but in fact she felt the Chevalier's malice.

That court contained, as well as fools and libertines, many men and women of cultivated intelligence and wit. But no courtier, whether rich or poor, ignorant or wise, held themselves aloof from the game of scandal and intrigue that formed the matrix of life there. It was a fine art, at which even the average gentleman and lady excelled. And so, when Madame returned to her letter-writing with an air of dismissing the Chevalier, there was not one person present who did not, under the guise of normality, watch almost breathless to see what would happen next. And this is what happened.

The game resumed but Lorraine himself did not leave Monsieur's side. And after the briefest interval, so that no one could miss the connection between Madame's denial and whatever it was he then said, Lorraine bent and whispered something in his master's ear which seemed to cause them both amusement.

The insolence of the Chevalier's behaviour took my breath away, and one could see clearly that it was not lost on others in the room, who half concealed here a smile behind a fan, or there a cheek with a sudden spot of colour. The implication was clearly that Lorraine had some reason to link the name of the Chevalier de Sinsanet with Madame, but until opportunity loosened his tongue he would not be able to carry the speculation forward.

For another twenty minutes Madame continued to write. From the way she did it no one could guess that she gave enough importance to whatever insolence Lorraine could produce to be unsettled. Courage is the same, whether it's a question of the battlefield or the drawing room.

When she had got to the end of the paragraph she looked up, and there were Lorraine and his cronies still hanging on her husband's neck. And among the courtiers at large, as soon as the opportunity arose, Lorraine's insinuations about the Chevalier de Sinsanet would be analysed and passed from mouth to mouth. And Monsieur was notoriously fickle. He would lend an ear to any nonsense if it was put in a certain way.

But Madame had not only been raised at court; she had been loved a great deal when she was a child and this, I have noticed, gives certain people strength in their later lives. Madame also out-ranked everyone in the room except her husband. These certainties were like a shield that she could hold against attack, and she did so with a sang froid that won the respect of those in the room who were keeping their eye upon her.

She stood up, saying that she was going to visit Mademoiselle de la Vallière. I should have stayed where I was, in order to listen to what was said when she had gone; but I lost my head. Anxiety for her well being overcame me, and I could not bear to let her out of my sight. Accompanied by the Maréchale de Clerembault who was the governess of her children, she left the room. A moment later I followed her, and taking another route, I arrived at the apartment of the King's mistress before her.

CHAPTER SEVEN

It was not just in order to escape from the unwholesome atmosphere created by Lorraine that Madame visited Louise de la Vallière that afternoon. It was planned, and had been prompted by kindness, because la Vallière had, the previous evening, been insulted by the King, and everyone knew about it.

At this time, although she was still *Maîtresse en titre*, she no longer monopolised Louis' affections. He had allowed his attention to wander from Louise to Athénaïs de Montespan, who was a member of Louise de la Vallière's own household and the governess of her children. By fair means or foul, as witness the murder of my poor birds, de Montespan used even witchcraft to ensnare the King, and by now she had so far succeeded that she had already borne him two children and he had transferred all his affection to her. This is not an unusual sequence of events. It often happens that a man's desire is triggered by the frequent sight of another woman in his household occupied with the children, and Louis XIV did this three times.

But although seduced by the Montespan, he insisted on keeping to the same domestic arrangements as before. La Vallière was still his Maîtresse en titre; Athénaïs was still a member of La Vallière's household; and to some extent this cruel arrangement had led to the scene which had so upset Louise de la Vallière, and scandalised the court.

Madame de Montausier was one of the very few who were pleased by the incident, because she adored the Montespan, and she showed herself still entirely capable of the hard hearted silliness of Les Précieuse, whose leader she had once been.

"My dear, the King was only retiring for the night," she said. She had the habit of turning morsels of gossip into recitations, on this occasion adopting the role of faux naif and playing it like she did her cards, with little flourishes.

"Alone?" said someone else.

The Princess de Conti laughed.

"Naturally, not alone but with Madame de Montespan."

"Do you mean he had her by the hand?"

"Oh, Monsieur le Duc!"

"I did not mean to imply that he held another part of her, Madame. Only that the King, who as we all know adores the lady, certainly had his hand on her somewhere."

"In which case how can he have been carrying the dog.? You said he had the little creature in his arms, and now you are recounting it as if he was holding Madame de Montespan."

"He had the dog in the crook of one arm, like this, and Madame de Montespan in the other."

"How awkward."

"I was there," interjected Sidonie de Freines, "and it looked easy to me."

A courtier I didn't know got up because he was called.

"So why was La Vallière in tears?"

"Wouldn't you be, Madame, if you were obliged to watch the man whom you adored going off to bed one of your own ladies of honour?"

"I might the first time," she said, with a wicked little sigh. "But not after it had happened every night and most afternoons for three years."

One of them suppressed a giggle.

"But then, the King..."

"What did he do?"

"He threw the dog – you know that little dog; the one Monseigneur gave him – into La Vallière's lap, and said 'that's good enough for her!'"

Despite their intentions to preserve a humorous note, the company fell silent. The bitterness of loss on such a scale, when a beautiful woman who had been universally admired was humiliated in such a way, aroused an almost religious awe. But it is scarcely surprising that a woman who used sorcery to get the King into her power would have the means to make him cruel as well. The days were long gone when she needed the help of such sorcery and wicked devices to secure His Majesty's favour as had caused the death of my poor birds, and yet she had not given up these means. Far from it. They caused her downfall in the end.

Louise de la Vallière, who was still as beautiful as ever, and still loved the King, submitted without complaint to whatever he did. This afternoon her apartment was crowded because others, like Madame, came to demonstrate their fondness for her at a time when she needed it. Athénaïs de Montespan held court at one end of the room, while La Vallière herself received her friends at the other.

Being by now much better habituated myself to company, I was already sitting talking to one of Mademoiselle de la Vallière's Maids of Honour who was a particular friend when a moment later Madame entered. She did not look around generally but gave all her attention to La Vallière, who got up and crossed the room to welcome her. La Vallière limped, of course. Curiously enough, this limp only added to her attraction. Blond curls like an angel, a gentle and modest expression, and sweet manners distinguished her. Her beauty only served to attract attention to these other qualities, which then became the anchor of one's affections. The same was even true for the King before his infatuation with Athénaïs de Montespan corrupted him.

Madame smiled very warmly and kissed La Vallière, and settled down beside her to have what she called a good gossip. She paid no attention at all to the Montespan, positioned at the other end of the room and seeming to be out of humour. You would have thought, to contemplate Athénaïs de Montespan's sullen looks, that it was she who had been rejected by the King, and who had lost both her position and her heart. She looked pale, and her very red lips and dark hair made one think of ripe fruit in a tapestry. Mme. de Vieuville was paying court to her, and a number of others. She answered them curtly, tossing her head and seeming almost close to tears, and of course she noticed that Madame gave her no greeting.

La Vallière who had so much more cause for discontent, bore herself with an air of sad but gentle dignity. Madame de Sévigné's nicknames for them as the Dew and the Torrent seemed particularly apt just then. As soon as the King arrived, La Vallière rose again, as we all did, and her skin, that was so pale and beautiful, took on an even more transparent tone. Otherwise she was composed. She didn't twist her hands or make any sudden gestures, but gave him a calm and graceful greeting which he almost ignored in his haste to approach the Montespan.

Madame looked very plainly at it all, her chin drawn in and her eyes wide open with an expression that reminded me of a peasant child I saw once whose father was drunk and attempting to conceal the fact that he had smashed a basket full of eggs. Unaware of this the King, striding across the room and radiant with energy took the Montespan's hand, kissed it, and then said to the company in general that they were going to play ombre and to gamble in the drawing room and that whoever wished could join them.

MALICE

Many of the company followed, but not La Vallière. She, however, looked after her former lover with an expression of such adoration and submission on her face, that it was almost shocking to see. Is it right to love so much? I wonder. If Summer flowers paid no attention to the frosts of Winter, but continued to bloom, what would we think?

And then with a faint smile La Vallière said to her friend the Duchess, "I am very fortunate in having the pleasure of your company, Madame, when I have so little entertainment to offer, as you see."

Madame took her hand in both of hers, and having stroked it gently for a moment said,

"Come. Sit down again. I haven't told you of Monsieur's latest idea for the decoration of my bed chamber."

Soon afterwards I withdrew; and it was precisely because I left just when I did and without any purpose more urgent than going to look for Ernst, that I stumbled on Lorraine and discovered the intended sequel to the slanderous attack on Madame which he had launched that very day.

I chose the darkest passages and the quietest stairs as I went, as usual. At the time the Court was still housed in the palace of Saint Germain, the palace of Versailles being not yet completed. In St. Germain there were a great number of dark passages, intricate corridors and small staircases to connect the different parts of the building. These routes were very useful for anyone who wanted to move around unseen, and particularly so on this occasion, because in the narrow passage that went from the tribune into the corridor of the old wing I discovered the Chevalier de Lorraine who was standing with Madame de Coetquen in his arms.

Neither of them saw me. Just in time I shrank back, but I realised at once that they would certainly not have been able to hear me. There was a tremendous noise of silk and linen cloth being tossed and crumpled as the Chevalier almost seemed bodily to swim into the tides of the lady's voluminous garments in order to part them and make way for himself.

She was wearing what were called wide skirts, which was a style the Montespan had introduced to conceal the evidence when she became pregnant with the King's children. I was suddenly struck with the irrelevant thought that the Montespan must be pregnant again, because to support her, when she was breeding, all her ladies wore them at the same time. No matter that, as Madame so amusingly remarked, the dress itself had become the equivalent of posting the lady's condition up on a notice board, Madame de Montespan still clung to it.

That apart, the fashion was clearly a convenient style for concealing other things that were going on as well as a pregnancy. The Chevalier had got the lady into such a position that it almost looked as if he was wearing her clothes, so absolutely swathed was his body in the piled up fabric of her skirts. He had his back to me and she, with her face and closed, eyes turned up as if she was swooning, was making a rather lovely little sound between her clenched teeth. I was young, of course, and very interested in what was going on. I shrank into the shadow of the corner around which I had just emerged, and watched with fascination for a good while.

Eventually the Chevalier put the lady down. You could tell from her voice that she was pleased and smiling. However, it wasn't of love that she spoke when she had got her breath at last..

"You really need not fret," she said eventually. "Killing her is wild talk. It's absurd to imagine that Monsieur could ever prefer a fat German woman to you."

Her words had the same effect on me as a hole in the road has on the wheels of a cart. As for Lorraine, he was tidying his clothes with absent minded care, and although he smiled, the corner of his lip was pulled down in contradictory bitterness. He put forward another suggestion in a tone that implied a desperate hunger for blood, but Madame de Coetquen clearly thought that it was partly in jest.

I knew otherwise. I carried the burden of his villainy with me everywhere, because I knew, and others did not, that he had engineered the murder of the little Duc de Valois. Of course he, and not the women, had been the real perpetrator of the deed, just as he, not d'Effiat, had procured the poison which d'Effiat then somehow used.

"An indisposition, then."

"No, I'm telling you."

He flicked something off his sleeve, and just for a moment there was something physically repellent about his hand and that dirty finger. There was a brief silence, and then his voice said softly and cruelly,

"Madame de Sévigné's grandchild has smallpox."

Coetquen made a gesture like slapping him in play.

"I'll plant the letter for you, but I won't go further than that," she said. "Give it me."

There was a longish silence. Then the lady said, reading from the paper, "To the Chevalier de Sinsanet? Who copied this? It looks like

Madame's own hand. And that's a German way of spelling." Silence again, and then a laugh.

"Don't look so cross," said de Coetquen. "I am all admiration, I assure you. If Madame were to speak ill of the Queen – which she never does, one must admit that I suppose – the words in this letter that you have cleverly made are just the ones she'd use. And all this about the Chevalier de Sinsanet! You have been quite clever, my dear."

I melted further from the corner, because she had taken a step in my direction.

"The King will be very angry when he sees this," she said.

Indeed, the very thought of it made my blood run cold. How would the poor Princess be able to explain away such a convincing calumny when joined to the whispers already started by the Chevalier's remarks in the drawing room? Her position at court would be disgraced. Louis, with the power to make Madame's own country, the Palatinate, the most wretched place on earth because his armies were engaged at the time in watching His Majesty's interests in that area would, if he took action against the populace, demonstrate politically that the Duchesse d'Orléans no longer had any influence at the court of France. Madame would feel it to the very bone. She who had nothing but good will and loyalty towards her husband would be humiliated before him and before her relations throughout the courts of Europe. It seemed that Lorraine's plan, for the moment at least, was only to make Madame despised and miserable. Perhaps when he had done that he need not stoop to take her life. Truly, he was a most dangerous man, and far more so than Madame de Coetquen suspected.

The pounding of my heart was almost loud enough to make me miss the valedictory tone of de Coetquen's voice as she gaily spoke her last words, and only in the nick of time, like a shadow without a sound, I slipped out of my corner further down the passage and fled before her. But not too far. I wanted to know where she was going.

The sliding sound of her little steps as she tripped along in the court manner were well behind my own when I came to a convenient loose tapestry before the stairs, and there I concealed myself until she passed.

Emerging once again, I followed her openly as she entered the gallery thronged with people. What opportunity would she find, I wondered, to give this vile forgery which she now carried in her pocket, to the King? Or would she give it to Monsieur? Would she attempt to do it directly? I followed her into the drawing room where the King was still playing at cards with Madame de Montespan surrounded by members of the court. Madame was in the next room with a large company looking on as she played cards with the Queen. De Coetquen stopped, and looked around her. She did indeed have the letter in her pocket; but she had her hand upon the letter.

After surveying the room carefully for a while her attention seemed to settle on Monsieur Lully. Always dirty and usually drunk, it was a puzzle to make out how the Master of the King's Music could be useful in the context of the letter she carried, and getting it shown to the King. But in fact he was not her target. She started to make her way across the room, allowing no one to distract her, but when she arrived it was to Philippe Quinault, the writer, who stood beside Lully, that she spoke. This gentleman had, not so long ago, bought the post of *valet de chambre du Rôi* for three months of every year, which entitled him to make the top part of the King's bed. He would be able to present the letter that was even now being surreptitiously handed over to him by Madame de Coetquen, to the King at his *coucher* that very night. Where would the conflict between love and duty – the main theme of Quinault's writings – be then?

I could charge him with it once de Coetquen had gone.

I could say, "Monsieur Quinault, the King favours your writing and insists that your words must be the ones used by our august Master of Music for his operas because of your high moral tone. And yet you've got a forged letter in your possession there."

Or alternatively I could just pick his pocket.

I chose to do the latter.

Once I had it, all that remained was to keep it safe until I should have an opportunity of passing it to Madame with an explanation of how I'd found it. But fortunately I had the idea of not keeping it in my own pocket. I hid it behind a certain piece of tapestry when no one was looking, and then I went to pay court to Madame. She was still in the room, no longer playing cards but in lively conversation, surrounded by ladies and gentlemen, the Queen having retired to her prayers.

Climène, my half sister, had also just come in. She looked very tired but was kept standing by de Fontequieve, whose job it was to bring forward a *tabouret* stool for her. Theobon had noticed my arrival. She said to me in an undertone,

"He is a lazy fellow, that de Fontequiève. It is excessively spiteful of him to keep Climène waiting for her *tabouret* when she has paid so dearly for the right to sit in the presence of members of the Royal Family. Now that she is a Duchesse, and considering her vile tempered ugly husband, no one should grudge her the privilege."

Madame Theobon never minced her words, and what she was referring to, of course, was the pitifully ugly and deformed man Climène had married. The man's ill nature and depraved character was more important than his hump back, or the eye he had lost through smallpox. When one thinks of it, my half-sister's taste in lovers, from the incident in the cupboard some years before to this of her marriage, was not good. When on one occasion I was brave enough to say to her, "Climène, do you think you can really be happy with the Duke d'Autour?" she said, "What exactly do you mean? D'Autour is one of the richest dukes. I shall take precedence over Madames de Freines. I shall have a *tabouret*, and... Oh really, Berthon."

I said "You don't love him," And first she let her mouth open in a way that was not at all natural, and then she laughed.

I looked longingly at Climène now, because I loved her, and it was painful to see her changed looks. Her face was pale and her hair was dressed with two great *touffettes de Dinde*, which did not suit her. If it would have gladdened rather than mortified her to be served by someone like me I would have fetched her *tabouret* myself. In the end Madame called out to de Fontequiève, and he came at last with the stool.

As usual, there was a great deal of laughter wherever Madame might be. Her sense of humour – blunt enough at times – would set everyone in an absolute roar, and she was recounting the story of how the Princess de Harcourt was beaten by her maid. When she described the prelude to this event, and the many times that the Princess beat her servants, Madame pointed at the ceiling with her hand over her mouth, referring to the fact that the Princess's apartment was directly over her own, and therefore we all had heard the commotion caused at various times by these beatings that went on.

"And then again she dropped the stick on the floor," Madame exclaimed laughing, "or perhaps it broke in half, and we heard it bang bang bang, just above our heads." Her audience rocked with laughter.

"And then this time – Oh, Dou Dou (turning to her friend) have you seen this country girl. The very fact that the Harcourt's take such care of their peasants in the country is exactly why they should learn to stop beating them at Court. This well fed girl (even last Winter they didn't starve in Brittany; not if they were on Harcourt land; they dish out soup and bread every day) so she is a big girl with strong arms, and she took the stick out of the hand of the Princess, and I heard –" she put one hand partly over her mouth to pretend to hide her laughter, and looked over the top of it with her eyes wide; "We all heard her shout out as she beat her mistress, 'This is what will happen again if ever you try to hit me in the future.' And the Princess has not dismissed her!"

Madame had not noticed the Dauphin's reaction to all this. Usually he hung on her words and laughed whenever she did. It had not occurred to her now, that making a joke of a peasant's discourtesy towards a member of the aristocracy might offend him. Which was surprising too, since Madame herself was meticulous about matters of precedence and rank. If the Princess d'Harcourt had not had the apartment directly over her own so that the beatings had becomes a regular ritual which we all could not but hear, Madame would not have allowed a joke on such a subject.

She looked doubtfully at Monseigneur, clearly wondering what to say. She tried a humorous, slightly admonishing, smile, but he did not respond. He had been sitting beside his mother the Queen until she left, and stayed afterwards for Madame's sake, but she had forgotten that he was there. When she got to the point in her story where the peasant woman attacked the Duchesse he looked quite scandalised. And since Madame did not happen to notice, his colour darkened and by the time she finished he was the only one not laughing,. Obviously he was thoroughly offended by the misbehaviour that had so amused Madame.

Everyone's attention was now turned on him. Even Madame Gordon had given up her whispering and was covering her lips with her hand to avoid showing her teeth. Madame tucked in her chin as she did when about to make a riposte, but fortunately Monsieur came up at that moment to ask her to accompany him to the play, and we all left.

I had not for one moment forgotten the matter of the letter, and I was torn between deciding what to do next in that desperate connection, and the need to wait until the next day should bring an opportunity to speak to Madame in the comparative privacy of her drawing room.

Others were going to see the play. It was to be *Britannicus*, and not in the King's theatre at court, but in Paris, where the stage would be crowded with a melee of people. I was not at the time as enthusiastic for Racine as Molière. One way and another I should not have gone either from inclination or convenience because, needless to say, I had no coach of my own nor, as it happened, a ticket. But as I was about to leave, the husband of one of Madame's ladies in waiting, namely Monsieur de Labertière, appearing to speak on impulse just as I was near him, offered me both.

"I have another appointment," he said.

If he had been more polite I would have been suspicious. He looked down at me sideways, skewed his mouth up, said something about 'do me the honour' and I followed after him because it was very rare for anyone to even speak to me, apart from the small group I have already mentioned. His servant came forward, and led me to the coach.

It did not occur to me that anyone had seen me steal the letter, or deduced that I had because I was nearby. Perhaps I occasionally attributed too much to my own skill in avoiding notice when in reality I needed to remember to attribute some measure of the fact that I was ignored to a reluctance to speak to or acknowledge me, whether they saw me or not. In this case there could be no doubt that I had aroused suspicion in connection with that letter, because as soon as I got into the coach and before I was even seated the collar of my coat was seized and I was roughly dragged onto the floor. I realised that I had been deceived by Labertière.

There were two ruffians in the carriage, but they were thrown momentarily off balance themselves as the horses set off. They were masked of course. I did not even recognise a voice. But I knew at once what they were after. I would have had precious little chance of hanging on to the Chevalier de Lorraine's letter if I had not hidden it behind the tapestry. While my pockets were being searched I refrained from giving the Chevalier's messengers any trouble; but when they found they were frustrated they began to turn their malice on my person. Then I fought as hard as I could. I even had an advantage in such a small space because I could twist and turn where they could not, and in the end, when the carriage stopped at the theatre, I fell out of it onto the pavement but still managing to keep in my grip the collar tied around the throat of one of the villains. My arms are very strong and I had made my mind up not to let go, even if the second thief tried to hack my hand off.

That was exactly what he attempted. There ensued a tremendous commotion, and I would have been killed if M. de la Reynie's officers had not been present to guard the Royal visitors, and the ruffian was taken off me.

I was propped up for a while on the stone pediment by the railing. The common people were very interested. They had the insolence to gawp at me, but I could not really blame them. My usual appearance was not excellent, and this was deplorable. It made matters worse that I had changed into my best court dress. Take my shoes alone. I had been wearing the highest I had, and one of them was broken. I had also been wearing a very high wig, which was unrecognisable but which someone, perhaps with the intention of restoring my dignity although it had the opposite effect, had put back on my head. In addition I retained, of course, that which must always be of greater interest to any stranger than articles of dress which can be put on or off at will, however absurd; namely, my hare lip and my hump.

When I could stand I was approached by the Captain of the Guard attached to Madame, who informed me that her Highness the Princess Elizabeth Charlotte, Duchesse d'Orléans, had sent him to be of assistance to me. And so I returned home, soothed very much by this attention and also by the knowledge that I had foiled my attackers.

CHAPTER EIGHT

The following morning I was no worse than I usually am, except for one bruise on my face. I went to Madame's room after the *grand lever* was over. The Maréchale de Clerembault was there as usual and Theobon and various others while Madame's hair was being dressed.

The busy scene of which Madame was now the centre seemed unaffected by recent events, except that my adventure of the evening before had been talked of. Madame ordered me to come and be looked at for a moment, which gave me an opportunity to thank her for having ordered de la Reynie's men to assist me, but I was cut short by the little Duc de Chârtres, who had started to cry. The Maréchale de Clerembault, who was governess to Madame's children, was just leaving. Strangely enough, the children loved her. She was not so taciturn with them. Even so, this morning the little Duc de Chârtres was crying because his mama could not play with him.

I stopped and gave the boy a sweetmeat out of my pocket. He stopped crying instantly. Madame noticed and smiled half sadly, half in amusement. I knew that what she was thinking of – and indeed she said so later herself when there was no one nearby to hear – was my gift to herself a few days previously of a consignment of fresh sausages from the Palatine that I had managed to procure in Paris. She asked me whether I thought all sad hearts could be cured with food, or only those belonging to Germans!

Now Madame said, "You have not yet told me anything about last night's adventure, poor goblin. Monsieur said the thieves were spies and set on you by mistake."

"Did the Chevalier tell him so, Madame?" I asked.

Vienne – for it was he who was doing her hair – begged Madame to keep still, and so she rolled her eye around the corner of her cheek at me and said, "stand here," pointing at the floor just beside her chair, where she could look at me without turning her head.

I advanced and stood there. Vienne dressed the King's hair before coming to Madame and he was a great gossip. We all knew that His Majesty asked Vienne for news and kept himself intimately informed of all the goings on at court through his hairdresser. I was rather aware of this fact as I prepared to tell Madame about my adventure because if the

King came to hear of it, so much the better.

"The Chevalier?" Madame queried. "Did he have a part in it?"

"Why, yes Madame," I said. And I proceeded to describe, as politely as I could, the scene that I had witnessed in the passage, and its aftermath. The first part of my story made one or two of the ladies laugh, but they were more shocked by the second. The room was utterly silent except for my own voice, and had my tale been less important I would not have dared to speak in such a way. When I had finished Madame, who had been quite still for five whole minutes, spoke.

"I should like to see this letter!" she said, and although she moved her head right out of his reach as she said it, Vienne noted the sternness of her voice and made no protest.

"May I have the honour of presenting it to you, Madame," I said. And with that I took the paper out of my pocket and gave it to her.

This amazed her. She held it up wonderingly and at first I could see that she thought it really was one of her own. The writing was astonishingly well done. There was even a crossing out where she might well have made such a mistake. She wrote so much that she dispensed with the formalities of starting again if she had to correct an error.

When Madame had looked for some moments at the contents of this paper she became very angry. Her face changed. The plumpness of the ripe cherry suddenly turned into heaviness. The muscles and even the colour of her face prefigured its look in middle age and she said to me, in that threatening tone which princes use towards the messengers of bad news,

"Monsieur de Brisse. What does this mean?"

"I think it means, Madame…" I began, but she interrupted me, saying, "Have you read this?"

Before I could speak, she repeated, "Have you had the impudence to read this?"

"No, Madame," I said. Alas, I was lying, but there are limits to anyone's courage.

"How did you get hold of it?"

I told her. I had already given an account of what I had seen and heard, not excluding what the Chevalier had been doing with Mme. de Coetquen in the beginning. Now I recounted how I had followed Madame de Coetquen afterwards and retrieved the forgery from Philippe de Quinault's pocket. The others present, namely Mme. de Clerembault who had returned, Ernst, who had grown into a fine fellow, the Abbé Dubois, the Duchesse de Ventadour, the Duchesse de Villars and I forget how many others, kept very straight faces until Madame burst out laughing. But then they began to be as merry as linnets, which I thought rather premature.

In the very midst of this merriment Monsieur come into the room. At the sight of him, or rather of the Chevalier and Madame de Grancy, who entered behind him, Madame's face resumed its serious expression. She said straight out, and before Lorraine had had time to properly enter the room, "Ah, Monsieur de Lorraine, I have an item of your property here which I will take some pleasure in returning to you."

I was utterly dismayed. This would not do at all. But I dared not interfere. The Chevalier, who was kept lithe by the continual practice of mischief and foul play of one sort or another, took in the situation with lightning rapidity and was ready to take advantage of Madame's impetuosity. He bowed, came forward with his hand held out and in the instant he was about to take hold of the letter.

In that moment I decided it would be better to die than let him get the paper in his own hand before others had seen it and heard where it had come from. Theoban stood nearest to Madame and I, almost hidden behind her skirts, darted down and bit her ankle. As I bit her very hard she let out a sharp cry, stumbled, and came between Madame and the Chevalier so that he was stopped in his tracks.

No one had seen me. They were all so taken up with events at a higher level, and I, with my heart thumping in my chest, stood as calmly as anyone else by the time they turned their eyes on me. The Maréchale, of course, blamed one of the dogs, and a hunt ensued for Motte who had been under the table all the time, and got a beating. As soon as order was restored inside the room the Chevalier asked again for the letter and held out his hand, but fortunately Madame had thought better of it..

"I am not so sure," she said, much to my relief. She stood there very haughtily, holding the letter with both hands flat at about the level of her waist. Her fingers didn't tremble. I was shaking like a leaf myself, but she only directed the most quelling look at the Chevalier, who for once looked anxious.

"I will give it to Monsieur." she finally said. "He knows that I am not deceitful, and a forgery that is so cleverly carried out in the writing will not deceive him when he sees what it is about." With that she handed the letter to her husband.

Monsieur took it, and as soon as his friend had it in his hand the

Chevalier seemed to recover all his confidence. He even had the insolence to make a play of reading the letter over Monsieur's shoulder, and after a few moments, to titter. Madame rounded angrily on him and demanded that he should stand further off.

"But how can I tell what the paper contains unless I read it?" he demanded.

"You know very well," she replied, "since you wrote it."

"I – wrote *that!*" he exclaimed. And he snatched the letter out of Monsieur's very hand and showed it to the Grancy, saying "Madame de Grancy, whose hand is this?" Monsieur began to look angry. But not in the direction we expected. "What do you mean by writing such stuff?" he said to his wife.

"I? But I am telling you, I wrote no such thing. This friend of yours, this fellow, has forged it, as God is my witness. Or rather Monsieur de Brisse is my witness. Where is my goblin. Come out at once and tell Monsieur how you came by the letter."

I am ashamed to say that I had been hiding behind Madame. When she was in court dress I could, without needing to bend, be completely hidden while standing beside her. Not, I have to say, if I wore my best wig and high heels, but that morning I had not got them on.

I stood forward now, and in a hasty voice recounted how I had come by the letter, and added the fact that my attackers of the night before had been in search of it, having deduced that I had had the opportunity to steal it. It would have been better if I could have had Monsieur's whole attention in order to impress the scene on him as vividly as possible, but unfortunately as I spoke he was torn both ways by the contemptuous interruptions of the Chevalier and by the scornful fury of Madame. When I had finished she demanded the letter of Lorraine, but he said he didn't know where it had got to. He held out both his hands mockingly, to show that he hadn't got it, but I had seen him pass it to Madame de Grancy. When I said so, Madame challenged her and she made as if to have, in all innocence, only just heard that it was wanted. She passed it over to Madame with a little self conscious squint of regret at the Chevalier.

Madame held it at arms length and said to her husband, "Monsieur, surely you would not suspect me of disrespect towards the Queen as it states here? As you know, I never dissemble, and the Queen is particularly kind to me and we are the best of friends. And this, about our living a cat and dog life is not true because although I am not worthy of so excellent a husband you said to me only yesterday that you loved me quite well and were grateful once again for my help with the diamond buttons. And why should I spy and try to pass deceitful information to the King? Indeed, this letter is nothing but a wicked forgery. Before I ever came to court there was mischief making of this kind, I have been told, and I would have thought the Chevalier de Lorraine would have learned his lesson."

This was a daring reference to Lorraine's past behaviour which had led to his exile from court. Madame waited for an answer, but for several seconds Monsieur was silent, and no one else dared say anything. He seemed to be at a loss, fidgeting with the braid on his tunic, until finally with an awkward gesture of mingled impatience and mockery, he said, "I have had enough of this now, Madame. I don't want to hear any more about it!" And with that he left the room.

His particular friends prepared to follow after him, but the Chevalier de Lorraine let them all get ahead of himself and then paused deliberately to look at me. I tried to assume a posture of casual dignity, but it was difficult. The contrast between Lorraine's superb manhood and myself, as he towered over me, would be very noticeable to an observer, but was even more emphatically obvious to me as, with a galling inability to even get onto level ground with my two feet, it half broke my neck to look up at him.

For a moment he held himself absolutely still, but without any hardening of the muscle, and I can only say that something to do with this combination, added to his expression, was quite terrifying.

"Monsieur de Brisse!" he said. I waited, assuming a determined expression of resistance. He let the corner of his lip curl very slightly with contempt. "You will not live," he said in a whisper. Then he left the room. And I must say that the way in which he went through the door – the strength of his legs combined with the need to conceal his encounter with me from Madame giving his movements a special significance – made me think of the gait of a rat. Perhaps this was the first glimpse of corruption spreading from his heart to the visible outward frame of this man.

Madame meanwhile had been talking to Theobon and Félicité de Blonde who was also there. Now she turned as if to say something to me, but at that moment a message arrived from the King asking if she would walk with him to see the new statues he was having set in the garden, and so she also went out. But took the letter with her.

CHAPTER NINE

While Madame was walking with the King, with the exception of one interruption which I will disclose later, I was able to spend the time on reflection. I thought that Madame would make good use of her opportunity to speak to the King about Lorraine's treacherous forgery. And she had the letter in her pocket. She could show it to him. Quite obviously, this incident, if properly handled, should be used to establish her security and put an end to the ambitious malice of her husband's favourites, and I earnestly hoped that Madame would be aware of this. De la Reynie still held the louts who had attacked me. They could be made to say who had hired them and why. Lorraine's invention of this letter could be proved and such low dealing treachery, exposed, would perhaps be enough to alienate that villain from the King and even taint his influence with Monsieur. Or he might consider it politic afterwards to court Madame's favour rather than plot her ruin.

But alas, Madame was no strategist. When she came in from the garden she seemed to have forgotten all about the entire affair, and for the moment she also overlooked the fact that I myself had any hand or interest in the matter. Such frivolity was an unexpected contradiction in her character, because no great personage could have been more aware, or more delicate in the observance of, the obligations and entitlements of rank, and the serious aspects of court life. But in her, this dignity was offset by a sense of fun and a lightness of spirit which betrayed her now because she seemed not to realise the danger she was in. Or she may have thought that it was enough to have thwarted Lorraine's scheme, without carrying the point further.

I stood of course when she entered the room, but she did not appear to notice me. She spoke only of Coysevox, the sculptor of these two statues of Fame and Mercury, with which the King was so pleased, and went on to ask the Maréchale de Clerembault whether she had seen the bust of the King commissioned by the Hôtel de Ville. I preferred Girardon, by the way, and the Maréchale agreed with me. Although she had an indefatigable appetite and memory for court gossip, and an ability to foretell the future by means of computation and divination in the dust which certainly did interest Madame a great deal, I think it was this mutual interest in the arts that formed the bedrock of their friendship. Listening to their discussions of the arts was always a pleasure.

But where was the letter? I was impatient to know what had become of it. The Maréchale was also restless about something, because at such times she had a little habit of screwing the inside of her pocket. Either she was becoming anxious about getting to the gaming tables, this being an absolute obsession with her, or alternatively she also was curious to return to the subject of the Chevalier's forgery.

"Oh, by the way," she said, when she had a chance, "Lorraine sent Madame Gordon back after you had left, Madame."

Madame sat down in her chair. "Go on," she said. "I cannot believe that even she could be so stupid as to think she would see the wretched letter lying on a table where she could steal it."

"No, I don't think that was her idea. She gave a note to Monsieur de Brisse."

Madame did not look round at me. I think she was smiling, but she thought that she could conceal this fact provided that I did not see the actual curve of her lip. But if great people chose to find it amusing that their interests should be defended by one so small and unsuitable as myself there was nothing that I could do about it.

The note was a challenge, as it happened, from the Chevalier. Or rather, he had not sent me a challenge as such. It was more an order to make myself available to be killed at a certain time and place. He said that he was going to set his dogs on me, since he could not demean himself by touching me even with the point of his sword; but to avoid causing too much of a disturbance he required my presence in the lower courtyard before supper on the morrow. I had consulted Ernst already and sent my answer.

"Come here, little goblin," said Madame. I stepped forward and bowed. The expression on her face was mischievous. Her skirts had piled up as they do when a lady sits down abruptly, and almost hid the hand that rested in her lap. To call me little was an endearment with her. If angry or merely on business, she called me goblin only.

I stood forward and bowed. "This enemy of mine," she said, referring to the Chevalier, "would like to take everything I am fond of from me. But he shall certainly not have my goblin, and that I swear here and now."

Those were her very words. It is what she actually said at the time. And then she added, "Where is the note he sent you?"

I took it from my jerkin and handed it to her. I might have had the wit to keep it locked up in my own pocket if I had not been made dizzy by the charm of Madame's kindness just before, and her calling me her little goblin. The Maréchale, of course, did not miss the importance of the note as a piece of evidence, in that Lorraine, by seeking revenge for the exposure of himself as having forged the letter, admitted his own guilt.

"The man's a great fool," said Clerembault, "to provide you, Madame, with such concrete evidence of the truth of Monsieur de Brisse's story. We only have to tell the tale here and there today, and show this little piece of paper as proof that the Chevalier is involved, and he will be the laughing stock of the whole court."

Madame gave a little bounce in her chair as she was sitting, in the way she did when she was excited or amused. She laughed, and then stood up. And they went off there and then, taking my piece of paper with them.

Fool that I was, I still thought that Madame would make good use of it. In this encounter, now that the Chevalier had, as it were, drawn his sword, Fate had dealt very generously with us in allowing the friends of Madame – mainly myself – to stumble upon the means to defend her. But to set too much store by that was to forget what I had observed myself earlier on; Madame was too honest and light hearted to compete in such devious intrigues where her enemy had recourse to a depth of treachery that she, despite the fact that she heartily disliked him, was not aware of. You will see how she misused her opportunities so that even by default her enemies gained the advantage.

As for the challenge, I might as well admit that I was terrified by Lorraine's threat to set his dogs on me. He could not have known it, but unwittingly the Chevalier had hit upon the worst possible punishment from my point of view. I should have infinitely preferred to have had my head cut clean off with a sword. The enmity of large dogs had always disgusted and frightened me because my strangeness aroused their aggression at the same time as my body was not fit for flight or defence.

Perhaps Madame, who had rather allowed herself to forget the fact that she was the chief target in his malice, because my predicament diverted her – perhaps she thought that the Chevalier was joking. He was not. Despite the outrage of Ernst and his young friends, whose training in the use of the sword they imagined would be more useful than I could realistically hope because they were still only very young men and Lorraine a skilled and mature fighter, I was rather at my wits' end for what to do.

Consequently when Climène sent me a message asking me to go with her in her carriage to the race in the afternoon where I should see how she had made a plan to extricate me from my troubles, I readily agreed. My need for help made me credulous about the direction from which that help might come, and I imagined that even Climène might hit on some means of saving my life.

This race was one that had been arranged between a horse of Monsieur de Vendôme, and one of Monsieur le Grand, and had been planned to take place by the river. It had been in prospect for some time, everybody had placed bets, and feelings ran high. I had certainly intended to go anyway. I would not have missed it for the world even if I had been set on by ten men the night before, not two, and the Chevalier had the power to unleash Cerberus himself to devour me later.

Madame set off early in the afternoon with the Maréchale de Clerembault and Monsieur Tiladet in her carriage. I climbed into Climène's carriage while it was still empty, and hid myself by sitting on the floor, as she invariably insisted that I should. My sister was kinder to me these days than she had been before she married, but she did not go as far as wanting to be seen with me in public. But she said that her husband conferred a great blessing on the rest of mankind, since in contrast to himself they all resembled angels.

There was a most tremendous crush between the many carriages when we set out. At one moment I was afraid that Climène might not appear, and at another that her coachman would get his wheel caught in the hub of a carriage into which four ladies had crammed themselves, including Madame de Fiennes. I did not want that lady's cruel wit descending on Climène if she should discover that I was in the carriage. I kept well hidden, and eventually Climène herself was handed up by none other than her husband. Her skirts hid me from him for so long as he was standing, but what if he should get inside?

He was in an amiable mood apparently. He called her by some endearment or other which I cannot bear to bring to mind, and muttered some louche remark, Climène remaining completely silent throughout. He had the most unpleasant voice I ever heard. It was rough, as if his vocal chords suffered some malformation in keeping with the rest of him, but he was inclined to pronounce his words as if the instrument they were played on was glorious instead of ugly. He strung out his vowels. He landed with gloating heaviness on one syllable, and then ate the other. To my relief he made his farewells. He signalled to the coachman and we were carried off.

Immediately I crawled out from under the seat, but still remained on the floor where I could not be seen by passers by. To my dismay I thought that Climène was looking very ill. "I have vomited," she said.

I said nothing but just looked the question that was on my lips.

"What else?" she snapped. "I know it. I shall have to bear the child of that monster. Oh God! If only I was out of this court, living as a washer-woman in Paris, or sewing lace!"

I laughed. A year or so ago she would have slapped me for such insolence, but now she restrained herself. "Berthon," she said, (her name for me), "Could you poison him? You are so good at finding things out. Just for me! You could go to La Voisin. Have Athénaïs de Montespan followed. She uses her. Or ask Madame Gordon. She knows what concoction was given to Monsieur's first wife, and she died in agony I have heard. Oh don't look so stricken, Berthon!" she snapped. "What's d'Autour to you?" Indeed, nothing. It was not him I was thinking of.

"How do you know that?" I said. "You've never spoken to me of Madame Minette before? Who told you she was poisoned?"

"Of course she was. What else would you expect to happen in this horrid place, if some wretched woman came between Monsieur and his friends?"

My heart dropped like a stone.

Climène was drying her eyes as she spoke and the lurching of the carriage had made her smudge her cheek. I knelt on the floor and told her to bend down so that I could mend it. I held my kerchief of lawn to her lips for her to lick the cloth. While I was at it, I gently rubbed some colour back into her skin, and used a trace of unguent from the silver box I kept, to smooth her lip.

"You should not wear *toufettes de Dinde*," I said to her. "The style doesn't suit you." She was so beautiful that in fact she could wear anything.

"Let me pull the hair out slightly here," I said to her, and she held her head further down and turned her neck. She looked better then, in every way.

She sat up. "If only I loved someone else," she said. "But I do not."

"You loved the Chevalier de Lorraine once,"

She didn't answer. Then she remarked, "I am not going to let him kill you, Berthon. Listen to what I have arranged." She was silent for a moment, biting her lip. "It is a little complicated," she said, "but Fallongues, who is the one who keeps Monsieur le Grand's horses, is the brother of Anne Colombe who was my aunt's cook and who loved me, you remember? I have paid him to start a quarrel."

"With whom?" I said stupidly.

"Good heavens, Berthon!" she exclaimed, "With Lorraine and his brother of course. Men are always quarrelsome when they are racing, and Monsieur Vendôme is notoriously quick tempered."

I couldn't for the life of me see how this was going to further Madame's cause or mine, or keep me alive.

"Yes," I said.

"Do you mean to say that you don't see what it could lead to? If he does it well, there will be a fight, and when everyone is taken up with the fray Lorraine is going to be killed."

"Killed!" I said. I was so astonished I allowed my tone to be completely unguarded and for a moment I thought Climène would indeed slap me.

"What is it?" she demanded. "Does he not deserve it? You exasperate me, Berthon. Don't you realise that Lorraine means what he says? If he says he will set his dogs on you he means it, and then he will make out that it was an accident and that he never threatened any such thing. Oh no! You just think I could not possibly have arranged anything to save you, because I am too heartless, or silly. Well let me tell you, ugly and horrible though you are, I thought this up entirely to help you, and I had to surrender to Fallongues the ruby clasp my foul husband gave me when he discovered that I am pregnant. Don't stare at me with your mouth open like that Berthon! Oh, if I had known life was going to be so annoying I would not have let myself be born!"

By this time she had got into such a temper there was no knowing what she would say next, but I assumed that whatever plan she had tried to make it would not do any harm, or any good either. These things are not so simply settled. Nor so complicatedly. Luckily, at that point we arrived, and with a sudden change and her face all smiles, she jumped out of the carriage onto the grass.

There was such a crowd on the bank that Le Grand's servants had to beg some of the ladies to stand back, or the horses couldn't run at all.

But the course was well laid out. They would gallop up river to a certain point before turning and coming back.

Madame was also there of course. She was accompanied by both Theobon and Clerembault, the latter with that ridiculous little mask, called a *touret*, clutched between her teeth as usual. And the Dauphin, of course, joined her among the spectators, together with many others.

I had already placed a bet on Monsieur le Grand's horse. The fact that he was the Chevalier de Lorraine's brother didn't deter me, because if I could make money out of him I would. I had heard the day before from Captain Sinsanet that the horse was very good. But now that I was actually at the spot, stumbling in my awkward way on the turf and looking through gaps between the coats and skirts of others to see the horses, it was the English servant riding for the Duc de Vendôme who worried me. The moment I caught sight of him I simply knew because of the way he stood, that he was exceptional. Even if the mount was not so fast, a man like that riding her could beat a more ordinary man on a bolt of lightning. I wanted to take a closer look at him, and wove my way between all the legs and skirts that crowded the grass.

The Englishman was standing receiving last minute instructions from the Duc de Vendôme. I had already put Climène's fanciful story out of my mind, and gave all my attention to the wager. I watched Vendôme's rider anxiously. I can't tell you why it was that I knew he was so good before I even saw him mounted. What I certainly did not know at that moment was that we were destined to become friends.

He had sandy coloured hair which he wore in a very plain style, and yet he did not look like an ordinary servant. He held the bridle in his hands, and struck a pose that was altogether elegant, whilst the horse, scenting the race ahead and shifting around in the way they do, was nevertheless quiet and nudging this man against the shoulder from time to time. The moment had almost come for the race to begin, and I saw him mount. As he swung his leg over the saddle I was still watching how he moved, and I gave up hope for the forty pounds I had placed on Lavalle riding for Monsieur le Grand.

Now the two horses, both magnificently keen and well groomed were led side by side to the starting post. I was almost knocked over at the crucial moment by one lady running excitedly right past me in skirts big enough to sweep me into the ditch. By the time I had righted myself the race had began, and both of those wonderful creatures were already thundering away and along the river bank.

Dozens of the spectators set off after them, but I couldn't shift on that ground and I had to stay where I was. The horses turned at the point where the river bends towards the village of St. Germain and came thundering back again, and then I had a better view. To my eye they were neck and neck. But then, inevitably, I was knocked aside and my view blocked again as everyone rushed to see the finish. I did not know how he achieved it but le Grand's horse was declared the winner, so I had a successful bet after all.

In all the commotion of the finish, I saw Madame noticed me and beckoned me to her. She was flushed with excitement and she and the Duchesse de Ventadour – the lady whom she calls Dou Dou – were having some fun at the expense of the Chevalier Tiladet which I could not understand, but it involved the losses he had on this race. The Dauphin, who had watched the race with Madame was preparing to go for a ride on the other side of the river when the rest of us returned to the palace. The Maréchale de Clerembault stood, haughty and silent at one side as she often does. She had bet heavily of course, but one knew nothing of that either, since she could not or would not talk. I should have thought, with the daylight beginning to fade, she could have taken the *touret* from between her teeth and ventured to let the air onto her face.

"Goblin," Madame said, "Here is a gentleman who has lost so much perhaps he would be glad to earn a few pistoles by acting as your body guard. Because I have to tell you that I am afraid I lost your piece of paper before I could show it to anyone. I have no doubt that the Chevalier learned from you, and picked my pocket."

"What's this?" said Tiladet, his face wearing that odd expression of a man anxious not to offend a protégé of royalty, and yet reluctant to share conversation with me. "What paper, Madame?"

What paper indeed! Ah well, I thought to myself, it is gone now. And without it nothing stood between me and the revenge of Lorraine, because I certainly did not credit Climène with the necessary seriousness to make any real difference to my plight. Not noticing any effect that her words might have had on myself Madame was entirely taken up with telling the rest of her story to Monsieur Tiladet, and so I left them.

As I turned away I found the Chevalier de Lorraine himself was standing just behind me but with his head turned the other way. For a split second nothing more surprising was to be seen. Nothing untoward.

The next moment he turned his face, and I saw his expression almost unrecognisably darkened with an angry flush. At first I thought myself the object of his rage, and was about to give myself up when I realised that not I, but someone else was the target of it. He was about to hit somebody. I thought with horror that surely he had not overheard Madame's words and be mad enough to strike the Princess, but of course not. He swung back round and struck a blow with his fist in a man's face. I think it was Lavalle. A violent quarrel had broken out between Lavalle and the Duc de Vendôme exactly as Climène had predicted. Le Grand had made a cutting remark which I just caught the edge of – not the sense, but a fragment of his tone, and the unmistakeable kaleidoscopic shift of men's bodies when suddenly they are at war. The Duc de Gramont was also standing in the group and he with his rough skin and shaggy brows, was already in a fury and I saw the spittle fly from his mouth as he shouted at Monsieur le Grand. And who was Monsieur le Grand's brother? Why, the Chevalier de Lorraine of course, and it was Gramont that he had meant to hit, but Lavalle got in the way. He struck again, hitting Gramont this time, and so hard in the face that his wig fell off. Even as he staggered back Gramont reached for his sword, but of course he, like Le Grand and many others, had taken it off to disencumber himself when following the race. At that point I was knocked over. I scrambled up again in time to see the Chevalier de Lorraine rushing to throw himself bodily between his brother and Gramont. Above all the shouting, and the cries of alarm from the ladies and the yapping of dogs Le Grand called Vendôme a liar, and Vendôme screamed that he saw Lavalle cheat.

All the time my mind was racing with the thought that Climène could not have engineered all this. And yet there was Vendôme shouting at the top of his voice that Le Grand's rider, Lavalle, had cut in on the Englishman. And Lavalle's brother was married to Anne Colombe.

It was extraordinary to see men so enraged. Many of the onlookers were frightened and had retreated under the trees. Monsieur de Marsillac, in an exquisite coat that must have cost him the equivalent of my income for a year, saw the Chevalier de Lorraine trying to separate the two men, and he went to help him and was immediately splattered with mud on one side and his pocket ripped off on the other. Gramont was too enraged for Lorraine and Marsillac to hold him.

His servant had run to fetch his sword for him, and he drew it although the Dauphin himself was still present, and Madame too, which is an inexcusable offence at Court. Such an indiscretion alone could have resulted in his exile. He flung himself on Marsillac, but the unevenness of the ground mercifully threw his aim wide. And at the very moment when Lorraine, distracted by all this, had no eyes for anything else, a servant of the Duc de Gramont suddenly ran at him from among the onlookers scattered some distance away on the turf, and on the pretext of mistaking him, or so it seemed, for le Grand, he attacked Lorraine with a knife. He should have succeeded in killing him, the move was so completely unexpected. Lorraine was taken absolutely by surprise, but he was as quick as a snake and he just succeeded in defending himself. His attacker, having failed in his attempt on Lorraine, then dropped his knife and fled; but the Chevalier went after him.

Lorraine's features were red and knotted up with fury as he raced across the turf on those great long legs of his. In disbelief and terror I saw him catch the servant's hair in one hand, while swinging back his sword arm, and then he landed him a great gash across the face. I couldn't make out for sure if this man had been the one bribed by Climène, but it turned out to be the case, and in my view such punishment was a costly quid pro quo for a ruby clasp. He would be lucky if he lived.

The servant fell in the grass, whether dead or not. And Lorraine with blood on his sword, turned immediately back to the centre of the fray where one of Monsieur le Grand's attendants was now attacking the Duc de Gramont, and coming close to killing him but for the intervention of another gentleman. Their clothes were torn, their wigs were off. They were dirty. Many of the onlookers got involved in the struggle, and the prettiest among the ladies fainted or rushed about with little cries. Eventually I think it was the Duc de Villeroy who succeeded in forcing Le Grand into his coach, and someone else doing the same by the Duc de Gramont put an end to it.

In all this *mêlée* Climène was nowhere to be seen. If it had been of her making, then she had failed because Lorraine had survived; but my feelings were bewildered at the thought of what she had perhaps dared to try. And now I realised that everyone was going, and most had already gone. Two or three coaches which were the last to leave went by, and suddenly the field of battle was all but deserted, and I, unfortunately, had been forgotten by my friends. I decided reluctantly that I would have to walk home. I began to lurch slowly back under the trees in the way that is peculiar to me, my mind in a state of absolute confusion.

I sometimes think that if I could walk on my hands instead of my legs I would be better off. I saw an acrobat once who could do it so easily he looked designed to be that way up. And my arms are very strong. But to walk any distance on my legs involves a feat of invention to complete every step. That is why I took so much trouble to master the art of riding later on, and had my own saddle made. But at the time of this event I had not yet done it. And so I walked.

A deep melancholy settled on me as I struggled over the grass. The remaining carriages passed indifferently by. I calculated that by the following evening, when I was destined to meet the Chevalier, the sands of my life would be down to their last few grains. Madame, having lost the note of challenge, could not now give warning and proof of what the Chevalier had threatened, in which case he would not have dared to do it. And even if, with her exceptional kindness, and the extraordinary alertness of her cast of mind, which was so charming and merry, she would have wished to protected me, I had no doubt that the interesting scene that we had all just witnessed would put it clean out of her thoughts. No one at court would talk of anything else for days.

I gave my thoughts over to the contemplation of my disgusting fate. I had always feared dogs. Little ones like Charmille, were different. But the large breeds and the hounds used for hunting, terrified me. Consider my position. I am near the ground, on an eye level with some of these beasts. Men call them brave, and I suppose they can be, but they have a predilection for attacking something weaker than themselves. I keep away as much as I can, but I have been snarled at. I have looked, eyeball to eyeball, at a wolfhound that growled at me with its jaws open, and the teeth running with the saliva designed by nature to help digest its food. I have been chased, and only escaped by hauling myself with the strength of my arms alone, up a hanging. It makes a human being feel utter despair to know that his body, miserable as it is, deserves no better than to be devoured.

Even so, it was unusual for me to be so melancholy. Perhaps the twilight shadows that settled their cool grey fingers on the ground as I went, and snuffed out the daylight, affected me. Also that cold and alien breeze which sneaks through the gap between day and night ran through the grass, looking for mischief and everything that has no love and only malice in it. I've heard it said that sorcerers and witches set great store by the hour when that wind comes, and they will trap it and use it for their own purposes. They call it the wind of power. There is never an evening when, just after the sun goes down, this little breeze does not spring up. But if one is protected by well being, or the walls of a house, it matters very little. On this occasion I was exposed to it, and I remember it.

Just as I was going along sadly reflecting on all these things, I heard the sound of a horse's hooves behind me. I did not look round. Some yards before he reached me, the rider slowed his mount from a trot to a walk, and drew level. I turned, and stepped back a pace to make it easier to look up at the rider. In the half light I saw at once that it was the Englishman.

"Monsieur," he said, "You are alone."

Ha! I thought to myself, I've always been told these people choose their words very carefully.

"I myself am rather tired of riding today," this extraordinary man said, "whereas for another person a ride home, even on a horse's back, might be welcome. Shall I get down and help you up, Sir?"

I bowed slightly. He jumped at once onto the grass. I smiled, covering my mouth with my hand.

"You are very kind," I said, catching at once, although us yet unaware of it, the man's own aptitude for the *mot juste*.

I accepted his offer to place one foot in his hand, and from that with a very neat movement he managed to get me into the saddle without handling the other side of me. There was a strap and a buckle on the back of the saddle and he rolled a cloth he had and tied it there so that I was held in place comfortably. I thanked him, and we started off, he leading the horse by the bridle.

To make conversation I said to him, "You have had a hard day." I meant the quarrel and the fight after the race. And then I realised that I was very interested to know the cause of Vendôme's argument with Lavalle, and asked him for an account of it.

"The other rider," he said, (that was Lavalle) "cut against me and hit my horse on the neck. I'd have won even so, but his mount was better than mine."

This sounded like Climène's plan.

I said, feeling ashamed because this man would have lost money if he had been cheated, "Most Frenchmen would behave differently to Monsieur le Grand and his brothers."

"I don't doubt it," he said in a tone that gave his agreement something in addition to the simple words I'd used.

In the brief silence that followed I turned over all the observations before me in my mind: his voice, the deepening shadow, the horse's steps and his swinging with effortless strides together.

"May I ask," he said, "do you know the Chevalier de Lorraine well?"

How should I answer a question like that?

"Yes," I said. "I know him well."

"I'm sorry if he is a friend of yours, Monsieur," he remarked. I thought this was a preliminary to some other statement, such as "I'm sorry if so and so is a friend of yours but I do not like his verse, or his music, or his wife." But he left it at that, and added nothing. I realised that this meant that he was actually sorry to understand that I had made a friend of the Chevalier. Odd though I knew it was, I felt the need to set him straight on this matter.

"I am not his friend," I said. "In fact, although he would consider it beneath his dignity to hate me, he will kill me if he can." And thereupon I told this man about Lorraine's intention to kill me with his dogs.

"You don't need to worry about dogs," he said. He left it at that for rather longer than most men would without any further explanation. And then, just when I was about to challenge him, he glanced up with a dry smile, and added, "If you had not met me it would have been a different matter, because a dog can be as dangerous as an assassin. But I will show you how to quell even the fiercest of them. It is a trick that I was taught at home. I'll gladly let you have it for a fee."

I was still very young; only a boy. I was confused by his sophistication, seeing that he was only a servant. I was also shy. And untrusting. When I looked ahead there were only a couple of hundred metres to go before the gates of the palace. Some lamps were already lit. I wished I was there already. Surely no man, however odd, would like to lie with me.

I said, "Name your fee."

My tone gave him pause. He was surprised, but then said, "I wish very much, to make the acquaintance of Climène, the Duchesse d'Autour."

First I was relieved, and then I was astonished. He could not know that I was related to Climène. He was not a courtier. Then I realised he'd seen me get out of her carriage. And I felt disappointed, because this must be why he had stopped for me on his way home, when I imagined that kindness or fellowship, but not self interest, had been the spur.

Now once again I noticed who he was; a servant. I considered offering him money, not because I thought he'd take it, but to annoy him. I let him wait while I considered my answer. I decided that it would do no harm to find some pretext for an encounter between himself and Climène. He little knew how quickly she would dispose of him. Presumably he had seen her pretty face, and knew nothing of the sharp wit and angry heart that God had seen fit to dress up in such a way. And she was proud. What business could he think to have with her?

But if he truly had a secret that could protect me from wolfhounds and brutes of that sort, it was worth my while to trade what would be useless to him for what could be so useful to me.

"Very well," I said. "How shall we arrange this?"

He had his answer all ready. He would meet me in a certain small court behind the riding schools at noon the following day. I dismounted at the bottom of the Great Stair and left him. I didn't thank him again. I felt that the encounter had merely been one of commerce.

CHAPTER TEN

An hour later I went to Madame's apartment, where her ladies were at table, attended by Ernst. When he had first arrived as a little page, Madame's ladies used to kiss him because he was so pretty. But now that he had grown so much, the two youngest and newly arrived of them eyed him in quite a different way; which was not to say that they were less inclined to kissing than before. They no longer did it at table.

The talk was all about the race and the quarrel. I had not yet been able to find Climène to verify her part in it, if indeed she had any. I could not help smiling at the very idea, and yet it could – it must have been – Fallongues who told le Grand's jockey to cut in, and it was certainly he who muttered something to the Duc de Vendôme. I saw him. And if Lorraine was not killed it had not been for want of trying.

"What are you smiling at," Theobon said to me. "Are you so pleased because the Chevalier de Lorraine is in the Bastille?"

"The Bastille?" I repeated, astonished.

"Where have you been, Berthon?" said Theobon in that very sharp tone, with her thin voice, which earned her such a reputation at court for being a scold when in reality she was kind-hearted to a point of absurdity. "The King has sent him off and his brother with him. You know how His Majesty despises quarrelling, and they drew their swords in the presence of the Dauphin. The Queen told Madame that she asked the King to send them all away from court for abusing the respect due to the Royal Family, and Monseigneur himself agreed."

"But it's just the Bastille after all? Not exile."

She was in an impatient humour, and didn't answer me.

"How long for?" I said.

"Two or three nights? Not more, I fancy, because that fiend can charm the King as much as he does the other. You're standing on the hem of my gown!"

I lifted Charmille off. It was she, not I, who did it, but I didn't waste my breath with an excuse.

"The Duc de Vendôme and the Duc de Gramont have been sent as well. They have all been arrested. "

Then in that case Climène's plan had not gone so awry after all, since the Chevalier could not now keep his tryst with me. There was much that I could do in the meantime to disarm his plan. Even without the written evidence of his note, which Madame had lost, if there was time for the story of his threat to be passed around among the Court he would have to desist. He could not risk the King's anger again if he was known to have incited his dogs to attack a courtier with the result that he was killed or injured.

So it was with a much lighter heart that I went to my meeting with the Englishman the next day to find out what tricks he knew to protect me against an attack from a hound. To his credit, the Englishman made no mention of Climène before taking from his pocket a small object like a pebble with a hole in it. He placed it between his teeth and seemed to blow, but no sound emerged. He was amused at my expression. And then he explained to me – a matter about which I felt some scepticism – that the sound produced was at too high a pitch for a man's ear, but audible to a dog, and that if it was repeated the tone was painful to the animal and it would, in the end, lie down at the feet of whoever made it. But in addition, he said I should learn two gestures. One was merely to imitate the movement of a man picking up a stone. The other is too complicated for me to explain because it involved a combination of gesture and attention. But he would not let me go until he was satisfied that he had taught it to me.

During this explanation I, to some extent, fell under the spell of this man's charm again. There was, without any doubt, an extraordinarily pleasant air about the way in which he did everything. I asked him how he came to speak French so well, and he said that he had been taught as a boy by a French tutor. I said that such sophisticated tricks were not taught to the children of French servants, and he asked me, with a quizzical look in his eye, who could have told me that his father was of low birth.

"But," I said, "If he were not, why would you be the Duc de Vendôme's lackey?"

At that point he looked at me very steadily, but with his head a little on one side. I swear I had the impression that I had disappointed him in some way, when the previous evening I had definitely thought it the other way round.

Did I mention before that his hair was of a sandy blond colour? He wore it very plainly tied, and it did not curl. A gentleman would not have put up with that. And yet, if one had stood him side by side with a nobleman of our Court – Monsieur de Lauzun for example, who dressed

MALICE

appallingly so that he could scarcely be said to have an advantage of
that kind over anybody – then a stranger might well assume that Lauzun
was the lackey and this Englishman was the lord.

All this went through my mind, and I found myself overcome with
embarrassment because I did not know how to behave towards him. I
also became acutely embarrassed at having let him see the full extent of
my deformity in such an open way, and in full daylight. I could only just
restrain myself from hiding my face. I should wear a mask of black
velvet like Madame de Clerembault, and like her, avoid foolish talk by
holding it in place with my teeth.

Struggling with these feelings of embarrassment and remorse, I
finally said that to fulfil my side of the bargain I had invited my half
sister to go with me to Versailles in the afternoon when the King and
Madame went hunting. I did not tell him that she had been thoroughly
delighted with the quarrel and had, indeed, been responsible for
arranging the entire event, including, of course, the rider who cheated. It
quite bewildered me to think she should take so much trouble on my
behalf, until I found it impossible to stop her talking about it and
detailing to me a host of new plans to do with arranging for the Duc
d'Autour to have to go abroad, and for her friend Dou Dou's daughter to
have a fall out hunting when her cousin's horse was near so that he
would pick her up and fall in love with her.

"Lorraine was not killed," I said, pretending to complain. But she
responded with something like the touchy vanity of that Field Marshal
who so annoyed the King outside Compiegne. "Lorraine is at least in the
Bastille, Berthon. You should be grateful. He can't set his hounds on
you while he is there. And it was my first venture. I had no idea that it
was possible to intervene to put the patterns of life together as one
wants. It is easy! I wish that I had realised before I married. My mother
always told me that we are helpless in the hands of Fate and the
Almighty, but she was wrong. You can see that."

"Of course," I said.

"And you promise that if I agree to walk with you in Versailles we
can drive there in Madame's own carriage? She really has given her
permission?"

"Yes."

This was because Madame was being taken by Monsieur, who never
hunted, in his carriage, but would need her own to return after the chase.
To complete this complicated arrangement, Climène's coachman would

drive her carriage empty to Versailles, in order to be there to bring her home.

"And you will sit on the floor, "she said. I nodded. "Very well. And thank me please, Berthon, for the quarrel. "

"But I certainly do. With all my heart," I said. And she was so pleased with herself that she clapped her hands together and laughed, and then left me.

The Englishman, when I gave him news of this arrangement, asked me where I should advise him to walk in the hope of an encounter. I said that Climène would refuse to walk with me at all if there was too much company, because naturally she would not want to be seen to be escorted by myself. But that he must hope for as many courtiers as possible to stay away, and then I would walk with her either on the terrace in front of the Galérie des Glaces or on the parterre of Latona. But I warned him that Climène would walk exactly where she liked, and if that happened to be elsewhere, he would have to come and look for us. I left him then, and went to lunch with Ernst.

CHAPTER ELEVEN

That evening Bonhomme handed me a note from the Marquis d'Effiat telling me that the Chevalier de Lorraine could not attend his meeting with me by reason of his imprisonment in the Bastille. But, when all is said and done, I knew that this was just a temporary respite. The Chevalier de Lorraine was not the sort of man who would forget an injury if his first attempt at vengeance was thwarted.

You might imagine that someone like myself, who for a long time certainly had no friends, would not mind an enemy. Oddly enough, this is not the case. Specific enmity is different from impersonal cruelty, and I was surprised to feel how keenly my spirit recoiled from it. Although frequently treated with contempt, I had never been attacked except by the two thieves in the coach, which was a different sort of thing. That a gentleman, and one as strong and as malicious as the Chevalier de Lorraine, would from now on actively seek opportunities to harm me, gave me sensations which were new. Like a nightmare that repeats itself, an amalgam of sensations and half forgotten details to do with my earliest understandings of the difference between myself and other men haunted me afresh. It even overshadowed my anxiety over the conspiracy against Madame. To some extent her high spirits and apparent carelessness deceived me into imagining that, for the moment at least, she was safe and I was not. My own fate loomed large.

One morning several days after the race my spirits were still overcast. Towards mid-day Bonhomme was busy with a jerkin of mine in the corner. He whistled between his teeth as if it was a horse that he was grooming.

"What's that you're putting on it?" I said.

He seemed startled that I had noticed him. I remembered his reaction most exactly later. His pale face with its leaden skin and his shifting uneasy stare was printed on my mind as if some painter had done it.

"There was a stain on the cloth," he said. "This powder can clean away almost any mark."

I told Bonhomme that I was going to walk in Versailles, and would put on my new coat of green velvet, with the tunic of grey, embroidered with silver. He left his grooming and went to prepare these things, and when I was ready later I went to await Climène in the coach.

After only a moment or two she appeared. I watched her descend the steps. She had a waiting woman with her who I hoped would not expect to accompany us. In coming down, Climène's skirts caught on the steps because they were made of a heavier cloth than usual, and I could see that knots of embroidered flowers were sewn in at intervals. The effect was enchanting. She had taken my advice and did not wear the lime green silk lace trimming which was not flattering to a pale skin, and instead the bosom and sleeves were edged with a silk gauze, cross-woven with silver.

"It will rain," she said. "I don't want to get my shoes wet, Berthon. They are new."

I assured her that there was no need, and she did lean on my hand in order to mount into the carriage. I got in after her as best I could, and the coachman drove off.

No sooner were we on the road than as usual we gossiped like two old women. Of course she wanted to tell me all over again how she had arranged the famous quarrel, and I was as generous in my praise and thanks as she could wish. Or almost. She had heard from Félicité de Largues that the King had ordered the release of the recent prisoners from the Bastille, but although this struck a chill in my own heart she had no further interest in it because the situation between Monsieur de Lauzun and the Princess of Monaco had caught her attention. Now that she regarded herself as a mistress of intrigue she was bent on a scheme to reconcile Lauzun with the King, although I told her that in my opinion a fiery Gascon like him would sooner die that let anyone, even his great friend and master the King, get the better of him in love. He would sooner die himself than see the Princess de Monaco, his own mistress, flirting yet again with His Majesty, and even Climène could not manipulate his rescue. Everyone knows how he deliberately trod on the Princess's hand with all his weight when she was sitting on the floor with other ladies around the King, and they all heard the bone snap.

By this time we had arrived at Versailles. Fortunately the dampness of the ground made Climène anxious to walk on the terrace in front of the Galerie des Glaces. I kept my eyes open for the Englishman from the very beginning, but there was no sign of him.

Among the very few to be seen there was one gentleman standing at the head of the steps leading down to the parterre. As we drew closer I realised to my astonishment that he looked familiar. He wore a wig the colour of his own hair, that is to say a sandy blond, and a buff coloured coat with emerald buttons and almost no gold except for a kind of sarsanet with lace tied very elegantly across it. His jerkin beneath was of scarlet, and his hose sable coloured. None of this can convey, however, the impression of style, dignity and grace that his appearance conveyed.

I was not the only one struck by it. Long before we were within range of any greeting, Climène had already noticed him. I could tell because she became suddenly silent, and when I looked up at her she was preening her shoulder and glancing repeatedly, with a long neck and an abstracted expression, in the direction of the steps. A moment later she remembered me and said crossly, "Berthon, don't follow me so closely."

We had almost reached the steps, she pretending not to know me, when the Englishman came forward, as I knew he would, and touched his hat to me. I stopped. I had no idea of the man's name. I bowed to him also, and was aware of Climène beside me so full of impatience that it crossed my mind that she might reach down any minute and pinch me like she did years ago once when I annoyed her. As if to ask her permission to present the Englishman, I half turned to Climène, giving him time to produce his own name. Immediately he bowed again, and sweeping off his hat, said, to my profound astonishment and Climène's delight, "My name is Francis, Viscount Alltwen, the eldest son of Lord Claydon."

I was too surprised to say a single word.

CHAPTER TWELVE

I saw nothing of Climène after this encounter for several days, much as I wanted to hear more of my extraordinary friend, and of Climène's own conversation with him. On the day in question I had left them together, and returned to St. Germain alone.

A few evenings later Lorraine was back at court, and attended the King's supper. No doubt when this memoir is read these ceremonies will still be identical because such things do not easily change. Even so, I will describe this supper in some detail. Madame was seated next to the King, who had the Queen on his other side, and the rest of the Royal family were all present, ranged along the far side of the table and both ends, The courtiers stood as usual, most of us facing the table from a distance of eight or ten paces.

Madame was in good humour. She looked radiant. I realised with my mind only – because there was such a fixed opinion on the matter at court and because Madame herself always insisted that she had no beauty – that in every one else's opinion she was plain. But with my own eyes I could not ever entirely understand such a view, even when I tried. If she was plump, her figure nevertheless had an inimitable grace, and if she was at all heavy, then it was only just so much as was needed to convey the majesty that was absolutely appropriate to her station. Her eyes were not particularly large, but they sparkled and her lips were beautiful and even, and naturally red. I loved to watch her eating. She was clean and pretty in the way she did it. If she was greedy – which she sometimes was – she reminded me of a child's famished need for sweets and favourite food, in the way that she devoured sausages from the Palatine, and the German butter which she swore was so delicious and better than the French, and even cream brought specially for her from her own country, wrapped in ice.

I watched her on this evening as she spoke very pleasantly to her husband, and also a great deal to the King. He laughed heartily several times, as he always did in her company, and also discussed some detail of the chase which had shown up the prowess of a gentleman newly come to court who rode very well.

The Queen, on His Majesty's other side, ate only her special dishes loaded with onion, garlic, cloves and chocolate, and spoke hardly at all, except to her dwarfs, who stood just behind her chair. In short, it was a supper like any other except that the Chevalier de Lorraine, instead of standing in the first ranks of those who were grouped about in attendance, facing the table, was content to keep in the background. This at least was his strategy.

The King did not fail to notice him, even so. Lorraine bowed with a touching affectation of humility when the royal gaze passed over him. At the same time Elizabeth de Grancy changed her position in the room. With mincing quiet steps, a whisper here, a small obeisance there, she arrived finally at his side. She had something written on a little slip of paper which she showed to d'Effiat in passing. I felt the wretched stirrings of anxiety at the sight of them, wondering what progress their insatiable ill-will might make towards the constant ambition of harming Madame. At one point Lorraine peered around the room, looking for someone in the crowd of courtiers. Clearly they had some intrigue on the boil as usual. There was never any peace when these people were on hand, and if not the actual product, then the undercurrent of possibilities set in motion by their restless malice was quite enough to poison the atmosphere wherever they were.

The King ate well. After three platefuls of *soupe Colbert* he had a whole pheasant, a partridge, and a dish of hashed mutton with garlic, together with a salad. And even then he had two slices of ham, pastries, fruit and sweets. I had long ceased to wonder at the appetites of whole men. But the King himself, every facet of whose being was so noble and splendid, ate like a hero, hungry after a day of exercise and work. He did not eat tid bits between meals, like Monsieur for example, and he had hunted for three hours in the afternoon.

When the King left the table, Madame was about to follow the Queen to the card tables, but Monsieur detained her. Lorraine waited at Monsieur's elbow while the Prince spoke to his wife and despite the fact that he had been in disgrace and had scarcely had time to clear his throat since returning from the Bastille, Lorraine was clearly hatching some new plot. Madame was bound to be the target of it.

After a brief interchange, they left the room with the Maréchale de Clerembault in attendance on Madame. I followed without being seen. When they arrived at Madame's drawing room Monsieur, Madame and the Chevalier continued from there into her cabinet, leaving the Maréchale to wait outside.

After a few moments Monsieur d'Effiat entered the room, and stood together with Clerembault in icy silence. Not a word was spoken. With her unyielding expression the Maréchale conveyed, involuntarily, the awful fear that must have been in her heart. Courtiers develop an instinct for disaster, and she must have known that however much Madame was Lorraine's ultimate target, she herself was about to be sacrificed. As for myself, my heart instead of beating faster seemed to have stopped. Suspense and worry over Madame would kill me in the end. There would be no need for Lorraine to do it.

Eventually Monsieur and Madame came back into the drawing room.

Madame was deeply upset. She knew very well how to behave with dignity, so that at a time like this her youth and her simple nature were quite overlaid by an assumption of the dignity of her rank, and the common signs of distress were hidden. Only the stiffness of her body and the complete absence of the light that was usually visible in her eye told a different tale. But as she came into the room she did touch the corner of her eye with her finger. My heart jumped like a rat in a trap as I saw it. If I had been born a man instead of such a figure of fun I would have thrown myself at her feet there and then and dared anyone – even the King's brother – to cause her the slightest unhappiness. And then I daresay I should have been executed for my pains and done her who I so longed to serve, no good at all.

While my blood boiled with all these thoughts, Monsieur said something to the Maréchale de Clerembault. She responded with the same icy calm but that was not unusual with her. He elaborated. The Maréchale was to be dismissed from court, and the reason given was that she was accused of trying to encourage a liaison between Madame and one of the artists she patronised, as well as being too familiar herself with her mistress. Such an expression of cold and angry contempt settled on the Maréchale's face when she heard this that she looked, just for an instant, as if she had been turned to stone. She said something addressed more to Lorraine than Monsieur, but the words were few and fell with such sharpness from her lips that they could not be heard a yard off. Nor did I hear the name of who was to replace her as governess of Monsieur's children. A moment later Monsieur left with d'Effiat and Lorraine. Madame took the Maréchale into her own closet and closed the door.

The next day there was simply no sign of Madame de Clerembault. At first everyone who came to Madame's apartment asked after her in astonishment. Theobon had the task of answering, and she was as tight lipped and sharp as you would expect. If it was the season for dismissing favourites she might have to look to herself. And the disappearance of a lady so obviously loved by Madame as was the Maréchale de Clerembault was an deliberate insult to the Princess and an indication of how her influence with her husband was not to be compared with that of Lorraine. He who would have been the first to proclaim that no other way of life could possibly compare with the one from which Clerembault had been so ruthlessly cut off, namely to reside at Court, remained to enjoy the artistic, the intellectual and the social life that had been the life blood of the Maréchale. And Madame, who ranked above all the women in France except the Queen herself and whose wishes should have been set before all others, was her dearest friend, and loved and valued her company, and wished to see her every day. And yet neither could save themselves or each other, simply because Madame's husband was the King's brother and he was manipulated by the Chevalier de Lorraine as easily as the wind blows a leaf off a tree. The Maréchale de Clerembault was dismissed from court and would never return. And since her absence would so bitterly grieve Madame herself, this was clearly the real reason for her being sent away.

Where had she gone at such sudden notice? Apparently she retired to a house in Paris; in the Marais of course. But she and Madame were forbidden to meet or communicate with each other. Part of the forged letter had dealt with the fabrication of too warm a friendship between her and Madame, and some ludicrous nonsense about the Maréchale and the sculptor Bernini.

I said to Theobon that I ought to have done differently myself in connection with that letter. I should have burned it. Madame was too outspoken and good humoured to deal with a matter like that effectively. She had failed to establish the fact of the forgery with her husband. Others knew perfectly well how to think of it. When it came to be spoken of in court subsequently no one doubted the dishonesty of the Chevalier de Lorraine, and I later learned that the King was well aware of the forgery. But Monsieur allowed himself to be duped. Or rather he allowed himself to be used in order to please the Chevalier de Lorraine by forwarding his plans and his secret strategy.

Instead of the Maréchale de Clerembault, Madame d'Effiat now had charge of the children. She was not an evil person, like her husband, but she was nothing to Madame. And it went without saying that her allegiance, however constrained, would be to her husband and Monsieur. Very shortly after, d'Effiat himself was proposed as the governor of the little Duc de Chârtres. Madame was hemmed in by her enemies and but for Theobon and myself in her immediate circle she was almost cut off.

But if Lorraine and his friends had hoped to see Madame diminished or quelled by her treatment they were disappointed. Even those who looked for signs of it the very next day could not spot any diminution of her kindly manners and liveliness. It was even slightly astonishing to me. If one had not know how she grieved in private one could have been deceived into imagining that she was heartless, but almost all her friends knew very well what lay behind it. And such spirit, combined with her exalted rank and the favour of the King, brought new and often devoted friends to pay court to her every day, so that the conspiracy now so obviously undertaken against her by Lorraine reached a stalemate in this; her basically regal status, and her natural resilience.

The first Duchesse, by all accounts, had not had these qualities. She was like a delicate piece of English china compared to a fine strong German beaker moulded out of silver. I placed as much faith as I could in this material difference simply in order to have enough peace of mind to sleep at night.

Lorraine and his friends showed no hesitation in presenting themselves in Madame's apartment just as often and as confidently as before his confinement in the Bastille and his obvious implication in the banishment of Clerembault. Various people at court expected him to be abashed, but on the contrary. He and his little *cabale* of friends had no shame. It made my hackles rise to see Lorraine strut in Monsieur's train with as little concern for the fact that he was in Madame's drawing room as if she was a person of no account. How thoroughly one can learn to hate a man!

When he came into the room for the first time after Clerembault's dismissal, Madame, who normally tolerated his presence with apparent indifference only stared at him as he made his bow, and the maximum acknowledgement she could be said to have given in reply was a minute movement of the head. But it apparently meant nothing to him. There were courtiers present who, if they were received in such a way, would shortly afterwards leave the room. Not he. If Madame intended him to feel her scorn, the nasty glissade of his blue eyed smile threw it off with as much ease as oil repels water. He directed his flattering attention at Monsieur who, for his part, responded with all the warmth needed to contradict his wife. But Madame sat with Madame de Villeroy, or Dou Dou, and the Dauphin, and hardly interrupted by that momentary notice of Lorraine, she was the centre of lively conversation.

I watched all this from my usual place which I will now describe to you. There were three sets of windows. The table at which Madame wrote her letters was at right angles to the wall between two of them. Between the third and the end wall of the room a little nook was created by the obtruding side of a cupboard that occupied a prominent position on the end wall, and moreover, the hangings of dark crimson damask which fell to the ground were often caught up on a footstool sometimes used for Charmille, and this was where I belonged. The corner was always rather dark. I did not know that the Chevalier de Lorraine or any of his crew had ever noticed that I was there.

He had. He knew where I was. And now I saw that he seemed engaged in some little game or other, bending first to one person and then to another and whispering to draw their attention to where I was. He was doing what I most dreaded; destroying my invisibility. Once my presence was made obvious, to have me sent away would be easy. If he were to have me excluded from Madame's presence, as he had the Maréchale, I would die. I would not be able to survive elsewhere. And if my body persisted in living, my heart would not.

I felt a noise in my head, like a wind that buffeted my brain with bewildering force so that my thoughts were knocked against each other without sense. But then I forced myself to master the reaction. Monsieur, following his favourite's eye, nevertheless looked at me quite kindly. It was not really in his nature to torment others unnecessarily. And of course, that I should be capable of being either useful to his wife or a comfort to her was not likely to occur to him.

But I needed to put the Chevalier, who knew otherwise, off the scent. On the spur of the moment only the device of cowardice occurred to me. If I pretended to be afraid of him, he would no doubt be cruel but perhaps he would not mistrust me. It was his apprehension that I was capable of being deliberately useful to his enemies that I had to overcome. He could perhaps be persuaded to think of my intervention over the letter as a freak of chance unlikely to be repeated.

Therefore, mortifying though it was to my pride, I ran away. I stepped with seeming timidity around the edge of the wall and slipped through the door. I heard him laugh behind me, and in my imagination I ran a dagger through him, the blade of which sliced him into pieces.

I was in such a rage following this scene, that to find consolation I took myself up onto the roof, to be with my birds. It was a fine day. In early spring our country is the best in all the world – not that I had at that time been to any other. I could look down to where the river glinted in the sun between the trees towards the village of St. Germain, or see the horses and coaches gathered below, or watch the road to Versailles.

I arrived breathless as usual. At the last moment I was additionally distracted by having caught my right foot as I emerged from the small hatch and therefore I was slow to notice another person already sitting on the leads. It was the Englishman.

He had taken off his smart clothes and was a lackey again. This was a fortuitous distraction from the pain I had just suffered. If Climène had told this man where to find me, it looked as if the introduction that had been brokered as my part in the bargain had prospered where I had thought it bound to fail. In which case I was extremely interested to hear about it.

"Did Climène tell you I came here?" I asked.

"She did."

I nodded to him and went straight over to the boxes, and also looked up into the sky for Bronzine and Salamandre who were missing. I could just make them out on the trees by the mill. It still surprises me how one can recognise the wing pattern of one's own birds at a distance. Then I picked up Michette to examine her flights. She had a small deformity which I controlled by sometimes clipping the edge of a feather with my knife. But I was thinking all the time about his meeting with Climène, and wondering what had happened and what had been said after I had gone. No sooner had she exchanged five words with Francis – Viscount Alltwen – that afternoon on the terrace in front of the Gallerie des Glaces than Climène had dismissed me with some whispered comment which made it very clear that she wished to be alone with this gentleman.

The Englishman made no further comment for a moment or two, and then said "I have come here to give you an explanation."

"About Climène, perhaps?"

"I should find that rather hard," he said, laughing. "It is more on my own account that I feel the obligation to dispel a mystery. There is nothing hard to understand in an exquisitely beautiful creature such as

Climène D'Autour being adored. Her conversation has the charm of Molière and La Fontaine both together. She is as lively as sunlight, and as changeable. But since I have been so fortunate as to win her friendship, I should do you the courtesy of thanking you for the introduction, and explaining why I am obliged to live as I do." He made a gesture with the back of his fingers as if he was brushing dust off his livery.

So he had won her friendship. How much of it did an Englishman mean to imply he had got when he smiled like that, without any guile whatsoever.

I was not used to being considered with such politeness by any one, least of all on the basis that I could claim any right to know the business of my sister and I scarcely knew what to say. And at the same time I had to remember that this erstwhile lackey had laid claim to nobility, even if only that of an Englishman. In all probability he ranked above myself.

"Have you seen her since?" I said. "I have not."

I was having difficulty holding Michette at the same time as my knife, and Francis said, "Shall I hold the bird for you?"

I was about to decline but he apparently knew exactly how to do it. He took the bird with her head facing in towards his body and her legs between his fingers exactly as I had, and she stayed quietly in his hands while I trimmed the feather. It made me smile. I couldn't help it.

"Do you tame bears as well?" I said. "And have you the right dress for that too?"

He looked down at his livery, which was that of the Marquis de Bellefonds not the Duc de Vendôme. He rode for the Duc de Vendôme because the Marquis de Bellefonds suggested it.

"I wear this livery," he said, "because for the moment I am in the service of my friend, the Marquis de Bellefonds. I had better tell you how that came about. He was in England as the Ambassador of France. My father is a madman. When I was a small child he was quite different, but something gradually changed him, and then he could no longer look at me without getting in a rage. Eventually I ran away but he had me hunted down, and when his men were about to kill me de Bellefonds' carriage came into the mews because his coachman was lost. I have been in his service now for three years. It is not a bad life."

Naturally I was astounded.

"When my father dies," he said, "I will inherit his title and estate. But until then unfortunately I can never see him, and I must be careful that he never finds out where I am, because he would do his best to have me killed."

"Why?"

"He's mad. I said so. No physician and no priest can reach that part of his mind which has become totally distorted. My mother's dead; my brothers and sisters live in a state of misery but not actual danger." For fully a minute he said nothing. Then he sighed and added, "I remember him before he went mad – when I was about seven. Laughing. Trying to teach me how to catch a butterfly without harming its wings. Have you finished?" referring to my work on the feather.

Unconsciously I had dropped my hand, but Michette remained quite content in the grip of this unusual man. I recovered my wits, neatened the cut quill, checked that the pinions now stacked correctly, and then asked him if he would set her down on the leads, which he did. After a moment he took a deep breath, looked up at the sky and said, "Would you mind if I sit a while? It is too delightful up here to hurry down. And besides, I must tell you how your sister has stolen my heart right out of my body. I will marry her if I can."

Then I did look at him in utter astonishment.

"Don't men have affairs in England?" I said.

"Of course. Especially when the lady is married already."

"Climène is married."

He sighed as if it was the first time he had heard of it. But then laughed, and said, "Berthon," – using the name by which no doubt he had heard her speak of me, "I only want you to know what I will do in the end. I can see perfectly well that it can't be done in the beginning. Your sister keeps offering to poison poor d'Autour, but that isn't necessary. I'm flattered by her impatience, but I consider myself too happy in this immediate present to press it."

"She will sting you for that!" I said.

"Yes!" He threw back his head and laughed so loud that the birds all exploded upward with a clatter. The idea seemed to absolutely delight him.

But I also wondered why he wanted to make me think he intended to marry Climène. Or was it true? An Englishman was capable of anything. And many of them having deserted the Catholic church, no doubt they had become confused about the practicalities of matrimony as they had about the ability of bread to be transformed into the true body of Christ at the moment of communion.

I sat patiently through a long monologue in praise of Climène which would have bored most men; but as well as agreeing with him he had a great facility to make me laugh.

Eventually, when he was ready to talk about anything else but Climène, I asked him where his father had his estates. In something called the Midlands, apparently. He described an area equal to the lands held by the Duc de Vendôme, but over territory that was flatter, with a great deal of woodland and very harsh winters. While he had still been young enough to live at home he had spent all his spare time in the stables and it was a coachman who had taught him about birds.

He stayed on the roof with me for more than an hour talking. It was a rare delight to be treated as an equal and a friend by another man of my own age or a year or two older.

He told me stories that made me laugh and described opinions that astonished me, as well as persuading me on my own account to explain my views on the English monarchy and the claim made by our own Louis XIV on the Palatinate. From that day onwards I called him Francis whenever we were alone, and I remarked that it seemed rather ill luck that he should have to wait for two men to die before he could have what he wanted in life; that was, if he wanted Climène for his wife, as well as to be able to live safely at home.

There was a lot of activity on the road to Versailles at the time because the final preparations were in hand for the movement of the whole court to take up residence there. As Madame de Sévigné wrote in those letters that she was so eager that the court should read, *'Tout le mond va et vient á Versailles.'* The to-and-fro of wagons with all sorts of equipment and materials was almost constant and looking down on it as I listened to Francis, I remember it as part of the story repeated to me. Although the two may not go together at all, that dusty track with the flat thick fields on either side and a line of tall trees stubbornly cleaves to my impression of the part of England he described.

Before we parted, Francis said, "Lorraine is back. I hope you've learned my lesson well. He is the sort of man who does exactly what he threatens."

"How can he set his dogs on me now?" I said, although I was not as confident as I pretended. "He has attracted the King's anger by his violent behaviour at the race and he will hardly dare to allow even his hounds to be responsible for harming another member of the court so soon."

Francis also asked me if I would be interested in buying a horse, because he knew of one that would suit me well.

"I can't ride," I said. I told him that I could sit a horse that was being led walking, but that was all I could do at that time. My mind was not on the answer I was giving. It was too much occupied with other things.

CHAPTER THIRTEEN

The next day, at one o'clock, I was in Madame's apartment to attend at her luncheon, which she ate alone. When I say she ate alone, there were at least twenty, Ernst included among us, in attendance, standing talking to her when she chose, or silent. She ate a great deal of German food when she could get it. Any visitors from the German court would be likely to bring her supplies of sausage and cheese, and, as I mentioned before, even their cream packed in ice, which she thought so superior to ours. On this day the fact that her table was particularly laden was the first indication that a large company of Germans had just arrived at court accompanying Madame's half brother, Charles-Louis of the Palatine.

The meal being over, Madame returned to her drawing room, and was greeted by a number of these visitors, the chief among whom was her half-brother; a very striking man, and no less so than reputation had painted him. He was more than six foot, blond and well made with that sort of strength that, if a young man can control his excess of energy and not fidget but remain fairly still, can be intimidating.

I already knew well enough the importance of not allowing strangers to catch sight of me. I entered the room only in the wake of Madame Soissons, and remained entirely in the background. But the Raugrave, as they called him then, saw me. He looked as if he would take offence; but in his sister's presence checked himself. All the same, his eye returned to me from time to time until eventually Madame noticed it. To my dismay she then called out, "Ah, this is Monsieur de Brisse. Come here, my goblin."

Alas, it was her idea of rewarding me for the service I had attempted to do for her in getting hold of the forged letter. It also pre-empted the Raugrave's likely inclination to offer me some sort of insult, although I didn't realise this at the time. By noticing me publicly she did me a great honour, and I was aware of it. But I would have preferred obscurity. I thanked Providence that I had put on my best wig and my highest heels as I took five or so steps into the room and made my bow. One of the Germans tittered. They were all massive.

"Monsieur de Brisse," Madame said, "has been of the greatest possible service to me lately."

Her brother looked amazed by the idea, but said nothing.

"I assure you it is true," she said. "You know how I am plagued by the enmity of a small group of Monsieur's special friends, and in particular the Chevalier de Lorraine."

Her face held an inimitable expression as she pronounced these words in such a relatively public manner. She looked both mischievous and regal at the very same time. Dou Dou suppressed a giggle in anticipation, caught the quelling eye of Theobon, and quickly looked away.

"If you please," Madame continued, "the Chevalier forged a letter and was about to pass this scurrilous writing off as mine."

The Raugrave drew himself up and glared like an actor on cue, but Madame went on.

"You can imagine that in it I was made to say all sorts of impertinent and dangerous things which I would not dream of. But it was so ingeniously forged that if the King had been shown it by anyone other than myself, it might have been believed. Fortunately, however, Monsieur de Brisse heard about it, stole it and brought it to me."

The Raugrave had lost interest in me and transferred his whole attention to the story of the letter itself. His companions broke into German, and although I couldn't understand the language, their threatening looks were unmistakeable and they were clearly furious at the malicious duplicity of Lorraine. And then it was at this very moment that Madame Gordon came into the room, closely followed by the Chevalier himself.

Madame looked straight at the Chevalier with a smiling face which brought him immediately into the centre of the room, and at first he was unaware, as he made his bow, of the peril he was in. "Here is the Chevalier de Lorraine" she said to the Raugrave, and to the Chevalier she added, "I have been telling my brother how skilful you are with your pen, so that you are even able to imitate my writing well enough to deceive Monsieur."

For once Lorraine's *sangfroid* deserted him, because the Raugrave Charles-Louis had already taken a step towards him, as if to issue a challenge there and then. The Raugrave had not yet said anything, but the tinge of red in his golden cheek – I call it golden, because his hair was a reddish blond, and his beard, which like the King he only shaved every other day, began to show through the skin and gave it this colour – and his fierce and haughty look was enough to quell anybody.

The Chevalier let his mouth fall open for a moment, he was taken so by surprise. But then, when he did realise the situation, he did what I never thought to see; he turned tail and ran.

In fact, he walked of course. But he simply left the room at once, and without any excuse. He tried to put the best face on it afterwards when Madame Theobon obliged him to give an account in front of Monsieur, by referring to it. He wasn't grateful to the Countess for mentioning it, of course, but a very quick glance of spite in her direction was followed by that elegant laugh that he could produce at will no matter what disgrace he should have been in, and he said,

"My dears, what should anyone expect? Madame does not love me, alas, and the room was simply full of great big Germans who, as everyone knows, can't take a joke."

The laughter that followed his words was in sympathy with the Chevalier, merely because of his deceptively open manner and his wit. A series of events that could have destroyed the reputation of some men, beginning with the scurrilous and ending with the ridiculous, had been turned by him in his own favour. He was a snake of a man who could cut and twist with the same speed as others go forward, and arrive at a point where he was not expected before his enemies could intercept him. And that reminds me how apt my simile is because poison had been his chosen weapon before. And for my own part I should never have forgotten – even for a moment – that he had given his word to set his dogs on me and in this sort of bargain, if in no other, a man like the Chevalier would keep his word.

On the afternoon following the scene described with the Raugrave, I was alone, crossing one of the paved yards leading between the stables and the kennels, when the King's hunt returned from Versailles. I was still preoccupied with the miserable scandal of the Maréchale de Clerembault's dismissal and the effect on Madame of having been deprived of such a close friend, and in a manner that humiliated her personally before the court.

I followed the cycles of Lorraine's malicious intrigue against Madame with one predominant objective in mind; to detect the moment when, satisfied that he had weakened his enemy enough to dare the attempt, he would strike at her life. Should that moment come, I staked my life that I would be before him. Because naturally the pretext for

Clerembault's exile was well known, and in treating one of his wife's ladies in such a way Monsieur exposed Madame to contempt as well as danger. Words could not describe the bitterness with which I hated Lorrain as I walked, deep in thought. I paid little attention to the grooms and horses as they briefly passed me by.

Then, with an almost supernatural suddenness, as I was about to cross the small empty quadrangle from which the staircase leads up into the west apartments, my path was blocked. Standing there was a massive hound, one of the animals being brought back from the hunt, who must have silently doubled back on his track and stood confronting me.

I recognised the creature. Among the King's favourite pointers and setters such as Diane, Blonde, and Mitte, there had recently appeared this wolfhound called Camargue. He was reputed to have a very docile nature but he was twice the size of myself and I never went near him. For some reason he now had his hackles raised and his mouth drawn back in a deep guttural snarl as he unmistakeably confronted myself.

My blood froze. The intentions of the animal were clear. With my eyes jumping out of my head I looked for somewhere to run. There was nowhere. Behind me was a large empty yard, with no other human being in sight. The hound would catch me before I had crossed a quarter of it. The animal was the same height as myself at the shoulder, the head higher, and every muscle in his body seemed strung and standing out with the tension of menace. I knew that whether this was the King's hound or not, I faced the revenge of Lorraine.

I didn't move. I was frozen to the spot. The animal was silent for an instant and then drew back its lip and uttered from the back its throat a deeper and even more blood curdling growl. I heard, in the next yard, like a distant reverberation of sound from another world, the everyday noises of the kennel master in charge of the other hounds returning, the yelp and patter of other dogs. I should have liked to call out. But my voice was stuck in my throat. I tried to remember my lessons from the Englishman.

I bent to one side and picked up an imaginary stone as if to throw it, there being no real ones to hand. The beast snarled and made a flinching gesture, but one which only ended by increasing the angle of its incipient attack.

And then it sprung. With one bound it landed on me and fastened its teeth into my back. Fortunately – or so I thought until I discovered otherwise – I was wearing a certain thick jerkin under my coat, and for a moment it protected me. I hit the ground and the animal let go of my back, and came for my throat. Thanks to my wits, which functioned independent of conscious thought, I remembered the Englishman's second lesson and from where I lay I executed the gesture he had taught me with such desperation and apparent exactitude that the animal recoiled for a moment. In that instant I felt the pebble in my pocket. I thrust it between my teeth and blew with all my might. I heard not a thing, of course, but the hound heard something. Starting from a position where his foul head was poised over my own, so that his very breath, foetid with the chase, was mixed with mine, and repellent drops from its muzzle had oozed already onto my cheek, the cur froze, and then let out a single whine. I blew again and again, and incredibly, the knotted muscles twitching under the close cropped hair of its shoulder and straining against the skin, it held back; it whined again; it turned; it crouched down miserably just as a huntsman appeared through the opening into the next courtyard, and with a cry of amazement ran over to where I lay.

I was in no condition to stand. As I took out of my mouth the pebble that had saved my life, blood from my hand and wrist poured over my face. Almost my last thought was of pushing that precious stone back into my pocket. I let others lift me. I was carried up to a room, and laid on a palette where someone cleaned me and bound up the wound in my back, which bled a great deal.

For a week I suffered a fever which threatened still to put an end to my life and even now the fantasies that haunted me during those hours are still vivid in my memory. Camargue predominated. But almost equally, an image of the Chevalier de Lorraine fastened on me, because I knew that although the King's dog, and not his, had attacked me, Lorraine was behind it and only he had somehow achieved such a diabolical manipulation of an animal that had been famous until now for his gentleness.

I was so badly injured that the King himself, and not merely in my fevered imagination, did me the honour of coming to see how I was, and sending to enquire on two other occasions. When I was well again, I was honoured with permission to attend his *coucher*, and even an invitation into the Cabinet on one occasion. In this way, His Majesty expressed his regret that an animal belonging to him had attacked me, and I felt more than recompensed for the pain I had been caused by the courtesy the King showed to me. Neither did I consider it to be pain at all when I remembered that it was in the service of Madame that I had incurred this punishment. I had succeeded in thwarting – or partly, and only for the moment, thwarting – the malice of Lorraine just when he had produced a potentially very successful trick with that letter. And although Madame had not made good use of it, my intervention had protected her in some measure.

Of course the Chevalier de Lorraine kept well away from me while I was sick, but I had an opportunity to speak with him in private one evening when I was back on my feet, and we came face to face, he alone on his way somewhere and I also. He would have walked past me but I spoke his name.

He stopped. His tall and beautiful form was remarkable. He was dressed in blue velvet, and the decision to halt and answer me was accompanied by a progressive relaxation of his joints and muscles which had the exactly opposite effect in that it made him look ready to spring. It was only with an effort that I avoided cringing. He said,

"Thing!" as a way of acknowledging me, and while he waited for me to speak he took a little pinch of snuff.

I said, "Chevalier, I have written a letter for the King, and if you try again to kill me and succeed, he will know you are to blame."

With almost a smile, he replied, "Are you challenging my ingenuity? Because I had almost lost interest in you, but such a wager could be amusing. I can think of many ways in which to prove you wrong."

I saw the trap I had fallen into. But in a moment of inspiration, I laughed. I know that I am very ugly when I laugh, and I also know that it is the one weapon a mortal has against a god. I could not bring myself to laugh much, but it was enough. The Chevalier stiffened, turned on his heel and walked away without looking back.

When others at court continued to express amazement at the behaviour of Camargue, which they considered to be so out of character with the usual nature of the animal, I took very little notice at first. It was painful for me to be aware that dogs which regard most men as their masters are likely to mistake me for their natural prey, and although I was convinced that Lorraine had had something to do with it, I had come to the conclusion that I would never know how he had done it.

But one day I happened to overhear the Comte de Lauzun talking with Mme. de Sévigné about herbs. As everyone at Court knows, Mme. de Sévigné's daughter has gone to live for the moment in Provence and her mother is always talking about her, her health, the habits of that part of France and so on. On this day she was discussing a plant called the Dragon Arum which can be gathered there in Summer, a preparation of which is very effective as a purgative, and asking Lauzun whether, coming from that part of the country, or near, he had any knowledge of it. He had, and they talked for some time; but then he mentioned a very curious thing. He said that certain dogs go wild if they smell the powdered root of this Dragon Arum, or Dracunculus vulgaris, and he had heard it mentioned once that Camargue, of whom there had been so much talk a little while ago, was roused to fury if he smelled it.

They then went on to talk of other things. Climène would have been interested, because Madame de Sévigné told yet again that story of how nearly her daughter was drowned when crossing the Rhône at the very point where Climène's husband would soon be travelling.

But I left the room, and went thoughtfully back to my own apartment.

I will tell you what ideas were occupying my mind. I had remembered Bonhomme rubbing my jerkin with a powder which he said was to remove a stain. I had not worn that jerkin until the day I was attacked. Then, it was the very garment I had on. I called Bonhomme as soon as I reached my door.

I said, "Bring me the jerkin I had on when the wolfhound attacked me." He pretended not to know which it was. "Surely," I said, "it was torn and you will have mended it." He made a great play of calling himself a fool, and then went out the door, promising to fetch it from some person to whose skill he had entrusted the repair. He said he would return with it in a few minutes.

I waited for half an hour, and then I went to the servant's room of Monsieur le Grand. Bonhomme did not even know that I was aware of his friendship with Culotte, one of Le Grand's men, and so he had assumed he would be safe in there. I forced him out, and because I think I had gained some very small status at Court following on the King's show of concern for me during my illness, he did not dare to resist me.

Once back in my apartment, I insisted that he showed me the powder he had rubbed on my jerkin. He said that he had none left. I said, "What? Are you not anticipating ever again having to clean off a stain?" He looked sour, and said nothing.

"What did the Chevalier pay you to rub the powdered root of Dragon Arum on my jerkin?" I said, with an expression of contempt. "Did you know that it would madden the wolfhound Camargue and cause him to attack me?"

An expression of pure shock lit his eyes for a moment before he could suppress it. I knew that I had made a hit.

He wouldn't answer. I could see that if I continued to question him for hours he still would admit nothing. It was the only satisfaction he could have. I rather pitied him for it when I looked at his face, because he was such a miserable pinched sly looking man, and I told him he could go. I said I knew enough anyway, and I had the patience to do without something if I could see that it was of no real value to me: like the account by a dishonest man of an event that I had more or less pieced together for myself. Something like a tear sprung into his eye at my words, and he turned away. It surprised me.

CHAPTER FOURTEEN

While I was still recovering from the attack on me by Camargue I received many visits from Climène – a matter that surprised and pleased me almost as much as those from the King. Her usual conversation went as follows:

"Berthon, it is not my fault that His Majesty's wolfhound attacked you. I know that perfectly well. And yet I feel very disappointed, when I took so much trouble to save you from the Chevalier de Lorraine once."

At this point I would tend to thank her again for the trouble she had been at for my sake.

"Please Berthon, don't be grateful," she said with a little return to a more snappish manner. And then suddenly soft again, "But I am allowed to be grateful and I shall be, because you introduced me to Viscount Alltwen. How extraordinary that he should have met you in such a way. It was fate. The good angel who looks after me arranged it all: the race, the quarrel that delayed everyone returning home, your walking back alone."

"Is that why it all happened?" I said. "The servant who died, I think I heard, and the three noblemen who ended up in the Bastille, not to mention the coats torn and the wigs ripped up – this was all for your sake?"

But Climène took no offence. She merely smiled at me and said, "Yes. Without all that I should not ever have met Francis. And he is a really remarkably handsome man, don't you think, Berthon?" A very brief moment peering into my face with her own eyes on fire. "You don't look very well, Berthon. Are you faint? "

I might have been about to say I was, and that I needed a glass of water which was within her reach, but to make sure I didn't she commanded, "Don't interrupt me. Do let me tell you. You know that horrible husband of mine. He asked to see my ruby; the one I gave Fallongues. When Francis heard about it…"

"You told him!" I couldn't help exclaiming.

"Why not?"

"But you bribed a servant to cheat against him during the race."

"Only to help you, Berthon. Otherwise I would never do such a disgusting thing. And let me tell you, Francis understands that far better than you do. He absolutely laughed at the very idea. Have you seen him laugh? Don't you think he has an enchanting laugh. You've noticed the crease that cuts across the end of his mouth when he smiles. Isn't it wonderful. And he bought back the ruby from Fallongues, so that I should not get into trouble with that ogre I am married to."

From such talk as this – and it was the same each time she visited me – it had become quite plain that Climène was in love. In the subsequent melancholy days when, having escaped death itself I fell into the maw of despair because of my weakened state, I could not help comparing my life to hers. She was made to be adored. How could the same man – our father – have produced two such disparate off spring; one made for love and the other doomed never to know that sort of joy. I had reached an age some time ago now when I had become keenly aware of the beauty of women. But I supposed that never ever in my life would I be blessed in the way that Francis was with Climène.

I knew love well enough. I knew it because of my devotion to Madame. But that feeling which I had for the Princess was a sacred and elevated one. I saw her very much as a woman, although I would not dare to admit this to any courtier. Everything about her enchanted me; her mouth, her smiles, her moments of anger, her rude humour, her regal dignity. But at the same time, for example, as being aware of the softness of her skin – because I never forgot the moment I described in the beginning of this story – this softness had sunk into my mind like the voluptuousness of sky itself; the last thing a sane man would want, would be to possess it. I would have unhesitatingly leapt into the jaws of death to save her from danger, or perhaps even discomfort. I adored her so completely I wouldn't even have thought of it. But such feelings belong to deities, and although they are stronger than any other it is as if love is vaporised in that atmosphere; an intoxicating fume without carnal sequence of any sort.

But on occasion my thoughts would stray in the direction of another kind of love altogether, with a woman of my own rank whom, if I had a normal body, I might have hoped for. Then my imagination would flinch, as if the wing of my mind had briefly touched a flame, that singed the edge of it.

So I had a particular way of regarding women once I was a grown man. I appointed them a place in my consciousness that was cut off from the common circulation of my emotions. When Ernst and his friends began to talk of nothing but women, I took no notice. I visited the Pont Neuf like anyone else, but I was not such a fool as to imagine I would ever get satisfaction for my body without paying for it, or that any woman that I, with my sort of mind, would admire, could return the feeling of a man with my sort of body. I armed myself against the illusion of true love.

However, Fate is no less keen to take advantage of a man when he is in a weakened state than is a courtier. They could learn from each other. And so I, when more or less restored in body after the attack of Camargue, but still enfeebled in spirit, was ambushed by this other enemy and my heart was sucked out of me before I had time to defend myself.

It happened because Ernst had the idea – which I more or less agreed with – that to be constantly entertained at the theatre would help the progress of my recovery. And then, at a performance of Phédre one evening by the theatre company in Paris, a new actress came onto the stage. Her name was Fanette d'Estrier, and she played the part of Aricie. Her opening lines are, if you remember: *'Hippolyte demande á me voir en ce lieu? Hippolyte me cherche, et veut me dire adieu?'*

She was dressed exquisitely as an Athenian princess. At the end of the third line she struck a pose, as was the style appropriate to the drama, and I had time to observe the perfect shape of a small gold Greek sandal. The outline – the shadow – of her body under the draperies of her costume, was more beautiful than I have any hope of describing. I leaned forward without breathing, and felt my heart crack against my ribs as I strained to inhale every detail of her body. She had dark hair knotted with what looked like thongs of turquoise. When she spoke there was a little catch in her voice – a roughness; a flaw – that acted on my heart like certain cadences of music against which one has no defence.

The essence of what moved me so deeply was caught somewhere in all this. The most that I can tell is that I simply felt a sudden desire for her that was as overwhelming as the desire for food which I remembered when I was starving as a child. Before I even knew that I had strayed from my usual path I was lost in unknown territory of the heart and there was no hope of getting out. I could not undo that coil of her hair, or unhear her voice. I could not remove my eyes and peel away the image that seemed to have stuck agonisingly to the retina like the wing of a lace fly sticks on water.

When the performance was over and we returned to St. Germain I couldn't sleep. The next day I was not much different except that the needle of my uncompassed heart seemed to have swung to the opposite pole. I struggled with a most unreasonable sensation of happiness. If I forgot for one moment to compose myself I let my mouth stretch open in a broad smile which is something I should never do. I was only brought to my senses by one of Madame's maids of honour who let out a little cry and covered her own face when she saw me.

Then all of a sudden, my spirits plunged into the depths of despair. I made as rapid a descent from heaven to earth as a hawk fixing its vengeful eye on one of my birds. Because if the sight of my face when I was happy was enough to make a maid of honour scream, I would never ever be able to speak to, and know, the lovely person whose presence in the same world as myself had suddenly made me so joyful.

Once when I was on the roof I did see a hawk almost level with me and stooping ready for the kill. I threw my hat at it, and it flew off. I wished that someone could throw their hat at my terrible deformity, and that it would vanish, like the bird of prey. With such a deformity it was futile for me to fall in love. I had made my mind up when I was quite young, as I said, never to do it. But look at me now.

I did not tell anyone about this disaster. Luckily young men of Ernst's age are not particularly observant. His friends thought that I suffered a relapse because the play was long and we had not dined. In the meantime Climène had been appointed a lady of the bedchamber to Madame and I began to see more of her, which would have pleased me very much if I had been in my normal frame of mind.

"Berthon," she said to me one day, "What is wrong with you?"

We were playing cards in a corner of Madame's apartment, and I made some mistake due to inattention. It was not actually a game as such, but a method of telling the future by laying down cards in certain patterns.

If the Maréchale de Clerembault had still been at court, I wonder if I should have had the courage to ask her to use her skills at divination for me. She had spent hours in the past with Madame. She would first lightly stir some dust with a stick and then, as it were, read it. She foretold the death of the little Duc de Valois, Madame's first born child, in this way. She warned Madame to take especial care of him.

Madame had talked about little else for the rest of the day. She had sat by the window which was full open, and the breeze – quite a cold one – fanned the soft tendrils of hair around her brow.

"In the Palatine," she said, "infants are looked after differently. Here in France I am extremely afraid of habits like bleeding, and the food and the treatment of infants' clothes. Look how often they die. It makes my heart beat with fright just to think of it."

"Madame," Madame de Freins said, leaning forward and shielding her mouth with her hand, "the Maréchale de Clerembault is very proud of her skill in divination, but did you hear that she told Félicité that she would give birth to a boy and it was twin girls."

Madame said "Oh!" and held her lips in that little circle for several moments after the word. Then she brought her hands up with the fingers laced under her chin and said, "This must have been before I came to court."

"Yes Madame. But it shows that she can be wrong."

Madame had nodded thoughtfully. Theobon who was standing nearby gave a snappish look at the open window, rubbed her arms, and stood further off.

"Even so," Madame had then said, "how I wish the care of my children could be given to a German woman. I mean no discourtesy, but every nation has its special skills and where I was born the mortality of infants was far less than here." Her brow darkened – literally – at the thought. When disturbed by something or someone that she regarded as an infringement of her proper position her complexion would change, as it did now when confronted with the fact that she was powerless to take the management of her children out of the hands of those to whom her husband insisted that they should be consigned. She took a deep breath, tucked in her chin. Her body had an extraordinary ability to take on different qualities according to her state of mind, and no woman could look more regal than she if she was displeased. She had absorbed some habits of French dress at court and followed Monsieur's advice quite often. But if she was disturbed, her appearance reverted at once to that of a German Princess.

"I will ask Monsieur again," she said.

All this happened years before the time when I, now in my lovelorn state, was sitting with Climène. Time had passed. But it had passed with the muffled tread of a determined assassin, whose steps I listened to everyday in fear of the moment when they should stop behind Madame. This had not changed. I was the same person as that young boy who watched from behind a screen as the little Duc de Vendôme had been poisoned. And on numerous occasions – the letter, the dismissal of the

Maréchale, the attack of Camargue and so on – I had caught the flash of the knife and only just in time. But now, I was in love.

"Berthon!" Climène exclaimed again now, and I was brought back to the present by the sharpness of her tone. Her voice was so sharp, in fact, that Madame, who was sitting on the other side of the room with Athenais de Montespan and the Dauphin and some others whose names I forget, looked across at where we were. "Berthon!" More softly. "If you don't pay attention you can go. You have put the Queen of clubs on the six. This is important. You know very well who it is I want to see, and who I want never to see again."

"Yes. You want your husband, who is having to travel to Provence on business for Monsieur Colbert and the King to find the Rhône in flood when he has to cross it, and drown like Madame de Sévigné's daughter so nearly did the other day. "

"And," she interrupted me, "the confluence of Mars and Venus which is expected soon is dangerous for madmen. I told you that I heard that it often drives them into extremes from which at last they die. I don't want you to forget Francis' father when you are setting out the cards, Berthon! "

The Englishman's father was an object of equal interest to her. If he died, Francis need masquerade no longer as a servant, and he would be free to marry her when the Rhône had done its work. To see Climène sitting there on the floor, her skirts of peach coloured damask and underskirt of blue piled up around her, her nail between her teeth, her brows drawn down, one would not guess what a viper in the bosom of longevity she was; or would be if she had the chance. Having said which, she was breeding of course. Her belly was beginning to swell. When it pressed her, she knelt on a cushion.

I did not need to tell the cards for myself to know whether or not Fanette was likely to love me. Nor, for that matter, whether Francis loved Climène. If I saw either of them I heard of nothing else. Climène, who could never have been accused of unworldliness, seemed not to mind the indignity of entertaining a gentleman in private one moment who the next would be riding on the outside of Monsieur de Bellefonds' coach. If I made any jokes she glared at me.

I said to her now, in order to make her forget her irritation over the cards, "What about the Chevalier de Lorraine? You thought you loved him before."

She cast her mind back. She never objected to this kind of

conversation. She loved to compare one man with another, and one occasion with another. She pushed against her closed lips with her tongue so that they looked as red and plump as Madame's, and she said, "The Chevalier thinks that he is irresistible but I have discovered that the proportion of his thighs to his shin and ankle are not at all pleasant. There is something graceless, when his leg is compared to that of another. The other has a very long, straight, hard leg and that I like very very much."

This was the sort of talk I was used to with Climène. I was perfectly well at home with it. If anyone had let me, I should have carried on in the same style about Fanette.

CHAPTER FIFTEEN

Perhaps it was a lucky coincidence that the removal of the Court from St. Germain to Versailles fell at just this time and provided us all with alternative distractions. The new palace was ready for occupation and the King had decided that any work remaining to be done, such as in parts of the gardens, could be completed with the Court in residence. Consequently there were practical matters in plenty to occupy the mind of an individual in love who might otherwise brood on his hopeless prospects too much. And it was noticeable that Lorraine and his friends applied their mischief elsewhere for a time and left Madame in peace.

In Versailles, my new lodgings were in the north wing. Even if my apartment was extremely small I was most grateful for it. I thought it was very much nicer than my attic in St. Germain. I had no one over my head here either, but the walls and ceiling were completely regular and very pleasant in proportion. My neighbour on my right was Ernst, and on my left a distant cousin of the Comte de Lauzun, so for the first time I was among friends.

Francis helped me to transfer my pigeons. I was very hard pressed to think of how to keep them from flying back always to St. Germain, which by nature they would do. But fortunately Bronzine had just hatched some chicks that were not yet fledged. So by bringing them in the nest I ensured that she at least would fly to Versailles. And then her mate, Salamandre, followed suit of course. Francis told me that perhaps I ought to play the same trick on the others, and thereafter whenever any of them had eggs, by keeping a close watch on the little colony that remained at St. Germain, I gradually was able to transfer nearly all of them.

Finding a quiet space on the roof was more difficult, because the King liked to walk there. In the end I mentioned my birds to His Majesty. I had the opportunity in the gardens where the King walked. It has always been his custom to greet every courtier that he encounters when walking, either touching his hat, or taking it off, or bowing, all depending on rank, and then he would speak a few words. If the King then bowed again, one was expected to retire; but otherwise, he might invite one to walk with him some way.

I waited where I thought he might come, and after a few attempts one afternoon I saw him approach, walking with the Dauphin and his wife, the former Princess of Bavaria. I hardly dared expect His Majesty to notice me, but in keeping with his habitual concern for all his subjects, however insignificant, he paused and touched his hat. I bowed to him and to the Dauphin and Dauphiness. "Monsieur de Brisse," he said, "we are glad to see you have recovered." I thanked him. But I was very anxious to bring up this other matter before he should bow, and thereby dismiss me.

"Your Majesty," I said, and I drew out from under my coat (we wore very splendid ones at Versailles right from the very beginning, and mine was embroidered all over with coloured silks) a little pigeon of purest white which I could claim to be my own since this bird was hatched from two others mated under my care and fed by me. I had tied a blue silk ribbon to her leg, and now bowing I presented her to the King, and said, "May I please have the honour of calling this bird Lyse, and showing that she is your majesty's loyal subject, as am I."

"Oh," said the King, smiling a little. "What a pretty bird."

"By your leave," I said, and I released her from my hand. She did what I had hoped she would do. She flew straight back to the roof of the palace, the blue ribbon fluttering in the air. A prettier sight could not be imagined, and the Dauphinesse clapped her great big hands, while the Dauphin exclaimed "Well done, Monsieur de Brisse."

In the following conversation with which the King honoured me, I was able to explain the short history of my birds and how they were transferred from St. Germain, and to ask his permission to keep them on a corner of the palace roof. He granted my request, and he even said that he would mention them to Mansard, who might design a pretty structure for them low enough not to be visible from the ground. This never happened, but the idea alone was generous, and I was amply satisfied with the permission just to keep them there. Then the King bowed, and passed on.

I went and told Francis of my success, and he helped me with the final adjustments. We were just making the last of our journeys up to the roof again, with a small bag of hay from the stables, and a little sack of meal. He had also told me that powdered garlic was good for them, and there's no doubt that the gloss on their plumage had improved. I sat down rather wearily when we got there on the leads. The climb had made me sweat, and I took off my coat.

Francis whistled between his teeth as he laid a very small portion of the hay in a wire cage open on one side and just big enough to hold it. We had to think of the unobtrusive dimensions that all these arrangements needed to keep.

"Climène told me that Monsieur de Bellefond is going to England again," I said. "Is that true? Will you be going with him."

"Yes," he said, smiling broadly. A great crease appeared the length of his cheek when he laughed, and he had the most excellent teeth. "She is not pleased. Your sister has a witch's temper."

I can't imagine why he thought that so attractive. But then, come to think of it, she has abused me often enough, and I am more or less her slave.

"You had better not go for very long," I said. "The baby will be born in two months."

"Monsieur de Bellefond is not planning to leave for another ten weeks," he said over his shoulder, implying that he could therefore do nothing about it. "Fortunately the late flooding in the country has delayed Climène's husband, the Duc d'Autour, in the provinces, otherwise he would be back. I only hope that, spurred on by paternal enthusiasm, he throws himself into the Rhône when it is in spate and drowns himself."

We both laughed. When later on this was exactly what happened, Francis was overcome by the pangs of conscience, as if to wish for a thing conferred some responsibility for the event itself. But at the time I am describing, he considered it to be an ideal solution. A moment later he sat down like myself, with his back against one of the chimneys.

"Will you see your family?" I asked.

"Oh yes."

He had about five sisters and brothers, the boys younger than himself. The two older sisters who were married he would see in London. A visit to the country would be more difficult, but he planned to make it in secret, and I had all at once in my mind's eye, almost as if I had been brought up there myself, the picture of a large mansion in grey stone, very stern and elegantly decorated with a number of angles leaning where age had settled the foundations. And my friend here, his hair curled like a gentleman but simple nevertheless, wearing perhaps green velvet, which I knew he liked, going eagerly along, looking to right and left like a boy who has been away from home and is noticing everything just as much as a man who wants to avoid being seen except by the objects of his visit.

"I wish I could see my father," he suddenly said. He didn't look sorrowful, like an ordinary Frenchman might, but if anything even less sentimental than before. The lucid glint in his eye had nothing to do with tears. One could have had the impression that his feelings were cold, or repressed, but of course the very opposite was true. It was just a trick of the landscape of his spirit, and perhaps typical of all his countrymen.

"He is not an evil man," Francis added, speaking of his father. He paused, looking intently through the slightly lowered lashes of his eyes out across the roof. "He is a man who is alive, except that suddenly one night, as if a rat stole into his bed and ate half his mind, he awoke not knowing properly where he was in the world or who was his friend. Even if I had a chance to see him I'd be very unwise to take it."

He dangled his hands between his knees as he spoke, playing with a bit of string. It was some time before he put these thoughts aside, and he gave no hint, with sighs or gestures to convey the inner movements of his heart. He seemed to hold his feelings in still balance like someone who can look into a depth of water without the impulse to disturb it with a stick or by casting in a pebble. Eventually he first turned his head in my direction, and then got energetically to his feet, saying, "Now I have something here for you, Berthon. Look at this."

He took a sheet of paper from his pocket, unfolded and put it in my hand, and then moved round to look at it over my shoulder.

"Do you see?" he said, pointing at a rough but well executed drawing. "It is a saddle. If you had a saddle made to this design, you could ride as well as any man; long distances and with a better balance for speed when you required it. Do you see how shaped it is here? I have tried to get the dimensions right."

I was fascinated. I wanted to ask him how he had learned to draw so well, but he was too engrossed in explaining his idea to tell me. I decided to commission the saddle on the spot, and he estimated that it could be made in time for him to teach me to ride on it before leaving for England.

I had never particularly wanted to ride for pleasure because it had seemed impossible, and one learns to school one's desires to avoid foreseeable disappointments. Take Fanette, for example. I had decided that morning that instead of haunting the theatre in order to see her, I should act now to destroy, if necessary, that part of myself that was most vulnerable to the madness of love that had taken hold of me. "If thine eye offends thee, cut it out." So I would not see her. I would make myself stay away from the theatre, and then build on the indifference to which abstinence had made a beginning.

"Berthon," Francis said. The corner of his eye was creased. He had come round to the front of me without my noticing him move, and was crouched on his heels, still holding the paper. "Did I ever tell you that one of my brothers – the youngest in fact – has a way just like you, of disappearing into the landscape of his own mind from time to time. A complete dreamer. And here am I with this invention, worked out entirely to please you, and I might as well be explaining the fine points of it to thin air."

I made all the necessary apologies. He went on; "Did you hear what I said about this buckle? Or the sliding clasp for varying the stirrup length when you need to relieve your cramp, but without dismounting?"

Something about his manner warned me that he guessed what preoccupation had made my mind wander a moment ago. But I really was very interested in his idea for the saddle, and in fact I began to be quite delighted with the prospect of the freedom that such new found skill would give me, enabling me to ride like any other gentleman. We went down together there and then to the stables to get the work started, after which we went our separate ways.

Is this how danger creeps up on those whose friends and servants imagine that their vigilance creates an almost invincible barrier against misfortune, and yet in the end their own common interests distract them at that very moment when the assassin's knife is unsheathed? Because I loved Madame even more than all these others, but from time to time I forgot the danger she was in. Or I thought it might be partly of my own imagining.

CHAPTER SIXTEEN

Once the court was established in Versailles with a return to past routines, there was still much energetic shoving around for place and precedence in the new palace, with anxious courtiers running to make sure that their old privileges were still held for them. In all this of course, Lorraine was foremost, and if Madame had managed to relegate him to the back of her mind for a few weeks he and his friends returned now with a vengeance. I wished that that familiar device of good housekeeping, whereby the removal from one house to another gives an opportunity for the removal of unwelcome parasites, had applied to them, and they had been shaken out like so many lice or fleas. But alas, they were carried over to the new place as if in Monsieur's very clothing.

Madame particularly despised Madame de Grancy. There was no doubt that some men found her attractive, and I think it was to do with the fact that she was both pretty and dirty, which is a curiously seductive combination, but to Madame she was repellent. In certain things, such as her person, Madame was fastidious in a manner that she herself described as German, and the Grancy's slovenly habits – her spitting, her soiled clothes – particularly disgusted her, quite apart from the woman's spiteful and greedy nature. I believe that she was the inspiration behind the plot involving the Chevalier de Sinsanet – the gentleman Lorraine had referred to some time back in his attempt to cultivate a slanderous rumour against Madame – because I witnessed a particular scene between them, the outcome of which might well have been that Mme. de Grancy desired to do Sinsanet harm for his own sake, as well as using him to do harm to Madame.

This gentleman was the Captain of the Guard, who rode out hunting with the King. One evening perhaps as much as six months ago, de Grancy had taken a fancy to this man. She singled him out when Madame was playing cards with the Queen and there was a great crowd in the room. In the insinuating way she had, the Grancy stood very close to the gentleman. Her little fingers flutter here and there because she likes to touch the men she talks to. It is a habit of hers. Sometimes it must have been successful because she has had numerous lovers. But in this case not. De Sinsanet took a step back, and the expression on his face was one of consternation mixed with disgust. He is a very tall man, and the lady particularly short so that her fidgeting little hands seemed to be threatening him in an embarrassing place. With an angry flush, he said something to which Madame de Grancy responded with a little laugh – the sort that passes off very well if the other person can be persuaded to follow suit. De Sinsanet merely glared at her. The next moment he virtually turned on his heel, and de Grancy was left standing there with a smile on her face that changed in mid-air from gaiety to venom.

Anyone who was unwise enough to be delighted by this interchange – Madame for example – risked paying more for a momentary pleasure than it would turn out to have been worth. If one minute that foul woman Elizabeth de Grancy was humiliated in a way she deserved, she would be revenged the next.

Lorraine and his friends had already dabbled in the invention of an affaire between Madame and de Sinsanet, but the slander had been allowed to go cold, and perhaps the Grancy's little show of lust explained why. Perhaps if the gentleman had sacrificed himself he could have protected the reputation of Madame. But this is just speculation. What actually happened was that in an intensified and spiteful concentration of rumour, the four friends of Monsieur began a new campaign of slander once the court was settled in Versailles. Lorraine returned to the attack when he came with Monsieur to Madame's apartment one morning, after she and the Royal Family had returned from Mass. She was particularly well attended. A number of courtiers who would usually have been elsewhere were present. Monsieur le Duc de la Rochefoucauld, for example, came in and Madame asked his opinion of the play, but her husband waved him aside because he had no intention of being drawn into a discussion of literature. The Duke came then and stood directly in front of me, without realising that I was at my usual post rather hidden in the corner of the room. After a moment or two his faithful friend Madame de la Fayette came and stood beside him. Immediately I heard her say, "I spoke to the Chevalier de Lorraine. He swears that it is true."

She looked shocked, and her voice was grave.

The Duke replied, "Madame's chief – perhaps, to my mind, her only virtue – is her fidelity. I cannot believe that she would throw it away."

"My dear, a plain woman made love to is worse than a pretty one."

Madame de la Fayette turned as she said that, and looked

thoughtfully over to where Madame was standing.

"What do you think the King will do?"

"And Monsieur?"

"The King is the one. I should think he will send him to the Bastille and never let him out again."

"Not for…"

"He will devise some charge, of course, that deflects harm from Monsieur's honour."

"I pity the lady."

"I don't."

"Ah, but you are a man. Madame has enemies and more of them than she deserves. What hope will she have against them after this?"

"It is Sinsanet I am sorry for," said de la Rochefoucauld. "When he is out hunting with the King he has no choice but to give attendance to Madame, who rides immediately behind him. He has to frequently assist her in small ways, and if she seeks to extend these services beyond what is essential he can hardly protest. He lifted Madame in his arms after her fall!"

So he did! But the illicit passion now described as having been provoked by it was all an invention.

"He's a handsome fellow," said Madame de la Fayette. "He's the one with the blond whiskers, like her brother. With so much family pride, she probably thinks that such features deserve preferment."

There was nothing I could say. Like a mule tethered to a post I had to bear witness to something without being able to do a thing about it. All this time Madame, who was adorably dressed in a gown of dark lavender silk ordered for her by Monsieur and therefore exceptionally well suited to her dark hair and rosy face, was smiling and talking not far off, in a way that should have disarmed any observer. And yet Madame de la Fayette, with all her intelligence and her sympathetic nature – after all, it was she who wrote the story of the Princess de Clèves, and was therefore clever; and who was such a close friend of Madame de Sévigné, and therefore had a lot of patience – could pass on, with such brittle naïveté, the spiteful and dangerous inventions of de Grancy and Lorraine. And she rattled on, while actually looking at Madame. She had a little fan of painted silk, and having made herself quite hot with excitement over this imagined liaison she plied it vigorously. It made a tiny noise, like thrushes when their wings frip the air. I heard it, separately from the murmur of the room and the dominant sound of the conversation around Monsieur and Madame, and Madame's laughter. When I heard it in the country during that long journey which I had to take later, a shiver went through me, and I followed the tiny body of the winged bird that burst from one bush and fled into another with the eyes of a young man who saw a woman, her pretty face flushed with gossip, and wielding a fan.

I could not get out from the corner where I was, nor did I want to, until Madame de la Fayette and her great friend, the Duke, stepped aside. I waited to see if she had more to tell. But she only said that the Chevalier de Lorraine could not be blamed for protecting the Prince's interests. She said it for all the world as if she believed that that was what he was doing, and then they both moved away.

What can you do when you become aware that some little sparks which you thought had been put out had in fact smouldered unobserved, and suddenly a full blown flame bursts out before your very eyes? I was horrified. My first thought was to consult those friends who were most likely to help me to save Madame. I saw Theobon, but she was surrounded by others and I could not possibly run to her straight away. I was so agitated that it was impossible to stay where I was. Madame still stood among the same people in the middle of the room, and still looked as lively and as lovely as before. A second later I caught sight of Ernst at the other side of the room. But so also had Monsieur d'Effiat.

D'Effiat was up to something. His steps through the crowd were necessarily circuitous but unpleasantly purposeful. Even if Monsieur le Grand, or Monsieur Vendôme, or Madame Gordon stopped him for a moment, as I saw them all do, he slid out of each diversion with very little pause, like a snake progressing through a forest. He was fond of wearing black. I think I mentioned it before. On this day his waistcoat was embroidered on black velvet.

Finally he reached Ernst, and there he stopped. I was not yet within hearing myself, but I saw the colour rise in Ernst's cheek and that fellow leaning over him like an incarnation of the devil. I never saw a man with redder lips than d'Effiat's, and yet they were very thin. Near the corner of his mouth on one side he had a little tracery of blue veins that gave his skin a look like sour milk. You can get a mark like that from being hit, and by all accounts his father thrashed him within an inch of his life many times when he was young.

Ernst had told me about this man's persecution of certain boys and young men. It was difficult for those who were relatively poor, or who

MALICE

were under the care of lazy governors, to resist the approaches of a man like d'Effiat; a favourite of theKing's brother, and rich as well. I, who had very early on in my life learned how to digest gall and wormwood had been spared this particular problem for obvious reasons. Ernst, on the other hand, had grown into a handsome youth and why should a courtier, who had, by all accounts, debauched the King's own son without losing the friendship of His Majesty, hesitate in his attempt to coerce a nephew of Madame? At that moment, to make matters far worse, the Chevalier de Lorraine appeared from the other side of the opening. Between the two of them the boy struggled to appear at his ease.

I was close enough now to hear d'Effiat say "Even if I ask you?" He said it in such a tone that someone who did not know better would assume that certain favours had already been exchanged between them. The Chevalier laughed. To my rage, I saw that under cover of pretending to be crowded against him by the press of people he had put his hand on the young man. He seemed to have forgiven Ernst for having supported me in connection with the letter. Or else, more likely this was his revenge. It would go further.

I had no idea what I planned to do when I reached his side, but I think I would have stuck my knife into whichever part of d'Effiat's anatomy was on a level with my thrust. Indeed it could have been a very bad thing for him.

Fortunately just at that moment, Monsieur was seen to be coming across the room. He had decided to play cards, and was followed by Madame on her way to see the Queen. As everyone cleared a path for them, Ernst stepped back and very nearly knocked me over. I got a handful of the cloth of his coat in my fist and determined not to let go of it until I had him safely in some place where he could tell me what was going on.

"What is wrong?" he said looking with surprise at my face. And then, "Oh!" and he laughed that great happy laugh that was blond, like his hair, so that Madame de Harcourt looked sharply at him as she passed, as if she thought she might be the butt of his humour. It transpired that d'Effiat wanted a model bird with moving wings carved for his nephew.

Nothing more. I myself had taught Ernst how to make these toys.

"Nothing more?" I said, still not amused by all this. I had had two frights in one morning, and the first one would not be so easily forgotten.

But we were walking now towards the yards. I might see Francis there and it was a good day for riding. All at once the image of Maud, the horse that he had found for me to buy, cantered gracefully into my thoughts, and away from the stifling press of cloth and limbs I stretched out my arms and felt happy again for a while. It was because of this that I put aside so quickly that discovery which had first aroused my anxiety, and whose shadow lingered and deepened when I had turned my back on it. I refer to the conversation between Madame de la Fayette and the Duke de la Rochefoucauld.

CHAPTER SEVENTEEN

I can tell you another reason why Lorraine's plot got so thoroughly hatched before I could take any action to protect Madame, and that was the birth of Climène 's child.

For the last three weeks of her pregnancy Climène would not look at me. She said it would be bad luck, and she did not want the baby, saddled already with a loathsome father, to have a hare lip as well. When she sent for me, which she often did if she needed something, she would keep her back to me while I was there, or insist that I faced the wall.

Her impending confinement occupied her mind day and night. In addition to the advice from other ladies at court and from the doctors, she wanted news of any drug to control the pain, and any potion or liquor to soothe the stomach or soften the skin, that might be discovered. I was employed by her to gather information from every corner of Paris. I even visited a former colleague of La Voisin taking with me a lock of Climène 's hair. I discovered the most exotic apothecaries whom no other courtier had even heard of. I found my way, masked and wrapped up like a *djinn*, into the doorways and staircases of ancient houses near the Seine built by sailors who had spent all their lives in the east. I bought one matchless remedy for the fever that often follows childbirth from a beautiful woman reputed to be eighty years of age who reclined on a couch covered with cloth of gold infested with lice. She had lived for years as a slave in Africa and sold me a stoppered glass full of oil which cost me as much as my horse, but Climène said she had to have it. She kissed my hand after I had given it to her.

By this time Francis was due to leave very soon for England, and still the baby didn't come. Torn between the dread of giving birth and the fear that he would be gone before the event took place, Climène was beside herself.

Two of Madame's ladies of honour were particularly kind to Climène, but by far the most important was Theobon. That lady had a very quick temper as you know, and being so close a friend of Madame she shared Madame's opinions on the subject of doctors. She stood guard by Climène's bed, and even the King's own physician was turned away by her when he tried to bleed Climène minutes after the birth. I would have stayed outside the door, because I could not bear to see Climène in pain, but at a certain point I heard my name being called by her so loudly that I allowed myself to be bundled into the room among the dozen or so people who were gathered there. I was masked, but Climène, who seemed to have taken leave of her normal senses entirely, seized my hand and wouldn't let it go.

Madame had refused to give permission for Francis to enter the room. She said that unless the subterfuge of his passing for a servant of the Marquis was given up publicly and he was presented to the King in his proper rank, then he could not be permitted to be present at the birth as if he was a courtier.

I found the experience truly terrible. I wept. The sound of Climène's voice acted on my flesh like a knife. I did not see the birth. I heard one last sound from Climène that I will never forget, and then the stifled noises of a tiny infant, not screaming, but sounding like a cat shut in a cupboard.

I kissed Climène's hand, and crawled out from the *ruelle* between the bed and the wall. Trembling, I took out from the folds of my clothes the oil of clove and also the distillation of poppies that I had prepared. I soaked a cloth in the latter and held it near Climène so that she breathed easily. A little of the oil of clove I asked Theobon to spread on her forehead and her thighs.

There was a tremendous bustle meanwhile with the infant and it was some time before I looked at it. I wanted to hurry outside and give Francis news of Climène. That was what was in my mind as I was about to step off the dais, but at that moment one of the midwives handed a bundle to the wet nurse, and I caught my first glimpse of the child. Something happened to my heart. I'm still not quite sure what. And then I went and informed Francis that Climène sent her love to him, and that she was well. Neither she nor Francis had any interest in the baby. A little girl, by the way. I don't think either of them looked at it.

After the birth, all the ladies of the Court visited Climène. She recovered her health very quickly, and she enjoyed the attention and the opportunity to appear in the most lovely silks and laces as she received visitors lying in her bed. She no longer needed me, and sent word through Theobon that I was on no account to come unless she sent for me.

On the other hand, she wanted most ardently to see Francis, and in the end it was being deprived of his company that induced her to cut short the period of lying in. At this point the imminent return of her husband threatened her happiness, and for those who do not believe in Providence the account of what actually happened in connection with him should be enough to bring about a conversion. You know how absurdly anxious Madame de Sévigné was about her daughter when in March she crossed the Rhône during a storm and her boat was thrown against the one of the piers of the bridge so that it could have been smashed or overturned. It was now a time of year when d'Autour on his return journey to Paris should have been safe enough from a repeat of such weather, but an extraordinary thing happened. In the south west there were several days of heavy rain at the end of Summer. The dry ground could not absorb the deluge and the rivers rose, including the Rhône. D'Autour was in such a hurry that he insisted on trying to cross and a heavy barge, also caught in the tide, hit his boat so that it was cut almost in half, and the Duc drowned. Climène made very little effort to conceal her delight at the news, and Francis, with that slight reservation I mentioned before, was no different.

I began to grow tired of this love affaire, and to realise how repetitive these things are. If I met Francis on the roof, or in the yards, or if he found the opportunity to ride with me, the conversation these days was always the same. Much as I loved Climène, I could not talk about her for ever. And with Climène it was the same. There was one subject on which I would have dearly liked to have spoken to her, and that was her baby, but she was utterly indifferent. I do not think that Climène could have picked her own child out if someone had shown her two or three to choose from. And when I tried to raise the subject, or to talk in any way about this little creature who had so caught my fancy, Climène would tell me to be quiet. Instead, all she wanted to do was to sit on the floor in Madame's apartment talking for hours about Francis; what she should wear when she saw him, what he had thought of what she wore last time, whether he had noticed other admirers who courted her and so on.

I would have been happy enough with this gossip, repetitive though it was, had it not got so in the way of others things that were going on. Theobon had told me that the slanderous rumour started by Madame de Grancy and Lorraine against Madame was not only being discussed in every part of the palace, but each day this invented affair gained credibility and it could only be a matter of time before Monsieur and the King were brought into it. I was at my wits end to know how to contradict the story. No one would listen to me.

One day, when I had escaped Climène and been first to Paris and then Saint Cloud in attendance on Madame I returned to Versailles as darkness was falling. It had been very hot, and with the coolness of twilight my heart fell into a melancholy stillness. Long before the day when the King formally took possession of the completed palace and we all processed together for the first time up to the magnificent facade cleared of the debris of work and with all the pieces of sculpture in place – long before then everyone had been constantly going backwards and forwards to Versailles. There had been numerous balls, and there had always been hunting at Versailles. So you can imagine that all the approaches to the palace from every direction were continuously more or less crowded, and remained so.

By what chance I found myself alone on this particular evening is a mystery. Normally I might also have had Bonhomme riding behind me. He was sick. There would have been carriages and men on horseback on their way to and from the theatres or other gatherings. There were none.

It would have been an ideal opportunity for Lorraine to have disposed of me if he had known about it. When I looked behind me up to the turn in the road the path was empty. Some distance ahead the palace of Versailles was still partly concealed by trees. I let the reins slacken against the neck of Maud. She slowed her pace and stood. As the comparative coolness of the night air settled on the baked earth, the leaves and grasses stirred. Maud stepped aside, lifted her head, and stood very still for a few moments. Then she began to crop the grass. All at once it seemed as if my life had stopped and I would never move away from that place.

CHAPTER EIGHTEEN

Jours d'appartement took place on Mondays, Wednesdays, and Fridays, when the King and the Royal family entertained the court with supper, dancing, music and cards, and it was lucky for me in one way, that my brief descent into melancholy was closely followed by one of the most splendid of these. On the other hand, it marked the moment when Lorraine and his friends made the decisive move to set the noose around Madame's neck which, in the end, they hoped would choke her.

I went to the Kings antechamber at six o'clock with all the other gentlemen, and on into the drawing room with the Queen and the ladies. The crush was immense, but as usual everyone was in the best of humour, and the crowding was soon eased by the dispersal of those who wished to dance into the next chamber; or into the King's throne room, to listen to concerts.

In the next room – the bedroom – three card tables are always set out: one for the King, one for the Queen and one for Monsieur. The Queen loved to have Madame at her table, and so this is where we went. I stood as far away from the Queen's chair as possible because the smell of garlic and cloves which surrounded her repelled me. Madame had no objection to this at all. She liked it. But I also found it very disconcerting to stand near the dwarfs. Her Majesty placed her cards very slowly. She often asked advice, and when she won she never smiled.

I was preoccupied. I had heard yet another courtier mention Sinsanet's name together with Madame in the anteroom at the very moment that we all came through. I had heard during the day from one of the ladies of honour attached to La Grande Mademoiselle that they had now started to say that Theobon was suspected of acting as a go-between in this imaginary affaire.

Madame herself, although privately very angry at the slander, insisted on laughing at it even to the closest of her friends. True her laughter was tinged with contempt, but she insisted on treating the rumour as being beneath her notice. Theobon tried to say that if your enemies are up to tricks, it could be unwise to be too proud to notice what they are doing. But Madame wouldn't budge. She gave Theobon that look of hers – a prolonged pause, without a smile and her back straight as a ruler. Theobon was very tempted to argue. She drew breath; but then tightened her lip and said nothing. More than once this ritual was enacted, and after one such, Theobon encountered Lorraine in the anteroom alone as she was leaving and he was approaching the drawing room. She stopped right in his path and whispered,

"May God curse you, Chevalier. You are the most spiteful liar in this court."

He seemed to enjoy it. He cast a smiling eye first to the right and then to the left, as if to invite any other person nearby to notice what was going on, whereas Theobon had a different intention entirely. But in fact even this relief to her feelings would cost her if not her life, then everything else she had.

"Why, Madame de Beauvron," he said. "It is some time since I have witnessed this famous temper of yours. What are you going to do next?"

She could do absolutely nothing. She wanted to slap and pinch him, but what point is there in a woman trying to hurt a full grown man? If she used every ounce of her strength it would only be like a fly landing on him. It is extraordinary, when you think of it, what a difference this one fact has made to the whole span of civilised history; namely that a man can always physically coerce a woman, and almost never the other way round. Having said which, it hardly needs reminding that at court such methods were not employed. Theobon simply had to curb her rage.

Madame meanwhile played cards. Her lips smiled; her cheeks were pink from hunting; her arms were plump and she appeared to be strong. Such a mien is probably one of the most effective ways of discouraging attack from ones inferiors, and it warmed the hearts of her friends. Not enough, however, to raise false hopes if they had happened to be nearby the week before when Monsieur spoke sharply to her and she was seen to turn away with tears in her eyes. The robust defiance with which she could often dismiss Lorraine played no part whatsoever in her feelings towards her husband, whose unkindness wounded her deeply. No doubt Monsieur was already suspicious of her loyalty as a result of hints dropped like poison in his ear.

Just now several of Madame's hunting companions were standing around the table, unfortunately including that officer de Sinsanet. You could not imagine a more straight forward and honest looking fellow, but Madame should have asked him to absent himself until Lorraine's vicious slanders had been silenced in some way. However, she preferred to treat the whole affair as being beneath her notice. She shared the same reckless courage that made her uncles so successful in battle. But the rules of engagement in court life are different from those in the field.

It started like this: a query arose at the card table as to whether Madame de Lafayette had to discard a black or a red, and in the most natural way in the world Madame turned and asked the Chevalier de Sinsanet his opinion. He is a good player after all. But no sooner had she turned back to her hand, than she was confronted by Madame de Grancy who, to everyone's astonishment, appeared from another part of the room as if she had flown there.

De Grancy's entire appearance was scandalous. She looked heated, as well she might when she was about to make public the infamous falsehood she had been busy cooking up in private. She struck a pose, the two red spots in her cheek darkening by the second, and said in the strangest tone to the Princess, "Do you know this man you are speaking to, Madame?"

Sinsanet had drawn back with an expression of angry surprise, but Madame was perfectly calm. Everyone else became completely silent, and not only in our part of the room.

"Of course I do," Madame was gracious enough to reply to her. "I see him and his brother officers riding beside me almost every day at the chase."

Stern displeasure showed on her face, but she did not turn her back on the woman. Had this scene occurred in her private apartment Madame would have dismissed her without an answer and the Grancy would have had to leave the room, in all probability never to return. But on the *jours d'appartement* the King and all the Royal family consider the courtiers to be their guests, and different rules apply. For example, no one has to rise when they enter the supper room. Madame de Grancy pressed home her advantage with quite astonishing insolence.

"Then he is one of your friends," she said.

Everyone at the table, including the Queen herself, maintained a shocked silence. Madame de Grancy preened one of her shoulders in a way that made me long to slap her, and cast a look backwards towards where Monsieur was not too engrossed in the game at the other table to notice her.

"Since he is your friend, Madame, as you say," she carried on, "was it for your sake that he insulted me at the ball last night?"

Madame gazed at the atrocious woman and said with an air of frigid condescension "I was not at the ball. Did he annoy you?"

"He certainly did," she said. "I invited him to dance and he told me I was too old!"

Madame let out a little giggle, for which I rubbed my hands with glee. But the Grancy was making a point, which provoked some at least who were there to wonder if Sinsanet's deliberate rudeness was an act of vengeance by a gentleman who loved Madame, even if only in the perfectly proper way that a courtier loves a member of the Royal Family he serves.

During this interchange the Chevalier de Sinsanet stood to attention as if he was on parade, and only the fire in his eye gave witness to the way he felt. Madame, seeming to stifle her amusement, made a solemn face, and then gave her attention for just a second to the cards in her hand before making a remark of apology to the Queen for the interruption. Only then did she look back at the Grancy, whose expression was twisted into a mixture of bitterness and triumph. But alas, everyone else in the room had heard the exchange and with the help of the Devil they would make of it exactly what Lorraine intended.

"Would you like me to speak to him?" Madame said.

"Oh Madame!" exclaimed de Grancy, with a little simper. "We all know that you will do that with or without the promptings of a simple lady like myself."

Theobon, whose face was white with sheer rage, let out a little gasp. Madame herself was caught off balance, and could scarcely believe what was happening, and yet she was under restraint from the understanding mentioned before, that during jours d'apartement the courtiers were guests of the Royal Family. Neither did the Princess fully understand the gravity of the scene at the time, because for all her irritation at what she had heard, she had not been forced to listen to all the whispers going around the court as we had.

Even so she turned to Theobon and said to the Countess, using her formal name, "Madame de Beauvron, please ask this lady, Madame de Grancy, to withdraw."

The silence in the room was now absolute. With her head held very high, despite her pinkness the Grancy looked, if anything, triumphant as she made only the slightest of curtsies, turned with insolent leisure and walked away. She had succeeded in giving the court an opportunity to observe how artlessly Madame had admitted to feelings of friendship for the officer, and how likely it was that a lover would resent his mistress's enemies enough to insult them, as she had been insulted at the ball.

Shortly after this scene, and before Madame left the table Ernst, having apparently looked for me for some time, suddenly appeared and insisted that I join him and his friends at a game of backgammon in the next room. I was in such a daze I let him draw me away. I let myself be distracted for a while playing there. I can beat these young men at such games. Not every endeavour in this world depends on straight limbs and if they challenge me with dice or cards I get as fast and as far ahead of them as they would me in running. I simply empty their pockets.

There was always some new scheme afoot to try to even the score between them and me and this time the young Count I mentioned before, Clément Cardinale, was sure that he could catch me out. I got the better of him after a brief trial. We went in a body through to the next two rooms where the food and wine was laid out on huge tables, and one eats and drinks standing. I like Italian wines and negus, but I am careful not to drink too much. Nature has abused my body so mercilessly with no help from me that I decided when I was only eleven or twelve that I would not add to the ill effects. I also eat sparingly although it is difficult on these occasions when the tables groan with the delicacies laid out on them.

Throughout this entire time the scene between Madame and de Grancy was in the background of my thoughts. I could not get it out of my mind for a second. Eventually I left to return to my own apartment. My feet hurt me. It is not easy to walk in shoes as high as mine even if your legs are straight, and I longed for my bed and for solitude in which to reflect on what had happened. The passages are usually lit on *jours d'appartement*, but something must have happened. I called for a servant to light me to my room but no one came and I set off in the dark. As I was approaching the second staircase I passed the apartment of Monsieur Moreau, and it happened that the lights were on and his door was open. I had become friendly with this gentleman because he had that extraordinary collection of paintings which I had asked his permission to see after hearing about them from Madame. At that moment as I passed I heard, to my surprise, the voice of Monsieur d'Effiat in there. Naturally I stopped to listen. But what I heard was a conversation between him and Moreau about Cicero. D'Effiat was returning a book. He was, after all, a learned man; a scholar. When not engaged in ruining the happiness of those whom he did not regard as his particular friends, by acts of greed, vanity and malice, he immersed himself in literature and the arts. When not debauching a young man he could teach him very well. How strange human nature is.

CHAPTER NINETEEN

That night I scarcely slept. Over and over again my imagination enacted and re-enacted past and future deeds of malice performed against Madame as compared to the scene created by Madame de Grancy. Over and over again I attempted to evaluate the threat posed by Lorraine. He carried forward his campaign to destroy Madame's reputation and happiness with remarkable persistence and cunning. He controlled the collective strategy that he and his friends employed so that each move got them a little bit closer to the desired end, which was to strip Madame of all honour and happiness. When recklessness was called for they could be reckless, and when patience, patient. At this rate they would succeed, and soon. If the King or Monsieur gave any credit to their inventions the result would be the isolation of Madame from all her friends at court, and she would be at Lorraine's mercy.

The following day I found an opportunity to talk to Francis, and asked him what he thought of the rumour of Madame's love affair. "What do you think?" I asked him. Naturally he had heard of the scene last night at the card table. Everyone knew of it by the morning.

"My dear Berthon," he said. "Surely Madame's virtue can hardly be questioned?" This was an unworthy attack on her appearance with which, apart from anything else, I did not agree. Besides, it was a ridiculous assumption, considering what I had told him before, and I was angry.

"She could die," I said, "before others like yourself would take any notice!"

He realised suddenly, that he had come close to offending me. He stopped tapping his foot and looking about him all the time as if expecting someone else; no doubt Climène. He looked down, instead, at me, and put his tongue between his teeth.

"You know, don't you," I said, "that these friends of Monsieur got rid of his first wife by poisoning her?"

"But that's a rumour, like this other one that you so object to," he answered. "Isn't it?"

"I'm not sure" I said. "How can I be sure of that? But what is certain is that Minette was much loved, by all accounts, and was very kind. And yet she is dead. No one would help her; not even His Majesty."

"The King would never countenance poisoning!" exclaimed Francis.

"Of course not!" I raged. "And Monsieur can have known nothing of it either, although the deed was done by his closest friends. They were very careful to make sure that he had no idea what they were up to. They poisoned her secretly, just as they are now poisoning the happiness of her successor, and may yet kill her. "

"Do you mean to say that they are planning to poison Madame?"

I said, "I am not sure. Would Lorraine dare to repeat that particular crime? Perhaps it is his intention this time simply to destroy her happiness and her reputation so thoroughly that she becomes isolated from the court and has no influence at all either with Monsieur or anyone else. Then perhaps he might murder her as well, at his leisure."

I added that last comment out of despair, but there was truth in it.

Francis said thoughtfully. "I've seen it done elsewhere."

"I'm at my wits' end," I said. "Madame has no guile. When she has an opportunity to expose their wickedness she squanders it."

"But Monsieur, you say, does not suspect Lorraine of having poisoned his first wife? What would have happened if they knew the truth?"

"Lorraine and the others would have been executed I imagine. Certainly exiled permanently from court. What would I not give to see that happen!"

"My dear Berthon," Francis said, "Find that proof. I'm surprised that you did not think of it before."

I looked up at him. He was smiling. I was not sure if he was still inclined to take a light hearted view of this whole wretched business.

"I mean it, Berthon," he said. "It might be possible to find out where he got the poison from, and from whom. If you paid enough, whoever sold him the poison might testify against him. If you are clever enough, there might be other evidence; a letter, someone who saw him, some event that looks like a coincidence. And then imagine how utterly beaten the man will be. I'd like to see it myself. He would be in terror of his life. "

He was beginning to sound like Climène. And yet there was a very tempting element in his idea. I began to wonder about it.

"I'm sorry that I seemed indifferent at first," he added, "to a matter that causes you so much pain. I'll ask Climène what she thinks."

I looked at him open-mouthed; and shortly after, we parted. You see how absolutely fruitless it was for me to attempt to get help from other members of that court. Intelligent people fell under an enchantment there and lost all sense of reality. A satin ribbon could inflame feelings of jealousy as sharp as wealth and honour elsewhere, and a grown man with a sharp mind and ready wit could suggest taking counsel from Climène on a matter of life and death simply because he was besotted with her. Meanwhile malice was being used to cut a convenient swathe through the protective surroundings of Madame, until once exposed she could fall before the knife. Her friends could apparently do nothing.

And yet that notion of entrapping Lorraine with proof of the first crime in order to make it impossible for him to commit a second did appeal to me. I began to think about it.

The one person who could have helped Madame when these troubles began to overwhelm her was the King; but he had shown no willingness so far to protect her from the enmity of his brother's favourites. She had appealed to him in the matter of the dismissal of Clerembault but he refused to interfere. Now, perhaps, with this invented scandal of Madame's lover being talked about everywhere at court, he would have to act. And eventually, after a lapse of two or three days the King himself brought the subject up when walking privately in a gallery with Madame.

By now it was Autumn. That very day Francis left the country with Monsieur de Bellefond, and Climène had gone with them, having managed to arrange an invitation for herself to the English court. Ernst, also, had been sent on manoeuvres in Flanders. Their absence increased my sense of isolation and imminent danger. There are many people who have died comparatively happily because it was a clumsy friend who stumbled and knocked them into the river, or who accidentally set fire to their house. If I was going to have to witness the ruin of my hopes or suffer any other slow torture at the hands of Lorraine it would have been a comfort to have Francis and Climène and Ernst nearby, even if they did nothing to help.

I watched the King and Madame walking together. I had nothing else to do. Sunlight, rather darkly gold under some slate blue clouds, fell through the windows in strips across the already shining floors. The King's expression as he talked was affectionate and also amused in the way that only Madame provoked in him. He had only to set eyes on her for a glint to sparkle in his eye as if the very sight of her reminded him of something that had pleased him and made him laugh before. But when he saw that today she was serious and had some matter weighing on her mind, he became solemn, at least for a time. Even someone standing a long way off and out of hearing could have had no doubt of his sympathy. He bent his head, and listened very attentively while she described the way in which this slander to do with herself and Sinsanet had been set in motion by Elizabeth de Grancy and Lorraine.

"I know about it!" he said.

"You know!" She was astonished. Even some indignation flared up in her heart when she thought of her brother-in-law noticing such things and saying nothing to comfort her, or to regulate her enemies. But she did not dare to protest.

They had stopped walking and stood facing each other.

"I know for a fact that the rumours about Sinsanet are part of a plot to calumniate you," The King added.

Madame let her eyes bulge in a way she had, and puffed down her nose.

"Madame de Grancy is jealous of you, Madame, and so is the Chevalier de Lorraine. There is really nothing to be done about it."

He implied that there was no need. But Madame very much disagreed with him.

"If I am to be made a laughing stock, that is one thing and it is bad enough. But to be accused of having an affair is another matter, and Monsieur, if he believes it, will become angry with me. Am I to have no heart at all, if I am to be expected to live in a foreign court and not be loved and respected even by my own husband.?"

"Oh, Madame," Louis said, taking her hand and looking concerned, "My brother certainly won't believe any such thing."

"Why not, if he gets told these lies every day?" she protested.

He considered this in silence for just a moment, but she quickly spoke again and said, "If you, your Majesty, would tell Monsieur what you know…" But he shook his head.

"Why not?"

If she had been in her own apartment and speaking to anyone else she would have stamped her foot. She was really at her wits end.

"If I know it is a calumny, isn't that enough?"

She gave him a quick glance sideways, but in the end held her peace. Naturally His Majesty's judgement was all in all, and if he maintained friendship with his sister in law and demonstrated by that friendship that he had confidence in her integrity, it scarcely mattered what anyone else said. Unless, of course, a lady was weak-willed enough to want her own husband to believe in her, and not to be laughed at by others behind her back.

They had resumed their walk, the King reiterating his assurance of his own friendship but also his refusal to interfere. It was as if he did not realise quite how grave the consequences of this latest conspiracy might be. And presumably he thought that the first Madame had died a natural, if tragic, death, and had no idea of any deeper level in this sort of quarrel. Neither had Madame. But the sheer effrontery of her enemies and the thought that they were to be allowed to devour her reputation and her peace of mind with impunity made her quite distraught. She had really thought the King would help her when first she raised the matter with him, and to find that he not only knew all about the conspiracy but intended to do nothing to stop it was a bitter disappointment.

She turned to him again, this time with her hands clasped together, and tears began to run down her face. When she found she could not stop them she lowered her head to hide her eyes. The King couldn't see her suffer without feeling remorse. Also he had not forgotten the cruel business of her dead child, and the memory aroused his pity. Perhaps he thought that when her maternal feelings had been so attacked by fate, Lorraine should not now be allowed to attack her as a wife. And yet, even if those ideas did occur to him, he didn't act on them.

"Come with me," he said gently to Madame, and offered her his arm.

The remainder of the conversation, which took place in the King's cabinet, was told to me later, and went as follows. The Princess, as soon as they were alone, protested her complete innocence again, which she scarcely needed to do, since the King believed in her integrity before she even opened her mouth. But then, despite the fact that he had such a good friendship with his brother and Monsieur loved him so well, Louis absolutely refused to simply go to Madame's husband and warn him not to believe a word that Madame Gordon or anyone else, might say. And he refused to speak sternly to the conspirators, or to tell them that he condemned their malicious slander, and to command them to desist both now and for the future.

Louis said that Philippe would be able to reproach him with intriguing with Madame against him if he took a more active part and did anything more than merely warn her of her enemies' plans. I wonder how he would have reacted if he had realised that these conspirators had killed before. Then indeed he would respond quite differently to

Madame's plea for protection.

In recounting all this to Theobon, Madame made it clear that she couldn't understand the King's reluctance to intervene. But I understood it. The King, as well as being unaware of what Lorraine and his friends had done before, fell under the same spell with regard to them as did his brother. He also found Lorraine and d'Effiat and Gordon and Grancy amusing, attractive, and fashionable. His liking was more balanced than Monsieur's, but it was liking nevertheless. To the casual observer Lorraine was as handsome as an angel, with exceptional charm of manner, so that whenever he wanted to attach someone to himself he had only to breathe upon them and they were enslaved, as if they had inhaled some drug or other. The King himself felt this power. And d'Effiat, although he was the Prince of Hell where Lorraine borrowed his devices from the armoury of heaven, was almost equally attractive. Both together, and attended by those women, whom I have described ill if I have failed to mention their beauty and their enticing ways and the manner in which they were adept at binding friends to their service, were irresistible to those whom they chose to attract. Consequently when Madame appealed to the King, his powers of compassion were partly preemptied by this insidious alliance. And he thought that spiteful gossip marked the limits of the harm that they could do.

It is not permissible for me to criticise His Majesty, but the feelings of my heart are outside the jurisdiction of any Court, and I was disappointed.

Madame was so overcome with misery at the prospect of all this strife with more to come, none of which was of her making, that she began to think of retiring to the convent of Maubuisson, and she meant it. The idea made her completely miserable. Even the atmosphere inside the convent when she went to visit her aunt depressed her after a short time. She disliked the smells, which were all different from those at court. And as for the piety, the silences, the dullness, one could scarcely imagine a person less suited to it all. But when she talked about it now, although the very skin on her face seemed to swell slightly with suppressed tears, she insisted it would be better than having to endure the daily mischief making of the *cabale*, and the resulting enmity of her own husband.

No less desperate than Madame's idea of entering the convent was my own idea of murdering d'Effiat, Lorraine, Madame Gordon or de Grancy, and possibly all four of them, And I am not saying that it was

141

beyond me to do that. If I really thought that it would solve the problem, I could have crept into the bedrooms of all four of them and I would not have minded what became of me afterwards. But it was obvious that Monsieur would not have continued to love his wife if her distress inspired the murder of his friends. I should be doing the work of the conspirators in separating Monsieur and Madame for ever.

In the past Madame's apartment had always been full of laughter and chatter, but after this latest development she became so sad that it was noticed. Many courtiers were in attendance, and without this change some people might have thought that it was they who brought vitality and wit with them. But once Madame was silent, one could only marvel at the way in which the spark of entertainment was extinguished, proving how the lively warmth of her character would be missed. Monsieur began to notice it, and look as if he would speak to his wife, but then say nothing. Finally he took Madame's hand when they were standing by the window not far from myself, and asked her tenderly what was the matter. She lowered her eyes, and she was clearly moved. He was a loving person when left to his own devices, and with a kind enough heart. Besides, he was exceptionally good looking. I hope I have not omitted to make that point before.

"The Chevalier de Lorraine and Madame Grancy have started a scandalous rumour, Monsieur, saying that I am having an affaire with the Chevalier de Sinsanet, and everyone is beginning to believe them," she said. "It is making me very unhappy. And I am afraid in case you, too, may end by listening to them."

"How could I possibly be so foolish?" Monsieur exclaimed. "You are a loyal wife, and very dear to me, Madame."

"Oh!" she said. She began to raise her face, and when her husband saw her expression of timid hope, and noticed how pretty her lip was when the very beginning of a smile just caught the edge of it, he wanted to say more.

"I promise you," he said indignantly, "that anyone who has the insolence to try to make out that you have a lover will get short shrift from me. I know what a loyal wife I have."

The reward he had for this statement was to see her face turned fully on himself with an adoring smile, and although this was a familiar experience meted out to him by strangers and courtiers alike, it was one he never tired of.

"I know very well what a loyal wife I have," he repeated. "Anyone rude enough to suggest otherwise will not remain a friend of mine be they Madame Gordon or de Grancy or anyone!"

This brief scene brought an end to all Madame's unhappiness for the moment. She was never more merry. She was all smiles immediately. She told Theobon afterwards that even if Lorraine immediately thought up a new scheme to take the place of the one that had been frustrated, she was positively grateful to him for providing her with such proof of her husband's affection.

Theobon was always difficult to please when it came to any service performed by others with the objective of pleasing Madame. And one aimed at harming her, however benevolent its actual outcome, could only be expected to provoke one of her sharp comments. Usually these rejoinders made Madame laugh but this time she had no intention of listening. "Please do not try to convince me otherwise," she said, taking Theobon's hand. "And don't tell anyone that I can be made so happy by this show of friendship and affection from my husband. Those who believed you would be jealous and the others would think me a fool!" And she put her fingers in front of her lips in that familiar gesture of hers that implied suppressed laughter at an improper subject. Although as a royal personage it was her fate to be given in marriage to a stranger in a strange land, she had a simple heart and with the sheer courage of a great lady she planted the flower of her affections firmly in the ground that was given to her. It was fascinating to watch a Princess with this robust and homely character coming thus headlong into contact with the hypocritical subtleties of the French court. When she triumphed, it was indeed tempting for all those who loved her to throw their hats in the air, and be glad.

However, like Theobon I was still uneasy. It never seemed likely to me that any one turn of events would signal the end of Lorraine's treachery short of him being stretched out dead upon the floor. With him, frustration over one plot would only precipitate another more deadly. Unless of course the proof of his criminal behaviour in the past could be discovered and produced against him.

This idea, first raised by Francis, had begun to play upon my mind. But if the past was to be uncovered to incriminate Lorraine as the murderer of the first Madame, I would need help. Now the idea occurred to me that the Maréchale de Clerembault, still a devoted and resourceful friend of Madame, might advise me. Since her banishment from court I had regularly carried letters between her in her house in

Paris, and Madame. Monsieur had forbidden any correspondence, and so letters had to be carried in secret either by myself or de Wendt.

The next time I went to Paris on this errand I decided to approach the Maréchale on the subject of the death of Monsieur's first wife. Perhaps the Maréchale would know more of the matter, and have an opinion as to the cause of death, and if poison, who had administered it, and how.

It was on an afternoon when the sun had made a very early disappearance behind a massive bank of cloud, that I was sent with a letter. It was the day after the scene I have just described with Monsieur. The Maréchale's house was in the Marais, and premature shadow bathed the front of the mansion in a gloomy and thwarted stillness. And the atmosphere inside the house could easily be as bad as that outside, if the Maréchale was not in a good mood. She could be taciturn and cold and I would have no chance to speak to her about Madame. Or if she was gambling I would have to leave because I could not play with her. She did not favour the games which I excelled at, but preferred to pit her wits against naked chance. And then, fired with the lust to play and play again, nothing could stop her.

Inside the house – perhaps my own state of mind imposed this – the atmosphere was indeed funereal. The staircase ahead of me was of the grand sort, and I had to climb it. The late afternoon was humid. The density of the air seemed even to muffle the rattle of wheels in the street. I could hear no sound of voices. I had a copy of Jean Picard's last work on astronomy to give her, and also an account of the completion of the Canal du Midi the previous year, as well as the letter from Madame. You see how I ingratiated myself with her, knowing her secret scholarly ways which were, besides, very interesting to myself.

The servant had asked me to go into the Maréchale's bedroom, an apartment almost oppressively filled with a certain shade of dark honey damask, which she loved and hung everywhere. And books. As soon as I entered I saw that I had come at a good time. She was seated in the window, writing.

"You've arrived," she said, "at an opportune moment. Here I am completing a long letter to the Duchesse d'Orléans, and now you will be able to take it back for me. Let me see that."

I handed her the letter. I was struck by the beauty of the Maréchale's complexion at that moment. Perhaps as a result of her always using that mask when out of doors her face was luminous and almost unlined even years after this. The curious light of that particular afternoon, occluded as it was by whatever dust or humidity had got between us and the sun, caused her skin to almost shine in the rich and dim interior. The light behind her was dusty and yellow, but this oval of her face seemed lit with a light of its own.

She said, "You may sit, Monsieur de Brisse."

She had known me since I was eleven or twelve. Ten years previously, in Madame's apartment, this lady had put a cushion on the floor with her own hand and pointed at it. Such extraordinary kindness occurring in the character of someone who was also ferociously strict, was very touching. Although I was cautious in the presence of this woman – and I needed to be – I loved her. She now indicated a stool just beside her own chair, but before sitting on it I presented the book and the bound essay that I had brought for her.

"Ah!" she exclaimed. She was more interested in Madame's letter for the moment, and read it through once as I waited. As she read, it was clear that she was very moved; both angry and upset at the beginning of it, which told of Madame's meeting with the King, and apprehensive at the triumphant conclusion. I described the scene I had witnessed, when Madame had appealed to the King for help, and he had refused.

The Maréchale made a click of annoyance with her tongue and got up from her chair only to sit down again almost at once. This saved me from having to rise.

"So what will be the next step? Oh, don't tell me," she exclaimed sharply, spotting the fact that I had just drawn breath "Those fiends will think of a way round it if Monsieur is momentarily sensible enough to believe his wife. It makes my blood run cold to think how very much the same their behaviour was to the first Madame. I was not as friendly with Minette as I have had the good fortune to be with the present Duchesse. But she was a delightful woman and they killed her. When they find that this scheme is thwarted for the moment, they will fabricate some new evidence. I shall send money to Claire-Amant (I had no idea who this was). I shall have news for you when you come again but I beg that you will be watchful in the meantime. Tell Theobon to give the men servants plenty of money so that they can't be bribed. That may help to keep her safe."

Without being asked she had already answered the question which was uppermost in my mind. She said that "they" had killed the first Madame, and she considered the present Duchesse to be in danger of her life. The fact that she took the same view as I did, both horrified and comforted me. But she allowed me no time on that occasion to discuss it. There was always this other obsession of hers to be accounted for. Namely, gambling.

She looked now at the clock and said,

"You'll have to go, Berthon. I've wasted much too much time." She will have been expecting visitors from among her gaming friends. But she smiled and said, "You must not think me ungrateful. If I sound like a bitter old woman it's not because I don't appreciate your gifts. Come and see me again soon. Bring me more news."

"But I do most urgently need to talk to you about what can be done," I protested. "We cannot simply wait for them to kill her."

A clatter down below gave warning of new arrivals in the house, and the Maréchale got to her feet.

"Not now, Berthon," she said. "Come again tomorrow. But wait."

She turned rummaging in a little cabinet, finally saying, "I wanted to give you this."

She held out a little jewel set in a crown of gold leaves, with pearls and mounted on a blue enamelled circle. I was astonished. This lady was universally known for her stinginess, and I never expected her to give me anything in her life.

"You can give it," she said, "to that little child you're so besotted with. What's her name? The Duchesse d'Autour's baby. Make sure the wet nurse doesn't steal it. It's valuable you know."

I thanked her very warmly. She gave me rather a chilling look. I know why. When mean people part with anything they are longing to take it back until you are well out of the room. "Oh Madame," I said. "Keep it. The fact that you wished to give it to me is enough. I do not need the jewel now."

I meant it. My heart was touched. For a moment she hesitated. But then – equally rare event – she smiled. I don't know why she didn't smile more often. She had good teeth. And when she actually smiled it gave her whole person an air of sweetness.

"Don't be a fool," she said. "Take it. And you have my permission, if you prefer, to give it to that actress, Fanette d'Estrier, now that she is back from Flanders. I hear that she knows you love her, and when some fine fellow tried to tell a joke at your expense (by your leave) she cut him dead the next evening. Go on now."

And having in this way thrown me off the very perch of my life, so that I was dumbfounded and could not move, she simply said again, "Go on now," and I had to leave. I crossed the room somehow. I was half way down the stairs before a servant came after me with the letter for Madame.

CHAPTER TWENTY

The last two minutes of this interview with the Maréchale had a shattering effect upon me. Fortunately Bonhomme was waiting outside the Maréchale's house, and helped me onto my horse, otherwise I think I would have stood there in the road until I fell down. The remarks made about Fanette had acted on my brain like a violent purgative. I don't think I had a wit left.

It was all very well for the Maréchale to tell me to be watchful of Madame at court if at the same time she turned me into an idiot. I forgot that I had planned to visit Climène's child. I forgot that Maud always wanted to turn North at the intersection of the Rue St. Paul and Celestins because she had foaled in the stables of the old Duc de Berry. I forgot even about Madame's predicament. My mind was on fire with the thought of Fanette. After all these months it was as if each desire to see or think of her denied in that time had been so many pieces of fuel heaped onto smouldering ashes. Along came this little wind, this whisper of gossip issuing from the lips of a lady extremely given to such opportunities for provocation, and with an impact that shook my body like an explosion the whole thing went up in flames. My resolution. My courage. My grasp on reality, as in knowing myself to be utterly unsuited for love. All that my brain could hold was a chaotic image of Fanette herself, like a reflection in a glass being carried along a path by a frightened child; and those words of Madame de Clerembault: "I hear that she knows you love her."

I had not mentioned my infatuation to anybody; not even Ernst. Or not seriously. And not recently. The humiliation of thinking my sentiments to be known would have made me kill myself on the spot if it were not for those other words: "when some fine fellow tried to tell a joke at your expense (by your leave) she cut him dead the next evening."

When I found myself back at Versailles, I remained in my apartment the whole evening and never ventured out. All the devils of hell seemed to have been let loose in my body.

I pay too much attention to the sensitivities of those who conform to a physical pattern of normality and are more or less whole and acceptable to their friends. I avoid disturbing them with any fear that I could have feelings like theirs. I am afraid to disgust them with the involuntary thought of my face, my twisted legs and hunched back lying against the beautiful form of a woman like Fanette. But the fact was that in this context I did not feel like the creeping crawling version of humanity that I had been born. I felt like they did. Like gods. Something in my blood took wing regardless of the inability of my pathetic legs to follow after. And I adored her.

Throughout this annihilating experience when I could scarcely recognise where I was or put two thoughts together Bonhomme took care of me, and politely too. His manner to myself had changed in the last couple of months. Not that I had given much attention to him, but I had noticed that he tended to seek out opportunities to be of service to me when, on past form he would have made himself scarce. My reaction to the first faint awareness of this change was suspicion. I had never greatly like him and he had helped another man in an attempt to kill me, probably for money. What would you expect? But now it was being borne in on me little by little that a more subtle difference was at issue here. He said nothing. He looked as unprepossessing as usual, not that it behoves me to find fault with another man's appearance. But his spirit, or his state of mind, or something on those lines was altered.

He had always been inclined to be slovenly. Finding that I became fastidious about dress, he complied with my wishes, but always with a dismissive air, as if stating the obvious by his manner; I refer to the fact that any attempt on my part to minimise my ugliness was a waste of time. His own clothes he disdained to clean. He would scarcely put his linen on straight. But then, sometime fairly recently to the events I have described, he began to change.

At first, he only did this: he would be waiting for me when I returned to my apartment. In the past he was usually absent, and if I wanted his services I either did without or waited or went looking for him. Nowadays he seemed always to know when I would be returning, and there he'd be. And then, if I had some errand, like this to Paris for example, he would offer himself and I was beginning to get into the habit of making use of him.

When finally we got back to Versailles the never forgotten image of Fanette dressed as Alcide rose up in my mind and obliterated all hope of rational thought returning, like a shaft of impossibly bright sunlight in a dark room. I blundered into the furniture. I couldn't eat. I have a dim memory of Bonhomme manhandling me into my clothes one morning –

whether the next or the one after that I do not know to this day – and then he put a glass into my hand and said "Drink this."

I hoped it was poison. I drank it. Then I felt drowsy, slept a while, and woke in my rational mind. When I sat up I had no idea if it was morning or evening. Bonhomme was lurking in a corner as usual but when I stirred he got to his feet.

"What o'clock is it?" I asked him. It was only ten in the morning. I put my hand to my head. I remembered what had ailed me, and I heard a great sigh which came from my own breast; but at the same time I got to my feet. Although he was short for an ordinary man Bonhomme was head and shoulders taller than myself.

I said, "You can go, Bonhomme. I need nothing."

He stepped back a pace and said sulkily, "If you are hungry, Monsieur, I have prepared some food."

I was not hungry. But then, because I was beginning to feel responsible in some way for the cumulative effort that he was suddenly anxious to make on my behalf, I roused myself and said that he could bring me something. When next I noticed him he was putting the finishing touches to an unexpected array of little delicacies which included some of my favourite food; crayfish for example. When I ate them, I found them cooked in the spiced sauce I liked best. And there was an excellent soupe Colbert and several other things. Although all the courtiers and their servants had access to the food from the King's kitchen, Bonhomme had been involved in some trouble getting and arranging all this.

When I had finished eating I sat back, conscious of feeling very much better than I had before. Also something else soothed me. After a moment's reflection I realised that it was Bonhomme's kindness. I could have laughed out loud. Who else in the entire court was so absurd that, a mere six months or so after being nearly killed as a result of a man's treachery, he would take food from the hand of that very servant who had so despised him, and feel moved, what is more, by gratitude. And as for kindness, was it 'kind' of Bonhomme, or merely his duty, that he did what he now did? That my heart had this absurd low melting point, as the alchemist Henig Brand of Hambourg might have said (the Maréchale had recently lent me a copy of his latest work), was one more deformity to add to all the others. But at least it was a deformity I could hide.

I hardened my heart against Bonhomme, who was watching me out of the corner of his small watery eye. But above all my resolve to avoid the humiliation of being seen to be in love was suddenly reborn with even more force than before the Maréchale's fatal words had so destroyed me. I thanked Bonhomme, but no more. I told him that he could take the empty dishes away, and I got up intending to put on my hat and hobble down into the gardens. I wished that Ernst was back from manoeuvres; that Climène was not in England; that Francis was returned. And I wished with all my heart that, like other young men of my age, I could go and see the woman I loved, touch her lips with mine and be free to express my feelings without shame, or fear of contempt. Another sigh must have escaped me unawares because I heard the sound of it and realised Bonhomme was watching me.

I was about to dismiss him when he said, "Monsieur, I would like to help you."

Just like that!

If he had expressed himself in any other manner I would have rounded on him with anger, but how can one man reproach another who makes such a plain remark. I didn't know what to say. Finally, "It's a private matter," I said. "But I thank you."

He put down the dish he had in his hand.

"Monsieur," he said. "It would be a great honour for me if you were to trust me with your confidence. I have reason to want an opportunity to show that I can be a faithful servant, as I have been an unfaithful one."

I was amazed. And disgusted. And why on earth should he want any such thing? He had been happy to have me murdered a few months ago. I tolerated his continued service because I was uniquely dependent and no one else would do it. My indignation was such that I couldn't speak straight away. I looked, speechlessly at him, and then I saw how his hand trembled; the one that had held the dish. One side of his mouth, too, was caught down as if upon a thorn. I could not read the signs of such emotion – emotion so like my own – without pity, even though he was only a servant.

"Don't trouble yourself, Bonhomme," I said in a much kinder tone than I would have used. "As I said, it is a private matter."

He continued to look just as agitated, if not more so. He was fumbling around in a pocket of his miserable jerkin, until he took out a paper. He couldn't bring himself, evidently, to put it in my hand. He pressed it down on the table, and then took his hand away.

After a moment's pause I took a step forward, and with my eye on him rather than the paper, took it up. It had been a tidy sheet at one time before spending so long in his pocket or wherever it had also been. It held a very brief message. I read, "To Monsieur de Brisse. Thank you. Fanette d'Estrier."

"Where did you get this?" I said.

"The lady's servant, Sir."

"When?"

"Just after... well, just after..."

"Camargue."

"You were ill. Too ill. I put it in my pocket."

There was a long silence between us. I said, "Have you any idea what it refers to?"

"Yes," he said.

For a breathless moment I said nothing, and then I shouted,

"You scoundrel!"

I hit him. I never would have thought that I would hit a living soul, or an animal, in my life. What I used to hit him with I have no idea. I must have succeeded in reaching his chest perhaps. I hope so. Even in memory I do not like to think of myself thrashing my servant, possibly with a cushion, and around the buttocks.

The indignity that I was inflicting on myself, rather than on him, brought me to my senses, and I remember flinging myself round so that I had my back to him, and hearing the panting of my own rage, and for a moment no other sound. It took several minutes for me to master myself. When he spoke again I kept my back to him. He said, "It's not my fault, Monsieur. The lady herself told me, and I mentioned it to no one else. She found out that you were the one who paid to have her uncle put in prison, Monsieur."

I did. It cost me half my year's pension. The facts of the story were as follows; Fanette, owing to her poverty which was aggravated by her refusal of many lovers, was forced to live with the uncle who had brought her up. This man was a devil, with a violent temper and a sadistic pleasure in beating and injuring a beautiful woman. Fortunately he didn't desire his niece; only her money, such as it was, and the pleasure of beating her. He also was a drunkard, and a thief. When Fanette tried to leave him he would find out where she was, and drag her back. Because she appeared on stage he always knew where he could lay his hands on her.

One night, during a performance of Tellemache, she appeared so bruised and battered that at first the stage manager gave her a mask. But the audience booed to force her to remove it. Then when they saw her face, which despite all the paint she could use was still not prepossessing enough in the circumstances, they booed again. I was there. She stood alone on the stage, because the others were frightened and ran away. Only she stood her ground, without defiance I have to say; a modest, quiet air that silenced the audience in the end. For the time that she held the contemptuous attention of the whole house, I felt as if my very soul had been pared out of my body and put to stand beside her. I remembered my debut at Court. It was not as if I ever exactly forgot it. But that terrible confrontation – the accumulated magnificence of all those courtiers, each one so immensely richer and stronger than myself, who directed the concentrated disdain and contempt of their attention on me – I remembered that.

I left the theatre and sent word to de la Reynie himself that I wanted to see him. You recall that he was the Chief of Police at the time. He also knew me slightly because of that other incident I mentioned before, and he knew that I enjoyed the friendship of the Duchesse d'Orléans. Consequently he saw me, and agreed to charge Fanette's uncle with the vengeance of the law. I did not pay de la Reynie to do this. He was incorruptible. The money I spent was all on witnesses. Once the uncle was in prison I went to see him and told him that if he ever laid a finger on his niece again I'd have him murdered.

I cannot describe the rage I felt at Bonhomme knowing about this. When I confronted him again he said,

"It's not generally known, Monsieur, I assure you."

I was calmer now. I began to let my thoughts settle. I perceived Bonhomme might be telling the truth, and that he was not guilty of indiscretion. But in that case, what had prompted the words of the Maréchale de Clerembault? No doubt the very incident that she had precisely described. Apart from that, the facts which mattered to me were only those concerning Fanette. These very simply consisted of the business of my intervention to rescue her from her uncle, and that she knew I had done it and thanked me.

I said to Bonhomme, "If you ever mention this again to me or to anyone else, I'll have nothing more to do with you." He looked disappointed. But then he was a thoroughly disappointed man in the first place. I told him to go, and he went out of the room.

My heart was heavy but the rage of hope, shame, excitement and despair that had reduced it to ashes seemed to be burnt out. With an effort I tried to put aside thoughts of Fanette and to return to my true duty, which was to keep watch over Madame and to serve her. I went to pay court to her.

Madame was busy when I arrived. Her apartment was full of people, and I retired quietly into my usual place. Theobon was there. When after a little while she noticed me she came to speak to me.

"Where have you been?" she said. And, "You look ill, Berthon. What's the matter?"

Not more than half an hour later there was a general move, promoted by Monsieur, to go and play billiards and most of the ladies went with him and the gentlemen, except for Madame who excused herself saying that she would write her letters.

When Madame's little dogs were all in their accustomed places, one on her skirt, another under her left elbow and so on, she began to write. Two of the ladies in waiting were painting a fan at a table some distance away. The room was quiet enough for the busy scratching of Madame's pen to be heard. If I moved at all, Charmille, without stirring a hair of her outstretched and sleepy body, rolled an eye in my direction. Motte made as if to jump down until restrained. Madame continued to write. She had her bottom lip caught between her teeth and a little frown on her face.

After all my anxieties and fearful disappointment, the very sight of her was balm to my ruffled spirits. I could not help feeling soothed when she was nearby. There was a Dutch painter whose name I forget but I saw one of his portraits, and Madame reminded me of her. A little.

She was wearing court dress that day. Theobon had told me that Madame had invented a most ingenious method of tying various parts of the skirts and underskirts together so as to be able to get into court dress with the least possible trouble. She laughed about it. No other lady would have been so original. Now, when, with a flourish Madame started to write another line, something in what she was putting down caught her fancy and she gave a little laugh before finishing with a great stroke of her pen. She knew that I had my eye on her. I hoped that she was going to tell me some part of what she had written, as she sometimes did when it was a joke, or an anecdote that she thought particularly amusing. And certainly she wrote with great vigour and life in her words. I have read worse writings in the King's library, and often.

Madame had already half turned to me and drawn breath, but before she could say anything the quiet of the room was suddenly disrupted with a loud noise of clattering steps – unheard-of at Versailles where we walked in a particularly graceful style – and the harsh, almost ripping, sound of cloth that a lady in court dress can cause by rushing between doors. The peaceful atmosphere was changed in an instant to one of fearful commotion. I leapt to my feet, but Madame only drew herself very upright as she still sat.

It was Theobon herself, having left the room some time ago, who now came rushing back like this. Her face was quite red and she was distraught. She threw herself at Madame's feet and burst into tears.

The playful expression that had been on Madame's face a moment before was replaced with one of horror. But as well as alarm and pity she took instinctive refuge in her own majesty. The playful air of the young princess who had been so peacefully and humorously writing a minute ago, was gone, and in her place sat that manifestation of Madame's character which showed her regal nature, and the resolute strength of her ancestry.

"What is the meaning of this?" she said to Theobon. And then again, unconsciously amending the tone of her voice, "What on earth's the matter?"

It brought Theobon to her senses to hear the tone of Madame's voice, and she attempted to control herself, but couldn't. She looked up from the floor, and tried to move her lips. Eventually she managed to bring out the words, "I am dismissed."

"Dismissed!" exclaimed Madame. "Who can dismiss my friends from Court except myself?"

Theobon hardly dared reply. She still crouched there looking right up with her wet face and soaked red cheeks, and her mouth with its rather thin lips stretched open. The other two ladies in the background were frozen like statues.

Eventually Theobon said "Monsieur!"

"Monsieur!" Madame repeated.

Theobon couldn't repeat it. She simply folded her face into her bosom and wept and would have stayed there for ever if Madame had not done something. Madame bent down and took her hands and insisted on placing her in her own chair. Theobon clung to her, sobbing violently.

"I have to go," she said, with the most dreadful moan.

"Why?" Madame demanded. There was firmness in her own voice because whether or not she dreaded hearing the explanation she would certainly show no fear. Theobon responded at last to this.

"They have told Monsieur," she said, "that I take messages between you and the Chevalier de Sinsanet, and that I try to embroil you. The Chevalier de Lorraine has persuaded Monsieur that Madame Gordon is telling the truth when she says that I was carrying a letter which I dropped and she read it."

Madame's expression was rigid with indignation. And she felt the most bitter – the most cruel – disappointment. Theobon's words struck her to the heart, because if this were true, her husband would have broken his promise. Had not Monsieur promised, only last week, never to believe a word that anyone might say in this connection to impugn his wife's honour? In fact she couldn't believe it at first, and she said,

"Has Monsieur himself dismissed you? It is not a rumour? Not some story told by others?"

Theobon knew very well that for Madame to be told that her husband had taken action against yet another of her closest friends, and for such a reason, would make her very unhappy. So she tried to hold back the answer behind her teeth, but in the end she had to say it was Monsieur himself. She said, "I have been told to leave the court today. I am not ever to be allowed come again. Oh, Madame!"

It was fortunate in a way that Theobon concentrated like this on her own distress, because it aroused anger and pride in Madame who might otherwise have found it hard not to weep herself. She had her back to the open door and did not see the first movement of shadows beyond the ante room which gave warning of the arrival of others. I took the liberty of alerting her whereupon she did not turn at once, but prodded Theobon on the arm so that she fell silent, looked, and stood up at once.

Monsieur himself was by now walking across the ante room and not, of course, alone. He would need the support of his friends for the scene ahead of him and he had it. Lorraine and Gordon and Elizabeth de Grancy were with him. They had all adopted a serious air, as if constrained, perhaps not exactly against their will, to take part in an execution. Secret satisfaction nevertheless, lent a putrid tinge to their manner. One could almost smell it across the room.

D'Effiat came in a moment later pretending to be very deep in conversation with the old Duc de Malin, who would never have willingly participated in such a drama but he was too deaf to keep track of what was going on.

Madame turned slowly when she judged that her husband had walked for long enough towards her as she held her back to him. She moved with such a regal air that I shivered. I don't know how it could have affected Monsieur. The figure of Theobon, her face ravaged with distress, the skirts of her gown almost knotted around her, flanked Madame on one side whereas I, alas, stood on the other. It was very unlucky that I happened to be visible.

Lorraine, quick witted as ever, stopped with a little curvette of his body and held both palms of his hands half up as if to admire a particularly remarkable grouping. I hoped Monsieur would not see him, but he did. At once the expression of solemn alarm with which he at first faced his wife was broken. Fed with this little joke, he brought a more flippant and determined eye back to face his wife and said at once,

"I have dismissed this lady, Madame. She is no longer to appear at Court."

The Princess, deeply hurt though she must have been by such a betrayal, looked calmly at him and said, "I presume she has offended you, in which case I wholeheartedly accept your decision to be rid of her, Monsieur. But may I know what she has done?" Monsieur seemed rather at a loss for a reply. But prompted by a little titter, quickly suppressed, from behind him he said, "I do not feel that to discuss our private business before friends is appropriate. So you must just accept my decision, Madame."

"She has transgressed then, in some personal way, Monsieur? Am I to infer that she has behaved improperly toward yourself?"

The idea was so ridiculous that he said so. But then, seeing the trap that she was setting for him, he became genuinely angry. This Prince who with all his ability – because undoubtedly he had talent, and was brave and not slow-witted – and with all his wealth and power and handsome person, was apparently yet so greedy for self-gratification that he was allowing himself to be manipulated into attacking two harmless women as part of what he must have known was nothing but a game of scandal. His wife generously and sincerely loved him, but he was quite ready to make her miserable on a pretext that he must have know was sheer nonsense.

Since no one will see this memoire until I am beyond the reach of earthly punishment I can mention that I longed for him to be transformed, while conscious of the magic that afflicted him, into a tailor's apprentice, or a gardener. He needed to be whipped, and to taste the bitterness of the sort of food that I had had when I was a boy.

When he got started now, with his speech, he was very fluent. His story of Theobon's role as lovers' go-between came easily to him. Madame reminded him of his assurances of only days before but he had thought of a way out; because he said that the integrity of his wife didn't stop a certain type of woman from carrying messages, and doing everything that she could to promote disloyalty.

Madame would not plead with him. At a certain point she just fell silent. Theobon let out a great sob. Perhaps Monsieur disliked, on aesthetic grounds, the spectacle she was making of herself, and perhaps he had simply tired of this event, but he turned on his heel at that moment with an expression of finality.

However, he was not rude enough to keep his back to Madame when she spoke and Madame did speak now. He turned to listen again, and must have been struck by her words and her manner. In spite of all that people said of her, and in spite of what was her own opinion, Madame was capable of beauty. And when that grace touched her, whether because of a particular light or her state of health, or an expression, it took an unforgettable form. Simplicity, majesty and humour are not naturally companions of each other. In her these qualities were uppermost and in those moments of charm she was truly unforgettable.

On this occasion humour was replaced by a dignified sadness, and she looked more royal than her husband, or indeed anyone else that I have ever seen. If some great man could have painted her at that moment – Rigaud I suppose – it would have been a good thing. But let that rest; I have the image in my mind for ever.

She took Theobon's hand while continuing to face her husband.

"This lady," she said, "is my dear friend. I came from a country far away to assume the honour of being your wife, Monsieur, and I still consider myself fortunate. And if you require to take my friends from me you must do so. Only keep yourself my friend, and I shall not complain."

Monsieur was struck. Even Lorraine and Gordon, standing behind him, were surprised into a fleeting moment when their faces showed admiration. I thought to myself, "Will they also love her in the end?" But d'Effiat was made of sterner stuff. He said something to the Prince in an undertone. It was an example of impertinence that he said anything at all at such a moment, but whatever it was it broke the spell, and with one last uncertain glance and the very slightest bow to his wife, Monsieur turned on his heel. But just before going out of the ante room, he sent his gentleman, Choin, back again. That person, with his face red and his eyes upon the floor, gave Madame the message that Theobon must leave at once, and all communication between her and the Princess must be at an end. He stepped back to allow Theobon to precede him from the room. Madame took that lady in her arms and kissed her. Her cheek was smeared with the tears of her friend but her own eyes were dry. Almost fainting, Thebon made her way out of that room and never once came back.

I can vouch for the fact that she had never arranged a single meeting between Madame and any gentleman in private, nor took any amorous messages. Madame laughed about court intrigues, of course, and made merry with her friends about all sorts of adventures and even allowed her ladies-in-waiting to have lovers, but she herself maintained the integrity of a royal person, as she saw it. She knew that her reputation and happiness resided with the success she could achieve in her marriage. But if a Prince like Monsieur chose to believe that Theobon had done what she was accused of, he could take from her her livelihood, her home, and her friends, and this he did. And deeply embarrass and upset his wife into the bargain.

I saw Monsieur later that evening, at the King's table and at cards after, and his good spirits were untouched by the misery he had caused. He laughed like a child. He had invented a new game with small plaquets of lacquered wood and he played it with his companions until three o'clock in the morning.

CHAPTER THIRTY-ONE

The scandal caused at court by the dismissal of Madame's Lady of Honour threatened to destroy, once and for all, Madame's reputation not only in France but elsewhere. Lorraine and his friends might have achieved the first step in their plot to destroy Madame, since it was inevitable that accounts of Theobon's exile and the putative reason for it should be carried to foreign courts, with the most mortifying consequences to the blameless Princess who was her friend. This would not fit the convenience of Monsieur, if he ever allowed himself to be sensible enough to understand it; nor, I thought to myself, the King.

At the centre of it all Madame was as sad as she had been before. But this time there was a greater pride in the way she carried herself; and neither did Monsieur need to enquire why she was unhappy. Presumably His Majesty deliberated for a while. He could either intervene, as a good and powerful judge might rescue an innocent person from the scaffold, or of course he could sit back and let his brother's wife be destroyed as the first had been.[

]I wrung my hands over this triumph of Lorraine and his friends, that had put Madame in such a vulnerable position, from which I began to think that the next step might well be the attack on her life that all her friends dreaded. I could have been wrong in imagining that Lorraine would not dare to kill Monsieur's second wife, and would prefer to merely destroy her in other ways.

When letters arrived from abroad, Madame had the mortification of finding that her virtue was being discussed and her influence was assumed to be reduced to almost nothing. She wrote to her aunt in Hambourg to complain about it and sent the letter by de Wendt in order to avoid it being censored by the Abbé Dubois. And although the tone of voice she used was never without a twist of humour nevertheless the entire business was so humiliating and painful that her thoughts began to turn seriously again towards the idea of entering the convent of Maubuisson. Dou Dou laughed outright when she said it, but her amusement died away when she could raise no answering smile on the face of Madame. These other friends – Dou Dou and Monsieur Tilladet in particular – could not supply the place of Theobon who had a particular quality of devotion. Lorraine qualified as a most cunning strategist, when he succeeded in removing both Clerembault and Theobon from Madame's entourage, just as a soldier intending to attack a city first cuts down the guardians at the gate.

I took to attending on Madame even twice as much as I ever had before. I never left her if I could avoid it. I worried my mind from morning until night with the subject of how to master and disarm Lorraine. And more and more the idea fixed itself with me that if his guilt over the death of the first Madame could be proved and evidence presented to the King and his brother, as Francis had suggested, even Lorraine could not expect to be pardoned. He would be either executed or, at the very least permanently banished. But as for getting such proof, that was another matter.

I was dragged from my obsessive watches at last by a message from Clément Cardinale begging me to visit him. He had been sent back early from Flanders with a broken foot. I went to see him at once, taking a book on falconry which would amuse him. But I was too preoccupied to be a good companion. After a short while Clément abandoned his attempts to interest me in tales of the camp, and asked instead for news of court. He asked if it was true that the Countess de Beauvron had been dismissed by Monsieur, and of course the whole story came out. And I also confided my belief to do with the death of the first Madame, Minette; namely that she had been poisoned by Lorraine.

Clément's father was Italian by birth although two generations of the family had already lived in France. His eyes were very long and dark and set under extremely soft brows that curved like one of the portraits I had seen when I visited the rooms of Monsieur Moreau.

He said, "My mother told me once – or rather, not me, but one of her friends when I was near by – that she had secret information about the death of Monsieur's first wife."

"Did she say what it was?"

"To do with a certain monastery. We have a family connection with it – in Italy, near Lucca."

"How should a monastery play any part in the death of Monsieur's first wife?"

"This monastery is famous for the study of all herbs, and also poisons," he said. "They cultivate their reputation for healing, but I can tell you they have had a hand in as many deaths. My mother said so, and she is too devout to lie. Because the monastery and the land around it belongs to my family, she gives them money, but not enough, and they supplement their income in this way."

I was looking at him sharply while he said all this. If he finished with some inconsequential remark about the lineage of his uncle, or the food in Italy being superior to that in France, my patience would not stand it.

"And so?" I said.

"My mother told a friend of hers once when I happened to be listening, that Lorraine bought poison from a certain monk in that monastery during the period of his exile. She knew it because the Abbot received a complaint about the monk from one of his brothers."

"How many people know about it?"

"It will have been kept secret," Clément said. "The Abbot is greedy, and determined to enrich the monastery in any way he can. Minette died so suddenly that people talked as you say. But because everyone drank from the same jug of chocolate as she did, Lorraine was able to convince the King and Monsieur and others that her death had nothing to do with him. But what of her cup, her clothes, her napkin?"

All this made me very thoughtful, as you can imagine. My heart began to beat fast. I thought I saw my way to making a beginning on this business.

"You mentioned a certain monk," I said to Clément. "Do you mean that your mother actually knows his name?"

"I had the impression she did. I would have to ask her."

"And will he still be there?" I said, half to myself, but Clément answered readily.

"They don't move around very much!"

I decided there and then that I would find the means to extract a confession from the monk who had sold poison to Lorraine. I questioned Clément for more than an hour on every detail and possibility. He had other useful connections which he was anxious to place at my disposal. It was a matter merely of constructing the best plan of action and having the means to carry it out.

Being a young man and temporarily immobilised by this injury to his foot, Cardinale transferred all his thwarted physical energy into this scheme to entrap Lorraine, and I agreed to return to him after my attendance at Madame's table.

"You will have to travel to Italy," he announced almost as soon as I came back into the room. "How will you pay for it, Berthon?"

I had no idea.

"I will ask my mother."

"Do you want to get me killed?" I exclaimed. "Do you think if Lorraine gets to hear of such an enterprise he would let either me or the monk live?"

"My mother wouldn't speak of it."

I just looked at him. He blushed very slightly and bunched his lips like people do sometimes when they are embarrassed. I remembered Francis offering to ask Climène's advice recently when I attempted to confide my anxieties to him. Cardinale was just at that age when he had not yet transferred the acme of his confidence from his mother to some other woman. And was I to be surrounded with friends who could think of nothing better to do than to run in that sort of direction as soon as there was a problem needing to be solved?

"I will find the money myself," I said. "Just be sure that you never speak of it."

"If I can't speak of it, how am I to find out the monk's name?"

"Don't sulk," I said, but smiling. "You Italians are known for your cunning, so let no one but me know the direction you are searching in."

At some point he said reflectively, "Can you imagine, Berthon, how Lorraine must have been enraged. When Minette complained about him to the King, and the King consequently sent Lorraine into exile for two years, he must have been beside himself. Two whole years separated from the source of all his power, his special luxuries, the furtherance of his ambitions. Two whole years kicking his heels in the court of Spain, where life is as dull as you can imagine and all the women are guarded and locked up; and in Italy where no one knows him. No wonder he killed her!"

This gave me a new idea; namely that perhaps after all the King had his suspicions. And if he had even the slightest notion that Lorraine's revenge could be dangerous, just possibly his apparently complaisant neglect of Lorraine's ill treatment of Madame was designed to protect her. But it was a line of thought I did not pursue. I could not be sure of the King's opinion now, but I could be absolutely sure that concrete evidence – proof that Lorraine had poisoned Monsieur's first wife – would cause him to put aside any personal liking of this man and his friends, and it was very unlikely that they would escape execution. And what is more, Lorraine would know that.

I returned to my apartment and found that Bonhomme had brought back a message from the Maréchale de Clerembault that I was to visit her. I told Bonhomme that I would go into Paris for that purpose the next day, and he could accompany me if he wished. Accordingly we went together. I made a point of arriving in the middle of the morning when the lady might be dressed but not yet given over to cards or backgammon. I passed a gentleman kicking his heels in the hall who I later learned was her son. But she didn't like him. I, on the other hand, was not kept waiting. In a manner by no means designed to conceal the fact, I was led past this other man, and shown up the stairs.

"You have taken your time," she said. "I want to hear about the Comtesse de Beauvron."

I sat on the chair that she was pointing at. She showed kindness to me always in letting me be seated as long as no one else was present. I described the scene to her of poor Theobon's dismissal. She punctuated my narrative with comments of her own and several times I could have laughed at the words she chose. No one who could avoid it should ever have made an enemy of her. Not even Lorraine and d'Effiat.

"Madame," I said. "I have an idea which might be made to serve the Duchesse d'Orléans by putting an end to the mischief making of her husband's spiteful friends; but I need your opinion."

She fixed me with her eye, saying nothing. I remember she stretched her right arm slowly, adjusting the hem of the sleeve and the lace that fell from it with the fingers of her left hand. She settled with her finger on her lip.

"It has to do with the death of the first Madame."

She still waited in silence.

"The rumour at court has always been that she was poisoned by her husband's friends." A small movement of the eyebrows. She thought she was about to be disappointed. "It is not that I imagine that merely warning them will make them stay their hand now," I said at once to counteract this.

"Good," she said dryly.

"But then, if I have understood correctly, whatever they did do Monsieur was definitely not part of it. They did whatever they did in secret, and it was essential that they should be able to convince him and the King, afterwards, that they were innocent of any crime."

"Yes."

"Some information has come my way, Madame, and I think that if poison was administered by Lorraine or any one of the four, I may be able to prove it. There is a man whom I can approach, and I may be able to get concrete evidence to put before the King. And Monsieur. There is no doubt that if the King had the crime and Lorraine's guilt proved to him, he would punish him severely. At the very least all those involved would be forced to leave the court for ever."

"They would be exiled a good deal further than the river Loire I fancy," she said with a bitter laugh. She meant the river Lethe, which is indeed far enough away for anyone. "So what do you think of my plan, Madame?" I said.

"What plan?"

My goodness, the woman was contrary. How did her husband ever get her consent to anything, leave alone the begetting of children.

"I mean," I said, "the plan of finding the evidence to prove them guilty."

"Surely it is too late," she remarked. "The other people involved may be dead. I know for a fact that Minette's young footman died not long after her. He was run over by a coach."

"What footman?"

"The one who found Monsieur d'Effiat with her chocolate cup in his hand shortly before Madame came into her apartment with Monsieur and some other friends an hour or so before she died. D'Effiat had taken it out of the cabinet, and produced some feeble excuse about noticing that it was dirty, and cleaning it. The footman took it from him, so he had no opportunity to put poison in it. If that had been his intention."

"You were not present yourself, Madame?"

"I was not such a friend of the first Duchesse," she said. "Very charming though she was. And Theobon was a Maid of Honour to the Queen then."

"Who else was present, I wonder?"

She thought a while.

"I think the Comtesse de Soissons was there," she said. "She certainly talked enough about it afterwards. But how will you get her to talk to you about it now? She is stupid enough at the best of times. You must see her often trotting around in the wake of Monsieur and his cronies and yet I would be prepared to wager that she has never noticed you."

"I fell against the hem of her gown once," I said.

"Ah! I should have lost my money. I hadn't stipulated any difference between the rough and the smooth edge of her tongue."

I smiled.

"Don't do that, Berthon," she said. "We are old friends, and I have to tell you that even after all these years the disfigurement of your mouth catches me by surprise. You should always hold your hand up if you smile."

I burst out laughing, unable to restrain myself. But I did as she asked. A very slight curve of the lips showed that she was amused.

"If you were not so extremely talkative," she said, "you could mask your face with a *touret*. As I do."

I declined to argue about how, with my mouth, I could hold the stick of the *touret* between my teeth for any length of time. I returned to the subject of Madame de Soissons.

"Here is a good example," I said, "of what I have in mind. It will not be necessary for me personally to speak to Madame de Soissons. I can get Ernst to speak to her when he returns from manoeuvres, which he will in a day or two now. She will say anything to a young man."

"That is true," she said. "I begin to see your plan. But what about the poison?"

"It happens that the family of a friend of Ernst, who I spoke to recently, comes from Italy. His mother is particularly friendly with the Italian Cardinal, Alberoni." Clément had discovered that this was the source of his mothers knowledge of the events which interested us. And the Cardinal was currently at the French court.

"The Duc de Vendôme – that impossible cynic, but really he is a friend of mine – he is the chief patron and friend of that same Cardinal, here at court."

"There you are Madame!" I exclaimed. "And this man knows the name of the person who may have sold poison to the Chevalier de Lorraine. My friend Clément tells me that outside a certain village in Italy there exists a monastery which has been renowned for years as the chief source of obscure and lethal poisons. In Catherine de Medici's days apparently they were at their height and were enriched by the regular demands made on them by the Queen of France."

I received a rather cold stare from the Maréchale, but ignored it.

"His mother – the mother of Clément – has a cousin at this monastery. It seems that a monk there was most likely the direct contact of Lorraine and will have sold the substance to him. In this way – one person, who knows another, who knows another – I can find out the truth in the end."

"And are you to be doing all this while still remaining in Paris?"

"No, Madame. I will travel wherever I need to go in order to ferret it all out. But I will do it."

"And without any money, I presume."

I allowed myself to be silenced by this remark as she intended. I was perfectly well aware that I would need a patron but I had not been such a fool as to imagine that someone as stingy as she should be approached. Notwithstanding her gift to me on my last visit, I thought she would not part with anything.

"I believe I am considered mean," she said, reading my thoughts with a disconcerting lack of humour. "But have you also heard it said that I am a devoted friend?"

She rose from her chair. At her first movement I, of course, sprung to my feet. Or perhaps 'sprung' is not the right word. From underneath the cloth of Clerembault's skirt a small cat, who had clearly not stirred for hours, made a slow and luxurious process of uncurling. Once on her feet the Maréchale de Clerembault stood still. I assumed that she intended to lecture me, and she did.

"You may not realise," she began, "that I have been at Court a long time. When the present Madame first arrived from the Palatine I was appointed to her household. It was an honour which I was prepared to value for its own sake. But then my heart fell into an enchantment. I saw the Princess, and I do believe I fell in love. I like the minds of men, and their conversation, but very little else about them. Up until that time the great love of my life had been my sister, as you probably know."

She continued her extraordinary speech with an almost dream-like composure, looking over my head as she spoke. I did not move a muscle.

"The Princess wore a gown of pale blue silk, even though it was Winter."

I knew this. I was as unlikely to forget as she.

"To my mind, the moment that I saw her, the combination of her plumpness, her red lips and shining eyes, her pretty accent, her laughter..." She stopped and breathed deeply, like someone in a garden breathing in the scent of a rose. And when this memory had filled her lungs with the air of remembered happiness, she breathed it out again in a long sigh. I thought she was about to break off and resume her progress toward whatever part of the room she had in mind. She did look down, and single out a little key from a bunch hanging on her waist, but then stopped once more, as still as I was.

"Do you know," she said, "that Madame used to romp around with her step children like a child. She was nineteen, but so young in that way. She loved playing. Carllutz used to play with her as well, and the little Prince Eisenach, and I remember how she used to throw pétards into the skirts of that old lady who hated bangs. What was her name? Of course, you wouldn't know. Madame de Freins. That's right! Madame de Freins. Oh!" She laughed. She seemed to be looking at actors on a stage. Somewhere behind me where I dared not glance, the bright figures of the past were moving in front of her very eyes. "Madame de Freins used to run after the children – I mean after Madame and her playmates – and try to hit them, and Madame thought it was the greatest fun." She waited, her eyes still fixed on that spot where perhaps the shadows of her memories laughed at her as they faded. But in the end she looked again at me. She shook her head very slowly from side to side – a sad movement – and said, "Do you think that I would not let my body be cut in pieces and every penny I possess thrown into the ditch if either could save her from unhappiness, or secure peace for her?"

I was moved more than I can say. And shocked. A little. The love that she described could not be mistaken.

For her part, she had now said all that she intended to say, and had made the impression on me that she intended. She walked quietly over to a cabinet, the door of which she unlocked. She returned with a leather bag in her hand and gave it to me. It was so unexpectedly heavy I nearly dropped it. It could have been full of solid gold coins. In fact of course, that was precisely it, but at the time not what I had expected.

"For so long as you are occupied on the business that you have just described to me," she said, "I will give you as much money as you ask of me. I think your plan may have a chance of success. I have racked my brains for a solution but never thought of anything that seemed at all likely to help, until you mentioned this. If you are right, and if you succeed in finding and bringing back proof that they poisoned Minette, Lorraine and his friends will be at our mercy. When this money is used up, send for more. Send Bonhomme if you can't come yourself. He used not to be an honest man, but he is now. And when I ask you to come and see me in future, come at once."

She said this last with a small ironic smile that was at the same time very kindly, She could no doubt see that I was struck dumb. "Don't forget that I am possibly your best source of information as well as of this other," (indicating the gold) "and I have been as good at finding out the truth in my day as you clearly are and I hope will be."

I hadn't yet found my tongue.

"Madame loved me to do divinations for her," she continued after a slight pause. "Do you know that I foretold the death of the little Duc de Valois?"

That can't have given the Princess much pleasure! I bowed. In fact, at that moment I very much revered this extraordinary lady.

I said, "May I kiss your hand, Madame?"

She drew herself up quite sharply.

"Don't be ridiculous, Berthon!" she snapped, snatching her hand back into the very folds of her skirt as if afraid I should get at it. But then, perhaps seeing the expression on my face, she said very kindly, "My child, I am a silly woman. I don't like boys. But you have a heart and a mind which are much more present to me than your body. Count yourself lucky that your ugliness is so well off-set by these, and that you have other friends beside myself who look at the one and not the other."

And so I left her.

CHAPTER TWENTY-TWO

When next I visited Madame I could not get the memory or the image of the Maréchale de Clerembault's extraordinary confession out of my mind. I had always thought that sort of love – I mean the passionate love of one woman for another – to be an affectation; a sort of emotional game not really meant. But the feelings described by the Maréchale could not be mistaken. Of course, it did no harm. Madame was too simple to suspect any such dimension in the affection of her friend.

"Madame," I said.

She was writing letters and no one had been invited to remain in attendance. Her heart was heavy. Most likely she had forgotten me. When her heart was heavy it altered the lines of her face. Those who were forever describing her as Germanic and plain could have a field day pointing it out. The fullness of her lip was increased by the unaccustomed dullness of her expression, and the fact that the corners of her mouth were not drawn up in laughter. Her cheek was not pink with animation, but sallow.

She gave me permission to speak only after a full paragraph of continuous writing. "Madame," I said again, "I have an idea which I think might serve you. May I speak of it?"

She nodded, but carried on writing. Charmille was trying to attract my attention by snapping at my coat, and I took a step backwards.

I began my proposal. I described my plan just as I had described it to the Maréchale.

The Princess had begun to smile by the time I was half way through my narrative. After a moment she put down her pen altogether. She shifted her gaze once or twice between myself and Charmille, whose ears she began gently to pull. I could read her thoughts. She was intrigued; amused because this idea came from me, and dubious on the same account.

"And so how will my little goblin find this out in order to be able to present evidence to the King after all this time?" she said. "La Voisin has been executed, and is gone, together with all her skills of divination and magic, if in fact she ever had any. And I don't know who else can have taken her place."

"Madame," I said, "I will depend on my own powers. Lorraine and his friends think their secret is safe – if in fact they killed her. But secrets can always be found out and used by a man's enemies." I had not mentioned all the details that I had described to the Maréchale. I was not sure that Madame could be discreet if Lorraine or any of his friends annoyed her and she was tempted to tease them.

She nodded. She also gestured to the cushion, which was on the floor for Motte to sit on, and I gratefully took my place on it.

"But who talks about Minette now?" she said. "You would have to find people who could tell you what they had seen or overheard, and you would have to persuade them to do so. Spying is very expensive."

I wondered whether or not to tell her about the gift of the Maréchale de Clerembault

But decided against it for the moment. She would not have believed me. I might not have believed it myself, if someone had told me that that notoriously close-fisted woman had given them a large sum of money.

"I have what money I need. I will find everything out in time," I said. "I have been told the name of a monastery in Italy where the study of poisons has earned them more money than the relic of the bleeding heart, and apparently there is a monk there who sold poison to Lorraine."

"Oh!" She looked quite astonished. And very young again, with her eyes wide open. She made that little gesture of shuffling her body more deeply into the chair she sat on, as she did when very taken with gossip and affairs.

"How did you hear of it?"

"From Clément Cardinale, a friend of Ernst," I said. "His father is intimate with Cardinal Alberoni."

"Oh, does he say the poison was definitely bought?"

"Not exactly. But it remains for me to find out where Lorraine went, and what contacts he did make. If he visited this monastery, or had an assignation with a certain monk from it, I shall find out."

"I remember something," Madame said. "They are lines which were written by La Fontaine for the marriage of my husband and his first wife." Then she recited:

"O couple aussi beau qu'heureux,
Vous serey toujours aimables;
Soyez toujours amoureaux.

Sad, is it not?"

I did not know what to say. After an uncomfortable silence I declared, "Those who destroyed her happiness shall not destroy yours, Madame. I swear it."

A little sigh.

"Well then," she said. "I think your idea is a good one, Goblin, but I hardly think that it will save me. But you have my permission to tell me whenever you have any news."

At that moment the younger Mademoiselle de Freins and other ladies of honour came into the room, and Madame dismissed me.

I got up and left her.

Within a day or two Ernst returned from manoeuvres and as soon as I had the opportunity, I told him of my plan and asked him to question Madame de Soissons about the last time she saw Minette alive. Knowing that she had been with her on the day she died, and that she was observant, and proud of showing it, I hoped her recollections would be useful. And it would be natural for Ernst, a young man and not at court at the time, to show some curiosity in connection with such an interesting story of the past.

Ernst was anxious to help, and began to cultivate the lady's company. Olympe de Soissons was suitably flattered by this. From my vantage point where I was unobserved in company, I watched Ernst approach her once again when, having just finished a game of reversie, she was about to get up and follow her companions elsewhere. Ernst took the opportunity to sit beside her in a chair just vacated by one of the players.

She was beginning to think that Ernst might be in love with her. I could see that. Age is no bar to the imagination, and as Ernst sat she let Monsieur and his entire train of followers leave her behind so that she could stay and talk to this apparently fascinated young man. She half closed her eyes and looked at him with little glimmers, tapping his hands with her fan, and not infrequently laughing, it being understood at court that Olympe de Soissons had a particularly charming laugh. And she was attractive. I could see that. And as Madame herself maintained, essentially kind into the bargain.

As they talked this time I was, I'm afraid, out of hearing and the room had become too empty for me to cross it unobserved. Which was a pity, because this was the very occasion when Ernst at last was able to bring the conversation round to the subject of the death of the first Madame. I had to depend on his account, and I hope he left nothing out. It was very like I had imagined before. It was extraordinarily similar to my day dream when I imagined that I was looking into the moving shadows in a witch's ball. But there were some differences.

She said that Monsieur and his first wife had been walking in the gardens with Madame Gordon, Minette's Scottish lady of honour before they returned indoors to drink chocolate on that fatal morning. Elizabeth de Grancy, and the Marquis d'Effiat, were also included in the group.

During that walk, Minette had quarrelled with Elizabeth de Grancy. The Grancy had picked a rose for Monsieur and asked permission to fasten it on his collar, the shade of the flower being exactly the same as his tunic. She was very clever like that. Always elegant; as you see her now. "Isn't she elegant, Ernst? More than I am?"

There followed some diversion.

When de Soissons returned to her story, she described how Mademoiselle de Grancy had lingered too long and too close over the task of pinning up the flower. But when Madame was annoyed, she picked another and insisted on pinning it to Minette's dress. She could not be stopped. And Olympe de Soissons laughed a great deal because, as she told Ernst, the Grancy was an excellent comic when she chose, and could render a situation deliciously absurd. She pinned a large pink rose to Minette's bosom, or attempted to, and in doing so scratched Madame on the neck. She was very sorry afterwards, and quite in disgrace, but de Soissons said that when unobserved she giggled.

Shortly after this they all went in to Minette's apartment to drink chocolate. There they found d'Effiat, who had left the garden a while earlier, waiting for them. After the events of that day the footman who had been on duty in Madame's apartment while Monsieur's party were in the garden and only the Chevalier was indoors, said that he (d'Effiat) had taken Madame's chocolate cup out of the cupboard and had it in his hand when the footman came into the room. "But why shouldn't he?" said Olympe de Soissons. That servant had challenged Monsieur d'Effiat in quite an insolent manner at the time, and until he was luckily run over and killed by a coach in the streets of Paris he had made a nuisance of himself on the subject. But even he had to admit that d'Effiat had no opportunity to poison the chocolate. All d'Effiat had done was to clean the cup with a little piece of paper because it was dirty. Anybody could do that. And the footman snatched it back I suppose.

At this point there was another long diversion while the lady questioned Ernst about his preferences for sweet or bitter chocolate, and even without hearing a word I could guess something of the dialogue between them. But then I saw he had brought her back to the subject of Madame's death because de Soissons became serious again and an expression even of rationality settled on her face. As I said, she was not without real sense and feeling. And this was a scene capable of penetrating the hardest heart. Apparently Madame, despite the scene in the garden, seemed quite at ease again. She sat and took the cup of chocolate which the footman had just poured within sight of everyone and from the same jug as he then used to fill the cups for others. But no sooner had she drunk from it than she said she felt unwell.

She thought it would pass. Madame de Soissons herself had taken the cup. Then Minette became very pale. And beads of moisture appeared on her temples and her upper lip. When she said she would lie down she rose from her chair as if she expected to be able to walk out of the room, but as soon as she was upright she found that she was dizzy. Two ladies had to help her to walk into the bed chamber and to lie down, and Olympe de Soissons was one of them. She said that within moments Madame was seized with terrible pain. She began to cry out. All the people in the room and in the adjoining drawing room were frightened. Servants were sent to fetch the doctors, but before they could even reach the scene of this terrible event Minette was dead.

"Mark my words," Olympe apparently said at the end of all this, "there are plenty of natural causes for death. My aunt died in a similar fashion and she had a growth on the liver. And there are sicknesses to do with the spleen and all sorts of bits of the anatomy that our doctors know about. Poison was never anything to do with it. I was there. There was no opportunity for nonsense like that."

When Ernst recounted all this, I begged to differ. Madame could have been poisoned when she was scratched by Elizabeth de Grancy who would do anything that Lorraine, in his spite and wickedness, might request of her, and if he sent poison from Italy for her to use she would do his bidding.. And there was that piece of paper the d'Effiat used to wipe the cup. That intrigued me. The Medici poisoned books and gloves. This wiping of a piece of china because he thought it not quite clean, as he told the footman, sounded out of character. I knew very well that both Lorraine and d'Effiat, who by all accounts felt towards the first Madame exactly as they now felt towards the second, would have been happy to see Madame sip her chocolate out of the gutter.

I was very grateful to Ernst. I noticed subsequently how kind he was to Olympe de Soissons. He did not drop his attentions to her immediately, and as he gradually drifted away, if she was disappointed she was not humiliated. In fact she remained a great friend of his until she fled into exile over that unfortunate business of her husband dying in suspicious circumstances many years later. Perhaps at our court it was more remarkable if someone did not die of poison than if they did.

I discovered that the sister of that footman mentioned both by Olympe de Soissons and the Maréchale, lived in Paris in the Rue Saintongue. So I decided to visit and question her. This being my first effort at this sort of task, I dare say my style was somewhat crude. I disguised myself by wearing a full mask and taking Bonhomme with me dressed in a suit of clothes designed to make him look like a wig maker. He came from the Auvergne, which is not that far from Gascony, so this was appropriate.

If in the normal way a man from court visited in Paris, we went to the Marais, where the great houses were in that day. In some of these other places I should have been as lost as a peasant from the furthest provinces. As it was, Bonhomme was accustomed to buy his clothes second-hand from the Place des Grèves, and in general he could find his way about with some additional help if the signs on the streets had not recently been washed off by rain.

Anne Villette, as she was called, lived at a milk woman's house. It was a wretched little place but not as bad as in the country. Her part of it was just a hole in the wall looking onto a yard. It took an age to make the woman understand that we wanted to actually enter her house, and once I got in there, what with the unaccustomed restriction of looking through my mask and the extreme darkness of the place I hardly knew how to tell whether the woman was in the room with us or not. I was at a loss for several minutes. If Bonhomme had chosen to speak instead of me I should have been quite willing, but the man was grown so respectful that he would do no such thing. In the end his behaviour alone was enough to terrify the woman into thinking that I was a great lord who would have her thrown into prison if she said anything at all. Or not enough.

I looked more carefully about me as my eyes grew accustomed to the darkness of the interior. I saw things to remind me of long long ago. There were some poor lumps of whitewashed plaster clinging to the walls in places, which had a very familiar smell. That smell is to do with a beetle that lives in the paste when it has dried out. It is a foul smell, at the same time both sharp and cloying. I was afflicted with a spasm of remembrance.

In the end my question, as I put it, about the death of Madame the first Duchesse was uncomfortably abrupt. I behaved like a new actor on the stage and couldn't remember my words. Anne Villette concluded that the more she could say the more likely she was to be well paid. There was nothing unpleasant about her and I did not resent her keenness, but it was inconvenient. She 'remembered' far more than was helpful. She remembered that there had been a tall thin man who took a vial of liquid out from a pocket and poured it into Madame's cup when the chocolate was already in it. Not only is d'Effiat rather middling in height, but the procedure governing the serving of the chocolate to a member of the Royal Family and in the environment of the court would preclude such a method of intervention.

Also Anne Villette depended on the sale of candles for her living. A sort of child kept calling for more bundles. Between interruptions she would search in her imagination for more morsels of fantasy likely to please her guests, and these varied from a poisoned pin that was stuck into Madame's dress by a tailor in the pay of Monsieur's mistress, to powder scattered on the sheets of her bed.

I said to her, "Have you always lived here?"

"Oh no," she answered me. "My father had a farm in Brittany. We lived very well there, but Jaques (the brother) persuaded me to come to Paris. He said that he would get me work at court, but he died first."

I took thirty sous out of my pocket, gave it to her, and left. I considered this interview a complete failure. But it was only a beginning. It was merely my novitiate in the art of spying out the truth. I would grow immensely better at it by and by.

On my return to Versailles Ernst was waiting to speak to me, but I asked him to come up onto the roof to inspect my birds and we could talk there. My reason was that when Francis left for England he had persuaded me to let him take Bronzine with him in order to be able to try sending me a message from that country.

I had been reluctant to involve myself with such an experiment. Bronzine was one of the first birds I had, and sure enough, his mate had pined for him. I had had to spend much time keeping her strength up and giving her additions to her feed. Daily I looked for the return of Bronzine, but had almost given him up. When Francis came back to France I should have something to reproach him with if he had lost me this bird.

Ernst had changed in the months he had been away. He was so tall he embarrassed me. I walked about at a level with his thigh. I couldn't bear to say so, but part of his speech was inaudible to me because of the distance between his head and mine.

Once we were seated on the leads it was better. The upper part of my body comes closer to being the size of a normal person, and I could begin to catch up with what he had been saying, which was about the manoeuvres; and I told him about my visit to Anne Vilette. He knew, of course, the basic details of the plan I was working on. I had warned him not to mention it to another soul.

Ernst was full of his experiences with the army. He could scarcely talk of anything else, and he moved like a soldier, and rested his foot on the coping of the roof like a soldier, and laughed like one, and tossed his head. He described his commanding officers as magnificent, and boasted about the feats of his companions. After a while I also busied myself with the few things I had to do for my birds while continuing to listen.

Ernst had been to a play in Flanders, because during the King's visit there was a performance of Mithridate in the theatre in Dunkirk. Apparently the actor apologised to the Dauphinesse (this was the month before last, just previous to her return here, when she fell ill) and the entire audience roared with laughed at such an interchange between the stage and the on-lookers. It didn't sound so hilarious to me. I was watching the clouds which were gathering in the west and it was very much in my mind that unless Bronzine returned this very evening, I should consider him lost.

I would make no claims for myself as a clairvoyant and in fact all my life, because of that wicked involvement of Mme. de Montespan with La Voisin which led to the killing of my birds long ago, I have had a horror of such things. To me, the barrier between this life and the next is too fragile. I have no desire at all to make a hole in it, or I hadn't then. Nevertheless, while listening to Ernst I poured out grain for the other birds in a little tin I had, because the sound of it falling on the metal would tend to bring various of my pigeons back from the surrounding fields and trees. Ernst's laughter at his own jokes was so loud, I gave the tin an additional shake.

In Autumn we often have clouds which are dark grey above, but with a long sliver of open sky just between them and the earth. The sun shining through this gap coats all the land with gold. It is iridescent, as if coloured already with the effect of the impending rain.

Ernst's story had got to the point where the Prince de Conti laughed so uproariously that he fell into the orchestra. In trying to save himself, he caught hold of the cord from the curtain and brought it down on the lights, which of course caught fire. Whether or not anyone was burned to death in this fracas I never discovered, because the denouement of Ernst's story was pre-empted by a shout from me that came to my own ears almost like a call from somewhere else, so thrilled was I. I had had my back to the village of Versailles, but turning that way to adjust the spring of a box, I saw Bronzine cutting across the last swathe of land from the trees to the palace walls. This light, that I have already spoken of, turned him into the very figure of his own name, and although the flap of his wings was laboured they were burnished with light and unmistakeable.

Ernst had jumped up. I hoped that he would stand still, because I anticipated that the bird would be exhausted and I was afraid that the least discouragement might turn him away. Not so. I can see the picture now, Ernst tall against the sky cheering loudly and waving his fists, and that bird unhesitatingly coming on and on, the sheen of his wings lit by the light I spoke of, against the background of pewter coloured clouds.

On reaching the stone parapet he landed, and I could see, wrapped around one delicate leg before he started to strut across the leads, that Bronzine carried a message. He took several steps, and stopped. He stood still, and then perked his head, as if posing for some invisible memory, until he reached the other birds, from among whom he at once separated with his mate.

I scattered grain for him, and put out a small handful of fresh straw. Ernst was generous in his admiration and very curious about the message. As soon as I thought I should, I held out my hand for Bronzine and he jumped onto the back of it. He crooned. I held him closer to my head and he rubbed his beak against my skin. Then holding him with his legs laced through my fingers I took off the ring.

I let Ernst read the message. It said: "Father dead. Married Climène last week. Returning tomorrow. Francis, Lord Claydon, formerly

Viscount Alltwen."

CHAPTER TWENTY-THREE

Naturally this story became the talk of Versailles, by which I mean not only the marriage of Francis and Climène, but also the manner in which the news had reached court. Suddenly everyone wanted to see my birds, and ladies young and old and a fair number of men too, came clambering over the leads, their great skirts, their ribbons and tunics sweeping the gutters, offering the birds grain in embroidered gloves, and playing games.

As with every fashion, it came and went, but it left me marginally more respected at Court, because the Court liked, above all, to be amused. One afternoon I even encountered my father up there. I think that he had either almost forgotten the disgrace of being my parent, or perhaps taught himself to overlook the very fact that I was his son. Certainly when I realised that it was he who was standing with a lady looking down on the landscape in the direction of Marly, I was taken aback. It seemed that he had aged far more than I had in the last fifteen years. Seeing him in the broad light of day and at close quarters I noticed, in the matter of an instant only, how his face now looked; his legs in a pair of plum coloured stockings; one hand from which the glove was missing. In all this time, if I had caught sight of him at all it had been at a distance, across a room full of other people, and shaded, or even by candle light.

He felt my eye on him, and turned; and at first his expression didn't change. But I suppose the full light of day did as much for me as it did for him, and also a few seconds was enough to repair his memory of who I was.

They say when a man is drowning, that in the moments of extinction he experiences all he ever knew of being alive. I can only say that in the sudden moment of this encounter with my father, in that second when we looked at each other, and before he, with a very slight bow, blushed and then turned away, I felt my whole consciousness ravaged by all the feelings of thwarted filial affection that must have been mine for years. I wished that I could speak to him. The kindly and humorous expression of his eye when first it was turned to me while still occupied with thoughts of whatever conversation he had been having, made me long to speak to him. I knew, for example, that he had taken an interest in the writings of Descartes because three or four years before this his name had been mentioned in a conversation among some gentlemen when I was listening. It seemed suddenly, to me, a delightful thing to be able to talk to one's own father on subjects of mutual interest. Or to take his advice if one had dangerous enemies at court, as I had. All at once I could imagine it, although I had never before let the thought enter my mind.

As I watched him walk away, and noticed the altered tension of his body – a slight awkwardness in his previously relaxed gestures – I would have liked very much to imagine that embarrassment was not the only emotion that affected him; but I doubt it.

After this encounter I went down to my apartment and sat in the armchair that Bonhomme had been kind enough to get for me from the estate of the Duc de la Rochefoucauld's head lackey when he died. They can become very rich, the servants of Dukes. Monsieur Moreau, after all, was a lackey. And his collection of paintings in the four rooms of his apartment, which I have mentioned before, included three by Poussin, among them *The Funeral of Phocion* which I admired very much. He had dozens of others.

As for this other man, take the silk that was stitched around the arm of this chair which was now mine. Between the fingers of my left hand I could count three exquisitely made roses worked in very fine point and with gold as well as silk thread. Besides, I liked the background colour which was a dark lavender grading to blue-black, with the flowers etched in crimson. How many times had that lackey, a complete stranger to me, rested his fingers where mine were now? I imagined the bone of his skeleton inside my hand, until my mind was sunk as deep in melancholy as a bucket in a well.

How long I had sat there I do not know, but I was reminded very suddenly of the present by the sound of someone scratching on my door. The light had almost faded from the window, and Bonhomme was not yet such a reformed character that he was capable of remembering to bring me candles. I called once and the door opened. Standing in the crack was a frightened little maid of about ten years of age, in a skirt of very pale blue cotton damask with an apron over it.

She made a curtsey and said in a voice so quiet that I could scarcely hear, that she wished to leave a message for Monsieur de Brisse. I was glad that it was dark enough for her to be unable to see me clearly. "Put it on the table there," I said.

At that moment Bonhomme appeared with a lighted candle, but he had the intelligence to make use of it to show my visitor to me and not the other way around. He took the message. "Who is it from?" I said.

The little maid whispered something to Bonhomme. The candle light on his own face lit up a sardonic twist of the muscle at the corner of his mouth. It exaggerated it. Or my mood exaggerated it. Everything that belonged to the morbid drama of life; whatever takes place in semi-darkness or in that part of a person's character from which the twists and turns of the mind have cut off direct light in the same way as a sharp angle in a windowless corridor cuts the light from a door, seemed at that moment to deserve attention from me.

If you imagine I had forgotten Fanette for more than five minutes together in all these days, you have not understood my feelings. And it was the fact, freshly brought home to me, that a creature too ugly to be acknowledged by his own father could hardly win the love of any woman, that had occasioned my present melancholy.

Bonhomme glanced across at me, the glint of his eye darting, like a live thing sent to take a wary look on its own account. He did not know how to broach the subject that lay behind the visit of this young woman. For my part, I was trapped. I did not realise that anything momentous was about to happen, but I felt I could not move out of the area of my pool of darkness for the familiar reason that if I so much as stepped across the room in order to give a few sous to this little messenger I should only cause her terror.

Bonhomme forestalled me. I saw that he was taking some coins out of his purse. I hoped he gave her enough. She kept glancing across towards me. I couldn't hear what she said. Then, to my dismay, with quick little steps, she was suddenly across the room and right before me. She curtsied and looked straight at me, and I swear I could have been an ordinary person for all the change there was in her expression.

"Monsieur," she said, "My mistress sent me to ask you to attend the play tonight. If you were not at home I was to leave the message. But if you were here, I was to speak to you myself. I hope that I have been obedient and done this correctly."

I was in the dark in more ways than the one. Who might the mistress of such a simple and small girl be? And what could she possibly have to say to a person like myself? I put this to her, but like a child repeating a lesson, she said that she had given her message, and was not authorised to add to it. So I let her go.

The whole incident had amused me, but for some reason I was extraordinarily slow at arriving at the hidden importance of it. The sluggish mentality of melancholy made me stupid, and I could see that fact reflected on Bonhomme's face when I asked him what was to be the play. Even when he said it was Iphigenie I was still unsuspicious, because Fanette had always acted in Paris and I had no reason to suspect that she had secured a place with the company at Court. But now, at last, although he did not dare to pronounce her name after the way I had behaved on that previous occasion, Bonhomme succeeded in making me guess that it was Fanette who was to play the part of Eriphile, the daughter of Helen.

I was so shocked when I realised what this meant that I had no idea what to say, and for some reason or other I made a great sweep with one arm which knocked a bowl of Chinese manufacture clean onto the ground where it broke in pieces. "Leave it!" I said to Bonhomme. An entirely impractical order, because after all, once a bowl is broken you might as well sweep it up. But it soothed me to be able to hear my own voice sound firm and commanding. He looked at me. A rush of heat went through my veins. I was about to say something like, "How dare you look at me?" but I forced myself to be calm. I turned back to the chair; sat in it.

"I will dress in half an hour's time," I said to Bonhomme. "My best brocade coat and the crimson silk embroidered tunic." He went out of the room, and I gave myself up to wrestling with my soul. As soon as the door was closed I sprang out of my chair, but found myself very weary and sat in it again. So this little maid had been in the service of Fanette, but why had she been sent to me? Why had Fanette sent this message to request my presence at the play? How could she encourage me to pay her attention? The possibility of mockery occurred to me, but I dismissed it, because I knew that it could not be the explanation. But I was equally certain that it could not possibly be her wish to have me as an acknowledged admirer. The very idea, and my mind flinched from it. What would the frivolous onlookers of the Court say to the spectacle of myself paying court to any woman, leave alone an actress of some note. I had visited the prostitutes on the Pont Neuf like everyone else, and it was true that public opinion was robust on the subject of incidental deformities which any gentleman might be obliged to put up with as his portion in life without expecting his attractions for the opposite sex to be compromised at all.

But I was a different case. There is no need to reiterate the details.

I had a mirror in my bed chamber which I went to, and stood in front of it there and then, dressed as I was, without any help from the reinforced framework sewn into my best coat, and the high heels and wig that I would wear to the play. I saw a particularly small and ill made person, but not, for example, dirty; the skin not marked, but in fact rather good than bad, and so on with a few other details. I had very carefully studied my ways of moving. Although I couldn't walk or do anything else with grace, I did all these things in an inward, quiet, way, which salvaged what dignity was to be had from the wreckage of my person. If I was prepared to be humble enough to let the world see me receive what I obviously did not deserve – I mean the attention of a beautiful woman – and perhaps accept some abuse for my temerity, then I could take my chance.

I stood confronting myself, so still and so locked in thought that I was unaware of the return of Bonhomme until I saw the reflection of his face behind my own. I nodded at him, and turned around. He had brought my clothes, and I proceeded to dress, with his help, in silence. I found that he had not prepared my tallest wig, but another which I had before.

"Do I look better in this, then?" I said.

"I think so," he replied, with a grave air. "Do you mind, Monsieur?"

"I'll take your advice," I said. There was a pause, then he said, "Were you planning to be accompanied by a friend?"

I had considered this point, but who could I press into my service? If I took Ernst with me, with his great height alongside my smallness I should be rendered even more ridiculous. If Francis and Climène had been at court that would have helped me, but they weren't yet arrived.

"I think I shall have to go alone," I said. I expected no other comment from him, and I wasn't looking at him. He was, indeed, silent for a few moments.

Then, "May I have the honour of attending you, Monsieur?" he said to me. I looked at him in astonishment. He met my eye with a new firmness. I could see that a slight flush tinged the sallow colour of his cheek, but he maintained a steady composure, made a slight bow, and repeated what he had said. I looked again, and now for the first time I noticed how he was dressed. This man, who had been used to wear the meanest of clothes which were never pressed or clean, was all of a sudden quite respectably got together. He had on a coat which while not new was not torn either, and nor was it put on so carelessly that one shoulder hung and the other clutched at his neck. He had linen of a sort, and it was washed. He looked capable of lending credit to the gentleman he attended, and so I accepted his offer.

Since my arrival at court, I had witnessed all sorts of wonderful things. For example, I happened to see the occasion, as a child, when Louise de la Vallière rode an Arab horse bareback in the Tuilleries gardens, watched by the King. To my child's eye she looked like an angel from heaven, with her curls flying in the breeze. She had only a silken cord as a bridle, and yet after trotting for a minute or two, she sprung to her feet and stood upright on the back of the horse, and she did that several times. The Italian ambassador stood by and was so rapt in admiration that he wrote about it. Perhaps it is his account that partly colours my memory.

And of course I had been to the theatre a hundred times; more. But this occasion eclipsed them all. The bewilderment and confusion that I had felt on first receiving Fanette's message had dissipated, and I felt a most enormous joy. My heart was nearly bursting out of my chest. I joined the noisy throng, hearing the chatter of my fellow courtiers as if it was music, and breathing in the many scents of the crowd; the odour of musk and roses from cloth, and the smell of garlic, cloves, the perfumed fans, the smell of the floor and of piss around the pillars. I loved it all, and I was followed by Bonhomme carrying my sword.

I had to wait until the second act before setting eyes on Fanette. Her voice was then the first to be heard. Have I mentioned her voice? She had a most unusual tone that had almost a little crack in it. She began: *"Ne les contraignons pas, Doris, retirons nous."* The lines will be familiar to you. But do you know, I even forget who was the actress who played Iphigenie; and Clytemnestra. It could have been Chamel and Beauval both, for all the attention I had to spare from the rapture of watching Fanette.

The play being over, the King went to supper and most of the court with him. But I had sent a message inviting Fanette to sup with me in my apartment, and she had accepted. In my note, I quoted Quinault's reply to the game of Love Questions on that occasion when the King invited him to play. It was the third that interested me. The question was 'Should one hate someone who pleases us too much when we cannot please her?' And the answer he gave was, 'Yes, but it would be difficult to do so.'

In my apartment, with Bonhomme's help I had assembled an excellent supper. After the play I hurried back there and stood in the dimly lit room like a man waiting for his execution. Or his transfiguration. For ten long minutes I could hear nothing but the beating of my own heart. The occupants of the adjoining apartments were all silent or absent. I felt as if, should Francis whistle to me from England, I would hear it. At last without any preliminary sound of steps in the passage way there was a little scratching on my door, and Bonhomme, who I had thought still on an errand to the cellar, appeared and opened it. Fanette stood on the threshold, with that little maid just behind her. After a moment's stillness, she smiled with the sweetest air, putting her face slightly sideways and saying just my name. She made the sort of curtsey that only dancers can, when every part of the body lends itself to the movement although I realise that I was so in love with her that if she had coughed I would have thought hawking and spitting beautiful.

With the greatest effort I broke the spell that was holding me speechless and unable to move. It was necessary, after all, that I should show myself capable of rational conversation.

She came into the room and said something to the little maid which I couldn't hear. I asked her to sit. I watched Bonhomme come forward with some wine, and I could feel my whole body trembling, but I was so confused I remember worrying in case it would cause Bonhomme to spill the wine, as if my wildly beating heart could knock the glass out of his hand. But in spite of all this, the fact was that I sat at table with Fanette, and we ate together, and she looked at me without appearing to be concerned at my ugliness. And we talked about many things.

When she had been with me only two hours she said that she must go. I felt bitterly disappointed. I could have wept. I couldn't believe that I would be able to bear the sight of the very walls of my apartment after she had gone. I thought I would die unless I could keep her with me. If I had been a handsome man, like Lorraine for example, I'm sure I could have persuaded her to let me embrace her and she might have stayed with me. And yet I loved her far too much to wish her to have such a fate as to take a very ugly man, and one without real wealth or importance, as her lover, So I accompanied her as if I could bear to let her go.

At the door, she curtsied while thanking me, and when in this graceful way she had lowered herself to a certain point, she took my hand and kissed it. I was beside myself. I said nothing. I watched her pass through the door, and I think Bonhomme took care of me and put me to bed. I thought to myself, do all men feel like I do then, when they love a woman? But I gather that perhaps the answer is no.

CHAPTER TWENTY-FOUR

I remained absent from court for several days. When Madame came into her drawing room from her bed chamber on the first morning of my return I could see that her health had deteriorated. She looked ill. At once all my store of bliss was knocked out of my heart like fruit carried in a basket which is overturned. If her skin was sallow before, it was positively sunken now, and even her eyes looked small and tired. No one could have looked at her without longing to comfort her. I cursed myself for my brief absence on business of my own, when she was surrounded by enemies who daily crept closer and closer. How could I have left her in such danger and thought of anything else!

Soon after the Princess entered the room the Chevalier came in from the ante room with Monsieur and his other friends. His manner illustrated his sense of his own power only too clearly. He carried on a whispered conversation with Madame de Grancy in a manner which everyone who observed it knew to be insulting. With deliberate insolence Lorraine did not stop his charade in order to greet Madame as he should, but produced instead an absent minded bow. She appeared not to see, but her face and her whole bearing showed signs of weariness and melancholy. There was an awareness throughout the room of the Chevalier's intention, which was done to belittle the Princess. And yet, at the very same moment, right down the side of his face the crease of his smile made a fold in his skin as if good humour was the essence of this man. Hatred and fear are foul emotions and I burned and froze where I stood, utterly tormented. For the moment I could do nothing to protect Madame but feel her pain as if it was my own heart that was being cut out. I tried to console myself with the thought of my plan for Lorraine's unmasking. There might come a day when he would awaken to the realisation that others also might conceal unexpected qualities from the casual eye. Little did he know that I was already assembling a trap for him which, once it was primed, would never let him go. The interview with Fanette might have delayed me a day or two. God willing the same business might delay me yet more, within reason. But not even she would deter me from the task I had undertaken to bring about the downfall of this man, who was Madame's sworn enemy.

Covertly, I looked from him to Madame and back again. To see her look so ill and so constrained – although she held herself with courage and dignity as usual – and that enemy so nearby and so glossy with his evil prosperity, was enough to enrage any man. Her ladies of honour, who were with her, happened to be very taken up with some tale told by Madame de Vieuville, but although at the same time they were politely attentive to Madame, their laughter was at odds with her mood. The Abbé Dubois had come in, and as you know his duties in connection with Madame's son, made him welcome when he would not have been for his own sake. But she listened to him with only half an ear. At this point her eye settled on myself, and an idea seemed to occur to her.

She sat down, but when the *tabourets* were about to be placed for those ladies who were entitled to sit on them, she said that she was not well; that she would return to her bedchamber and rest, and that they could all go.

There was the sort of reaction that you would expect. This courtier expressed concern, that lady offered to fetch a special herb, this one brought a glass of water. Little by little each suggestion was taken or set aside, and while Madame herself retired again into the next room, one by one the others all dispersed, except myself.

When they were all gone, a servant appeared at the door, surveyed the room, and shortly after Madame herself emerged again alone. This time, as she approached her chair she beckoned to me, and I came forward and seated myself on the floor at her feet. For a moment she looked at me with her tongue just visible, pressed against her upper lip. Those lips were pale. Her cheeks looked thin too, and yet with a heavier outline. I wondered if she had been denied the pleasure of hunting with the King recently. I waited for her to speak, as I should do. She sighed first. Then looking at me she said,

"Well, my goblin. Poor Theobon is gone, and I miss her dreadfully." She sighed heavily and I thought she might fall silent. I waited with my eyes fixed on her. Eventually she said, "When I saw you just now, I thought, I do still have one friend. Why should I not tell my troubles to my goblin, because everyone must have one friend to confide in."

"Madame knows," I said, "that I am as devoted as I am honoured."

"Still?" she said, with a little return of her former playfulness. "I heard that you were in love!"

This gave me a terrible shock. "Who told you, Madame?" I said.

She laughed outright. "How can you ask such a question in this place? I should think the very walls of Versailles could pass on a morsel of gossip that lacked any other messenger."

I could only stare.

"Well, is it true?" she said.

"It is true that I am in love, Madame, but the lady, although she was kind enough to dine with me in order to thank me for a small service I did her, is out of my reach."

"She is an actress," Madame said. The surprise in her voice implied that I must be mistaken.

"By your leave, a very beautiful bird perched in a tree is out of reach of the man who might wish to hold it in his hand, and not because the one is socially more insignificant than the other."

She said nothing. She put her head a little to one side. And then she said, "Dear goblin, you may find yourself mistaken."

I could not help smiling. I had to lift my hand to cover my mouth while I smiled because I simply could not keep it shut.

"Ah!" Madame exclaimed. She paused, and then added, "I know that I am plain, but by your leave, Goblin, you are more so. And I was born a Princess, and you are poor. But yet you are far happier than I am. My heart is so heavy I can hardly make my body cross the room while I have to carry it inside my breast."

I could not bear this. I said, "Madame, your happiness is worth far more to me than my own. Although I admit to being in love like any man might be, nothing – not even this – can take precedence over my devotion to your Highness. I am above all, your slave, and there is absolutely nothing that I would not do to serve you. You comforted me when I was a child, and when no one else pitied me. If I can help you in any way I will do that sooner than save my own life."

A tear ran down her cheek. She rubbed it away with her fingers, like a simple country woman.

"Would you believe it," she said, "that devil (she meant the Chevalier) told Monsieur that I sent a letter and 500 pistoles to Sinsanet, and he believed it. How could Monsieur believe such a thing, do you think? Apart from his promise to me that he would not believe any scandalous suggestions made about my behaviour, I never have such a sum of money to spend, except on New Year's day, and he knows it, since it is he who takes and spends all the rest."

I was well aware of this. Monsieur had the right to all Madame's money inherited from her father, and he spent it; often on the Chevalier de Lorraine, or costly trinkets for others who it was best not to mention. Such an accusation was typical of the frivolous cruelty that the Chevalier de Lorraine encouraged.

"It turns out that that imaginary letter was the excuse for sending Theobon away. They said that she carried it. Anyway, I have decided that I shall go and finish my days at the convent of Maubuisson. I spoke to my aunt when I was there last. I don't think she thought that I was serious, but I am."

I felt very anxious at this idea myself, but said nothing. "I asked the King's permission to retire from Court and enter the convent," Madame continued. "I explained to him that this was no sudden idea, but one I had kept for some time. He could ask my aunt to confirm it if he wished. I used to be convinced that it would be a terrible life to live as a nun, but now all I can think of is getting away from Monsieur's friends."

"It would be better to discover means of silencing them, "I said. "It would be better to have them afraid of offending you, and so that they dare not take any action to harm you."

She only sighed again, looking down at me out of the corner of her eye as she rubbed the nail of her right thumb absent-mindedly with a finger of her left. The day was very quiet. Sometimes before the onset of Winter nature seems to hold her breath. And indoors many members of the Court who had gambled through the night, or part of it, were still in bed.

"Madame," I said, "I am convinced the Chevalier poisoned Madame Minette."

"I think the same myself. But what poison could he have used? No one put anything into the cup except the footman, and Monsieur drank from the same jug of chocolate and came to no harm. The clothes she died in were burnt. What proof do you think you can get, after all this time? Nothing but positive proof can be of service, if I understand you correctly, and how do you imagine you can get that?"

"I will have to travel to Italy," I said. "I plan to go soon, and there I will track down the monk who sold the poison to Lorraine which he then sent to d'Effiat. I have found out enough already to make this possible."

"Do you think Lorraine will care, even for your proof?"

"He will have to, Madame, because otherwise the King and Monsieur will be told, and Lorraine must be well aware of how he would be punished. I am sure that he sent poison from Italy to d'Effiat, and Monsieur d'Effiat administered it somehow. Or possibly" I added, remembering the account given by Olympe de Soissons, "Madame de Grancy. Besides, spiteful and wicked people are also cowardly, and so we shall find the Chevalier and his friends."

She allowed herself the luxury of imagining for a moment that I might be right. And I, in the darker recesses of my mind, did my best to conceal the dread of leaving her alone at Court with these evil and cunning parasites who could so easily harm her while I was away. It made my heart grind in my chest. She was sad today. But she would forget this crisis later. Monsieur would become "kind" again, and Lorraine might see his chance. "Who knows?" she said now, continuing her train of thought. "Who will you take with you?"

I had also decided to take Bonhomme into my confidence, but had so far said not a word to him. She was silent for a few moments, and when she spoke again she had forgotten her question and spoke of something else.

"The King told me yesterday," she said, "that my husband has asked him, urgently, to persuade me to be reconciled with him. Can you imagine! I was so taken aback that I looked at His Majesty with my mouth hanging open. Here is Monsieur one minute accusing me of all sorts of hideous crimes, and sending away my dear friend Theobon, who will soon be in serious want unless the King doubles her pension. And the next minute he wants to be reconciled! I told the King that I couldn't understand it. If my husband had been unable to care for me when I loved him deeply in the past, how is he going to suddenly be my friend now? He promised before not to listen to calumnies but his resolution hardly lasted a week."

"I think he does love you, Madame," I said. "You and he are good friends when D'Effiat or Lorraine are not standing by to sneer. Look how happy he was when you played lasquenet with him last week and gave him a new set of ribbons. He laughed so loud at your joke about the street songs that I thought he'd never stop."

She smiled at that. Then said "He would like me to be pretty."

"I am not so sure, Madame. Monsieur is pretty enough for both of you."

She threw back her head and gave a great laugh, and then put her hand over her mouth like a child.

"A really ugly man like myself," I said, "is in a different position."

"Oh yes. And I hear that the beautiful Fanette will never speak to

Monsieur Le Grand because he made a disrespectful remark about you. You have touched her heart, Goblin."

I said, after a pause, taking a great risk because such a remark was very intimate, and I should only have made it to a friend of my own rank and age, "And that may have to be sufficient for me."

She understood entirely what I meant. She was silent for a moment, so that I was very much afraid that I had offended her; but then she said while looking past me, and not catching my eye, "From what I understand of the life of an actress, a patron is absolutely necessary. But even then, matters are precarious. Theobon tells me in her letters that your Fanette dislikes the sort of obligation involved with many lovers, and the shallowness of relationships of that sort. Perhaps she thinks that she may find in you, who really love her and who have shown charity without any hope of reward, exactly the sort of fidelity and comfort which is more important to her than a handsome body. Lorraine, after all has a handsome body, and who could find happiness with him for very long? And Fanette is learned, I'm told. There are ladies who would as soon read a book as eat mice, but she is different, and if she is clever think how she will enjoy the company of a scholar like yourself, Goblin."

I was astounded that Madame had taken the trouble to find out so much about my friend. Gratitude stifled me. I could not say a word.

On that subject: two days after Fanette had dined with me in my rooms, and two days having gone by in which I was alternately in hell and heaven, either full of joy at the memory of her visit or in despair because it was over – two days when I tried to occupy myself fully with plans for my enterprise to entrap Lorraine, I received a message from Bonhomme's hand. He came looking for me, and found me near the King's library.

I took the folded paper from him thinking it might be from Ernst. But no sooner had I started to unwrap it than I was first puzzled, and then enraptured and amazed to find that it came from Fanette. She thanked me for the entertainment of two evenings before and asked if I would honour her with a visit at her lodgings which were now in the village of Versailles.

I doubt whether any man before or since has stood on that place – that square of polished boards – and been so happy. I put the letter in my pocket where it lodged like a hot coal. I went back to my apartment and told Bonhomme to have Maud fetched and that I was going into Paris. It was my intention to buy Fanette the most beautiful flowers, to get her a square of silk from Limenage, to fetch a basket of dove's eggs. I almost forgot to answer the note, and I barely controlled my joy well enough to refrain from smiling at Madame Gordon when, in all my haste, I nearly fell over her on my way to the courts.

When the evening came I had worn myself out. I dressed with great care, letting Bonhomme decide one or two things, but above all I tried to compose myself. If, by some miracle, Fanette was prepared to overlook the deformities of my body, my mind was all that I could call upon to supply the deficit, and if I became so agitated that I behaved and spoke like an idiot, then it would be all over for me.

I set out eventually timing my arrival for when she would be back from the theatre. There was a cool breeze. The twilight seemed hung with jewels. Had she invited me because she felt herself to be in my debt I wondered? This possibility – this likelihood – tormented me. If I had been less in love with her I should have allowed that to be an ample bargain and helped myself just as I would have done if someone lent me his house or his table. But here I almost turned back towards home because I was so fearful of unwittingly extracting a sacrifice from her. Maud, in response to my body's involuntary recoil, stopped dead and waited. But then went on again.

When I reached her house, I was enchanted with it. She had the quaintest and most charming household. The maid who had come first to my room was a foundling who had been apprenticed to a cobbler in Murmansk, so she was not even French. Then she had been stolen by a gypsy to whom she was delivering a pair of boots, and he travelled with her thousands of miles, for what reason one cannot imagine. That gypsy habit of stealing children has always puzzled me, because small children are not so useful and they have to be fed. Perhaps they only steal unhappy children.

Her name was Isabel, and whether in consequence of this strange upbringing or not, she had the deportment of a mouse and the courage of a lion. I told you how she looked at me when first sent to my apartment with a message. And when I found her at home with Fanette she was running about, and a large black servant – would you believe it – had to carry out her orders, which he did with colossal good humour. I thought once or twice he might crush her by accident, but he was as nimble as he was huge.

Among the other gifts I had sent Fanette in the afternoon was included a basket of fish from the Pont Neuf, and this man had cooked it for our dinner in a way taught to him by his grandfather, with herbs and spices I had never heard of. But I found it almost impossible to eat anything, although it was delicious..

"The flavour is strange," Fanette said. "Not everybody likes it."

"I would like it very well," I said, "if only my heart had not so overflowed its place in my body that I have scarcely any space left for food."

When she heard what I said Fanette blushed. She looked so lovely I could not help staring at her. She dropped her eyes, and the lashes looked as if they might burn as they rested on the skin. After that she spoke very little.

I began to despair. There was a long silence, when the wind suddenly rattled a glass that was ill fitting in the window. At that moment the blackamoor came in again with fresh candles and another bottle of wine. This wine was of a different vintage than the wine before. I found it extremely good, and somehow whenever I reached out for my glass it was as full as it had been before I drank from it last, which I think was his doing. It made me talkative. I began to tell Fanette about my birds, and she had never heard of them and wanted to hear more. She sent Isobel to fetch a book which had apparently belonged to the gypsy, but which had been mostly torn out of its covers except for two exquisite paintings of birds from Africa. To look at this better Fanette asked me to sit with her near the fire. She patted the cushion right beside her and I sat down with the cloth of her skirt almost over my own knees. Then as she held the book, she let her fingers touch mine.

When I saw that her hands were trembling I took mine away. I could not bear the idea that I frightened her. But instead of being grateful, she seemed to hang her head, and in a moment a great big tear fell onto the picture and ruined it. I just had time to see a portion of the paint run before my stumbling wits rescued me from the idiocy of trying to dry the page with my handkerchief. Instead I raised it to her cheek. I felt very calm suddenly.

"Why do you weep?" I asked her very gently. I touched her skin just above her lip with the back of my hand.

"Because I don't know what to do" she said, looking down into her lap.

"You don't have to do anything," I said. "Truly, if you imagine that I have done you some service, you have repaid me a hundredfold by visiting me in my rooms, and by inviting me here. There is nothing else."

I had not taken my hand away, and I could not resist stroking her cheek once more. Then instead of remaining straight, she leaned her head sideways, to increase the pressure of my hand, as if she liked it. I felt as if, instead of a heart in my breast, I had a horse there who had just jumped over a river or a cliff. She took my hand and kissed it. Then she held it in both of hers, but with her face lowered, and clasped it against her bosom and said, "I had hoped, Monsieur, that perhaps you loved me a little."

I thought I must have misheard her. The very thing that I vowed not to do – namely, to lapse into the bewilderment of someone whose wits had completely forsaken them – almost overcame me.

"But…" I said. "But I do most sincerely adore you. How could I not. Is it not quite obvious that I love you utterly. So much, in fact, that I will not let you love me. I am not fit for love, being made the way I am."

"Oh!" she said. She half raised her head. Good God, she thought I was impotent!

"You misunderstand me!" I almost shouted. "I only mean that I am too ugly to be loved."

Her mouth was half open, her face raised, and then she laughed. Within inches of my own eyes, this radiant face, the blue grey eyes flecked with a darker tint, her shining small teeth, her lips plump and pink and laughing so that a kind of music suddenly broke out and rang around her head and mine. I slipped the hand that she was still holding into the bosom of her dress, and with the other I caressed her face and brought her nearer, and laid my cheek against her own. And she leaned into me like someone who never wanted to get away, so I gave up that idea entirely. I became hers, and she mine.

CHAPTER TWENTY-FIVE

To another man it might have been a source of anguish that such an event as this between Fanette and me should take place at the very time, or nearly, when we would have to be parted for several months. Because I could not delay my departure in pursuit of the proof of Lorraine's crime. When I brooded on the progress of the *cabale's* hostility to Madame through the years since her marriage, and took note of the intervals and fluctuations of their malicious energy, I detected such a quickening of their resolve and increase of daring lately that if I had thought that I myself could protect her I would have given up the idea of leaving France. But I could not. For all the reasons which must now be obvious, my protection was inadequate. Instead, I could use my wits and my cunning in her service, and for that purpose this scheme of going into Italy to bring back proof of Lorraine's purchase of the poison, and the discovery of how d'Effiat or the Grancy had used it to kill Minette was the only sure strategy I could think of. But I must leave at once. To go to Italy and return again would take me all the Winter and part of the Spring.

When it came to parting with Fanette for many months, I felt so overwhelmed with good fortune that she loved me and accepted me as her lover that from one point of view I think I could have let myself be shut up in prison and still be happy. If we were parted for a while, the fact that we should come together again would give me enough to delight my heart and feed my well being and keep me fat with happiness.

I talked to Fanette about these plans. I took her completely into my confidence and she knew everything about Lorraine and his friends, and his malice and his treacherous ambitions. She knew about Madame, and she said she loved her for my sake.

And she said that she would visit Climène's little daughter, Ange, while I was away. I went one afternoon before my departure, to pay the assistant of Fagon for a visit to cure a bout of sickness. The baby was asleep. She lay in a cot of rough white linen like a peasant child because Climène had sent no money for her and my own funds were running low. She had curls as blond and soft as La Vallière's had been. For a moment my spirits dropped at the contemplation of what might be in store for her when she grew up. She was unaware of my own peculiarities for the simple reason that life was full of amazingly strange things to her, among which I was no more a cause of surprise than a tea cup, or a sparrow. I could hold her in my arms without frightening her.

A week or so after that first visit to Fanette I called for Bonhomme one day, and he appeared, rather to my surprise. The weather had turned cold. I wished a fire had been lit, except that it would have smoked, because the wind was in the north west.

"Would you fancy a journey to Italy?" I said to him. My leg ached. I twisted it round to try to appease the muscle, but the pain persisted. It became sharp enough to make me sweat and I considered taking some opium. This was a herb that Fanette's blackamoor had recently given me, and it was very effective. I loved it.

When he saw that I was in pain Bonhomme's mouth took on that sour twist that had been so familiar to me. However, I had to believe now that it was an involuntary expression of sympathy, "I have decided," I said, "to take you into my confidence. Will you engage to tell no other person what I am about to tell you?"

He put his head on one side, drew his lips together in an unattractive way, and nodded. He actually said nothing, and at the end of it agreed to accompany me on my journey. Of course, at the time it never entered my head that everything I had told him was known to him already.

And if what I have related of this particular time – of Fanette, and Ange, and Madame's increasing kindness to me – savours of the ideal, consider this. Most people have at least one moment in their lives when the butterfly of happiness seems to settle on, or near them. And so it stays a little while.

I began to prepare with sudden haste for my excursion to Italy, convinced all at once that I had left it far too late I was very busy assembling the small armoury of names, bribes, letters of introduction and so forth, that my friends at court, and the friends of the Maréchale, could supply, and which should take me within range of my quarry. Winter was approaching, and it was the worse time to consider a journey across the country, but I had no choice. And also I profoundly dreaded leaving Madame unprotected. It made me sweat at night when in those hours familiar to any man with a bad conscience or an over-burdened heart, I lay awake and thought how likely it was that Madame would be attacked by Lorraine when I was gone. And with myself absent, what hellish tricks might the women play? They had such opportunities to be private with Madame. I had nightmares in which I lived over again the still awful memory of their visit to the sick room of the little Duc de Valois. Bonhomme woke me. He said I cried out. He held the candle awkwardly, being half asleep, and hot wax fell on my face. But when at last I slept again I hunted d'Effiat through the dark maze of my dreams, convinced that he carried a knife. Which of course, he did.

When Madame questioned me anxiously about my means, because the journey to Italy would cost a great deal, and ransacked her own scanty store in search of a few pistoles for me, I eventually told her that the Maréchale de Clerembault had undertaken to finance my journey. She was so amazed that at first she would not believe me. I could see the thought passing through her mind that perhaps she herself had been mistaken in me, and my intellect was, after all, tainted with my body's weakness.

"You will never persuade me," she said, "that Clerembault would do such a thing. She thinks that any money spent not on gambling is an extravagance."

I couldn't deny it.

"Show it to me then," Madame said. I went and fetched only one of the purses of gold.

She gazed open mouthed, and then laughed. But then, with an expression of awe she turned to me and said, "She must believe that you can be successful with this scheme of yours. I will write…"

"Oh Madame," I said. "Please. I beg of you. "

She drew herself up. But although I had interrupted her, she forgave me.

"You are right," she said bitterly. "They open all my letters unless de Wendt carries them, and he is still away with the army. Oh, how I wish I could visit my friend like any other woman could. When Monsieur and I are staying in Paris, I think that it would take me only ten minutes to walk to her house, and it makes me mad."

She butted the air with her chin and looked, for an instant, very like her brother. As I looked at her, I seemed to hear again the Maréchale's voice speaking in that dreamy tone she used when recalling her first sight of Madame. Naturally I said nothing about this, but I remembered it. To those who love, the statements of others in the same predicament are unmistakeable. I am not meaning to imply that Madame shared

Clerembault's feelings in the same degree. Apart from anything else, I think that she was too simple for such sophistications.

Two days after this conversation, Madame submitted to theKing's wish to arrange a peace between her and her husband, and she told me about it. The King also promised to double Theobon's pension. Then apparently having got Madame's consent, the King brought Monsieur to Madame's room and said, "Madame, I have already told you how much Monsieur desires to be reconciled to you, and how your own willingness to make it up with him was only inhibited by a longing to enter the convent of Maubuisson. Monsieur will not agree to that, now or ever, but he does most sincerely want to embrace you."

Apparently – according to Madame who told me of it after with an air of affectionate spite, if such a thing exists – while this explanation was being made on his behalf Monsieur looked very earnestly across the room for a moment or two until a new box caught his eye, enamelled with unusual skill by a previously unknown craftsman in Germany and sent to Madame by her brother. Monsieur actually was so absent minded as to very nearly interrupt his brother to ask Madame about the box, but remembered where he was in time. He looked at his brother out of the corner of his eye to see if he had noticed. The King had reached the point where he was assuring Madame that he intended to cherish her interests with his brother more carefully than he had those of the first Madame, and then after exhorting them never to have explanations between each other after disagreements because the practice invariably perpetuated quarrels, he wanted all three of them to embrace. He said that he would put his hand in the fire sooner than believe any of the scandalous stories that had been told about Madame, and his brother agreed.

"And so we all three embraced each other," Madame told me. She closed her lips in such a way as to let me know that if her mouth had not been firmly closed, bitter and indiscreet comments on that embrace might have escaped. But to me it was a comfort to hear all this, because if nothing else it would buy time of safety for Madame during my absence. It would be bound to set Lorraine's plans back a little for the King to have expressed his wishes so clearly in favour of his sister in law.

A day after this the Chevalier de Lorraine first, and then d'Effiat and Mesdames de Grancy and Gordon sued for peace. Madame d'Epinay, who witnessed the interview, said that the Duchesse d'Orléans accepted them, but coldly. She said that Lorraine was forced to ask twice for the honour of an acknowledgement from Madame, and as the King was watching he had no choice but to spin out his obsequies for as long as she chose to stare back at him; which she did. It is extraordinary that a lady with such a daunting presence, so full of majesty when the occasion requires it, can be so simple, so amusing, so given to laughter when in private and with those she loves. It is also surprising that this charm which conceals the innate power of her royal blood does not also harbour some of the bruising facility for combat attributed to her country. But the fact is that despite the occasional hint to the contrary, Madame absolutely needed the protection of her friends. Without them she would perish, and I knew it. I never for a moment imagined that the *cabale's* repentance was sincere, or that this episode of diplomacy brought about by the King would be enough to protect Madame from future harm.

Fortunately Francis and Climène arrived back in France at the beginning of that week. From my point of view, it was almost too late. My loneliness during the first phase of their absence had turned into a bewildering busyness which left me almost without a minute to myself. And Francis himself was beset with the whole court who all wanted to laugh with him about the disclosure of how he had disguised himself previously as Monsieur de Bellefond's servant, and to congratulate both him and Climène. The romantic nature of their story made Francis and Climène the favourites everywhere.

When at last he came with me to look at Bronzine and to have me point out the exact direction of his flight when he returned, I had my chance to explain my plans. At first you could see that Francis thought the journey itself would be beyond me. And also he was sceptical about the means that I might find to uncover the truth. But I was patient in the way that I explained things. I laid great stress on the fact that the saddle that he had invented for me made long distances as easy for me as for any other person. And I succeeded so well in setting light to his imagination when I described the route I must follow that at one point he flung one arm in the air and said, "By heaven, I think I will come with you!"

I laughed to see how his eyes shone. I think I was beginning to feel the same myself, but of course he could not, and did not want to leave Climène. On the subject of his father's death I never spoke to Francis at all. To this day I know nothing about it, except that it was sudden.

I noticed that when he was with Climène, Francis' observant sense of humour often caught at details in her behaviour which lit a spark of laughter in his eye, although he might not actually say anything. She, of course, was as beautiful and just as wayward as she had been before. She had returned with her hair dressed á la Fontanges – a style that poignantly survived long after the death of that lady; long after the day when, out hunting with the King, la Fontanges had hastily bound up her hair with ribbons because it had fallen down. The style suited Climène very well. She had used a ribbon that was exactly the same dark blue as her eyes.

When she saw me first she shrieked and said, "Berthon, I had forgotten how ugly you are!" But she put her arms about me and embraced me so tightly that although I knew she had her eyes closed I could not help being grateful. The King happened to be giving a ball the evening after their arrival, and His Majesty had put Climène's name on the list of ladies chosen to dance.

I had one more visit to make to Madame de Clerembault before I was ready to leave Paris. When Bonhomme returned from his last errand there, he brought an amount of additional money with him which was the most that we could, with any hope of safety, carry on our journey. Bonhomme busied himself with concealing all this gold in a dozen ways in our clothes and other things. He had an acquaintance who was a leather master, and the two of them stitched away in corners until our horde had vanished into belts, stirrup leathers, saddles, and shoes and only one remaining purse of gold was to be carried.

I then received a message from de Wendt to say that the Maréchale wanted me to wait on her the following day at eleven in the morning. I went. I knew that she would want to know every detail of my plans, and that she would probably still have some improvements of her own to insist on, but I was to be surprised.

At first she greeted me just as I had expected. I expressed the warmest thanks to her, and she cut me off with a reminder that I myself was not the object of her charity. She also insisted that I should avoid Saulieu which was on the route I proposed from Paris towards Dijon, because a coach travelling from Lyons to Dijon had been held up recently close to the forest of Empoigne, and six horsemen robbed the passengers of everything they had, including their lives.

It was not exactly easy to pick and choose one's route in those days.

The roads are much better now, but then there hardly were any that could deserve the name, and it was hard to see how I could follow her instructions.

"Very well," she suddenly snapped. "I can see that you are not paying proper attention, Berthon, and I will overlook it in this instance but absolutely not in connection with what I am about to say to you. Sit down."

I looked, startled, for a chair. There was only one available, but it was a *fauteuil*. The Maréchale glared, and pointed at it. Expecting at any moment to hear a shout of outrage, I climbed into it.

"Now listen carefully," she said. I did not dare to put my arms on the rests, but tried to behave as if I was seated on a stool. "As I have mentioned before," she said, "I have exceptional powers of divination. Everyone knows this, and I presume you, who know everyone else's business, are also aware of it. I mentioned before that I foretold the death of Madame's first child, but I have had many other proofs of my ability. You are not, presumably, a sceptic, Monsieur?"

"No, Madame la Maréchale," I said, perhaps too hastily.

"I see!" Her face, as she was sitting with her chair half turned to me, caught the pale light from the window and that renowned complexion of hers glowed like polished steel. Her voice was equally hard.

"La Voisin..." I began, but she cut me off. She silenced me with the look in her eye.

"Don't mention that absurd creature to me," she said. "Kindly listen to what I am going to tell you, and remember it. I have taken the precaution of looking into the future in connection with this enterprise of yours, because I need to know whether you will succeed or not since it is my money that is being used. Unfortunately, although I have tried again, the ultimate outcome eludes me. I think all will be well, but I can't be sure. However, I have seen various things which may or may not be important, but one which you need to know about is that Bonhomme will die on the return journey. From what I can make out, he will be killed. Now – "

She paused momentarily with a look of exasperation, and I closed my mouth and tried to compose myself.

"The only reason why I am telling you this," she said, "is so that you will see to it that whatever evidence of Lorraine's guilt you may succeed in finding in Italy, Bonhomme is not carrying it on his person on the return journey. Otherwise if he is killed and robbed, you will lose the very things that you have travelled all that way to find, and which I, may I remind you, have paid for. You will come home empty handed. Have I made myself clear?"

I was appalled. But then I reminded myself that delusions about dreams and fortune telling are common, and Bonhomme was just as likely as I was to return unscathed. I realised that the Maréchale was watching me closely, so I dissembled. She was so insistent that I was obliged to lie about my religious convictions and to promise (an undertaking that I could perfectly well honour) to carry home whatever treasure of proof we acquired in Italy myself.

When she felt certain that she had made her point, the Maréchale was impatient to be rid of me. Other concerns always gave way to her insatiable appetite for gambling and I thought I heard, a little while previously, the sound of some new arrivals in the house below. I climbed down from the *fauteuil*. Madame de Clerembault indicated the second door to me, which led out of this room into a circuitous passage and finally a narrow back stair. I had made so many visits to her now that I had become a familiar. Turning to bow again at the door, I found that she already had her back to me.

CHAPTER TWENTY-SIX

During the last busy days before my departure I had to be careful never to look as if I had any enterprise that I was engaged on. If the Chevalier de Lorraine or his friends, in their constant watching, should guess anything connected to my business, there was no knowing what they might do. In fact Ernst told me that he had been talking with Clément when Monsieur d'Effiat had overheard something, and asked so many questions that they had ended up inventing an entire story including a marriage of one of Clément's cousins, to explain away a chance reference to Cardinal Alberoni. Even then, d'Effiat was not entirely satisfied. He may have talked to Lorraine.

The next day the Chevalier stopped me himself as I was leaving Madame's apartment to go to make some final preparations in connection with Salamandre and the other birds. I must have let some appearance of haste escape me, because I found my way barred by him. He looked at me with the most unnerving quietness. He let his eyelids fall, and without a trace of his habitual mocking or elegant smile, he seemed to be attempting to strip my thoughts bare with his eyes.

"What a hurry we are in," he said. My heart leapt. I remember how he gave a quick glance to make sure that no one else was watching, and then he took hold of my ear and twisted it, until he brought my face up sideways. I heard the rustle of a petticoat and a laugh nearby, and he quickly let go of me, but as it happened still no one came exactly where we were. He said, "What are you up to?"

"Nothing that would interest you, Monsieur," I said.

"How do I know that? You crossed me once." I made as if to pass him, but without moving his feet he barred my way by shifting his weight to the left. I had an inspiration. "I am going to race my birds," I said. "I am taking certain ones away from Paris to see if they will fly home again."

This way, if he heard that I had gone on a journey, he would assume that he knew the cause of it and would enquire no further. He stared spitefully at me, and then said, "You may have forgotten that you owe me satisfaction for an injury you did me. But I very rarely overlook these things."

Then he stood aside, and I left him.

I still did not leave Paris at once. I waited until after the masked ball, because I wanted to see Climène dance, and I waited a day more after that, because Francis arranged for the Duc de Vendôme to introduce him to Cardinal Alberoni, of whom he was the patron at Court. In that conversation Francis mentioned me by name, and obtained a letter of introduction to the Abbot of that monastery where I was to look for the monk called Morel. And I had decided to take one of my pigeons – not Bronzine, because he needed to remain with his mate, but Salamandre – and Francis, for as long as he was in Versailles, would look after the other birds and be there to receive a message if I sent one by Salamandre. I had had a basket made. When I added that to all the other baggage we needed another horse.

I saw Fanette last on the evening of the ball where she stood for a moment in the Galerie des Glaces. All the candles were lit. The actual flames of the thousands of candles were soft and their light muted in comparison to their reflections, which sparked and glittered against the polished silver of their hugely branched chandeliers, and in the glittering glass, in the hard shine of the silver benches, and in the polished floor like fire in water. The whole scene looked as if there were sparks everywhere but with flames that burnt nothing. In a gown made entirely of green and silver gauze embroidered with pearls Fanette was standing beside one of the four silver tubs planted with orange trees which were placed between each pair of windows. And as if arranged for her portrait, the ivory silken folds of the curtains embroidered in gold with the King's cipher fell behind her. This was the last time I saw her before I left Paris, and it was the image that stayed in my mind most clearly when I was away.

I was afraid that it might well be the last time that I should see her as my lover, because in my absence there was no knowing what new proposals she might get from another man. Fanette had told me that to her, fidelity and a constant mind was far more important than the conventional appearance of a man. And I could see for myself how I fitted well into her unique household. When I looked at Isabel, the blackamoor, and myself it was clear that Fanette was a collector of curiosities. I merely exemplified her version of a husband; a man whose appearance was exotic, but whose heart was true and generous. But she was also beautiful, and now that she played at the theatre at court she would find a new softness among those who wooed her. It almost crushed me to think how, in my absence, another might take my place.

Such a crooked piece as myself would fit into the jigsaw of love in one place only, and yet I must put it at risk. But I steeled myself because my service to Madame was something I had promised long ago, and life itself contained no argument that could release me from it.

CHAPTER TWENTY-SEVEN

At dawn on the 19th of November I set out from Versailles to travel to Italy. Bonhomme drove the coach which Francis had insisted that he no longer needed as he had bought a new one for himself and Climène, and I rode Maud. Another horse on a lead rein trotted alongside the coach.

I remember how the sun, barely risen from a horizon tinged with black and red like a dog's mouth, half lit the landscape rimed with frost. I looked back when we were clear of the village of Versailles. The palace itself I had rarely seen from this distance to the south east, and never in late Autumn or Winter, when it was less hidden by trees. And in the village of Versailles Fanette lay asleep.

Then I turned towards the road again.

A man must be half dead who sits astride a horse in the early morning and confronts the world without exultation. I rode with such ease now, and my horse was so good I felt as if I could cover the whole earth without even getting tired. I looked with fascination at the fields as we passed by. The land was well cultivated here and there were large tracts used for the growing of vegetables. When other travellers appeared on the road as they soon did, I took a good look at each one of them from under my hat and marvelled at what distance some of them might have come; even perhaps from where I myself was going.

At mid day we stopped at a prosperous looking inn to eat our dinner early, and then set off again. And at some point shortly after that, like a door being closed quietly on someone who is unaware that they are being shut out, the civilised world was left behind us. This is no exaggeration. It was quite simply the effect when Paris and Versailles were suddenly out of sight, and we found ourselves surrounded by nothing but earth and emptiness.

I rode on for some time before becoming gradually aware that we were no longer passing other travellers, and then, like a man waking up from a dream, I strained my eyes and blinked at the land to my right, and my left. There was absolutely no sign of habitation anywhere. Suppressing my surprise, I concluded that either we would come across a farm or a village soon, or that those people who came to court and said that all of France outside Paris and Versailles was dead and empty of real human beings had spoken the literal, and not, as I had always imagined, the fanciful truth. We rode on. The short day waned. And not one single person or building was to be seen.

I cannot describe the melancholy of that part of our journey. In fact, at a later stage of our travels we came upon land even more sparsely populated, but here I was at the beginning and utterly habituated to the crowds and bustle of Court life. So this emptiness struck me to the heart. I looked around with increasing desperation as the light faded. Nothing. The whole world could have been an empty place; Versailles a dream, dreamt by a man deluded with an idea for salving his own loneliness. I could scarcely believe that it ever had existed, or if it had, that this vast annihilation would not swallow it up.

"Surely," I called across to Bonhomme, "there must be some provision for travellers on the road to Lyons. Or have we lost our way?"

And at that moment the road which we had been on, which was simple enough and only just supported the wheels of the coach, became suddenly no more than a rough track. I assure you that this was the case. The roads are much better now. This was before the time of men like Jean Charles Philibert Trudaine, the Intendant of the Auvergne, and others, who took the building of roads in their areas in hand and improved them so much that they are now unrecognisable. But then they were pitiful. Bonhomme, who at the first lurch of the coach thought a wheel was loose, looked ahead at what the road had become with as much dismay as I did. Fortunately the weather had been dry. But at some previous date it had certainly rained and it was from one point of view reassuring to see that other carts or coaches must have travelled this way through the mud if the hardened tracks gouged out by them could nearly overturn us now. We went on, and a mile or so further I saw, dimly because the light was fading, the figure of someone walking towards us. This man turned out to be a pedlar on his way to Paris. He said that five miles behind him there was a farmhouse close to the road that provided travellers with a bed. Bonhomme spoke to him. Then he continued past us, face to face with that wilderness, all alone.

I looked back more than once, and the last time the just discernable moving shadow of the man was swallowed up before my very eyes by the darkness. Shortly afterwards we came upon the lodging he had described, and we ate and slept the night there.

I have described this first day at length because it made such an impression upon me. For some reason I had always imagined that the wider country of France was a place where the same (or similar) sights and conditions as were familiar in Versailles and Paris were scattered rather more widely and maybe in a muted style, but there nevertheless. You will say my own childhood taught me otherwise. But I grew up thinking that that terrible place had been uniquely desolate. And so it was in some ways, but not as regards the huge unpopulated wastes of land, the charmlessness of various terrains out of season, the absence of cultivated life.

At the time our first night's lodging was loathsome to me. If I had not retained, in the shadows of my mind, memories of that wretched hovel in which I spent the first five years of my life, I might have been more philosophical. But here I was, a man who had not slept outside the palace of St. Germain or of Versailles in fifteen years, and with only one nightmare memory of the conditions that the poor might have to put up with. I saw poor houses in Paris very occasionally, as when I visited the late footman's sister. But essentially I was the most ignorant traveller that you can imagine. What is more, I was accompanied only by one servant, and in no position to bring my own comforts with me.

When I stepped down onto the beaten earth floor of that first farmhouse, dug down into the ground as they are to the depth of as much as three feet, I felt as if I was going into an animal's den. The bitter cold that began to settle on the country when the sun went down was here transformed into a foul smelling heat. No one who has been in the same room as Madame de Choin, however spacious, can reasonably complain of the odour in any other place. But perhaps even the Dauphin who later became de Choin's devoted lover, would have found this other stench annoying. Bonhomme told me it had something to do with the grease used in the candles. It also had to do with the fact that there was an old man there who was extremely sick and who lay on a palette close to the fire.

However gratefully we seized upon this refuge as darkness closed in on the empty country side it was impossible to actually enjoy it. Madame de Choin after all – although I don't know why I repeatedly come back to the subject of that lady – was very clever, witty and much liked. The smell of her rotting teeth and the garlic she chewed were quite familiar at court, and only remarkable in her because so strong. But at least she was very amusing. Here the farmer's wife, dressed in a filthy garment tied with hemp around the waist, her feet bare, could hardly have been less so. She had a voice like a dog, and used it in the same way. She barked about the bad harvest, the poverty of the local farmers and the burden of taxes. She nevertheless produced some dark bread and cooked ham from a huge cupboard which served the double purpose of an almost empty food store, and a partition wall dividing the animals from the living quarters. She had two half naked boys for sons; I couldn't guess their ages.

I thought we must have hit upon the wrong house when following the peddler's directions. He had said, after all, that it was a farmhouse not infrequently used as an inn. But as Bonhomme reminded me, the harvest that year had been ruined. It was now November. Destitution settles very quickly on the countryside in bad times.

I would have had to share my bed with Bonhomme if he had not insisted on sleeping with the horses in order to make sure that nothing was stolen. The next morning when I woke he was already standing beside me. He helped me to dress as usual, and I drank some fresh milk and ate some bread. We were ready to leave when a sudden commotion announced the execution of some poor beast in the adjoining stall. I positively leapt up onto the threshold of the outer door which Bonhomme was holding open for me, and the relief of seeing even that wilderness, and being out of the hovel was immense.

I mounted Maud. She had been well fed, Bonhomme assured me. We carried several sacks of fodder with us, but this time the farmer had had enough to sell us what was needed for the night. I looked with a warm heart at the steam made by the breath of the horses, and breathed in the sharpness of the air myself with a smile. "Bonhomme," I said, "I am not sorry to leave that place."

There was ice on the grass wherever the shadow of a bush, or a bank, or a tree shielded the ground from the light of day. The sun soon began to shine, but with a deliciously cold light. In one place I saw the image of a whole tree etched in rime and perfectly drawn on the ground behind a tall lime's protecting mass, as if some massive artists had been there drawing with a silver point. There was some very thin piping of birds. I was glad to be alive.

Even the monotony inseparable from long travels was exactly to my taste. I enjoyed letting my mind wander freely through the landscape of my past life much as my body was carried through the landscape of France. I remember being preoccupied with recalling the words used by Bossuet to His Majesty in a sermon five or six months before, when he preached on Easter Sunday. They were remarkable. He had said, "Sire, yourself, your victories, your own glory, this unlimited power so necessary for the management of the State, so dangerous to the management of one's own spirit – this is your only enemy. *Voila le seul ennemi dont vous avez a vous défier*." I was enraptured by these words when they were spoken in the first place, and now I played them over in my mind with all sorts of speculation about the spirit of our times. Those words seemed to epitomise the grandeur of an epoch dominated by so magnificent a man as Louis XIV whose own advisers should, like Bossuet, offer the noblest and most exalted ideas for his consideration. Naturally the King paid more attention to religion now that he was falling under the influence of Madame de Maintenon, but I think that enlightened and noble aspirations were really native to him, as a man.

I also thought, with strong emotion, of Madame. When I had said goodbye to her, Madame looked surprised, as if she had forgotten that I was to leave her. I think she had kept her promise not to mention this enterprise to anyone and she beckoned to her Maid of Honour and told her to admit no one. The door to the ante room was closed.

"Goblin," she said, "surely you were not going until next week?"

"Alas, Madame," I said, "I am late already."

"You will be very cold!" she said, as if having only just thought of it. "My God, but how will you eat? Is your servant going with you?"

I reassured her.

"Wait!" she said. She had something for me. She opened the drawer of her desk and took out a small packet about the size of the palm of my hand. I have rather large hands.

"Look at it," she said, so I removed the cloth. It was a small portrait executed probably as a preliminary sketch by one of the pupils of Rigaud. It was very like her.

Unfortunately my heart was so full I found myself unable to speak.

"Put it under your jerkin," she said in a very gentle voice. I did so. "I will pray for you," she said. "And provided that the Good Lord does not ignore everything I tell him as He ignores my pleas regarding my husband's closest friends, you will return safely to me."

She held out her hand for me to kiss, which I never had before. I did not touch it with my lips, of course, but I felt the small fingers and smelt the lavender water that she washed with. Then I left.

It was strange to leave all these things behind, and to feel the influence of what had been my daily life being drawn by distance out of the tangled skeins of my consciousness like weeds being pulled. The previous day when we started our travels, we had heard the sound of the hunt at Fontainbleau behind us. We passed by too early in the morning for the chase to be under way, but a little later the sound of the horns had come to us across the dry and wintry fields, and from time to time the clamour of the hounds. Now we were too far away, and I was anxious to increase the distance at the same time as feeling this sense of loss at leaving it all behind.

I could see from the state of the countryside around us that the unusually early onset of the freezing temperatures of Winter had already now, in the second week of November, dealt a blow that nature would not recover from until the Spring. Some late clinging leaves had that dark, cooked appearance that is paradoxically caused by early frost before the last green leaves had fallen. Then, mulched with death and not dry like those leaves that change colour and become desiccated and fall, these ones hang and hang upon the hedge or mark the miserable remnants of a smallholding. And the land was very dry. The dreadful ruts in the road were the hardened products of rain that dated back to July. At that time, when the land would have been better without it, not only did it rain but I heard that there were hailstones, and the crops, naturally enough, had not survived. The result was as I have described. At Versailles one might hear of starvation in the countryside, but without understanding.

At about three o'clock in the afternoon, when the light had already taken on a baleful cast, we were crossed on the road by a chaise travelling from Dijon to Paris. Bonhomme stopped the driver and asked news of the condition of the way ahead, and whether on not we should reach the house of a certain country gentleman called Villeneuve, where we planned to lodge, before dark.

While Bonhomme interrogated the driver, I, seated on my horse, was a pace or two away from the very windows of the public coach. With my cloak covering the lower half of my face, for once I could be seen by strangers without exciting any uncomplimentary attention. Curiosity, however, and admiration of a sort I did cause, as I could tell by their staring, and their almost attempting to speak to me. The interest was mutual. A woman, with her head in a bonnet the type of which I had never seen in my life and wrapped in an extraordinary garment which, although made of the coarsest cloth had pieces of gold lace sewn onto it at random, almost made me laugh. There was a fellow next to her in an old fashioned wig who peered from side to side to take a look at me. He must have been wondering why a gentleman – as my sword and, at that stage, other details of my equipment proclaimed me to be – should travel neither in the coach, nor with a larger attendance. I would have wondered the same thing myself.

For my part, I was curious too. Presumably this coach had come past the forest of Empoigne and the village of Saulieu, which the Maréchale de Clerembault had forbidden me to include on my route. For the sake of this embargo I should have to make a detour via Précis sur Thil and Vitteaux. And yet no one in this coach had been robbed.

We set off again and were able to continue until shortly after sunset, and only then did we come upon a house large enough to be the one we sought. After a number of small farmhouses and one more prosperous than the others which we considered settling for, the retaining walls of a sizeable property loomed out of the gathering darkness fifty yards or so away to our left. I was seated in the coach at this point, having become tired of the saddle. I watched Bonhomme exchange some words with a rough looking man at the gate. A boy was sent at a run back towards the house, which fronted the gate from the other side of a broad courtyard. Bonhomme then drove the coach up to the door, by which time a man dressed more or less like a gentleman appeared on the steps to welcome us.

I had not been looking forward to this moment. I did not mention how the night before my face had excited the most impertinent curiosity from those peasants in the wretched farmhouse. And I knew, from my experience at court, that I could hope for little better from a gentleman. However, this man bared his head, and I also raised my hat as soon as I had my feet on the ground, and executed a slight bow. But apart from a twinkle in the eye, which I swear was humour, my host behaved as if he knew me already and was not at all surprised by my appearance. He led me into a great hall which was warm and hung with some tapestries but rather bare as to furniture. But there was not a single other person in it besides himself.

I was astonished. I did not know what to say to him. I didn't know what misfortune could have befallen this man that he seemed to have no servants indoors and no household. I began to be sorry that we had stopped there, but it had been the firm advice of Madame de Clerembault that we should. If Climène had directed me there I would have imagined some trick. Or Lorraine, and I might have expected to be murdered.

Bonhomme had gone off to see to my affairs and I thought that I had better do my best to behave as if I was at my ease. Two chairs were drawn up before the fire. No more. Had someone vacated the second before I came in? Or had I been expected? The Marquis – for such I assumed he was – took a glass from a table and filled it for me himself, recommending the wine as vintage from his own land which he then went on to say had failed completely in the last two years. He also mentioned that he had only six bottles left from previous years. That surprised me too. A gentleman at court would not boast about having so little of something when it was a comfort in life. I drank it and it was good. "Very well," I said to myself. "It seems that once one leaves Versailles, or at least Paris, there is no knowing what to expect and I might as well enjoy it."

I sat down by the fire and was soon engaged in the most interesting conversation about that adventure of Giovanni Borelli when he attempted to use artificial wings for flying. That apart, he had lived as a distinguished scientist and my host admired other work that had been done by him. But seeing that my interest was less scientific and more literary, he passed on to discussing the legend of Icarus, and from that to very interesting comments on the skills of Daedalus and resulting commentaries on the science of French fortifications. I began to be very hungry, wondering all the time if the kitchens were as empty of servants as the rest of the house, but my host carried on unstintingly with information about the ravelin, the demi-lune, tenail, and double tenail. Some years later I did come across a learned work on the subject by Manesson Mallet, but truly this man could have taught him how to suck eggs.

In the nick of time, before my thwarted appetite could have made me overlook the obligations of a gentleman, an inner door was opened and Bonhomme himself announced that dinner was ready. We passed through into a large comfortable room very well prepared and there ate some of the best food I have ever tasted outside of Paris. The more my appetite was satisfied, the more mystified I became. I watched Bonhomme out of the corner of my eye as he served us. I could read nothing on his face.

My host was more in praise of the fare than I was. He commented on everything as if it had been a gift from myself, and that, I soon discovered, was exactly what it was. Bonhomme had used part of the provisions with which we had left Paris, and it was he who had done so well in making our dinner. My host himself lit me to bed some time later without my having succeeded, by a very small number of discreet questions, in winning any explanation from him. Except that he did, whenever the drift of my remarks gave him the chance, protest about the ruined harvests and the fact that he himself kept hardly any servants indoors because naturally (naturally?) he could not.

There was, however, one woman in the kitchen, and without her Bonhomme and I might have left without discovering the explanation for this extraordinary household. The secret was revealed the following morning, when Bonhomme came to dress me. He brought with him a well dressed servant whose duties clearly lay indoors. "Where was she last night?" I asked Bonhomme with astonishment.

I could see that Bonhomme was amused about something.

"If Monsieur will wait until he is dressed," he said, or something like it. I remember him using rather a ceremonial style, which I took for humour on his part – "Marie and I will have the honour of showing him something of interest." So I held my tongue, and he shaved me and the girl behaved very well, in that she brought hot water and was discreet about my person. When I was ready Bonhomme asked me to make as little noise as possible, and to follow him. He had a taper lit, and he opened a small door on the stairs from which another staircase led down to the ground floor and a cupboard-like space giving directly onto the court yard. This we crossed on tip toe until we came to a large barn that formed as it were a wing of the house, but separated by the corner wall. A huge door was barred with a mighty slat of cast iron, but a wicket door was cut into it, and this Bonhomme quietly unlatched. First he sent the maid through it, and then me. It was almost dark inside. A voice called out in a muted tone, "Has he gone, Marie?" The maid servant put her finger to her lips, opened her eyes very wide, and looked behind me at Bonhomme. I became aware that there were groups of people all inside the barn, but moving cautiously and with no voice above a whisper. As I peered the light from the sun only just risen pierced between some boards of which one section of the middle of the end stone wall was built. The rays of light, as well as picking out bars of air full of dust illumined the shadows of many people grouped on the floor. All this took only a moment, and was ended by Bonhomme stepping back through the wicket, and opening the bar of the great door.

Then what a commotion. As soon as the light showed the figure of myself and Bonhomme to the people in the barn, and them to us, there were startled exclamations and cries from all about. Followed by absolute silence. I looked in amazement. There was a trestle table set up covered with food. There were thirty or forty in the barn – men and women, and one or two small boys and maids. They were well dressed, all of them, and the most senior were sitting on chairs which I instantly took to be those missing from the great hall. And with the utmost consternation they were all turned toward Bonhomme and myself.

At last a powerful looking woman in a clean white apron and with her sleeves rolled to the elbow in spite of the fact that this barn was none too hot – and I can see her now standing on a pile of straw as if she had her own kitchen underfoot and the full authority of her position as Monsieur's head cook, which she was, to back her – "Maria," she demanded. "What have you done?"

Maria giggled. I was surprised at that. I should not have laughed if someone I feared asked such a question of me and in such a tone. But Bonhomme stepped forward and said to all the company, "Please do not be alarmed. My master, who you see here, is Monsieur Berthon de Brisse and not, as your master mistakenly imagines, the tax inspector. Nor is he in any way a spy for that man."

I began to see the light. Here were all the servants, quite a deal of the furniture, and, I now noticed, the silver and hams and wine casks belonging to my host. It turned out that the master of the house, forewarned of a visit from the tax inspector, had mistaken my arrival for that of the dreaded official of the *Taille* and the *Aides*. As a member of the nobility he should not have been taxed at all, of course, unless he had committed some offence. And so it turned out, resulting in the inspector attempting to tax this wretched gentleman like a peasant. But he hit on a cunning plan to hide all evidence of his wealth, including his servants, in order to pay as little as possible.

The assembled company still all gazed silently for a moment. My figure silhouetted against the open door through which the day light now came, appeared to them I suppose like any other. My deformities were not apparent. Eventually a fine looking man with leather boots and a jerkin of livery said, "Where then, does Monsieur de Brisse come from?"

"My master comes from the court of King Louis," said Bonhomme. "He is acquainted with the King, and is on a journey to Italy."

Then there was such an outburst of exclamations, of apologies, of anxious remarks from some and laughter from others. Realising that I could not be clearly seen because of the darkness in the barn and the light of the open court behind me, for once I felt free to laugh myself, and I did. I laughed heartily, and all these good people started to laugh as well. Bonhomme looked as if he had never heard my voice in his life before. And at that very moment our host, attracted no doubt by the noise, came up behind me and what sort of a scene met his eyes?

I tapped him on the arm as he came up, and said "Monsieur le Marquis, we seem to have misunderstood each other."

"No, no. I assure you!" he said. "I have never seen all these people before in my life."

I was amused and rather at a loss as to how to reply.

"And I assure you," I said, "that I am the friend of the Maréchale de Clerembault, and no tax inspector. I would not know how to estimate for the *tailles*. I am a private gentleman at the beginning of a journey to Italy."

He looked at me with his mouth open for a second, then frowned, and demanded why I had not disabused him before. I explained that he had managed the whole affair so cleverly that I did not know that he was abused in the first place.

"But I was brought news that you were on the road," he said. "Or rather, that a man whom we all know by repute as being a spy for the tax collectors, had left Dijon on his way here."

"I came from Paris," I said. He looked amazed, as if no one ever did such a thing. And as we stood gazing at each other I realised, and I suppose he did the same, that he had made such a strong assumption of my identity on seeing me that either I had been embarrassed and not clearly said my name or he had not heard it.

"Tell me one thing," I said. "What caused you to be so sure that I answered the description of this villainous individual?" I asked the question rather firmly because I guessed the answer. I looked him straight in the eye, and in my mind I said to him that a man I would respect would rather stick to the truth now. He read me correctly and said, though in a quiet voice, "He has a hare lip, Sir. I pray you will excuse me for mentioning it."

And so that was the end of the awkwardness between us. I took a step back, mentioned my name in full, and bowed, taking off my hat again, and he also did the same, at which we laughed and, arm in arm, went back across the courtyard together. He called over his shoulder to his household to come at once and prepare breakfast.

"But Monsieur," I said, "Don't let them bring everything back from the barn I beg of you. Your tax collector is no less on the road from Dijon merely because I have come from Paris."

"How right you are," he said. "Gaston, bring only what is needed for breakfast."

But this was interpreted in a generous style and I have rarely had a good meal more merrily served by a greater number of servants on more splendid plates in all my days since. The food was flavoured with many stories of the countryside round about, and not least of their efforts to avoid the predations of the tax collectors. I had had no idea that the countryside was so oppressed. Apparently such a man would come into the house of a peasant or farmer requesting food, as travellers do, eat and drink, and then far from paying for it, he would present a bill to his host that would leave the poor man with nothing left to feed himself and his family. He might say, "The wine we've drunk here costs so much, and I can deduce from it that there is this and this amount which you have not sold, and therefore there will be such and such an amount left which you will have in store for yourself when I am gone, on which I intend to charge you this much. So here's your account for the wine. Then the ham was very good, and the tax for the salt that you must have used for it comes to so much..." And in the end he hands the poor man a bill for two thousand crowns.

Even so it was only the peasants who were taxed in this way. I never discovered what unfortunate event caused Monsieur de Villeneuve to be used so harshly, but I made sure to avoid any enquiry about it.

When we left, with many grateful remarks and good humour the retreat back into the barn was already under way. And I was very relieved that it was so, because Bonhomme and I had hardly been on the road ten minutes, when a spanking little chaise coming along in the other direction gave us warning that here was the very man. I held my cloak well over my mouth, which was quite understandable, the cold being what it was, and stopped the driver, who respectfully reined in the horse. I touched my hat, with as accurate a copy of the King's manner doing the same on encountering a washerwoman from the village of Versailles at his gates, as I could manage. I did mention before how invariably polite theKing was to all grades of people. With Bonhomme, who was driving my coach, drawn up behind me, I said, "Tell me, Sir, have you come from the direction of Dijon?"

The man, who held his hand against his face in a casual manner, but

I could see he was the one whose description had been thought to fit my own, responded with alacrity. "Then," I said, "will I find on my way any respectable house where I may rest myself? I am worn out after two wretched nights. I have only just left the last house and I am half starved. I was willing to pay handsomely for my dinner and my bed, but the man has nothing. A poorer place I never set eyes on."

I could see that each word meant more to my audience than the mere facts I pretended to complain of. He looked rather disappointed.

"Do you mean Monsieur de Villeneuve?" he said.

"Why, yes."

He looked at me. He had very large eyes; grey, and the lids very loose. It is a type of face I rather like. I felt suddenly sorry for the man. However there was nothing I could do about it. "Well," he said, "there is an Inn between here and Dijon where the coaches stop. You will see it on your right hand at about..." he cast a leisurely calculating eye first at me, then my horse, then at my coach. Bonhomme was swivelled sideways in his seat and staring into the field with the whip in his hand. Apparently the tax inspector had made his calculation and he said with a little smile, "At about five in the afternoon. I wish you good day Monsieur." Then he removed his hat, bowed politely as he sat, and I moved on.

CHAPTER TWENTY-EIGHT

The further Bonhomme and I travelled from Paris the more wretched were the scenes of life encountered on the road. I had never suspected that life in the country at large could be so like my own particular childhood experience of it. One heard rumours. And of course, having lived in the country myself once, I should have believed them. But perhaps a child tends to accept his own circumstances as in some way inevitable and he looks for no reason beyond the kindness or cruelty of the adult people who have charge of him. I now began to learn differently.

Versailles already seemed not only far away in terms of distance, but part of another world. It is not that I ever forgot that the object of this journey was to find and entrap the man who had sold poison to Lorraine. In fact, I doubt the journey would have been so interesting or the hardships of it endured with anything like the same relish if there had not been this dangerous objective. Neither was Madame's predicament ever far from my mind. If ever I was tempted to linger, or spend an extra night with a household that entertained me particularly well – and there were some later on – a certain image would appear before my inner eye. I will tell you what it was. I would see Madame sitting in her chair as clearly as if she were before my very eyes. I could see the folds in her skirt, the plump whiteness of her hand, her rings, her dressed hair, the tip of her tongue between her lips as she wrote; and standing not at all far off and looking silently at her the Chevalier de Lorraine. I can not describe how much this image frightened me. I would absolutely put my spurs to Maud, or if I was riding in the coach call out to Bonhomme to drive faster, or stop altogether so that I could be mounted and set a quicker pace.

But when all this is said and done, there lay before me many leagues of land that had to be travelled, both going and coming back. And I was too young and too full of curiosity to pass over it with my eyes shut. Neither would it have helped us to survive, since no man travels far in this place without the risk of going a good deal further than he ever intended, and finishing up in the other world. The previous Winter had been so bitter that we could not keep warm even in Versailles, and even the King himself stopped throwing open the windows, but agreed to keep them shut.

Now an exceptionally icy cold season had already set in again. It had set in on a landscape parched of rain, and, as I said, where the harvests had been ruined. Four days out of Paris I saw men and women whose skin was blackened by the weather and whose clothes had been flayed to rags, gathering grass to eat. I could not believe that they did really eat it. They dug up certain roots as well, but nothing that a pig would have wanted to swallow.

We heard news, when we reached the outskirts of Dijon, of a woman carrying bread on the road, who had been murdered for the sake of it near Tonnère. Bonhomme was insistent that we should hire another man to travel with us, but I would not agree. How would we find a man that we could trust? If we made a wrong choice, he would have a better chance of murdering or robbing us than anyone else.

At Dijon I intended to rest for two or three days, but the question of where I would stay occupied me very much. Climène had told me that very few country gentlemen resided in town these days and I might have to content myself with the bourgeoisie. This was a new term to me, and uttered by her in tones of such contempt that I was determined to avoid these people if I could, and asked the advice of Madame. She had given me the name of a certain Chevalier de Druce; a younger son of a noble family.

When we reached Dijon, I found it a relief at first to be back in what I took to be civilised surroundings. This town looked no worse than the poorer districts of Paris, and when by dint of Bonhomme constantly enquiring we found the house of the Chevalier, it was in an area of considerable prosperity.

I had taken the Maréchale de Clerembault's advice and decided to use a mask, although not a *touret*. Instead I carried a mask that I could hold over the lower part of my face. Bonhomme had one good coat which I had bought for him. Considering the roughness of the previous week's travel it was a miracle that we could present ourselves as well as we did.

I remember that I was extremely nervous. I stepped down from the coach with my heart beating somewhere in my stomach, as if it had escaped its natural moorings. I was as yet unaware of how deliriously happy the provincials would be to receive anyone from court, and how this would cause them to overlook my personal shortcomings.

But on that cold December morning when the many unpaved and

frost bitten streets of Dijon cracked under my coach wheels, I was not yet aware of the degree to which my credentials as a member of Madame's household, and a courtier, would supply the deficiencies of my youth and my ugliness.

I nearly fell when getting out of the coach but Bonhomme was watchful enough to right me. I looked around at first without remembering to raise my mask, but the servant who stood on the steps did not notice my face. I climbed up to the door using a stick. It had become fashionable to use these, and from my point of view it was very helpful. In the hall the Chevalier's gentleman received me with great respect, and with awe when I mentioned Madame and her letter to the Chevalier. He went away, but returned almost at once requesting me to follow him. On my very heels another of the Chevalier's household was greeting another caller, and this time I heard him say that the Chevalier would be very happy to receive him, but not until he returned from Mass.

I myself accompanied the Chevalier and his family to Mass, which was solemnised in a little chapel attached to the house. By the time we returned, upwards of twenty or twenty-five were assembled in the hall waiting. Everyone was polite. The two young gentlemen who seemed more or less to belong to the Chevalier, in the sense that they behaved not unlike gentlemen in waiting, treated everyone who came with courtesy. The noblemen from among this crowd of people, many of whom showed signs in their dress that they were extremely poor, were invited to dine with the Chevalier and taken upstairs by Monsieur Heurlant. The other visitors who were not members of the nobility were invited to dine apart with the other gentleman in waiting. These other guests were some of them members of Climène's despised bourgeoisie. They held official positions, or were merchants or lawyers. I was surprised to see such people received in a nobleman's house, but so it was, and they did seem to behave quite well.

Those noble guests who were badly dressed and clearly very poor were, in inverse proportion to their wealth, extremely proud. I was seated next to one of these, with my host on my other side, and Monsieur Heurlant not far off. At a certain point Monsieur Heurlant leaned across to me and mentioned that he had many friends at court, but in particular the Chevalier de Lorraine was especially dear to himself and to his mother. Did I know the Chevalier?

I should have expected this sort of encounter, and prepared myself.

Then I should have either denied the acquaintance of Lorraine altogether, or implied only the slightest knowledge of him so that no one could imagine it worth their while to send news of me to Paris. Alas, I was unprepared. I readily admitted to knowing the Chevalier de Lorraine and I dared not even appear to be too reluctant to join in Monsieur Heurlant's praise of his friend. Monsieur Heurlant mentioned other acquaintance at court, but always returned, with dreadful pride, to this one. However, the dinner did not last for ever and once released I dismissed the exchange, for the moment, from my mind. But if I only thought this had been a small irritation and nothing more, I was to learn otherwise.

After dinner the bourgeoisie were asked if they would like to join the Chevalier and his friends for coffee. They were made welcome by the Chevalier, but greeted with insulting condescension by these shabby Counts and Marquises, hung about with their swords and hunting knives to make sure that no one could mistake their aristocratic credentials. It made no difference apparently that the nobleman was dressed almost in rags and the lawyer, or whoever it might be, was dressed in silk and furs.

I began even at that point to speculate, in my own thoughts, as to the relative value of these different groups in society. A lawyer, who entered into conversation with me on the subject of the rights and wrongs of the laws regarding hunting struck me as more civilised than the Marquis who had harangued me on the same subject, but from a starkly different point of view, at table. The latter had merely bored me with a string of anecdotes about his own prowess and adventures in the field. But the lawyer asked if I was aware that the peasants were forbidden to hunt even the humblest and most numerous game for the purpose of feeding themselves and their families. When I admitted that I had not heard of it, he mentioned the fact that, to make sure that they did not kill any animals for the pot the peasantry were forbidden entirely to bear arms. And had I heard how, in consequence of this law, peasants in those areas where there were wolves lacked the means to defend their flocks or themselves. This was very interesting. I could see how a man whose life shaped him in that direction could become engrossed in the restructuring of new laws as well as the administration of old ones, in order to correct such bad handling of government.

But when they were all gone, and the Chevalier had kindly left me to be shown to my rooms, I began to feel anxious again, about that conversation with Monsieur Heurlant. Surely, I remonstrated with myself, the mere mention of Lorraine's name can do you no harm here, out in the world and far from Paris. I had no need to be reminded, since the thought scarcely ever left my mind, that in my absence Madame was at the mercy of her vulpine enemies like those same sheep described to me by the lawyer. I wished that I could hear some fresh news from court, and if I had been told at that moment that a man five miles away had yesterday's gossip from Versailles even I would have tried to walk there. It was then no wonder to me that these provincials hung with such ardour on the lips of those who, like myself, were recently arrived from Versailles.

The next day in Dijon, my host sent Monsieur Heurlant with a message requesting my company for a tour of the town, and I agreed with alacrity. I certainly could not enjoy solitude when I was so anxious about events at home. I had not realised to how great an extent the very process of moving forward – of travelling – tamed the impatience and anxiety of someone involved in a great enterprise, and here I was kicking my heels in the household of a gentleman of Dijon as if I was in a frame of mind to enjoy the pleasures of the provinces. It had been a mistake to say that we would stay in Dijon for three days.

The Chevalier and I went on horseback for this tour of the town, accompanied by Monsieur Heurlant. Various servants also accompanied us on foot. No sooner were we out of the particular little enclave where the Chevalier's house was situated, than I found to my astonishment that the streets which had been relatively empty in the very early morning were now crowded. And it was an amazing sight. Within three minutes we stopped to watch the performance of some strolling players. Then across one street a wire was strung and tightrope walkers were performing on it as if they were walking across solid ground. I had never seen such a thing. One of them stood on the tips of his toes and then took his other foot entirely off the rope. He might as well have had the capacity to fly.

There were so many musicians playing here there and everywhere, that one could not hear what one's companions might say. Except, I must remember to mention, in the vicinity of a showman who was enacting Ovid's *Metamorphosis* with puppets. This man was remarkably talented, and his puppets were exquisite. In order to hear what he said the people surrounding him kept almost total silence, and when a newcomer approached noisily because of being unaware of what was going on, they were silenced roughly by the crowd.

Further on an impertinent seller of elixirs, of whom there had been several dozen, attempted to accost me on the assumption that I would believe his potions capable of mending my deformities. The Chevalier's servant had to beat him off, and I held my mask more carefully from then on.

Monsieur Heurlant mentioned that the town was so crowded because so many of the starving peasants had come in from the countryside, and some of the rich merchants gave them food.

"Coming from Versailles, Monsieur," he said to me, "you must have seen how wretched the peasants are between here and Paris. But when you get to Italy you will find they manage better, because of the climate. The Chevalier de Lorraine, when he reads of your visit in my letter, may wish to send advice to you on your Italian route, because he journeyed there himself some years ago."

"You have written to the Chevalier?" I exclaimed. He smiled with satisfaction, taking my surprise to be caused by admiration.

"A gentleman in our company last night," he said, "was on his way to Paris, and has carried the letter for me. "

He continued to talk about his letter and how interested the Chevalier would be to learn that Monsieur Heurlant and I had met, and that I was on my way to Italy, in the very same direction as he, Lorraine, had been before. I wouldn't argue with the dreadful man. I had no doubt at all that he was right. I made a probably futile attempt to suggest a morsel for his future correspondence which might conceivably pacify Lorraine's suspicions.

"I think I mentioned this tour to the Chevalier de Lorraine" I said, "because as you know, the main purpose of my journey is to try one of my pigeons out to see if it will fly back to the nest from so far away. At the time I spoke to the Chevalier, Provence seemed the likely limit of my experiment, and I did tell him about it. But I subsequently thought it just possible the bird could go further."

"Ah, I see," said Monsieur Heurlant.

He looked very sceptical, and I hoped he might think it worth his while to send another letter to Lorraine to air his own opinion of my plan to test the bird from as far away as Italy.

As soon as I could, I confided the whole miserable accident to Bonhomme, so that we could fret over it together. It was an unlooked-for disaster. We wore ourselves out trying to guess Lorraine's likely reaction when he received Monsieur Heurlant's letter.

That afternoon, having excused myself from staying longer on the grounds that I was anxious to cross the Rhône before the river became flooded with the waters that had apparently gathered upstream from two weeks of rain in Germany, I left Dijon.

It had become yet more necessary to waste no time, if there was any possibility that Lorraine might send one of his assassins after us, and both Bonhomme and I were anxious to put as much distance as we could between ourselves and Paris.

CHAPTER TWENTY-NINE

On leaving Dijon I took with me letters of introduction from the Maréchale to a certain Marquis de Chalon living at Chalons sur Soane, but in fact I had no intention of acting upon them. For fear of Lorraine picking up my scent, it was necessary to disappear between one place and the next, and consequently we decided to spend the night in a field near Tournus, although this was a danger of its own, not to mention the bitter cold.

We settled down to sleep in a little copse. Bonhomme showed extraordinary ingenuity in making us comfortable and I began to wonder if he had some gypsy blood, but he hadn't the right colour, although his complexion had lost the sour look always noticeable in Versailles; that cast like chipped white enamel or skimmed milk, which was also the skin colour of d'Effiat.

I sat in the coach while he prepared some food over a small fire. The coldness of the air starched everything. Even the outer fringes of the fur I was wearing became rigid. I was not cold myself. But even so Bonhomme insisted that I put dried bracken in my boots.

I sat there and watched him. He whistled between his teeth as he fanned the flame of his fire. I could swear that he was happy.

I think that he had stolen from the courtier he looked after before the advent of myself. From what I heard he was rather severely punished. Presumably that was what gave him his sly look. His eyes, that were very dark brown like my own, had a tendency to dart about. At other times he would just view everything with a very sullen steady regard. From time to time I would remember him brushing the powdered Dragon Arum onto my jerkin to attract and madden the wolfhound Camargue, and then any tendency to befriend the man left me. However, I admit I was beginning to like him. I noticed the firmness and skill with which he wielded his knife when repairing a piece of harness that broke on the road, or whittling wood to make a spit over the fire. As a servant at Versailles he could not be expected to do all this. Something else must have propelled him into this adventure in my service.

It might have seemed reasonable to speculate on the possibility that the motive might be money promised him by Lorraine if he slit my throat on some quiet road well away from Paris. But he had convinced me otherwise; and besides, the Maréchale de Clerembault trusted him. You remember what she said about his having once been a dishonest man.

While I pondered these thoughts I had inadvertently let my eye settle on the man himself. His legs were supple and springy, and he squatted on them as he worked by the fire, able to move from side to side or forwards to backwards at will as he attended to the food. I could not so much as sit on the ground myself, without becoming trapped by joints which folded the wrong way. Feeling my eye on him, Bonhomme looked up once quickly and then away.

I was very tempted to ask him if he was happy. But his expression had become sullen again after he had noticed me watching him, and so the question seemed no longer appropriate. But I should have liked to know a little of his feelings and his ideas at that moment. I thought then that at another time I would want to ask again. Later, having eaten, I lay down to sleep in the coach. By filling the gap between the seats with packages taken from the backs of the horses, Bonhomme had made a comfortable bed that was quite large enough for me. But he himself was planning to sleep in the open. He was very cold. I noticed that the nails of his right hand were blue and even if he replenished the fire it would burn out before dawn, at the very time likely to be most freezing.

"Take my fur," I said to him. "I don't need it. I am protected in here and I never have felt the cold. These woollen cloths and the sack of horse feed will keep me warm enough. "

At first he couldn't be persuaded, but then at last he did take it. He had hoped the horses would lie down, but they were all standing. However, if he could not get any warmth from that direction – and indeed he had to cover them and thereby lose a few more cloths – he at least built up the fire, collected a heap of dry bracken and lay down on that, covered by the fur. He thanked me more warmly than he needed to for the fur. After all, it was in my interests not to let him be frozen to death out here. Even if the impulse of compassion and friendship that I had felt towards him had evaporated for the moment, he was still the only servant I had.

In the end he must have slept very soundly because I woke at dawn alerted by some quiet movement or other which had not penetrated his dreams. The horses made a noise all night. Intermittently, they grazed and chewed and their great teeth ground away like rocks in a cave, and every now and then they would shift their hooves, and hit a stone or a piece of fallen wood. But this sound which had woken me was not of that category. It should not have woken me at all because it was so quiet. Perhaps the stealth woke me.

Be that as it may, I was suddenly very wide awake, and in the instant carefully raising my head enough to see out, I caught sight of four figures creeping around the embers of the fire. I could not believe that this had anything to do with Lorraine. Although I accounted him an apprentice of the devil, I considered this quality as figurative and not a scientific fact that might enable him to act on Monsieur Heurlant's warning with such incredible speed. These men were simply poor – and of course, quite likely murderous – thieves. One was about to untie a horse. The knife the other held – I'm not sure what his intentions were with it.

With one mighty shout I woke Bonhomme and landed somehow myself, on the ground, outside the coach.

What would have happened if I had been a normal man I do not know. Bonhomme and I could not have defended ourselves because we were unarmed and caught in our sleep. But we were saved by the fact that when the thieves or would-be murderers saw me in the pale dawn light – saw a preternaturally small figure twisted and gnarled like the true goblin my dear Madame had christened me, and with my mouth wide open and my face uplifted – they fled. Bonhomme had hardly time to stand before they were disappearing. And they had taken nothing.

Then I thought of how starving they probably were. Who is awake all night, drawn across miles of freezing empty countryside by the remains of a fire? If they had run away less quickly I would have thrown a sack of food after them.

The next day we continued along our road with the satisfaction of being ahead of our stated plans, and none the worse for the night's adventure. We persuaded ourselves that for the moment we were too far ahead for Lorraine to send anyone after us. There was a magic in the life of a traveller that delighted me, and at these times I hardly cared if Lorraine suspicions were aroused by news of our stay in Dijon or not. But there were also times when certain huge tracts of empty land weighed down the heart. Sometimes the country was so empty that, particularly when the light faded, one felt as if the history of humanity and the companionship of our species had been a dream, and there never had been any others except Bonhomme and myself. This sensation was not welcome to me. Solitude I liked but this edge of abandonment belonged to some other dimension.

On one such evening, in a storm of sleet, we arrived at the gates of Lyons after crossing the river without any of the adventures of Mme. de Grignan nor yet the Duc d'Autour. I had been recommended to stay with the Sheriff here and as usual Bonhomme made his enquiries – he would ask the way of a lackey on an errand, a peddler, or a merchant's servant with goods to deliver.

Within the walls of Lyons there were many splendid buildings, including a massive twelfth century cathedral with great towers at each corner which would have aroused anyone's admiration. But to the eye of travellers sharpened with their wanderings, and honed with the keenness of solitude it inspired awe. We passed it when the vesper bells were ringing. The sleet was sharp, cutting the air between the low clouds and the street into ribbons. I rode Maud, but I had my hat pulled down and my cloak wound round my body. And as I passed the west wall a small wicket door opened letting out a sudden clatter of light and a smell of incense which faded quickly and took on an almost ghostly air when the turn of the next corner showed a length of that same cathedral's walls quite ruined, although patched with wood. It occurred to me to wonder what it would look like three or four hundred years hence; the year 1980 maybe, if such a time ever came, or 2000. Will they have rebuilt that ruined wall; or perhaps levelled the building altogether? Will it stand for other travellers, who in some other age canter along this same path as night is falling, in summer maybe, or spring?

But to return to the journey of Bonhomme and myself, we arrived without much delay at the mansion of a certain gentleman of Lyons to whom Madame had sent word, and who received us very kindly. We felt glad of the promise of a comfortable bed for the night after such a day. If the weather had not turned so vile I should have released Salamandre to fly back to Paris some time ago, because I was very anxious to send Francis news of the turn events had taken at Dijon. He could keep a sharper watch over Lorraine, and who knew what opportunity Fate might produce by which Francis might save or help us. I told Bonhomme that if he was busy with the horses, he must bring the bird up to me.

When I took Salamandre from the basket which I did in my bedchamber, he stretched his legs and his wings and fluttered and I could see that all was still well with him. I had prepared a greeting to Fanette, and now I unwrapped it from a crease of leather in my wallet and read it again. When I thought of her I was always amazed; sometimes too much so for gladness. Also, when I left Paris, sad though I was to leave her I was, as it were, fattened with the enjoyment of her company. Now I was no longer so. I felt in my very guts a starvation quite different than that to do with eating food. I penned a brief note to Francis in addition, to tell him of the unfortunate result of the meeting with Monsieur Heurlant, and rewrapped it.

If only we would have fair weather the next day I would send Salamandre with this letter back to Versailles. Francis would be on the watch for him, and it would be he who would take the letter and deliver it to Fanette, as we had agreed before I left. How I wished that Salamandre could be induced to fly from Versailles back again to wherever I might be afterwards. If he carried nothing more than a piece of ribbon from her hair, I should have been in heaven.

Bonhomme was in great haste to dress me because all provincials ate at most unfashionably early hours. I haven't mentioned my host on this occasion and he deserves a word, because he was an excellent musician. At supper he wanted nothing but tales of Lully, and also Alessandro Scarlatti who, for some reason, he was convinced had come to the French court. But I knew he had not. I did my best with an account of Lully, but since he was, despite being a genius and Master of the Kings music, such a dirty greedy fellow as a man, it involved some imagination on my part. Why do lovers of the arts show such an avid desire to learn about the personal details of these creative giants of men? Between Lully himself, and his music there was, to my mind, a meaningless and unbridgeable gap. From the point of view of a lover of court gossip it was perhaps relevant that Lully had to be thrown out of the King's kitchen where, out of sheer greed he loved to go, and being drunk would fall on the floor and create all sorts of trouble for the servants there. But to a lover of music, this was surely not interesting. What difference did it make to Lully's beautiful opera *Isis* whether the composer had, in his role of courtier to Louis XIV, had the privilege of making up the top of the King's bed?

However, I kept these opinions to myself and gave my host as much gossip as I could in fair exchange for his hospitality. He had a very pretty daughter who played the violin, and he had bought for her an instrument made by Stradivari. I was to hear it after supper, and, what is more, he himself had one of the very first cellos made by that master craftsman. I wondered what sort of a performance I would hear. At Macon I had been taken to hear some music and although I did not think to mention it in this account, I still remember the misery of listening to it at the time.

When we left the table we all removed into what was called the music room where there was a harpsichord as well as more than one cello and several violins. Chairs were well set and I enjoyed the novel experience of being seated in a *fauteuil* in the company. At court I think Madame would have fainted if she had seen me so exalted.

The music began and at once I realised that we were to have a feast for the soul at least equal to that which had just been provided for the body. I began to feel real gratitude towards my host. His wife, who was not at all beautiful and who was clothed in a manner likely to emphasise that point, sat down at the harpsichord and played very well. At once, as if the keys she touched were the philosopher's stone she was turned to gold. Her figure was no longer ugly to me, I began to think being fat was charming, and her red cheeks were, after all, not much redder than those of Madame. I know that I contradict myself in saying this, because here I am building a bridge between the physical presence of the artist and the work that he or she creates, which a moment ago I was only too anxious to demolish.

But let me come to the violin and the cello. It is the most astonishing news that this craftsman in Italy can make such a difference to the sound produced by the same wood. I think it is the same wood. My host's daughter played a short piece by Scarlatti first on another violin, and then on a Stradivari and the difference was enchanting. The same was quite undoubtedly true of the cello. I did not know that Stradivari made them, but apparently he produced his first only two years previously, and my host had travelled to Italy to procure one.

The next morning when Bonhomme and I set out once more the skies had cleared and not a trace of cloud remained. The entire dome of heaven was one shining expanse of pure blue. So our exit from the town was as different from our entry as it could be.

"I fancy" I said to Bonhomme as we went through the wakening streets, "that I shall let Salamandre loose when we are out of the town. It seems a good day for it." He said something, but the clatter of the horses hooves on the paving caused me not to hear and I didn't ask him to repeat it.

Once out of the city the beggarly condition of the people began to be noticeable again. We travelled on the west side of the river, and then various roads began to climb upwards and we saw high mountains ahead, and snow. We were tremendously bothered by poor men and sometimes whole families begging from us. They would catch hold of the stirrup leathers and even pull at my clothes. If one gave a few coins it made as little difference as sipping a few drops of water out of a pool filled from a spring. At last we decided on a strategy. We stopped, and gave – or rather threw – a large number of coins to those who were asking for them, and then, while they gathered them together Bonhomme touched the coach horse with the whip and I spurred on Maud, and Bonhomme's mount followed after. This didn't rid us of the beggars entirely. There were always more, so we repeated the device whenever we needed to. And truly, I felt sorry enough for them.

If I were in their shoes – or rather their bare feet – I would try to cross these mountains that were before us, and come to country less harsh and a climate more forgiving where poverty is concerned. But perhaps they did not realise what land lay behind the mountains, and besides they were a barrier in themselves that no one could cross without resources of money and provisions for food and warmth and at least one or two mules to carry it.

In a little glade in the foothills of these huge peaks, at midday, I released Salamandre. I fed him first. His plumage was slightly dull, and Bonhomme remarked that perhaps it was well timed to send the bird home now. I placed the messages on the bird's leg in one of the rings that Francis had given me. We had chosen a spot away from the road in order to be sure to be alone. A group of saplings grew from a little stony heap that may once have been a shepherd's hut. The leaves were all gone, and there was a sort of soft whistling sound when the breeze rubbed the dry shafts of the grass together.

We decided to eat our own food at the same time as Salamandre, in the little caged extension which could be fitted on his basket, ate his. He kept looking at the sky. Drinking my wine and eating my bread, I watched how still he suddenly was from time to time, his head and shoulders locked into a position of extreme attention, the down of his underfeathers and his tail just frilled against the wind. He was inspecting the sky, like someone looking at a path to see where there are ruts to negotiate, or ice. He would travel that bright blue road with as much familiarity and ease as we all crawl upon the ground. I should watch him spread his beautiful wings and soar up from the earth, and I would not know whether I should see him again in this life.

When the moment came I, who am not at all devout, murmured a prayer. I hoped that if God heard me He would not, as due payment for my lack of attention at other times, do the opposite of what I asked from Him now. Salamandre, when he found the wire ceiling of his basket removed and himself free, looked about him, hopped onto the edge of the basket, and from there to the grass. He took a few steps, then spread his wings, and flew up. I thought he was off. I held my hand against the sun and watched him fly in a great circle.

And then he came back. He dropped onto my shoulder and in a detached way, but nevertheless unequivocally, he leaned his body against the side of my neck and my face. Then with a bracing of his claws which I could feel through the cloth of my collar, he sprung up again, and this time he was off.

CHAPTER THIRTY

The high passes through the Alps into Italy were said to be closed by October, and it was now the end of December. I regretted this because the route into Italy via Ventimiglia, although the only way to enter Italy in Winter once the Alpine passes were blocked, was much longer. So, when we came to the fork in the road where we should have turned left to climb up into the mountains, I hesitated.

Bonhomme had got ahead of me and was whistling. If he knew what a clear sign of his nervous anxiety was this habit of his designed to hide it, he might have kept silent. He whistled shepherd songs from the Auvergne, or so he said on the one occasion that I asked him. They were subtle tunes, very fast and complex, and his quiet accurate version of these would pipe very softly away sometimes for hours. I called out to him now to stop. He was riding alongside the horse which was in the traces, one hand looped through the rein. I dare say he hoped that I would be discouraged by the prospect of his having to turn the coach, or that I would believe that he was too far ahead to hear me. He was pretending not to notice that I had fallen behind. But at the repeated sound of my voice he halted and turned his mount around to face me. The coach horse simply stood. Like they do.

"Bonhomme," I shouted, "I still think we could make it through the mountain pass. If we find the road blocked we can turn round and come back. It could save us as much as three weeks."

He came towards me with a backward glance at the coach. On either side, before and behind us, the empty landscape stretched without a break. Devastated fields over to the west were still patched with frost. The rusted remains of dead stalks will have been making a rattling sound in the wind, but at this distance we couldn't hear it.

"If this weather holds up," I said, and at that very moment a bank of cloud which I hadn't noticed swallowed the sun in one gulp. I ignored it. "If this weather holds up we could at least attempt the shorter route through the Alps," I said.

"We should have got another horse. Even a light coach needs two on that road." "Mules," I said. "We need mules. We can get them at Falgere."

"Monsieur," Bonhomme began to plead. "Not one pass is open after

October. You were not there. You were dining with Monsieur l'Intendant and his wife and daughters in Lyons, but I was in the kitchen with a pedlar from Turin and he told me what the road is like in November. And even that month is gone now. The track is narrow, and sheeted with ice, because it is very high, Monsieur. If we could not go forward because of a fall of rock or snow, which is most likely, we couldn't turn either. How would we turn a coach, or even a cart if we went back to Lyons and exchanged our equipment for the sort of thing they use on that journey. You can't turn round on steep ice. And he said that even at mid-day the snow falls so thickly and the light is so dim that a man can't see further than a foot in front of his face. Monsieur because we are down here with nothing worse than a freezing wind and a hard frost..."

I knew perfectly well that it couldn't be done. I cut him off with a wave of my hand and gave Maud the signal to walk on. As I passed Bonhomme he watched me in silence and I nodded. He had done no wrong. It was just that the thought of what might be happening in Paris had begun to haunt me at night. Madame had other friends beside myself to watch over her; but none, I thought, dedicated and sharp enough to catch the warning signs of Lorraine planning a new, more dangerous, scheme. I tormented myself with these thoughts, which were increased by the anxiety over the chance that Lorraine would enact some devilry towards myself to stop me from returning to Paris. The incident of Camargue had given proof of how ingenious Lorraine could be. And although Madame's servants were fond of her, yet flattery and money can persuade a person.

"You are right," I said to Bonhomme when eventually he came alongside me. "We'll have a good enough taste of the mountains when this road climbs between Valence and Loriot. I suppose we may have even snow and ice, and enough to satisfy me." And besides, owing to Madame's friendship with Madame de Sévigné (and indeed probably without that, since hardly a single individual at court could have missed that lady's perpetual bulletins of her daughter's life in Provence) I had a curiosity to see the country on the other side of these mountains.

The clouds continued to devour the sky until there was none of it left. Gorged and heavy and a yellowish grey in colour they hung from horizon to horizon, pregnant with snow. We pressed on due south, but we could as well have been in Sweden.

I heard a description of that country once from the lips of the Queen

Christina. She was a very lively unconventional woman and caused havoc in the French court during her visit there. Had we intended to go as far south as Rome I should have called on her, because she spent most of her time there now.

Perhaps half an hour later, with the road climbing steeply, an icy squall suddenly billowed up from the ground and down came the snow. It was more like ice, sharp and at the same time very wet. In haste I called Bonhomme to help me dismount. We got a cover over Maud and the other horse. The carriage horse already had a cloth under the traces. Bonhomme could get some shelter from the overhang of the drivers seat, but I made no bones about getting inside the coach myself.

It became so dark that the road hardly showed ahead. As we climbed uphill, higher and higher, even I felt the cold and I could only guess at the misery suffered by Bonhomme. I had a bottle of some strong liquor which I handed to him. After midday we looked out anxiously for an inn or a house of any reasonable size and therefore likely to belong to a gentleman, but there seemed to be absolutely nothing. I was afraid to stop to eat in the open in case the horses should be killed by the cold as they were standing. There was no shelter at all. So we simply carried on.

Then suddenly, at about four o'clock in the afternoon, the sky cleared as if by magic. From dark it became light in a matter of minutes. The heavens were as blue as if they had never had so much as a puff of cloud upon them. There were even some birds. They sang a cold clanging song which was unknown to me. We had already arrived among the rocks, and they flew from these with sharp sudden flights that suggested joy; until you thought of the possibility of its opposite.

"Bonhomme," I shouted. "We can stop. We must eat." There was no response. The horse still plodded forwards. Maud and Bonhomme's mount were tethered to the rear of the coach. I shouted again and hit against the inside with my stick and this time there was a slow dragging halt and the horse stopped. But still no sound from Bonhomme. I started to dismount. Clumsy as I was at the best of times, it now took me a full two minutes to reach the ground.

I was calling him all the while. If he had frozen half to death and fallen into the road while the horse continued forward, and was perhaps lying miles behind us I would have the devils own job to reach him. I got round to the front of the vehicle and looked and there, to my great relief, he was sitting yet, but more drunk than I had ever seen a man. He had tied himself to the seat, which had shown some foresight on his part. His clothes were soaked as if he was standing in water up to his neck. As I looked, steam began to rise from them. His face was purple and grey, his hair frozen to his skull. He was trying both to speak and to untie himself but could do neither.

I had a mind to laugh for a minute. But then I set myself to giving the poor man what comfort I could. It was no good my trying to move him. I couldn't do it. I couldn't even reach him as I could not climb up onto the perch. Instead, I went back inside the coach and brought out bread, cheese, butter and water. I drew the coach over to the side of the road where there was a rock sticking up about a foot and I could just about stand on it. This way I could reach high enough to hand Bonhomme the food. The trouble was that he was too drunk to feed himself. I shouted at him, and gave him one mouthful at a time and very slowly succeeded in getting some nourishment into him. As soon as he had swallowed a few mouthfuls of bread and some cheese, he began to recover.

"Take the water," I shouted. He could drink now, although I could see him spill it down the front of his neck between his soaking doublet and his steaming cloak. I gave him more to eat. Then more water, more bread. Eventually he untied himself and half fell down onto the ground. He was trying to apologise to me, but if ever one man got drunk in the service of another, I think it was Bonhomme. So I put him in the coach, mounted Maud without assistance by using that same stone, and then went forward with the coach horse on a leading rein.

After an hour more of this weary travelling the mountainous rocks drew back from the road and I found that we had entered an area of high but flattish barren land. At some distance over to the left an immense castle stood in the middle of the fields, without walls or approaches of any kind except the narrow track leading to it. I decided at once that this would provide a suitable bed for the night, and so I stopped the coach, tethered the horses and went to wake Bonhomme.

He improved his appearance as well as he could, put on his hat and his dry cloak. Then I had him mount his horse and ride over to the chateau to announce my arrival. I had a letter – a kind of passport you could call it – from the Maréchale de Clerembault which served to make my own position at the court of Versailles clear if it was presented. I gave this to Bonhomme and told him that I would wait in the carriage a few paces along the turning that led to the castle, until he came back.

He cantered away and I settled down to wait for his return. I was able to watch the sky thicken once again, and although the rain did not turn to snow it nevertheless was icy, sharp and plentiful. By the time Bonhomme came riding back he was as wet as he had been in the first place. But neither so cold nor so drunk. He announced that the castle belonged to a certain Marquis de St. Hermitage, and that we were welcome. Good. He then tethered his horse beside Maud at the rear of the coach, climbed onto the driving seat, and in twenty minutes we were at the gates of this astonishing place.

Only now did I realise the immense size of the building. In such a featureless landscape it is possible to misread size and space, and I had computed the mass of the building and its distance in reverse to their true proportions. In reality it was further away than I thought, and once under its huge walls I saw that it was a building in which an army could be quartered.

I was received by the Marquis himself standing bareheaded on the steps in the rain. When, with Bonhomme's help, I had struggled to the ground, the old gentleman had had time to get extremely wet, and I felt sorry for it. I swept off my hat as I bowed to him, and put it under my arm, and once I had managed to climb the steps we went in to the hall.

Accustomed as I was to living in large buildings, Versailles was always full of people, usually brightly lit, and well furnished. Here the bare stone walls of the castle loomed between tapestries that could not cover their cold and massive fronts, and the furniture, although quite good, was too sparse. A huge fire so mesmerised me with its attractions that I had difficulty listening to what was being said to me. What would happen to us in this place, I wondered. Would we eat? Would we sleep?

Three huge dogs got up from the hearth as we approached. I felt my pulse quicken, and wondered if my host would be quick or strong enough to save me if it became necessary. The Marquis seemed to have a very phlegmatic nature. He told me at once that I was the first visitor that he and his wife had seen for a twelve-month. And yet he sounded neither satisfied nor regretful about it and behaved towards myself with a sort of dull and steady courtesy that ignored, incidentally, the peculiarities of my person. I never encountered a stranger before or since who showed such little reaction to an appearance which I know perfectly well is extraordinary. I could even have wondered, from his manner towards me, if some enchantment along that road that I had just travelled had refashioned me without my knowing it. However, when the Marquise came in, my mind was set at rest on that score.

A little while later, when the three of us had been together for perhaps ten minutes, a really charming young man came into the hall who was introduced as the grandson of the Marquis and his wife.

After another twenty minutes dinner was announced, and we went for a considerable walk from one room into another, until we came at last to one where a table was set. The Marquis was already in the middle of confiding a complicated law suit to me; an argument in which he and his neighbour each laid claim to the same small parcel of land which lay between the vast tracts owned by both of them. The neighbour and the subject of this dispute, together with the wars in Hanover, made up the entire diet of the conversation at the table, and afterwards, when they all led me back into the Great Hall. The grandson might go to Paris in the spring when travelling became easy once more, and lay their suit before Parliament. The claim derived from rights granted to the Marquis' grandfather by Henry IV but later called into question along its eastern boundary by a grant of land to a nobleman of Valence. I can tell you that it is hard to take the minutiae of another man's quarrel to heart when it has to do with something so dry as fifteen acres of bad grazing. However, I did my best.

Alas, in this small and interesting family there was none of the curiosity about court life that I had become accustomed to, and certainly no questions about fashion, or enquiries about the King. The Marquise had not heard of Madame de Maintenon.

Every now and then the young man would tell some anecdote about the hunt, or ask his grandfather if he might take a certain horse with him to ride into Valence. Clearly the two old people loved this boy, because they both had the habit of falling silent the minute he drew breath to speak, and then paying attention to him with small encouraging smiles and flattering concentration. What was more surprising was that the young man himself – Dagobert was his name – seemed so content with his lot. Here he was shut up in a gloomy castle with two old people and stranded far from the influence of society and never visited; and yet he seemed so blithe. I could not make it out.

Apart from these three the castle contained a cook, a housemaid, two footmen and a coachman. One hunter and two old mares were stabled in accommodation large enough for a whole regiment of cavalry.

For an eternity after we returned to the Great Hall the Marquis sat in dignified stoicism, one hand resting on the fingers of the other, neither embarrassed by the silence nor showing the least inclination to put an end to it. He sat in a carved walnut chair before the fire, but the old fashioned low collar at the back of his neck fanned constantly in the icy draught. I was in despair. The young man had disappeared. The Marquise seemed asleep.

However, there was suddenly a most tremendous noise emitted by a clock in the far corner of the hall. As soon as these thunderous chimes began, the Marquis and his wife both stood up and a footman came towards me with a branch of candles, to light me to bed. I said my farewells, and went very willingly. When we had been walking five or ten minutes through various passages and doorways, Dagobert suddenly appeared and offered to accompany me the rest of the way. We went up a great staircase and along a gallery hung with paintings the entire floor of which, for some reason was covered with overlapping layers of carpet from the Orient. All this showed up but dimly in the light of the candles. Half-way across it – I could see that the gallery continued as far as and beyond the reach of the eye into darkness – we went through another doorway and from thence to another stairway of stone leading up into a tower.

Dagobert happily told me what history he knew of all the visible features as we went, and said that I was to spend the night in the room known as that belonging to Queen Christina of Sweden, because she had slept there. What amazed me most at hearing this was to contemplate the Queen in this castle as a guest of the Marquis and his wife. How had that quiet grey aristocrat coped with the presence of a guest so lively, so unconventional, so noisy? He had been younger then, but he did not look like a man who changed much. When she was at Versailles – or rather St. Germain, because her sojourn in Paris was long before – she had turned the place up side down. Her flirtations, her intellectual adventurism, her appetites were each phenomenal in their way. I had heard that she indirectly caused the death of Descartes because when he was unwise enough to spend a Winter in Stockholm she made him attend her at five o'clock in the morning in order to teach and discuss his ideas. Dagobert laughed when I mentioned this. "Extraordinary!" he said. "That she should ever have been interested in a man who called one of his first works *'Regles pour le Direction de l'Esprit'*!"

I was so astonished to hear this comment from this young man that I missed my footing on the threshold of the room we were about to enter. I righted myself by taking hold of the footman's arm. He stood firm, like a guardsman on duty, the spilt wax dry on his fist as he held up the branch of candles for us to see the room. But my impressions were still overlaid by surprise at that remark of Dagobert. This young man had not uttered a single literary or political opinion throughout the evening and with all his pleasant ways I had assumed his mind to be quite dull. If he thought it so surprising that Queen Christina should have taken any notice of a man who wrote about Rules for the guidance of the spirit, then I thought it equally surprising that he himself should have read or even heard of the early writings – or any writings – of Descartes.

"I only meant," he went on, noticing my reaction, but attributing it to the wrong cause, "that Queen Christina never acquired a reputation for keeping to any rules."

I laughed as a means of providing punctuation – a full stop, as it were – to the interval that had proved so surprising, and Dagobert turned to the centre of the room. He threw out an arm and said,

"Monsieur, I think that you will not find yourself cramped during the night."

Lo and behold, there was a bed seven foot square, with curtains of crimson silk on the outside, and green gauze within. The corners of the bed were surmounted with great gilded carvings of cupids. In front of the chimney piece two chairs were drawn up on either side of a heavy darkly carved table, and a huge fire burned in the hearth.

The footman put down the candelabra on the table and withdrew, but Dagobert showed not the slightest inclination to leave me. Which suited my mood very well, because I was determined to get to the root of this man's extraordinary character and to know more about him.

In response to my tentative questions he unreservedly began to tell me the history of his early life. His parents had been murdered before his eyes when he was less than ten years of age by footpads who attacked them on the road from Rome to Sicily. They killed his infant brother too, and a girl of five whose nurse had left her for an instant to go down to the stream to fetch water. The outriders and servants who had been travelling with his parents had all either been killed or fled, and he himself escaped because one of the servants threw his cloak over the child and hid him when the attack first began.

I was amazed by this tale. Where, then, did this young man acquire his singularly tranquil frame of mind; his air of finding himself in a pleasant world in which he was completely at home? I drew our discussion from personal matters to literature and the arts, and there too he proved to be equipped with a fund of knowledge. His comment on

Descartes was not a coincidence. He had read all the works of that great philosopher. To this should be added Pascal, Racine, Corneille, Spinoza, Basile, Molière. But his main interest was chemistry. He had learnt English in order to read Thomas Willis.

Bonhomme had come into the room some time ago and was standing almost hidden by shadows in a recess. He was probably shivering with the cold, as we had let the fire burn down. At a sign from me he came forward, put another log to burn and replenished our two glasses. I noticed nothing unusual about the way he did this, but he must have put something in the young man's glass because suddenly, about a quarter of an hour later, in the middle of a sentence, Dagobert became quite still, fixed his gaze on a point somewhere behind me, and then abruptly collapsed into unconsciousness.

He would have dropped his glass if Bonhomme, unexpectedly near, had not caught it.

I made an exclamation and was about to hurry over to him when Bonhomme called out one word, and the door of the chamber opened to admit two men.

These were the footmen, but they had put their ceremonial coats aside, and now carried a stretcher between them. They came over to the young man's chair, with a brief bow towards myself, and proceeded to strap him onto it.

"Is he ill?" I said, horrified. "What are you going to do to him?" The incident had every appearance of being a familiar one to these men.

"Monsieur," Bonhomme said, in the middle of strapping Dagobert's ankles together, which I already thought a curious way of securing him to the stretcher. "If you will be so kind as to wait five minutes I will come back and explain all this to you."

Naturally I accepted. But I was full of disquiet as I watched the three of them carry the unconscious man across the floor, and disappear with him.

Once they were gone I took a dislike to the interior of my bed chamber. It was so vast. And cold. The light of the candles did not reach into the corners. The fire had died down again, but I threw no more wood on it, simply because I wanted the brightness of what flames there were. I realised that I was very tired. I crouched in the chair that I had been lounging in before, and waited. At last Bonhomme returned.

"Explain this to me, Bonhomme," I demanded the minute he came into the room. "That young man was perfectly well until he drank whatever it was that you poured for him. What intrigue is this? I thought we had left Versailles far behind. And besides, we have come here to find out about poisons, not the art of using them."

I think my solitary wait in that sombre room had unnerved me and loosened my tongue to some extent.

"I have a strange tale to tell you, Monsieur," Bonhomme replied.

"Well?"

"It is a tragic one in addition to being strange, because the young man is mad, Monsieur."

"Mad! Is that what they told you?" I felt my blood warm with indignation. "I have been sitting here this past two hours talking to him, and he is as sane as you or me."

"It is not my job to contradict Monsieur," Bonhomme said, with the return of one of his sour, furtive looks. In that guise I never wished in the least to speak with him, and I nearly ordered him to leave me to prepare for the night. But curiosity, and also, it must be said, the beginnings of friendship which I had really started to develop for him on this journey, gave me pause, and eventually I said,

"Let that not concern you, Bonhomme. Tell me what story it is that you have been regaled with by others in the household here. What do they claim against the grandson of the Marquis? And put another log on the fire."

He began at once to tend to practical things at the same time as saying to me, "Where shall I begin, Monsieur? Did he tell you, perhaps, about the murder of his parents?"

"Yes," I said. "And his sister and baby brother on the road to Sicily from Rome."

"That they were all killed by footpads who attacked them?"

"Yes."

"They were killed, but it was not thieves who did it. The young man himself murdered them all."

"But he was only a child!"

"Fourteen, Monsieur. He was fourteen."

I stared at him. "I don't believe it," I said.

Bonhomme was silent a moment.

"Why do you think no one comes here, Monsieur? The Marquis himself told you he had not seen the face of a stranger for twelve months. None of the nobility from Valence or the surrounding area either visit or hunt with them."

"This is a lonely spot," I argued; and then did not much like the sound of my own words. I'm no coward, but neither am I one of those who don't know the meaning of fear. "And as well as being isolated in this upland between the mountains, the character of Monsieur le Marquis is obviously not convivial. And yet you, I presume, would say that they are left alone because their grandson is mad."

"Not me, Monsieur," said Bonhomme.

"The servants, then."

He stood straight up, having caused an immediate blaze in the fire which lit the whole room once again. With the flames reflecting on the pale skin of his face which he held at an angle as he spoke, he said,

"The Marquis himself, Monsieur."

I was surprised. But apparently the very order to drug his young grandson and bind him up had come from the Marquis. Alerted by the servants to the fact that Dagobert had followed me to my room, he had summoned Bonhomme and told him what to do.

I stared at him in horror. I wished he would stand square on to me and look me in the face; not have such a habit of averting one cheek so that he addressed one always out of the corner of his eye. And the centre of that eye was so extremely small and black. As I gazed at him a thin smile curved the edge of his lip and he said,

"The young man was going to kill you, Monsieur."

"Me!"

"But yes. The pattern of his madness is that for weeks or even months he seems to emerge from all the ill effects of his last attack. He becomes, or so they told me, progressively more and more sane, as the world would say. After his madness has returned, and while it is on him he looks like a different man. But when he begins to recover, he gradually regains all the characteristics, both physical and mental, that you observed in him. He stands upright again. His skin clears. He allows himself to be washed. His hair is clean once more, and cut. They can put clothes on him one day. The next day he puts them on for himself; the next he chooses carefully, and asks to have his lace mended. And then he is back once more to his books, and his horse. He is the exceptionally charming young man you saw. But apparently, even when well and experiencing the wellbeing and grace of an interval of sanity, he seems instinctively not to seek to broaden the range of his activities beyond his grandfather's estate. Which is just as well, because he is so dangerous."

"And then?" I prompted him. "How can anyone tell when this fair weather of the spirit will break?"

"They keep a watch on him. There comes a time when he reaches the zenith of his perfections and then they know that the moment is very near. As they said, tonight he would have killed you, Monsieur."

I had nothing to say. Dagobert had sat in the chair I was looking at now; his smiling mouth, his gentle but enthusiastic manners, the keenness of his mind.

"He told me that he is very interested in the sciences, and chemistry in particular. Is this true."

"When he is well, Monsieur. He has written a paper but he cannot present it himself and so it has been sent to a member of the academia."

There was silence again. Bonhomme occupied himself with preparing clothes some distance away and then returned with my gown, ready for me to put it on.

I stood up. "Won't he kill his grandparents one day? Aren't they afraid of him?"

"Very likely," he agreed. "But they dote on him. Voilà!"

I slept fitfully that night. I asked Bonhomme to remain in the room, and he slept by the fire. I gave him permission to lie on the end of the bed because in all conscience it was big enough, but he declined.

As soon as it was light I rose. The surrounding countryside was so bleak and scorched with cold under the lash of rain that I felt my heart sink. I guessed that the Marquis and his wife would not neglect the courtesy of seeing me at breakfast, and when I said farewell to them how could I possibly tool my words? I thought about it.

When the moment came I thanked Madame la Marquise and Monsieur le Marquis for the hospitality of their house. And then, fixing my gaze on that nobleman's grave face, I said,

"Monsieur, I passed one of the most agreeable evenings of my life with your enchanting grandson. Whatever anguish the Good Lord has seen fit to visit on him, He has also given him a vision of bliss, and the grace to be able to share this at brief intervals with his fellow men. And I shall thank God in my prayers for the honour of having made one of them."

The old gentleman's eyes filled with tears; so full, in fact, that one escaped and ran down his cheek. After a moment's struggle he reached forward and seized me by the hand. And then, with an expression of positive joy, he and his wife accompanied me down the steps in the pouring rain, saw me into my carriage and stood watching over my departure until we could no longer see each other.

Now, whether killed by Dagobert or not, they must both be dead, simply because of the passage of time. But I have not forgotten them.

CHAPTER THIRTY-ONE

On that very day Bonhomme and I started our descent into the South of France. Any Winter traveller from the North who has not experienced the moment of arrival when the mountainous approaches give way to the balmy landscape of Provence has missed one of the most theatrical and comforting events in Nature. Even now – and it was the beginning of January – the air was soft. The colour of the earth had changed to red, the sky was blue, and olive and cypress trees were everywhere.

I had frequently remembered the single man walking towards Paris, who Bonhomme and I encountered on the road that first night. By now he would be in the city, privy to any scandal that made its way from court into the song sheets of the Pont Neuf, or the gossip of the wig makers. If harm had come to Madame, perhaps the rumour reached him, but for me messages only came in the form of dreams, which were usually bad. Or if Lorraine had put the worst construction on the news of my travels that he had received from M. Heurlant, so that he was assembling a whole regiment of spies and assassins to pursue me, perhaps this man heard a whisper of it. But I was cut off as effectively as if the miles I had travelled were thin air and Paris a distant star.

Bonhomme and I took to eating in the middle of the day sitting in a ditch together like two gypsies. I don't know if the softness of the climate and the charm of the landscape affected me but I found that the very last traces of my resentment, or perhaps it was distrust, of Bonhomme had melted away. As soon as we reached the south he started to put on weight and his skin, which had kept that grey enamel tinge of the north through all the ravages of wind rain and snow, became tanned a little. If I spent a day or a night when my anxieties about events at the French court during our absence weighed on me, I no longer kept silent, but discussed these matters with Bonhomme. And he turned out to be very knowledgeable. He had picked up almost as much scandal and gossip and private information around Versailles as I was accustomed to do, and as for Lorraine – whose name he never spoke without a certain embarrassment – he might as well have been living in his pocket all these years.

When I was discouraged – as I was for no particular reason just as we were crossing the border into Italy – and anxious as the moment approached when we should make contact with the first monastery at Genoa, he joked about the Spaniards that we should see lording it over their various dominions in Italy and reminded me of the visit of Philip IV to France, when a song which perhaps I should not repeat was very popular with the ballad-makers on the Pont Neuf.

I laughed. I had taken to wearing a mask as we travelled, because this seemed very acceptable to those encountered on the way who were accustomed to noblemen covering their faces if they wanted to. But at this moment I was not wearing it. I was just mounting Maud in order to ride across the ford of the Var, and what with the brightness of the day and the freedom of the road I had forgotten my scandalous ugliness or the need to hide it, and I laughed aloud with my face exposed and not even holding my hand near my mouth.

As everyone knows, an alternative method of traversing a shallow area of a river like the Var was to be hoisted on the shoulders of one of those men waiting to carry travellers who are always to be encountered in these circumstances. At this particular point on the Var a very remarkable old man, whose colossal height and knotted sinews reminded me of various antique statues and drawings, was just lifting an Englishman onto his back as Bonhomme and I arrived on the scene. He himself did not see me as I stood there laughing and waving my hat at Bonhomme, but the Englishman did. And at once he started to struggle as if he wanted to get down again, and was shouting out some words which later I realised was a version of the French language. Devil came into it; I hope nothing to do with myself. But anyway he decided that he was likely to drown and for all I know may have never gone into Italy for the rest of his life as a result. He certainly didn't that day. He and the carrier were arguing long after Maud and I, followed by Bonhomme managing to get the coach across with great skill, had risen splashing out of the water on the opposite bank. Luckily the river was low or we might have had to take the coach round by St. Martin.

From then on Bonhomme and I made our way along a series of rutted little earth tracks turning occasionally into broader roads and often within sight of the ocean. This last I had never seen in my life before. At the time I assumed that it looked the same in Calais although now I know differently. Blue, sometimes a strange green when the sky threatened rain, edged now with pines and now with groves of olives, lapping at the foot of cliffs or hemmed with fishing nets, pebbles and sand, it was far more beautiful than I had ever imagined. Added to all this, we never had any trouble finding lodgings for the night despite the fact that the dominance of Spaniards among the owners of the more important buildings and estates meant that I generally preferred not to risk their hospitality. But the sign of a rustic inn in those parts is a bunch of leaves or grapes hanging over the door and there was no shortage of these places.

It took us a week to reach Genoa. And I have to say that even though I have heard men say that it has declined a great deal since the Spaniards got there it still struck me, and must strike any visitor from my part of the world, as an exceptionally beautiful town. It is built on land shaped like a natural amphitheatre, facing the sea, and as well as the Via Balbi, flanked with sumptuous palaces such as the Pallazo Durazzo Pallavicini and the Palazzo Bianco – the latter still under construction when I was there – there is a labyrinth of small streets all backed by lofty hills. On our way we had picked up a French man who spoke both Italian and Spanish and who was waiting for us at the monastery attached to the Church of Santa Maria in Fontibus in Albenga. This man now led us through the ancient maze of buildings of which Genoa was composed, some extraordinarily tall, and curiously decorated and with sculpted gateways, until we came out at a Piazza that we should never have found on our own, and there in front of us was the Cathedral.

Viewed from the outside it was an amazing sight. These buildings which are constructed so slowly that the styles of architecture change radically from part to part have a strange beauty and fascination. It was a frequent phenomenon in Italy. In Milan the cathedral is still not finished to this day. Not far from the cathedral of Genoa we came at last to the monastery attached to the Church of San Matteo, where I should hand over the letter I had from the Italian ambassador, and make my first test of the plans laid down so carefully in Versailles. Our guide, Giuseppe Bruno, pulled the bell at the monastery door and spoke to the porter who opened the wicket. I handed over the letter but we were sent back to the church to wait for nearly an hour. This seemed, at the time, to be a potentially fatal set-back. I was afraid that we would never be called back to the monastery, and I should find, having come all this way, that my introductions, my passports, were useless, and a series of locked doors would put an end to all my ambitions.

There was a palmer in the Church where we waited; a strange fellow wearing a waxed cloak covered with shells. He understood French, and overheard me when I said to Bonhomme that the streets in this town were so steep I was afraid Maud would break a leg. He started to try to sell us a local horse in exchange because, as he claimed, horses bred on the Ligurian coast can climb like goats. It was true what he said. We found that out later. In the meantime I paced along the walls which were decorated with paintings by, I am sure, Castello among others. And I mastered my impatience to the extent of persuading myself that some formality to do with the daily time table of the Capuchins was the reason for this delay in our reception by the Abbot of the monastery. And so it proved. When Bruno returned to fetch us he brought the apologies of the Father Guardian who said that we should have been entertained in the monastery while waiting for Fra Bonaventura.

As we were leaving the Church, I didn't notice at first that another man who had been in the Church while we were there tried to slip out unnoticed between us. He started walking very close to Bonhomme towards the monastery, but after a matter of paces a group of Spaniards, very arrogantly turned out, came marching across the square.

The first shouted to him *'Venga usted con migo!'* at which the poor fellow turned round and fled back into the church as fast as a rat. There was no knowing what the Spanish officials thought he had done wrong. But I wished him well of his sanctuary. He would not starve. There were some very good paintings of food on the walls.

This Fra Bonaventura was not the monk who had sold poison to the Chevalier de Lorraine, nor yet a surgeon friar, but he was one who had spent several years in the monastery in Tuscany where Lorraine had almost certainly met the monk whose name was Morel. Morel was the individual known for his expertise in connection with poisons. This monastery, as Fra Bonaventura now informed me, was the Monasterio di Santo Stefano, north of Lucca on the way to Barga. I shall never forget the extraordinary style with which this devout man explained the complications of the situation to me; the way in which the fecundity of the land in that part of Italy combined with the nearness of the mountains had fostered an interest in rare plants and herbs that had, in time, given rise to an inherited expertise in the manipulation of their chemistry. He put it like this because he was determined to impress on me the legitimate use of this knowledge, and the fact that the Holy Church was responsible only for benevolence. He knew Fra Morel. If the Maréchale de Clerembault had not written to him, he would not have helped me on my way because the common failing of those ignorant of science was, in his opinion, to misunderstand the cognoscenti.

He had a humorous manner with which he tried to mask his own arrogance, but I was not deceived. I observed how extremely sharp his eyes were, although he creased the lids together with a smile designed to hide them. When he asked for the package that the Maréchale had given me to pass on to him, I did not let it go from my hand until I had extracted the last morsel of information from him as to our way, and exactly where I should find Morel, and an assurance that he was this moment at the Monastery in question. Because it would take Bonhomme and me – and also of course Bruno, now that we had to take him with us – two weeks or more to reach it. And I insisted on some token, in writing, from Fra Bonaventura to Morel. All of this he gave me; and I can only say that I thought the Maréchale had, as usual, struck a very shrewd bargain, since her gift to the monk consisted merely of a small box with a glass panel, of no notable artistic merit, but containing a dried piece of the skin of Saint Catherine. I hope it is not too offensive to one who reads this account if I say that my opinion of such mementos is rather low.

Not so Fra Bonaventura. He bowed his head over the package, so that I saw quite clearly the shaved pate of his skull fringed with dark hair, (this being the style of the Capuchins) and his fingers trembled.

I usually feel sympathy for the passions of other men. If some poor fellow is moved, more often than not I should be ready to feel with him and help him, in the unlikely event of his realising that I could be of any use. But in this case not so. I turned on my heel and would have left without kissing the end of the monk's cord if the ferocity of Bonhomme's expression had not warned me. As it was, I rejoiced to be in the open air again once we regained the little square.

It was growing dark. Bruno produced steel, flint, tinder and sulphur from a bag he carried, and lit a lantern. We returned to the inn where we had left our coach at the bottom of the town, and the next morning we left Genoa never to return. In spite of all my intentions, many aspects of those palaces and churches remained a mystery, and I never went back to verify the architecture of Bianco or the statues of Giambologna.

CHAPTER THIRTY-TWO

If I found the peculiar superstition of Fra Buonaventura, and the cleric himself, somewhat repulsive, I soon had to adjust my point of view to accommodate a populace who were very devout and extraordinarily fond of the priesthood. On our journey between Genoa and Sestri we passed through a village that was on the route of a certain Cardinal on his way to Parma, and the people had hung bright cloths from their windows and balconies, they had put flowers in their hair, they had tied ribbons on the trees. Our French habit of combining mockery with the necessary degree of respect for clerics was notably missing in this country. The fact that in this area, where the wool trade is reduced to less than half of what it was a hundred years ago before the Spaniards got here, so that the people are very poor, seemed to make no difference to their generosity towards the priesthood. Their enthusiasm was such, in fact, that when this much revered cleric later conducted a service in the Church at Rapallo an unfortunate young woman was crushed to death in the crowd that followed him.

Keeping to the edge of the ocean we were able to travel as far as Massa still with the coach and our own horses. But then we could only go forward on horseback and, much to my dismay, I had to leave Maud in the care of an ostler and take to those local breeds of horse mentioned before. Sheer rocks on which even vegetation often could not cling had edged our journey down the coast. I had admired these mountain ranges for their beauty. But it had not occurred to me – and I would have been horrified if someone had suggested it – that I might have to climb up into them, and that there might be no road. So it turned out. The monastery of Santo Stefano was deliberately inaccessible and only one route which curved right around Lucca could boast a road at all. We, on these local horses, would have to negotiate the bare rocks.

"What!" Bonhomme exclaimed before he could stop himself. "Where is the path? Do you mean that?" pointing at a rough staircase hewn into the stone at one place and ending where the boulders were piled one on top of another. I sympathised thoroughly with his feelings, but Bruno only laughed.

If a French man was about to take two others on an expedition which would almost certainly kill them, he might laugh with an edge of cruelty in his voice, but this Italian looked back at Bonhomme with an expression of good natured affection at the same time as he sang out against the rocks. When eventually he explained that our horses were used to climbing mountains and would not slip either on steps or boulders, the two of us could not believe him. The large mare that I was mounted on dropped her head to crop the rough grass between the stones. "It is the only way," Bruno insisted, and with that he spurred his horse on and mine, without any encouragement from me, lifted her head at once and followed after.

I had this advantage over Bonhomme, in that I was not physically capable of making my own way over such terrain, and where he threatened to dismount and use his own legs, I had no choice. I prayed that my saddle would stand me in good enough stead, because I saw Bruno's horse start on that flight of stone steps like an apprentice boy climbing the stairs to visit his mistress. To my astonishment I felt the mare under me launch herself up, her hooves clattering on the stones, timing each surge upwards behind the mighty hind quarters of the horse in front.

This first flight of steps was very steep and there were perhaps fifty of them before they finished in what I took to be a dead end of stone. But to my horror and amazement Bruno's horse, once clear of the steps, gave a great leap upwards straight onto the mountain. Before I had time to do more than loop my arm around the pummel of my saddle my mount also stood upright on her back legs and leapt onto the shelf of rock above. I was too astonished to feel fear any more. I rode that valiant creature like a mouse on a paper boat in a rough sea.

Up and up we went until the coastline laid itself down below us as if we were birds. We passed through villages where for fifty yards or so we could go on level ground between the houses, but then we would be round a corner and once again the horses would have to spring up a heap of boulders or clatter the precipitous range of another flight of steps.

These stone steps were very well cut, and used continually by mounted travellers as well as men and women on foot. We passed some mules on the way, drawing our horses heads into the mountain in order to avoid trouble. But I noticed that the mules were less adept than these phenomenal horses, and did what mules always do, which was walk on the very edge of the precipice. I wondered, with some pleasure in the anticipation of telling it, how this story would strike the ears of Francis when I got home.

When we had been travelling for maybe an hour and a half we reached relatively flat ground and stopped to rest. But then there were more rocks, and in the uneven ground between one part of the mountains and another, the necessity arose from time to time of descending them, which was in some ways even worse. Faced with one cruel flight of steps, Bruno's horse checked and refused to go down. Bruno dismounted and led it, and even then it would scarcely follow after him and I think he was afraid, from the amount of lashing of the reins and cursing that he did. I of course, could not dismount. Bruno called out to me urgently, and would have seized my mare's bridle but I would not let him. She rolled her eye and flinched noisily from the top step, but in the end I coaxed her down.

In this way we three travelled for several hours, stopping only to feed and rest the horses. I conceived a great enthusiasm for the valiant creature that carried me and would have bought her, ugly as she was with her unvaried dark chestnut colour and her somewhat brutal form. But then, once back in Paris what should I do with her? I did not want to go every night up to my apartment in Versailles on horseback. But I should have dearly liked to do it once!

In the late afternoon we came at last to the end of our journey. A mile or so short of the monastery we joined the road from Lucca. We passed a great castle over to the right on a mound above fertile fields grazed by sheep, and then a scattering of houses on one side of the road, and on the other the church and the monastery.

The castle belonged to a Spaniard. I met this terrible man later on, and if he had been able to do anything politely he might have held open the door between this world and the next and given my backside a kick as I went through it. But luckily the Spanish liking for dwarfs made him regard me more kindly. Even now I cannot bring myself to admit that anyone equated myself with one of those creatures. I had a horror of dwarfs. I know very well that it is unjust; for me, even absurd. But so it is. In all my ugliness, I could look at my reflection and see how nature, however gone astray, had been informed at first by the pattern of a normal man. My head was not out of proportion with my shoulders and although my legs were so short, they were also twisted and weak. They were not strong and compact, like those of a dwarf, and although if they had been they would have been more useful to me, even I had my vanity and preferred them as they were. This was a secret thought of mine. I was ashamed of it. Years later one of the dwarfs who stayed in France after the death of the Spanish Queen became a great friend of mine, and I overcame my stupidity.

But I am telling my story out of turn. On that evening, we passed by Don Roderigo's fortress without stopping, and not until the door of the monastery did Bruno leap to the ground and pull the handle of the bell. Bonhomme and I had a strategy worked out which was that we would approach Brother Morel's master, the Surgeon Friar, as purchasers of tinctures and herbs for cure of the plague in France. Armed with letters of introduction from Cardinal Alberoni, the friend of Clément Cardinale's father and also the protegée of the Duc de Vendôme I expected to be warmly welcomed, and indeed I was. For the benefit of the Guardian who received us, I dismounted masked, and leaned on my stick when Bonhomme handed it to me. I was treated by him with great respect, and a young monk was sent to fetch Father Ludovico, the Surgeon Friar.

We waited for his arrival in an anteroom sparsely furnished, and smelling of stone and herbs and the droppings of sheep. A small window looked out in the direction of the sea, and though we were now beyond range of any sight of the ocean, one could guess how the sun, that painted a quarter of the sky pink, marbled with a glassy blue, was resting with one rim in the water.

When Father Ludovico came into the room, I swept the ground with the brim of my hat, and kissed the cord that hung at his waist without any prompting from Bonhomme. And when I thanked him for his kindness, "Oh, Monsieur!" he said, speaking French but all tilted with exuberant Italian rhythms until I could only just understand him, "we are honoured to receive a friend of Cardinal Alberoni here. And a scholar, as he describes Monsieur, is even more welcome. As you know, we are a scholarly community here, and if some small measure of fame goes out into the world from our studies of plants and our few small discoveries to do with the mixture of minerals found in this area in the rocks and so on, …"

He was the sort of man who talks himself out of air, and every now and then for an instant his lips would move and no sound emerge until he caught his breath. I could not help liking him. He talked as he led the way along a cloistered walk to meet the Abbot, and still talked when an influx of the brothers who had been out of doors gathering herbs and working in the community began all to return, hurrying to be within the monastery walls before dusk, as the rule of their order commands. At one point they crossed our path rather like swallows, at the close of day, will dart across the sky one by one. But the very last of these was a great big fellow and I noticed him even then.

At the time I had the feeling that he had raced so fast to outdistance the fall of night in returning to the monastery that a piece of it had caught on his person, like a thorn. He panted, with his eyes on the ground as he passed us by, but I saw his skin was rough like some apples that Francis brought back with him from England; ugly fruit, and sour too, but he was proud of them.

At that moment a bell started to toll. Father Ludovico quickened his step, and his monologue turned to the need to return to recite sext in choir, and that the Abbot would meet us later but for the moment he would hand me over to a lay brother, for the finding of our beds for the night.

I at last came to rest in a small cell that contained a clean bed, a table, a chair and a bowl and nothing else. I had been standing in the middle of it quite bewildered as to what to do next when there was a knock at the door, and to my relief Bonhomme came in. He carried a full jug in one hand and my large case in the other. He knows that I need to drink water or else I develop a tick in my neck which sometimes plagues me. "Thank heaven," I said taking it from him. "I thought I was back in the centre of Paris and would have to pay two sous for a load of water to be carried to this room from the nearest fountain."

The sun had disappeared, and a dim twilight was all we had to see by. Bonhomme took a candle end out of his gown and lit it, and I think he must have left me alone again, and returned because he now had a jug of wine and a glass. "Drink yourself," I said to him. He must have been hoping that I would say that because he had another glass in his pocket. He stood by the window and I sat. There was the distant sound of prayers being sung. All at once a little cat leapt up onto the sill, settled, looked, and went away again. That is how I remember our first evening at Santo Stefano.

CHAPTER THIRTY-THREE

We stayed in the monastery of Santo Stefano for nearly seven days, in spite of the danger of Lorraine catching up with us, but I had no choice. In order to win the confidence of Morel and others, my visit had to seem to conform to a more sympathetic purpose than the real one, and I had made myself out to be a student of herbs beneficial to memory as well as to cure the plague.

Fra Morel himself turned out to be that very monk whom I had noticed on first walking through the cloisters with the Surgeon Friar; the monk to whose person the on-coming night seemed to have attached itself. As soon as I became familiar with the routine of the monastery, I noticed how this one man was often solitary; how he spent all his days collecting, drying, analysing and mixing herbs and minerals, which I would have thought would have earned him the esteem of the Surgeon Friar. And it did; but not his love.

In obedience to his superior Fra Morel would gather whatever herbs and minerals had been asked for, and there were certain roots that it took days to fetch because they grew where the rocks were almost inaccessible. Of the monks whose duties were focussed on this aspect of their work, Fra Morel was the one whose obsession with his studies caused him to outstrip all the rest. I have seen him returning with his robe torn and a great gash bleeding on his hand and forearm, but triumphant because he had, wrapped up in some coarse leaves in his pouch, a rare plant root.

The work of dissecting, distilling and studying these plants and roots was carried on in two adjoining rooms: a spectacular and quite extraordinary library, and a laboratory. Also plants were drawn, dried and still sometimes named for the first time, since travellers came to this monastery from all over the world to have particular herbs or flowers identified. While I was there two men came from the East. They could communicate only in Latin, which was good enough, but where their homeland was I never could establish. Only that they had sailed from Venice. But they had travelled for a long time before they got to Venice.

It was the visit of these two that gave me my first opportunity to get better acquainted with Morel. As I said before, he was not a friendly or an easy man. I had tried to open a conversation with him before, but he refused to be drawn, or even to answer in response to the most ordinary greeting. But luckily his morbid cast of mind prompted him to imagine that I might be of especial use to him in another way, although he had no intention of being open on the matter. It was only my watchfulness that caught him out.

Ever since the first day, I noticed how Father Ludovico simultaneously consulted Morel as an equal or even a superior in knowledge, but how this relationship was never free of a certain fastidious withdrawal. To take a crude example, I was present one evening when they were working together on a new combination of elements, using certain very delicate procedures. Only one phase of the task – and there were several others – involved heating a distillation already made, to an exact degree, while at the same time a powder was fired, and the residue added at the precise moment when the two, being of a perfect temperature for the purpose, would combine. But during this whole time, Father Ludovico avoided physical contact with Morel. He drew back when the other leaned across to reach something. He held his face at an angle. I should have already mentioned that Ludovico's character underwent a complete change when he was engaged in his work, and he talked and laughed less. But when Morel was with him, his communication was limited absolutely to an intense attention to the procedures. He seemed to try to be unaware of the physical man, and I only once ever heard him speak warmly.

That was when Morel injured himself as I described before. Seeing how his arm had been deeply cut, Ludovico was moved to express some sympathy, and in a tone I had not heard him use to Morel he commended him for such devotion to duty. But the look he got in return put an end to his enthusiasm. He promptly asked another monk to dress the wound and went himself into the library on other business.

If my observations are somewhat minute you must remember that my training in Versailles was all of watching men and women and what their secret thoughts were, and how in small ways they betrayed their real feelings and sometimes their intentions. It was useful to me here, because I was soon convinced that Morel had a study of his own – a particular project which he did not share with his superior, but for which he felt a passion that consumed him. This would be the interest that I could make use of in order to get from him first an admission of having sold poison to Lorraine (a matter for which he would have been expelled from the monastery if it became known) and then written and actual proof of it.

At first, when I noticed, or thought I noticed, that he watched me particularly carefully, I put myself in his way so that he could speak, as I said. But he ignored me. So I deduced that it was not to find an opportunity to speak to me that he watched me. One day I happened to have torn one of my nails, and when I took my knife out to pare and smooth it, lo and behold a minute later this man surreptitiously gathered up the fragments, and I saw him wrap them in a little cloth which he then put in his pouch. This was the first time that I realised he attributed powers to my deformity from which he hoped for a sympathetic effect with his experiments. I pondered this a while. I concluded that the correlation between the mutilated body and the twisted spirit which I had so often and so fiercely resented as an idea, was the one that would help me here.

I discussed it with Bonhomme and started from that moment to allow small instances of apparent duplicity or cunning to mark my behaviour when I thought that Morel was looking. But nothing could have prepared me for what I then discovered.

After about three days, following on a conversation that I managed to have with him, I saw an idea take possession of his mind which he knew involved some risk, and yet – with spite almost – he also smiled at it. Eventually he made his mind up, and he asked me if I would be interested to view a humble experiment of his own that he was carrying on in an adjoining room. This was when Ludovico was absent, as I have mentioned, with his Eastern visitors. I agreed. We went down a short flight of steps from the laboratory, which I had assumed led to store rooms. And so they did, but also there was another place. Here, on a long stone bench, this man showed me a line of cages. There were mice, two cats, a small mammal that I did not know the name of, and a dead thrush.

The bird was the luckiest of these poor creatures. The cat raised its head and made a very quiet whining sound when we approached, which was a noise I had never heard from a cat before. Morel had removed its tongue and one ear. I weep now, years later, when I tell you this. I cannot bear to describe the others.

But I felt Morel's eye on me, watching. And he was cunning. He watched my hands, not my face, which was too low for him to see where I was standing. I felt tears in my throat and a heavy feeling in my heart for all the world as if I would die of it there and then. But I realised that this moment was vital for my purpose, and no personal weakness of my own must intervene, so I steeled myself.

"What are you working on here?" I said, but in a tone that implied that I was interested in it, rather than horrified. I could feel him looking at me very intently. Being tall anyway, he was twice my height. Although I kept my eyes away from his, because I was afraid of revealing my true feelings, I could see him, as it were, with the nerves of my body. The glimmering calculation left his face when he saw that I was not afraid and that I was not, apparently, disgusted. The tone of his voice changed to one of morose explanation. "All creatures that live on the face of the earth are given to man," he said, "for his use. God said so, in the book of Genesis, of blessed memory."

"Of accursed memory," I said in my heart.

" And we are using these animals to make certain experiments and observations to further our craft, in order to help us cure the sick."

"Which diseases are they most helpful in?" I said.

"The plague. We had a terrible visitation here in Italy not long ago. You heard of it perhaps. If that happens again we will feed potions that we have evolved, to the mice here, and then a piece of that mouse eaten by an infected human being will cure them." I felt such despair, standing there listening to his words.

"And Father Ludovico...?"

Morel laughed. He rubbed the top of his shaven skull and said. "The surgeon Friar is anxious enough to use the results of this research, but he forbade it when I started. The Abbot himself had to rule on the matter, and after studying Holy Writ he concluded that mankind has the mandate of God to use animals for his own service in whatever way is necessary. And this is true is it not! Who can argue otherwise?"

I nodded. And then I said, "But yourself, Fra Morel? A scholar must have an ambition of his own. What is yours?"

I longed to leave that room, but I leaned my back against the stone bench on which these little animals languished, so that I could not see them. Morel had walked over to the corner where food was stored, and during the next few minutes he attended to the cages and gave all the creatures water as if caring for them, at the same time as talking to me. And what do you think it was, the great ambition that explained the whole tenor of this monk's life; that he took to be a sacred trust, but which must have been the work of the devil because it was consuming his soul? He swore me to secrecy before mentioning it. He said that I could help him, or he would not have uttered a word. And then he said that he thought that he was on the brink of discovering the unguents in which the cloths used to wrap Lazarus were soaked.

I was amazed. Luckily, like all madmen, he was ready to attribute my astonishment to admiration. "But how can I help you?" I enquired.

He stopped right beside me. Now that I was this close to him, I noticed that he smelled strange. The seeds of so many herbs and so many ground roots had been rubbed into the cloth of his habit that the mixture of the man's own dirt and these scents of nature were distinctive to such a degree that I have never come across it again. He told me, in simple terms, of a spell – it really could not be disguised as anything but an attempt at magic. He needed just one letter of the alphabet to put him on the right track to discover the last element of his study, and God would give him license, since this was all for His glory, to demand help from the spirit world.

I could already guess what this would have to do with me. He would need blood from one twisted and miniaturised like myself, just as the Montespan had needed the hearts of my two pigeons all those years ago. Maybe some cuttings from my hair. It was time for me to bargain with this man.

"Come," I said, "to my cell in half an hour. I will be alone, and I will have an answer for you."

I left the room, and found my own way back to my room. When I entered it, Bonhomme was there. He was leaning against the window, half looking out, but straightened when he saw me, and then started forward and said, "What's the matter?"

I had the sensation for a moment as if I stood with a wall of water towering over me, from which I could not possibly emerge without drowning. Only silence could hold it back. I decided to say nothing. I must see this man – Morel – first, and strike my bargain. "Don't try to speak to me now," I said. "Fetch me some wine, and help me to change my linen. Come back when you see Morel leave this place."

In the next hour I conceived some admiration for people who trade with the devil. I came near to it when dealing with Morel, and the experience used all the courage that I had. And yet he was the same man as had been working out in the fields; with whom I had spent one morning side by side, digging for roots near a little stream. He was the same man whose arm was cut by a rock, showing that he had blood and bone like any mortal.

I heard his knock on the door and called for him to enter. I saw at once he was surprised when he saw me. I had on my court shoes, my embroidered tunic, and silk coat. And I also had on my wig. I was scarcely the same man as had left him half an hour ago. I should have liked to say to him "Who do you see here?" And then I would have liked to drag the words out of him by prompting and interjecting words of my own until he recognised me as a nobleman of the court of France, And I would have said that I knew that he had met one other, and by that route come to the Chevalier de Lorraine. And so on. But Morel was not the sort of man that you can bully. He had that moroseness that does not respond to any lash, and therefore I had to resort to cunning.

I welcomed him in, and when he was standing gazing at me, with a little less security in his eye as to whether or not this new and grander version of myself was likely to be persuaded to help him as he had planned, I said,

"I have decided that I may be your friend."

This was not exactly what he had asked for, and he turned a puzzled expression on me, which at the same time was full of anxiety. I was reassured to find how desperately he desired my help with his silly plan.

"But," I said, "I also want something from you."

He continued to look at me.

"Some years ago," I said, "a gentleman from the Court of France came here to see you and bought poison." Morel said not a thing. "Deny it and I will have nothing more to do with you." He bit his lip and simply stared at me. I heard Bonhomme scrape his feet on the stone outside my door, but fortunately the monk heard nothing. Finally Morel said, "What do you want?"

"I want a letter confirming that you did this. You can sign it. And I want a measure of the same poison. "

"Is that all?" Morel said. He spoke sneeringly and I thought that perhaps I had lost him. I was afraid that I had miscalculated.

"You have nothing to fear," I said. "By the time I am back in France you will have completed your task here, and you will be free to move on. Isn't that true?"

"How do you mean?" he said.

"Rome, surely. Will you not wish to go and describe your findings to his eminence the Pope? Won't they be interested there to hear what you have to say? "

He looked doubtful. But the fact that I seemed to expect it lit a fire of anticipation in him.

"Besides," I said, "this proof that you will give me is not going to be shown indiscriminately. In fact, the very bargain that I wish to strike involves keeping it secret."

He looked doubtfully again. But it was true. I would use the evidence to blackmail Lorraine, promising to keep it secret provided he mended his ways. The only person who would know would be perhaps Lorraine himself. That said, I myself should not have liked Lorraine to know that I had betrayed him, even if I lived as far away as Italy. I hoped Morel would not think of this.

He had a way of standing that was very ungainly, as I said before. Something about his perfectly healthy normal physique repelled one almost, I swear, as much as my own but for different reasons, and those harder to describe.

"If the bargain doesn't please you," I said, "let's hear no more of it."

He hesitated. I smiled at him. I gave him the best view that I could of my lip split right up into the cartilage of my nose so that my teeth hung out, and then as if purely to admire the view I turned my side to him, for him to admire my hump. He capitulated.

"Then bring me a letter of confession tomorrow. Make it brief. I want the name of the Chevalier de Lorraine, and the date on it. And write the effect of the poison; how it kills, and how it is administered. That, and a small quantity of the poison itself, and I will then help you in the ways that you want. My servant Bonhomme will keep the letter and the package and neither the Abbot nor the Surgeon Friar nor any of your brother monks shall know a thing about it."

He looked at me intently. A distant bell had begun to toll and at first he seemed not to hear it.

"It's a fair enough bargain, isn't it?" I said. "Think of Rome."

The poor fool did that, and came to the conclusion that I spoke the truth; at which point he suddenly realised the bell was ringing and he should be at prayer. I do wonder what the Good Lord made of the words that issued from that man's mouth in the next half hour.

CHAPTER THIRTY-FOUR

I completed my part of the bargain with Morel – a childish caper which needs no description – and he completed his to me, which consisted of the signed and dated written evidence which I had demanded, and a parcel of small leaves of paper impregnated with the poison. He described, quite willingly in the end, how the paper if used to rub an object, would leave behind a residue which once touched with the lips or even the hand if there was the smallest scratch on it, would kill.

For the purpose of my ostensible mission, namely my studies with Fra Ludovico, these were completed and so at this convenient moment I was free to leave. But I wanted one more thing. Revenge.

Revenge is always dangerous. It is a forbidden fruit even more apt to cloy or embitter the senses than knowledge. But I felt such a taste for it as a man denied food will lust after meat. I wanted revenge for the suffering of the animals – the experiments – being carried out by Morel. Curiously enough, I became almost reconciled to the man himself in the end. He was a Frenchman who had wandered far from home when he was still a boy and had finished by losing his way in a profounder sense. But that Abbot of his, who had licensed the torture of the animals – towards him I felt a state of rage that would hardly let me sleep. Bonhomme warned me against any action that might annoy our hosts; above all raise their suspicion. But it was as if a hot coal had been ignited in my heart. I burned with passion when I remembered the suffering of those little creatures.

Let me admit here and now that I am not a good Catholic. I wasn't then, and I am not now. It was because of Madame, the Princess d'Orléans, that I first looked further afield in my philosophy. She came from a Protestant country, and whatever had formed part of her being was bound to be beloved by me. In the Palatine she had been brought up in an atmosphere of religious tolerance that allowed a man to think his own thoughts about Divinity, and without any prompting from her, needless to say, I nevertheless read and generally imbibed the opinions of her homeland. Just as she converted to Catholicism to accommodate the needs of her marriage to the Duc d'Orléans without any inner struggle, I transplanted my sympathies all the other way.

There are consequences of such a change of loyalties which are subsidiary to the basic alteration. For example, the next time I read, or heard read, the familiar passages from the book of Genesis I looked between the lines in a way that our good Catholic priests would have thought none of my business. I found some of these words of Holy Writ hard to stomach and none more so than those in which God gives dominion over all the animals to Adam and his descendants for ever. Frankly, I didn't believe it. As I am half way to being an animal myself in the eyes of some of my fellow men, I know what it is like to be despised. Worse, to be judged incapable of intelligence or feeling. And I have stood, helpless, spurned by the foot of some absent minded demigod who thought my mind and my heart empty when both were full of the poetry of Racine, or images of the sculptures of Michaelangelo. I am just giving you an example.

Is it extravagant of me to think that the same mistake can be made with respect to the animals? The idea occurred to me very early on in my life, and nothing that I observed ever corrected the notion. I saw the exquisite beauty of birds, of animals in the fields, even of Madame's dogs. I swear I read their thoughts. I perceived the need to have the same respect for them as for a person; the identical judgement, if you will allow space for the breath of Nature, which a wise man uses when he respects a compatriot who has education and intelligence but no money. Once this idea had occurred to me, my observation became more acute when in the company of animals, and in the end I could no longer think of them as deserving any less of comfort, safety, respect than myself. Added to that, their helplessness became almost painful to me. The carnivorous predators, in all their beauty, could better look after themselves, and as I said before I was afraid of large dogs. But the others had long ago, secretly, enslaved me. I loved them all. To tell you the truth, I didn't eat meat if I could possibly help it. Once the idea had occurred to me that the Divine authority for murdering my fellow creatures was suspect, I followed the example of King Louis and ate vegetables, fruit and eggs whenever I could.

I hope that this explains to some extent how moved I was, and how I could not wean myself from the conflicting passions of pity and revenge while we were still in the monastery of Santo Stefano. I was determined to give the Abbot cause to regret his heartless cruelty and his spiritual blindness, and I thought long and hard how to do it.

On the morning of my departure I had the honour of conversing with him in his apartment for about an hour. The purpose of this audience was meant to be for me to thank his reverence for his hospitality and to hand over a gift of money for the monastery at the same time as receiving some commissions for friends of his in France.

This Abbot was a man neither liked nor disliked by those who knew him. He owed his position to a wealthy mother and the fact that his great grandfather on his mother's side had been Chancellor under Don Gonzales Fernandes de Cordoba when he was Governor of Madrid. Perhaps he had some Spanish blood. He was an unusual looking man for an Italian. His pate was naturally bald, not shaven, and the fringe of hair still surrounding it was red in colour. He exuded an air of dissatisfaction, and I am sure that the monastery of Santo Stefano was more a stone for him to set his ambitious foot upon than a rock on which to build Christ's faith. It followed that any discovery that might enhance the renown of the monastery, already famous as it was for the study of plants and herbs as I have explained, was important to him. Hence his ruthless support of the study of an effective antidote to the plague.

It was on this subject that I was determined to attack him. I raised the matter almost at once. We spoke in Latin. I coolly referred to the animals I had seen and enquired of his opinion. He suppressed what little surprise he felt in the fact that I had penetrated so far into the many facets of work being pursued by the monks under his rule, and explained that the animals were a great help in testing and adjusting the powerful extracts of herbs, minerals, and plants studied here. I appeared to reflect on this. I wore my mask, incidentally, and he could only see my eyes. I kept them open, scarcely blinking. I had been seized with an utter coldness of the spirit as soon as I crossed the threshold of his room,

After a pause, I asked him if Our Lord's words on the protection of the innocent should be extended to harmless creatures of the animal world. He said that they should not be hurt for no reason, but that God had given them to Adam and his descendents forever, to have dominion over them, and therefore if their lives could be useful to mankind, they were legitimately forfeit. I chose to interpret this as a commentary only on their role as food, and questioned the suffering inflicted in these research processes.

My drift was already beginning to annoy the Abbot, but I maintained an air of such formal courtesy that he was forced to accept my enquiries as purely spiritual and intellectual. Even so, he threw back a rather heated answer. He asked me if I was aware how many poor souls had died in the last outbreak of the plague in Italy. Then he described the sufferings of these people for a few minutes, and concluded with a reminder that God himself had instructed Adam to use animals to work for, and feed and help him. This is what the Surgeon Friar and his monks were doing at Santo Stefano. If as a result of the work done with these animals a cure was found that would save future human sufferers from the plague, then it was right that that work should be done.

He had risen from his chair by this time. Irritation and tension combined with a wish to hint that our interview was at an end – I made out that all these signs passed me by. I had been standing in the beginning and I still was. I took a step away from the door. I smiled, and although the man could not see my mouth, he would hear it in my voice.

"Why, Father Abbot!" I exclaimed, and I made a graceful gesture at the same time towards him with my hand, in the manner of the court; "But I had not thought to find a follower of Macchiavelli here, and such a distinguished one."

"I?" he said, astounded.

"But of course. The end justifies the means. You have explained it to me very well. I also admire the writer of *The Prince*. Oh, come," I said, because the poor man was trying to interrupt me, and I made out to misconstrue his reason. "A man of courage earns the admiration of gentlemen like myself. If I were in your position I daresay I would be afraid to declare myself a supporter of one for whom the Jesuits have such inveterate enmity, and His Holiness, of course... But the vision of Macchiavelli is not incompatible with the Holy Bible, as you have just pointed out."

I thought the man would have a fit.

"I said no such thing!" he almost shouted.

"Oh, your Reverence," I said, and I made as if to wag a finger at him, but not quite. I did not want this interview to descend into comedy. I wanted the full tragedy of his vicious opinions to haunt him day and night when I was gone. I wanted him to see me travelling all the way back to France, a courtier with numerous important connections of which Cardinal Alberoni was merely one. And I wanted him to think of me as a talkative man; a dilettante with scholarly talents and an irresponsible sense of humour who would tell the world of how the Abbot of the monastery of Santo Stefano admired the writings of Macchiavelli. It would be enough, if it came to the ears of the Vatican, to debar this wretched fellow from preferment for ever.

MALICE

CHAPTER THIRTY-FIVE

One might be forgiven for thinking that my so-called revenge had not amounted to very much, and in fact as I set out from the monastery with Bonhomme and Bruno, I rather thought so myself. We started to travel the same path as we had used in coming, and I began to think of the dangers ahead because the more we talked of it the more convinced Bonhomme and I became that Lorraine, unable to stop us from reaching Italy, would do all in his power to prevent us on our return journey to Versailles.

After ten minutes the village was left behind, and some way ahead I could already see the Castel del Monte whch we had passed on our inward journey. From this angle it appeared forbidding, and one noticed how the landscape was broken up on the slopes surrounding it as if the massive rocks of man and of nature colluded in producing an impression of gloom. I was about to ask Bruno the name of the man who lived there, when a hurried clatter behind and to the right drew my attention to two men on mules who appeared suddenly in our road.

In broad daylight, and so close to the monastery and other dwellings, it did not occur to us that there was anything to be feared from these men until with extraordinary force and determination they suddenly attacked us. I was being dragged from my horse. Bruno was crouching not far off with his head in his arms and shouting in Italian, and Bonhomme received a terrible blow from a heavy stick which sent him flying. I stood up. I was not wearing my sword because it is too awkward for someone like myself to carry large arms, but I had a knife in my belt.

I attempted to set my back against a rock and I was determined to take at least one of these men with me if my journey's end was destined to be in the other world and not in this one. Whether I should have had any success I do not know. As I have mentioned my arms are very strong, and a knife can be a nasty weapon especially in the grip of someone small, like myself. I have seen people fight in this way, and normal sized men always crouch.

However, the individual with the stick was now free and he raised his arm to strike me with it in a way that would have cut me from the ground like a stook of corn. I am not one who can dodge. I threw myself forward on the ground and managed to pin the other villain to the soil with my knife through his foot, but more than that I knew I was quite unable to achieve. I expected death. I assumed that the next instance of my consciousness would be in another place.

And so it would have been if suddenly a number of other men had not come rushing to our rescue. There were six of them, and they put our attackers to flight very quickly. They were the most extraordinary fellows. They all had their hair bound in green nets which, I later discovered, hung over the left shoulder and ended in a large tassel. They wore loose wide breeches with the pockets full of knives, and were wielding rapiers with pierced brass hand guards. One of them picked me up in a manner I rather objected to and stood me again near the rock I had been trying to hold my back against in the first place. At the same time another, who seemed to be their chief shouted at Bruno, and receiving only a mindless babble of fear in reply struck him hard on the mouth with the back of his hand. This not only made his lip bleed but seemed to re-establish some connection between his mouth and his brain that had obviously been disrupted before. In answer to a string of questions he bellowed responses, not one of which either Bonhomme or I could understand.

I got tired of this. When one of these answers set our four friends in a roar of laughter I drew myself up and said to him that if he did not speak in French, I would kill him myself. This obviously was translated for the benefits of the ruffians who laughed again as if their sides would split.

Bruno, not knowing where to turn, remembered perhaps that I had not paid him yet, and told me that these four men who had saved our lives were bravos, belonging to Don Roderigo. I didn't know what he was talking about. He pointed at the castle, and I understood then, and more clearly later, that these men were members of a sort of bodyguard kept by the nobleman to serve his purpose in any way he chose. I later discovered that the authorities had tried to outlaw these bravos, but the Spanish noblemen ignored the proscription and habitually kept six or a dozen of them. They were called bravos, or cuiffi (a reference to their long hair). They would accompany their master as outriders wherever he went; and since the bravos were commonly ruthless and well armed they would not only protect their master, but enforce his will in any way he chose.

At this moment I could not understand why these bravos had come to my aid. They did not look like men who performed acts of charity. The leader, looking down at me as I spoke with an expression not altogether objectionable, prompted Bruno with a word of his own and it transpired that they thought that because I was a dwarf their master, being a Spaniard – and everyone knows that the Spanish are extraordinarily attached to dwarfs – would be pleased with them for saving my life and bringing me to the Castel del Monte. Bruno, no doubt from conversations with Bonhomme, knew that I would object strongly to this description, so that he cringed while producing it as if I might strike him. I thought of it. But after all, what is dignity compared to life? These fellows may have taken away the one, but they had given me the other.

I told Bruno to express my thanks to them for what they had done, and that I agreed to go with them. I asked Bonhomme to help me re-mount my horse, which he did but he was bleeding himself from a cut on the head that looked very bad. We all went in a troop up toward the castle gates. The leading bravo treated me with deference, and I was rather taken with him. He had great mustachios curled upwards at the ends, and in addition to all the other items I have mentioned, he wore a highly polished leather belt on which hung a brace of pistols. He also wore a small powder horn suspended round his neck. I never saw a man so armed before or since, taking into account the knives that were in his pockets and his sword as well.

There were some peasant houses clustered round the base of the castle which had been hidden from view by the angle of the ground because they were so low. A narrow path led up to the gate of the castle itself, and the great wall was pierced only with quite small windows placed high up and protected with heavy iron grilles. The door of the castle was closed, and this apparently indicated that Don Roderigo was at table, and not wanting to be interrupted.

The bravos threw themselves down on various benches and rocks to wait, and I dismounted. Poor Bonhomme, as soon as he had helped me get down, leaned over the side of the path and was sick. Blood from the gash on the side of his head had dried and the wound looked not severe, but I know how dangerous a blow of that sort can be. Finding out from Bruno that we expected to have to wait some time, I instructed him to tell the leading bravo that I was concerned for my man who had been injured trying to defend me. Surprisingly, he responded with homely sympathy, going up to Bonhomme and after peering into his eyes, hammered on the door until it was opened. After a brief discussion among themselves and shouted instruction at the old door keeper who clung onto the lock, we were led inside.

There were some terrible dogs in there. Great hounds came leaping and barking, but I was surrounded by the bravos and had come to the conclusion that nothing else could happen to me that day.

We were led through into a small courtyard and here suddenly there were seven ground floor windows with round arches bordered with a band of red beccia, and beautiful upper windows with trilobate arches and pilasters of white marble.

Across it was a portal designed on the principles of Roman architecture, although the arch itself rested on a series of little columns, with lions crouched on the capitals, which I took to be traces of an earlier stage in building. Through this we reached a room from which a great spiral staircase led to an upper floor. Four of the bravos stayed on ground level, and we with the remaining two, climbed up until we came to an ante room leading into a great hall resounding with the noise of loud conversation and the clatter of knives.

The leading bravo, assuming a posture of careful deference, went into the margin of the room, and after a few moment's pause there was a shouted exchange between him and his master. "What are they saying" I asked Bruno.

It was merely an account of the last hour's adventure, followed by Don Roderigo himself getting to his feet with loud exclamations which I took, from the good natured sound of his voice, to be words of welcome. He came towards me, an excited gleam in his eye, and with something between mockery and superstition he bowed to me, and I, with the most elegance that I could possibly muster, responded as if he had been the King of France himself.

He approved of this. He drew himself up as if I were a protégée of his who had performed some clever trick, and half turned to his companions with a smile as if to receive their congratulations.

"Bruno," I demanded, "tell Don Roderigo that I am a gentleman from the court of France, and that I am grateful to him in that his henchmen saved my life."

When he heard this Don Roderigo made a graceful reply, and then clapped his hands. A servant brought more dishes, and their Master led me, and Bonhomme as well, up to the table, where a couple of gentlemen who had been sprawling there vacated their chairs in our favour.

The chairs were huge. They were nearly too big for me to get into, but this very fact seemed to delight Don Roderigo. He began to converse with me using Bruno as an interpreter, and I told him how I had traveled from France to visit the monastery of Santo Stefano in order to gain some knowledge of certain herbs. The bravo interjected a word here, and Don Roderigo responded with surprise. Bruno, who was forever forgetting the reason why he was with me in the first place, translated when I prompted him, and said that the bravo said that our attackers were connected with the monks.

"Surely that can't be so," I said.

But in the next instant I remembered my revenge.

I broke off, and thought with some satisfaction of how well aimed my goading of the Abbot must have been. I had successfully made him so afraid that he had thought it best to have me killed. He would suffer even more when he discovered that I had got away and without injury.

The food that I was eating began to taste very good although it had gone cold since it was first prepared, but you know what they say about revenge. I drank a silent pledge to those little creatures for the sake of whose suffering, together with my own misery at such vicious chop logic contained in the scriptures, I had exacted this payment from the Abbot.

I started to take in the general furniture of the room with exclamations of admiration that I hoped would please Don Roderigo. Several great windows looked out towards the south in the direction of Lucca. Stone steps led up into the window embrasures, which on either side were modified into one vast ledge than ran right around the room. It was a very beautiful form, and after praising it I described Versailles to my host, and he listened entranced. Several times he asked me to repeat details of the great gallery, for example, and the King's apartment, and aspects of the gardens. He was an admirer of Bernini and Coysevox and could not hear enough, it seemed, of their work. He had never heard of Le Notre. But my descriptions of the fountains and the other water pieces in the gardens of Versailles almost brought tears to his eyes.

Noticing that Bonhomme was too sick to eat, I agreed that he should be carried into a room and laid down, but not that he should be given any cure, in case it had been prepared by our friends at the monastery. I said that I would sleep in the adjoining chamber, where a bed of the size and general trim of a cathedral struck Don Roderigo as being so appropriate that he was determined that I should have it.

I began to like this man. He was no scholar. But his soul was alive to art, and although he was dangerously powerful and would, I'm sure, be very careless of the well-being of anyone he didn't like, he was well disposed towards me and had already done me some service. So I decided to accept his friendship; and if he had a tendency to tap me on the head, or laugh delightedly when my size in relation to the huge dimensions of his castle and furniture gave rise to some difficulty, then I overlooked it.

For Bonhomme's sake we were obliged to stay with him for three days. Before departing I gave the bravos who had rescued me a good sum of money because apart from the fact that I felt I owed it to them Bruno warned me that they would come secretly after us when we left otherwise, and take it by force. Although their behaviour towards Don Roderigo was servile in the extreme they were bullies to everyone else. There was apparently no crime they were not prepared to commit for their master, and when he took horse or went in his carriage, as I said before, they accompanied him as outriders.

When we dined together on the eve of my departure I gave Don Roderigo a ring off my thumb which had come to me from Clément Cardinale in payment of a gambling debt. He was hugely pleased with it. He may wear it to this day. Indeed I had begun to worry in case Don Roderigo would have taken such a liking to me that he would not let me go; but news came to him of some hunting to be had in the next province and once he accepted that I would not go with him, he was quite willing for me to resume my journey.

CHAPTER THIRTY-SIX

We set out in the early morning. It struck me as a very excellent thing to be free once more, and on our way home. I began to want to see France again, and although the climate there would be vile compared to this, my heart yearned for Paris.

"Why, Bonhomme!" I shouted out to him as our horses hooves alternately thudded or clattered on the stone scattered ground, "We shall be home for Easter."

"Yes, Monsieur," he shouted back. "And will you remember that you owe me a bowl of fish stew at the Gros Caillou. Think of it! Carp, eel and gudgeon! "We had played cards one night on the road, and I had lost to him.

He looked back now over his shoulder, his horse being ahead of mine for the moment, and I noticed how his dark hair, that had used to be rather thin and skimpy, seemed to have thickened and in general he seemed much healthier. In other ways, too, he had become a man I liked. Before, I could not have told you his age partly because I had never asked it; but also because the uneasiness of his spirit crossed and recrossed the familiar clues by which one reads a man, until they were fouled beyond recognition. Now – it may seem a rather absurd point – but I knew that he was thirty-two.

And then – Then, at that very moment I remembered the prediction of the Maréchale de Clerembault! Those words in which she had warned me that Bonhomme would not return safely from this journey, but would be killed on the road recurred to me for the first time. When ruminating over the possible danger of encountering Lorraine or his agents waiting to ambush us at some stage of our return journey, it had not yet occurred to me to remember the Maréchale's words and put the two together. I was struck to the heart. How could I have forgotten? Now that I felt friendship for Bonhomme, and valued him, this fortune-telling seemed more vile and more significant than previously. Despite the fact that according to the Maréchale's prediction, I myself was destined to return safely to Paris and there would be no danger to our precious cargo provided that I carried it, I felt there was very little comfort in it if Bonhomme were to be killed. And furthermore, in the adventure that we had recently undergone, I had been nearly killed as well as Bonhomme, and they would have looted me as readily as him if our assailants had been the agents of Lorraine instead of the Abbot.

I thought again. If it was indeed the Abbot who was responsible for that attack, the other was still to come. But conversely, if this was the event that the Maréchale had foreseen, then perhaps her famous powers of divination were unclear in their detail, as these things often were, in that the blow dealt to Bonhomme had certainly injured, but had not killed him. In which case, the danger was over and done with. No more harm should come to Bonhomme.

These reflections took all the lightheartedness out of the morning for me. At the very moment when I liked him most, I talked to Bonhomme less. I rode silently, anxious about him and seeing him out of the corner of my eye. I decided that for the moment I would do nothing about the Maréchale's prediction, and my promise to carry the evidence of Lorraine's conspiracy with Fra Morel on my own person. I must think whether or not to ask Bonhomme to hand the letter and the package to me. I was most anxious not to offend him.

We kept Bruno with us until we got back to Albenga. He said that he would have liked to come to Paris with us, but setting aside the fact that we needed to have not only one, but several men with us to help fight off any attack, Bruno was a coward and nor could I afford him, and so we parted. And again, setting off only with Bonhomme, with the road ahead of us leading to home, and riding Maud once more my spirits rose. I pushed the thought of the Maréchale's gloomy predictions to the back of my mind, and we made a holiday of our progress through Provence.

The great charm of that country resides in the red earth, the groves of ancient olive trees with their blue leaves; and the sea. We rode along the very edge of it. We were like mules, we clung so absolutely to the rim of the land. Or when forced back by a spit of rock, or a village built in our way, we came back to the sea again as soon as we could. We bathed in the water, and we drank some excellent wine. The food was not as good as in Paris, but they had fresh fish and good cheeses.

Before Aix we left the sea, and rode up to that town and afterwards towards Nîmes, because we had decided to return home by a different route in order to make it more difficult for anyone to ambush us on a familiar path. Now that the worst of the Winter was over, Bonhomme wanted to see the Auvergne, and we would go north by Clermont and Vitry.

On a sunlit evening three days after leaving Aix, we crossed the wooden bridge over the Rhône from Tarascon to Beaucaire. It was our good fortune to happen to arrive when the fair was on, and the first hint we got of it was the overpowering smell of garlic from the Champ des Aulx. The western side of the Rhône before the town of Beaucaire is bordered by a broad piece of common land, and on this meadow at the time of the spring fair the entire harvest of garlic for the Southern region of France for the coming year is spread out. All those who grow the bulb bring their harvest to the fair to trade, and the wealth of that area is immensely enhanced by it. And then, as so often happens, prosperity follows on prosperity. Dealers in other goods began to come to trade and by the year that Bonhomme and I visited the place, it was famous.

One of the great pleasures of recounting a history is the opportunity it gives the writer to remember, in detail, pleasant times. And this was indeed a pleasant time for us. We had grown to be more like two brothers, Bonhomme and I. As soon as I cast my mind back to that moment in our travels, I see not only the thickening evening sunlight on the wood of that famous old bridge that crosses the Rhône out of Tarascon, and smell the garlic, but from the corner of my memory's eye I see Bonhomme on the driving seat of the coach just above and beside me as I rode Maud. The waters of the Rhône were calm and sparkling with light. Then as we descended from the bridge and subsequently mounted a little rise in the ground after the Champ des Aulx, for a moment we were able to look down on Beaucaire. For the duration of the fair the inhabitants of the houses spread huge sheets from all the windows of the top stories of the houses, entirely covering the tiny narrow streets that run between them, and giving an enchanting appearance to the town. It looks like a great sailing ship on land; or like the covering of an enormous parasol. At the moment that we approached it the sun's decline was almost complete and in the fading light the first candles and lanterns of evening were lit, and shone from under this cover like glow worms.

Once we were on a level and able to enter the streets, the fantastic impression was magnified a hundredfold. I never saw so many people in one place, the streets being thronged with travelers from every part of the world as well as the local people, and all milling through these covered ways, with lighted stalls and windows on every side. And although we kept our eyes wide open, always alert for any sign of pursuit from our enemies, Bonhomme and I were, after all, young men, and we enjoyed it. Even the danger was enjoyable, and the sensation of pitting our wits against the calculations of a man like the Chevalier. Above all this was such a motley crowd as almost any man could hide in and become invisible among such numbers. I saw men from Persia selling oils, and others seated beside stacks of carpets from Shiraz and Isfahan. From a place called Balouchistan a man had brought three slave girls. There was tea from China and china from England, sacks of coffee from Vienna, copies of songs such as you see sold on the Pont Neuf in Paris, Italians selling silk, others selling tufa.

A small man with a complexion like smoked snake skin sold me a printed copy of Sir William Temple's essay on government, which I bought purely to demonstrate to Francis when I got home that his countrymen have influence everywhere. And the noise, the music, the shouts of the traders. Only after several hours did Bonhomme and I return to the inn on the edge of the town where we had left the coach and the horses.

During our absence the innkeeper had told an Italian singer and puppeteer that he could share our bed. There was no arguing. The man had already parted with his money, and was at table gorging himself on a mutton stew with more beads of grease and garlic swimming in it than meat.

Wine is the solution on these occasions. I called for plenty of it, and refilled the glass of our future bedfellow whose first astonishment at my own appearance was soon sublimated in the fumes of the grape as was my own shyness at the thought of his immense night time company.

What I had not bargained for was his singing. You would have thought that after our sojourn in Italy Bonhomme and I would be familiar with the Italian's love of music and the strength of their lungs; but no sooner had this fellow gone before us up the stairs and while Bonhomme and I were still eating, than his voice could be heard through the rafters going full tilt at a song that I happened to know, by Guiseppe Aldrovandini. When you consider how much noise there is in a busy inn of an evening, with the serving of food and the tramp of feet, and the drinking of wine with shouts and loud conversation, you will know what to think of the fact that this man could be clearly heard singing upstairs. But then, after the first moment of astonishment and apprehension, I began to admire the noise he made. There was a timbre and beauty to his voice that was remarkable.

When he had finished one song, he began another. By the time that

Bonhomme and I were climbing the stairs, he was well into Cavalli. It happened that this was a duet that he was singing on his own, and to my utter astonishment as I walked through the door Bonhomme, beside me, took up the second part. I had no idea that he could sing. The opera was *Ercole Amanti*, that had been performed more than once in Paris, and although Bonhomme's voice had nothing like the force of our Italian friend, he sang with perfect accuracy and great sweetness of tone. The result was that I called for more wine to be brought up to our room, and also a dish of sugar-dried fruit from Sicily, and all three of us sang half the night, until, in fact, we were stopped by our neighbours hammering on the wall.

CHAPTER THIRTY-SEVEN

The next day, after we had paid our bill and said our farewells we set off again on our road north. I don't think either Bonhomme or I felt as merry as we had before. I liked this southern country, and despite my desire to be in Paris again news from travellers in Beaucaire of how the mountain passes were still, in places, under snow and ice, caused me to replan our route and for the next two weeks we kept to the Rhône valley. We then cut across into the Auvergne east of Puy. I wish we had never done so. I wish it were possible to slip back into a crease of time and unfold the matter differently. But since that is not an option, let me tell you how things fell out.

Bonhomme it was who was so anxious to see the Auvergne. It was something to do with his childhood and things he remembered. I would have travelled fifty miles or more out of my way to avoid revisiting the scene of my own infancy, and a time came when I had to do that once, and I did it. But Bonhomme was different. I think he had been happy when he was a boy. But there turned out to be other reasons for avoiding the Auvergne.

No sooner did we penetrate into that country than the harshness of life and the extreme poverty of the peasants became oppressive. We had long ago left the easy life of the south. Now we saw that the Winter months that had passed since we first journeyed from Lyons had sucked and gnawed even more bitterly on the empty breast of Mother Earth in this place. There were still beggars everywhere. More. Once we had to enquire at a hovel whether or not we were on our right path, and the family inside were all naked and bundled up together under sacking in their bed. It turned out that, being a Sunday, they had lent their clothes to a neighbouring family, so that they could go to church.

It is dangerous, also, to travel and to be well fed among such desperate people. We could not afford to have our lives put at risk on such different accounts; from sophisticated enemies at Court and from starving predatory peasants in the country at the same time. When you are young and well fed and riding through the sun you can keep your eyes about you and be watchful with a light heart. But when your path declines into sunless wastelands, without being a coward one can nevertheless find one's thoughts returning to any prediction of misfortune that has been made, and now I found that I could scarcely get the words of the Maréchale de Clerembault out of my mind for ten minutes. In the end the preoccupation began to make me sullen. I saw that Bonhomme knew that I had something on my mind, and he was not so altered that he could not remember how to look uneasy or sly. But how could I tell him that a prediction had been made that he would be murdered, and that therefore I, in cold blood, would have that packet off him which he kept so faithfully guarded under his jerkin?

The longer I took to make my mind up the more likely it was that I should offend Bonhomme if I demanded that he should hand over the package to myself for safe keeping. And the idea of causing him offence had become repugnant to me because I have taken such a liking to him. In the end I solved the problem of which of us should carry the precious package won from Morel in the worst possible way.

We had managed to find some miserable lodgings for the night with a so called gentleman – they called them *'hobereaux'* – and his family near Burt. We had a supper of hare stewed with garlic, which was passable; but the fellow also tried to convince us to try potatoes – a disgusting vegetable that no gentleman eats. Before our meal Monsieur le Baron, the eldest son, went out with his father, he to feed the cows and the old man to shoot something for the pot. To do his share of the work the son wore a brown linen hat and a patched smock, with straw wrapped around his legs against the mud and dirt. When he came in again he took off his wooden clogs and put on a pair of shoes, while his mother, a fat, loud-mouthed woman, came in from the mill.

It could not be anything but depressing to spend an evening with such people, especially burdened as they were not only with poverty but with their ridiculous pride. This man, and others like him, considered themselves to be aristocrats, and although in this case they reluctantly, and badly, did a small amount of work, I have known others where the family would starve rather than give up the slothful habits which they regarded as inseparable from noble blood.

The next morning, under a sky the colour of wet rocks and with a cutting wind, we set out again. But it happened that during the night I had had a bad dream which sharpened my apprehension of pursuit by Lorraine. I could no longer believe that he would sit in Paris and wait for us to return, knowing, as he must know, that if I had met with Friar Morel I might have such dangerous evidence against him. Also one of the Baron's two sons had set out while it was still dark on the only horse they had, and I wondered where he had gone to so suddenly if not to take sly news of our passing to someone who might be interested.

I mentioned my anxiety to Bonhomme and he reminded me of the fact that he had wanted to sell the carriage at le Puy. Without the carriage, of course, we could have travelled faster. I don't know why I had not fallen in with his suggestion, because now on the final quarter of our journey we were free to carry less, and what was essential would fit into two cases mounted pillion on Bonhomme's horse and mine. It did not make me sweeter tempered to feel so in the wrong.

As we set out one could see the faint imprint of the sun far behind the clouds like a skull looking through a sheet. Bonhomme said that we should have snow. He was right. Soon the clouds thickened with a yellowish cast and then flakes more like ice than snow began to hit the ground. I got into the carriage and we covered the horses and went on only very slowly.

I began to be afraid that we had missed our road because we should have come to the village of Randon, or if not that, Aiguepere. We reached a spot where one could just make out, at a distance of perhaps half a mile, the bulk of what was probably no more than a small cottage. Bonhomme said that he would ride over to it, buy food if he could, and otherwise make sure of our road.

"Very well," I said. I was sitting in the coach with Maud's leading rein looped through the window. I paused, looking at Bonhomme as he stood, where he had leapt down from the driving seat onto the track. I remember it well. He was blue with cold, as he had been before when we travelled in winter, and at these heights the early spring was, clearly, not much better.

I said "Take my cloak." He took it, and began to wrap himself carefully round, and as he pushed his doublet back to get the cloth hitched firmly over it, he felt the place where I knew he carried the packet from Morel, seeing that it was safe I suppose. I said,

"Bonhomme, let me carry that parcel."

He looked up in surprise; and because I knew that I could not be open with him as to my reason for needing to make this request, I was embarrassed and I think I tried to conceal it with an off-hand manner. A sharp look came suddenly into his eye. I tried to smile a little, and I held out my hand. I was very surprised at the bitterness in his expression as he gave it to me. He kept his eye on mine as he unfolded the cloak again, then he extracted the packet without looking at it, and handed it over. Having done that he roughly threw the cloak back over his chest, mounted his horse, and rode off across the dry and stony pasture.

He came back with the news that we had missed Aiguepère but if we continued along our path now we would come to Gannat. He gave no information about the people he had spoken to, or whether they had had food, but simply got back up onto the driving seat after first tying his horse to the rear of the coach.

About an hour later the weather cleared. Although the sky was still littered with big clouds flying before the wind, it was bright. The leaden overcast was gone, and sunlight, cold but glittering, slightly revived us both.

I rode Maud beside the coach again, and tried to engage Bonhomme in conversation, but he was still very silent. I thought his sullen mood must lift soon, and eventually I said that I would canter ahead with Maud for a while, and I did that. In no time the coach was out of sight behind me and the noise of Maud's hooves, and the lofty piping of larks was all the sound there was. I stopped and looked all around. There were still clouds in the sky but more and more the blue of heaven predominated. From time to time the shadow of a cloud would move across the dry stone scattered grass like the keel of a great ship dimmed with water. And then when it passed the sun itself seemed to be blowing, and swirls of light and shade moved everywhere.

I turned to go back, but kept Maud to a walk. On one side rather far off I saw some sheep, but not a single man or woman. I thought I must have gone further than I realised; that I had galloped rather than cantered, and that Maud had a turn of speed that made me proud of her.

Occupied with my thoughts, I first caught sight of the coach without feeling any anxiety at all. It looked as if Bonhomme had stopped for some reason. Then the thought struck me that something was wrong. But no, I reasoned. To pass one's fears backwards and forwards in the mind, to imagine Lorraine's sneaking assasin's footsteps printed in every blade of grass, to be for ever trading fearful imaginings was a path for cowards. I would not take it. But the human eye is so quick to compute details which leave the conscious intelligence far behind, and I looked again. I can't explain even now what it was. The coach was still too far away for me to see Bonhomme on the box or knowingly to judge how fast or how slowly it moved towards me or if it moved at all. And yet some part of my perception7 – perhaps the same that tells a man catching a ball to place his palm in a particular section of the empty air where that ball will fly to, when with his conscious mind he could not possibly work it out – that part of my awareness knew that there was something wrong.

I spurred Maud to a canter, my eye fixed on the road ahead. Bonhomme was not on the box. Where was he? The horse was not pulling the coach, but had turned aside from the traces to crop the grass beside the track. Had some of the harness broken again? Would I find Bonhomme sitting by the side of the road cutting and stripping a piece of leather with his knife and whistling between his teeth the folk songs that he knew from these parts?

As I got closer I thought that perhaps that was exactly what I saw. But if so he was working in silence. I got closer. He was not sitting on that rock beside the road, he was sprawled against it. In so far as he was upright it was not his doing.

I flung myself from the saddle in such a way that I could have broken my legs, and scrambled over to him calling out his name. His right arm, a part of his neck his chest and one eye were covered in blood. Most of his clothes had been stripped from him. His horse was gone. I thought that he was dead and I was struck with despair. But then he stirred very slightly, showing that he was still alive, and then I thought at once, "He will be well. He will be well!" I turned to the coach, stumbling and hitting myself in my haste, to fetch a glass of spirits to revive him. The coach had been violently ransacked but the very fact that no food or wine was taken made it clear at once that it was Lorraine's cut-throats who had caught up with us, and not just the starving peasantry. In desperation I found what I was looking for and turned back to Bonhomme.

When I tried to lift his head blood suddenly spurted from the wound in his neck. I managed to get a little of the spirits between his lips, but he looked not like a live man at all.

"Bonhomme" I cried out. "What can I do?" I was beside myself. How could he have come to such harm in so short a time? I flung my eyes in a rage around the surrounding countryside, but there was no one to be seen. No one. Tears fell from my face onto his and washed some of the blood away. I took hold of his hand in both of mine. "What can I do?" I said.

I saw one corner of his mouth curve with that ironic smile of his, and his voice spoke in a whisper. "I'm sorry, Monsieur," he said.

I couldn't speak; any more than he appeared to be able to speak again. I could see life flicker in his face like a candle that would go out. He was trying to gather strength to say something and I waited. I think I hoped that he might say that he would be all right.

But what he said was, "Why did you not trust me?"

"What do you mean?" I exclaimed.

I tried to wrap my cloak around him without increasing the bleeding, and with a corner of it I pressed on his neck thinking it might stop the blood.

"You took Morel's package from me."

I looked at him, horrified, and made an involuntary gesture towards where it was tied under my coat. Pity and despair silenced me. He said in a whisper, "Monsieur, I have never explained something to you, but I want you to know this. You know what it is like to have to live with a twisted body; but I had a twisted spirit. I learned the difference from you. Something grew up in my heart that made me want to win your respect, and it became the most important thing in my life. Lately, I thought that I had succeeded. Until you took the package because you still did not trust me."

I thought quite honestly that my heart would break. I began to tell him about the Maréchale de Clermebault and all her wretched predictions and conditions; how she had made me promise her to carry the package myself on the return journey precisely because of this. I had finally done as she ordered in case Morel's evidence was lost, but I had not dared to tell him of the reason in case her prediction was right.

His face cleared in a way that, even mutilated as it was, was almost beautiful. He had reason to believe what I told him. I said, "It is a long time now since I have learned to trust you entirely, and to love you as a friend. Have we not been like brothers. We have had a wonderful journey. Do not leave me now; please."

He began to speak. He said "Lorraine," and moved his eyes to where his own blood was running on the ground, and where the ransacked carriage stood. He wanted to tell me that it was Lorraine's men who had attacked him and that they were in search of the package that he had had, and which now I carried. I understood. But then something choked him. Blood, I think. My God, since then how much I have hated the sight of blood! I wish I had not any in my own body, or if I had to have it, that I could have given it to him. I took his hand again and kissed it. I felt his fingers try to grasp my own. His lips moved again, but he died. He died.

MALICE

CHAPTER THIRTY-EIGHT

I lay for a long time by that road with Bonhomme's body in my arms. I looked at the surrounding countryside through bitter tears. There, past that rise of ground, I had galloped on Maud until I was well out of sight. Bonhomme's attackers must have come down the track we were on and I guessed that the son of the miserable hobereau we had lodged with – the one who has crept so early from his bed, and rode off – had indeed gone to inform some agent of Lorraine about our presence there. And yet... But then in my uncertainty I looked again at the wine still in the coach and the sack of meal, and Bonhomme's good boots still on his feet where no starving peasant would have left them.

The light was almost gone when at last I remounted my horse. I could do nothing more for Bonhomme. Fortunately I am not a religious man, and so since I could neither bury him nor carry him with me I simply said my last farewells and left.

Then the night descended, both on the world and on me.

I could carry nothing with me, but my money and the precious wallet containing Morel's confession and the poison. I could not even carry a change of linen. I had one small bag slung from the saddle with some cheese in it. I had no fodder for Maud, and no appetite for the remainder of my journey. But appetite and an overwhelming sense of purpose are, fortunately, not always conjoined.

I was aware that any man in danger of his life is a fool of he thinks he is safer traveling in the dark than in daylight, but I felt driven to it. There is an attentive eye belonging to evil deeds that can see better in the dark. At mid day the figure of a man on horseback is just one more among many, but at night if an assassin asleep under a blanket so much as opens one eye and sees another man, at a distance, moving, it will attract his attention. Instinctively I felt most horribly conscious of this. But what could I do? I could not, in that freezing wilderness, stand still until the sun rose, nor did I dare to remain by the coach where the man who killed Bonhomme might yet return, looking. I left the carriage where it was, unharnessed the horse, then I rode Maud, with this other on a leading rein.

By dawn Maud was exhausted and so was I. Luckily by this time I was on the outskirts of a small town. I did not want to attract attention by appearing at an inn too early, and being asked how I was on the road at such a time as to have clearly ridden all night. I found a silent lonely spot to tether the carriage horse, and left it there. Then myself, still mounted on Maud, I stopped in the shade of a vast yew tree making a corner between two tracks, and drew my cloak up high and my hat down low to look as much as possible like an ordinary man.

It was to be a sunny day. The first shafts of bright light lay in strips across the loose earth with shadows the length of finger bones attached to small pebbles and gravel. Cocks were crowing. I was about to step back into the road when I saw the bulk of a carriage emerge at a distance between two gates and come towards me. Having no wish to be seen, I drew back further and saw, between the ragged black branches that this was no rough country vehicle, but a nobleman's carriage from Paris. I had not seen one like it since Bonhomme and I had stayed with the Chevalier in Lyons.

When it had passed I wanted to go to the house it had emerged from, but I was not sure if I dared. I might succeed in discovering the name of the man it belonged to, and that name might well be Lorraine, but what good would that do if in the process I was seen by someone who recognized me, or thought he might, and who would ride after the carriage, overtake it, and inform against me.

I waited a long time, and then seeing a country cart approach from one direction, and some milkmaids from another, I moved away, before my silently standing there could attract attention. I went into the middle of the small town before choosing an inn more or less at random. There I dismounted at a good serviceable block, and made up for the deficiencies of my appearance with largess from my purse. I ordered the stabling of Maud, and paid the ostler well to feed and groom her. Indoors I did the same again for myself. And in this way, riding a knife edge of despair for the murder of Bonhomme, and restless attention to the avoidance of my own, I ate and washed and slept. I bolted my door, and spoke to no one, and except for the serving men no one came near me.

From that moment onwards I looked on the final stretch of the road between myself and Paris as Francis told me the poachers in England looked on a stretch of the forest path where the landowner had laid man traps under the dried leaves.

Bonhomme died by the hand of a man, or men, who left three loaves of bread untouched in the carriage. I repeatedly reminded myself that starving peasants would have taken Bonhomme's boots off his feet, and as for pulling open the pockets of his coat but leaving it by the wayside, these were the actions of men in search of something else and not food or even money.

When the landlord sent me up a pie for my dinner, the man had to knock on my chamber door and I did not open it until I had taken a look at him through a gap in the wood. Then I slipped the catch, called out to him, and stood with my back to the room and looking out of the window. He tried to engage me in conversation but after a while, and still with my back to him, I told him my wife had died and I was returning from burying her at our country estate and grief made me unfit for company. I think that satisfied him. He went.

My thoughts then returned to Bonhomme. My heart longed for his company. At this time of year, every day lets loose a little more of the juice and thaw of Spring. I set out with Maud on the following morning, and I would have been glad whether I was a hunted man or not if only Bonhomme had still been with me. When I had left the last cottage on the outskirts of the small town behind me I stopped and surveyed the land ahead. If I calculated rightly, I would soon rejoin the path I had traveled on my way south. I would pass close by the house of the tax-evading Marquis, and this gave me an idea which rapidly became the basis of a plan. I knew I should be welcome there. This time I would explain something of my adventure to him, and I was sure that a man who went to such lengths to deceive a tax inspector would be no less ingenious at frustrating Lorraine's assassins. In fact what I would request of him was that he should hide me for a day or two, while sending one of his men on horseback to Paris with a message for Francis, requesting that he should come armed and if possible with Ernst and some others, to meet me on the road and get me safe back to Versailles.

However, I was not yet at his house and neither was I certain how to get there. And although without the coach I was traveling much faster than before, I was frankly undecided on whether I should stick to the more frequented ways or avoid them in order to escape anyone lying in wait for me. And whether to gallop across open stretches of ground when I came upon them or skirt their edges where I might be less noticeable; but so also would be an assassin who had as much interest in being unobserved as I had.

In the end I decided I would stick to the shortest route.

MALICE

The country was not as deserted as it had been in late November, and as I rode I passed on average one or two individuals an hour; traveling tradesmen, shepherds, and so forth. I calculated I must be about two days journey short of Paris, and these two days would settle the success or otherwise of my entire venture. And whether I lived or died; because if Lorraine or his agents succeeded in intercepting me and taking Morel's package, they would take my life as well.

My greatest good fortune was that at about mid-day I recognized the road I had traveled before, when I reached the crossroads where Bonhomme and I were stopped by the tax inspector in his carriage. I trotted along in the direction of the Marquis' house with my hat pulled down as ever, and my collar up. There was an empty stretch ahead. Then a small figure appeared in the distance and gradually enlarged into the shape of a tinker on a donkey. In my watchfulness I looked from time to time behind me.

I passed the tinker, who gave me the most searching looks, and saw ahead the walls of the house I was making for. I recognized it at once by three trees standing facing the gates from across the track. About equidistant from the house as myself two men on horseback appeared at that moment from around a bend in the road. I kept a steady pace towards them, so that they need not foresee my intention to turn into the courtyard of the house when I drew level with it. But at the last stretch I lost my nerve and spurred Maud to a canter. Almost immediately they did the same. My heart leapt, and at the same time as giving Maud a great kick so that she positively flew through the gate, I thrilled with astonishment at the realization that it was no fantasy of mine that Lorraine had the country crawling with his agents in search of me.

These two men did not pause before coming after me right to the steps of the Marquis' house. But I had the advantage there, because I began to shout at the top of my lungs, calling on my friend and his servants to come to my aid. The lad who was already there guarding the gate recognized me at once and added his voice to mine and gave the leg of one of these men a great thwack with his pole. At once doors opened everywhere and those men and women who I had surprised on my last visit hiding in the great barn came out of the house now armed with knives and sticks, and the Marquis himself with a firearm stood on the top of the steps and sent a fusillade over the heads of the attackers as they fled.

I had some explaining to do when I had dismounted. But the

Marquis gave me a welcome as warm, if of a different kind, as he had given to my would-be attackers. Apparently I had so undermined the confidence of the tax inspector when I met him on the road after my last visit, that the man was reduced to a shadow of his former self, scarcely questioned any of the answers he was given as to hams and wine and servants by the Marquis, had not taxed him at all and had made no attempt to come back since.

If the Marquis thought that he owed me a favour for this, it was convenient since I was about to ask him one. And he was as generous in his response as I could have wished. I saw the great gate closed and barred, a handsome gelding ridden out towards Paris with an armed man in the saddle, and I myself was attended by servants who provided me with clean linen and hot water and led me at last to a room where my host was waiting beside a table laden with good food and wine. There I told him my whole story, and since he was a man who enjoyed being entertained, although the part to do with the fate of Bonhomme was too tragic to be passed over, other parts of the story pleased him hugely and he urged me to repeat it many times, and asked innumerable questions.

That also was fortunate, because when two or three days later we looked for the return of the servant who had ridden off with my message to Francis, he did not come back. Another day passed, and another. The main gate was still barred and the Marquis servants were armed, but even so I calculated that if I stayed there long enough those villains would come back with reinforcements to have me out.

The conversation at table between the Marquis and myself changed to speculation on the delay of his man's return, and what might have befallen him. I could only think that he had perhaps met with some accident, or been stopped on the road. In the end it seemed plain to me that I must leave, and take my chances. I could not expose my kind host to any more danger on my behalf, above all that of boredom because by now he had heard all my stories twice over.

At first he argued but eventually it was agreed that I would leave provided I agreed to take with me a good firearm that he had, and one of his servants to accompany me for half the day before returning home.

This I did. We parted the best of friends, and while I had his servant with me I felt quite secure. In the afternoon the lad said his farewells, and I gave him some money and watched him on his way. Then I set Maud to a canter. I went unscathed until the evening, when I found myself near to a saw mill and knocked on the door to ask for food and a bed for the night. When I mentioned what I would be prepared to pay, the miller's wife redoubled the welcome she had already given me. I took Maud into the stable myself and did what Bonhomme always did before. I was no longer recognizable as a gentleman, and neither the miller nor his son offered to help me. In the lengthening shadows I was walking back to the side door limping heavily from weariness and hours in the saddle as well as my deformity when a sudden movement of two people just within the threshold checked me. I could give lessons to those who want to have covert conversations without being observed. For example, a too low voice or a whisper only attracts the attention of those who should not hear, whereas a normal tone is often inaudible and passes without remark. And then again, if a villain can learn to do what is wrong but with a graceful air, as Lorraine had for example, he would not peek over his shoulder as if afraid of being seen like this man did, and on catching sight of me scuttle round the corner as if that could undo the glimpse of him that I had undoubtedly had. The woman who was then left alone turned a very welcoming smile on me, and wanted me inside, and sitting down, and eating at her table for long enough for the other to go wherever he was going.

I debated whether to leave at once, or ask the woman whether her cooperation in catching me had been asked by anyone. But then she would deny it unless I gave her twice the money that had been promised her by the other. Might such a move tempt her to try to take the rest of what I had off me? Her husband, the miller, was quite large enough to do it, and so was she.

I sat down at her table. As I did so, and with her eye on me, I pulled my collar from my face, and with my eye steadily upon her brought up my hand with a gold coin held between my thumb and finger. She gave a little cry and stumbled backwards, and to make matters worse I smiled at her.

"Madam," I said, "the sister in law of the Queen of France says that I am a goblin, and such a great lady could scarcely be wrong, would you say?"

While she was still speechless, I caused the gold coin to disappear. I mentioned before that I was adept at such tricks.

"Now tell me," I said, "did someone come by asking for news of me, and say that he would pay handsomely for the information?"

Her mouth dropped open. I caused the gold coin to appear again. "You shall have this," I said. "Tell me who asked after me."

"Two gentlemen," she said.

"And they asked only you?"

"No. They ask everyone."

"Then," I said, "wrap that pie in a cloth for me and tell your husband to saddle my horse and tie a sack of oats to the saddle, and if this is done quickly enough you shall have this gold coin of me. And if it is not done, I will speak a word I know that will cause this house to burn down."

She backed away from me as if she dared not turn round. I could almost hear her heart beating from where I sat. I could not resist laughing at her. But, for a stranger, that was not a palatable sight either, especially since I was not feeling friendly. She tripped near the door where a stone was missing, but righted herself still never turning her back on me, and then scurried out into the yard. I waited. What else can we mortals ever do? And then my horse appeared saddled, so I stood up and walked out under the lantern that had just been lit. I climbed onto the mounting block, and from the block into the saddle, and held out my hand, all without a word. The woman gave me the pie which I put in my coat, and then with some care, because this was not the moment to get it wrong, I caused the gold coin to materialize between my fingers once more, and handed it to her. She took it with the tips of her fingers as if half afraid that it would melt when it felt the touch of an ordinary human hand. Then I left.

All this got me out of one difficulty, but I was back where I started. Another man could have changed horses and ridden without stopping into Paris. But I, with my unique saddle and dependence on the familiarity of Maud, did not dare to try without Bonhomme at hand to help me. And besides, it looked as if Lorraine in his determination to intercept me on my return, had corrupted the whole country.

I continued forward all that night. It was something I would not care to do again. I hate the dark. To my mind, all grace is withdrawn from the earth when the sun goes down. I read once in a scientific paper that since all plants depend on light for the processes that sustain them, their very life is suspended in the night time. They are in a state of suspended animation; a little death. And it is this which infects the whole earth at that time with the mordant spirit of decay. The fields around me, and then intermittently, the trees and hedgerows, rustled with dry twitchings in nature's uneasy sleep. I felt the tension in Maud's gait, her pricked ears, and increasing weariness. I was able to reach forward at one point and slide a nosebag with some oats around her neck. Then while she ate, I took the pie made by the miller's wife out of my coat, and consumed it.

After this lonely pause we set off again. From time to time when the track allowed it Maud would canter, but there was only half a moon and I was afraid of falling. Our way took us up a long hill which I did not remember from before. I had no memory for directions. It had been Bonhomme who kept us on the right path. But I began to wonder if, from the top of it, I might see some sign of Paris. In a great city, even at the dead of night, there are some lamps lit. On the top of the hill I reined in Maud and sat facing the chill wind and scanning the empty ground. The countryside was as empty as the moon. There was not a house to be seen, leave alone a city. Far on the left a wind-scoured bank of trees scratched against the sky, and I thought to myself that their bare twigs might make a squeaking sound, like sticks on glass, if I had been close enough to hear.

Not only my brain, but my skin and my mouth felt dry with tiredness. I thought I saw a gleam from a lantern in those trees for a moment, but when I looked again it was gone. It never occurred to me, exhausted as I was, that I could be seen where I was; that a horse and rider pausing on the brow of a wide hill with the night sky behind them faintly silvered with the light of the moon that only now declined, might be hung there for all to see like a painting on a wall.

We began the descent. Maud picked gingerly at the ground with her neck craned forward, pulling on the bridle. I felt my spirits dulled with disappointment when I had thought myself so near my journey's end. My thoughts were occupied with calculations of how far off Paris might yet be and how to gauge it, when suddenly the sound of galloping hooves hit my consciousness very much as if the mind were capable of being an entity that could be caught unawares and knocked over. I hadn't even time to find out from what direction the approach came before I was careered into. One man snatched my horse's bridle. The other tried to knock me to the ground, but that was not so easy. Even so, I couldn't get away. Maud reared up and struck out with her hooves, but the scoundrel on the left gave her such a clout over the neck that she whinnied and then stood still. Then he reached over and snatched my hat off my head, presumably to see my face. When he did that, I knew at once who his master was, and that he was no common thief simply in search of gold, but my enemy Lorraine.

"It's him," this man said to the other fellow. "Get him off. Search him."

Now I must tell you that the precious packet, for the sake of which both I and these men were taking so much trouble, was not simply lying in my pocket ready to be taken. I had learned from Bonhomme's fate, and had devoted some little time to hiding it inside my boot.

"You do it," shouted the first villain. "He bites."

I had my knife out and would do worse than that.

"Get him down by the bridge," the small one said.

They set spurs to the wretched nags they were on, and dragged Maud down the hill. All this took some time, and behind us the sun, or something like it, had begun to spawn some pale and sickly light.

Landing in a heap at the bottom of the hill, we encountered a third man who was waiting. All three of them set about me and managed to get me off Maud where, once on the ground, I was pretty much helpless. These three men were the roughest country idiots. I could almost feel sorry for them, their torn and filthy clothes and great cracked boots with holes in them like roofs with tiles missing. That they had boots at all marked them out as prosperous compared with some others, and it was a distinction they planned to build on apparently, as I soon learned that they expected a fat reward for catching me.

"Are you sure he's the one?" asked the small man.

"Look at him!" sneered his companion. "Look at his face."

"He's the one. What do we do?"

"We've got to take him or we won't be believed."

"Tie him up."

"How much are you going to get for me?" I said.

I did not have it in mind to attempt to bribe them. I was too much in their power, and neither could I enthrall them as I had the miller's wife, because they had already hit and felt me and knew that I was flesh and blood like themselves. But I had something else.

"Let go my hands," I said. "I have something to show you."

They thought I meant the package which they had been told I carried, and so they stood just slightly back a moment and I reached in among the folds of my shirt and took out, on its long golden chain, the locket that contained the portrait of Madame; the one she had given me when I left her.

"Look at that" I said, in a commanding tone and before any one of them could say that it was no more than a picture. "Look at that!"

They did look, since I made such a point of it.

"Do you know who this is? This is the King's sister. This is the Duchesse d'Orléans, who is married to the brother of Louis XIV. She gave it to me, as a token of her friendship. I belong to her. I belong to her household. Whose household do you belong to, gentlemen! If his name is Lorraine, let me tell you that he is very small – a mere pinprick – beside her. Harm a gentleman belonging to her, and just see how well Lorraine may be able to help you. If he even pays you you'll be lucky."

I doubt they had ever tried to rob a man who talked so much.

After a moment's absolute silence the small man said, "I'll kill him. Give me the knife."

The man who had stood guard on the bridge began to do as he said, but slowly. It was light enough for me to see his face, and there was doubt on it.

"Look out," the other one said. "There's a coach coming."

I could feel the ground underneath me growling like an animal, but the wheels were still a long way off. They had time to drag me into some trees, and waited there until it had passed. In the meantime, having reached some sort of a consensus, they threw me over the back of Maud, and I was knocked unconscious by the beating I had in being taken at a gallop for a mile at least before they stopped. I regained consciousness to find I was being loaded onto a cart. They left Maud behind in the care of a cottager and that was their undoing. Myself they tied with ropes and covered with a canvas sheet that must have been used for tenting goats, but although I was being transported to some other place to be murdered, I realized that I was going to have to die. I was in such a rage I don't think I was frightened for a moment.

"You fools," I said. "You were told to get the package were you not! It fell out of my clothes by the bridge. The great lord who is paying you for this will have you skinned alive when he finds that you have lost it!"

There was an uproar among the three of them even louder than the noise I was making. Two were for turning back and searching by the bridge. But one, and I recognized the sly voice of the small man, said they should take no notice of what I said.

"Then cut him loose and kill him and see if he's got it" shouted the other. "You're the one with the knife."

They would have done it too. One of them had half snatched back the canvas, when a shout from behind ordered them to stop. It was a voice so loud and so resonant that it had certainly been trained on the hunting field and I recognized it.

"Get the reins," screamed the small man.

There was a colossal lurch and the cart was suddenly moving at such a pace I could almost admire these charioteers who were able to get such mileage out of an old farm trap. I was in the infuriating position of not being able to see what was going on, but I could hear the furious sound of pursuit. The chase was decided before it was begun of course. But when that was over, and the horseman had caught up with the cart it was another matter. There were three of them.

"Francis!" I shouted from under the canvas. "Watch the small one. He has a knife." And I shouted to anyone else who might listen, "Let me out! Let me out! Cut me free."

On the contrary, one of the peasants got the cart going again and may have thought he could escape with me. There must have been another downward slope and very rough ground. Naturally the cart overturned and I might have been killed in that fashion in default of the assassins' knife, but chance decided otherwise.

I lay helplessly on my face on the turf, with my hands still bound. I caught a glimpse of a pair of boots not belonging to any peasant, that danced nimbly backwards and forwards rather near my head until the body of the first villain fell across my neck.

Then there was silence. I thought it was the silence of defeat or victory, but it was the silence of unconsciousness which, by this time in my life, I should have recognized.

CHAPTER THIRTY-NINE

I awoke at last in a hovel. I'm not sure that it may not have been the one in which I spent my first night on the way out of Paris. It smelt less terrible than before, partly I think because the old man had since died, and partly because, the weather being almost mild someone was standing at the open door, and when she moved instead of the sour smell that came from the skirts of the farmers wife, there was a waft of dried rose. I hoped that I was not in heaven; that Paradise should not consist of such half-hearted improvements on what was already familiar.

The next moment the angel spoke in the voice of Climène. She said, "If he is dead, why can't we go back to Paris? And if he is not dead but will recover, why can't we leave him here to rest, and we can go back to Paris?"

I laughed. It caused me some pain to do so, but I couldn't stop myself.

"Berthon!" Francis exclaimed, striding over the floor and standing over me.

"Oh Berthon!" said Climène. "I'm glad you are awake at last. It is so tedious here you would not believe it. Now that we've saved you at last we can go back to Paris." And she ran to the door and shouted "Gannon. Get the coach ready. We are leaving."

Needless to say, I was grateful beyond measure to Francis and Climène for this rescue. And also to Ernst, who had accompanied Francis to intercept me on the road and escort me back to Paris. The message carried by the Marquis' servant had reached Francis in good time and what accident had stopped that man returning home was unknown. Then Francis had set out with Ernst, but they looked for me in vain at first and had to wait, return to Versailles, and come again. Climène accompanied them the second time because Lorraine had become suspicious.

"If Lorraine heard, as he did hear – I made sure of it – that I was with Francis, well then my dear, "she said with a laugh, to me, "he would think there could only be pleasure in it!"

"Little did he suspect," I murmured, "that you could be involved in an errand where bravery and self-sacrifice were the real qualities required."

She paused. She was on my other side at this time, and facing the light. I watched through my almost closed eye. In speculation her lips fell open just slightly, and the light let form a bloom on her mouth that reminded me again of that Dutch painter whose name I had forgotten. For several moments she tested my words, thoughtfully tipping her head the other way, and repeating without any suspicion of irony, "Yes. Self-sacrificing."

I waited. She was too preoccupied to look at me. And then she said, in a matter of fact way, "And actually I am brave. I'm not afraid of anything, as it happens."

There she spoke the truth, I suspect. Francis said that when one of the men raised his gun at her and fired, she spat at him.

"And had Lorraine visited that monastery and bought poison?" Francis asked. I could have lit a fire from the spark in his eye, and two from the shout of triumph from them all when I tapped the part of my coat where the confession and the poison were now stitched into the lining.

Within a few hours I was rested more or less well enough to be carried back to Versailles with my deliverers, and it very well suited my state at that moment to luxuriate in the lighthearted comfort of Climène's gossip and the affectionate companionship of Francis who, with the restraint for which his countrymen are so renowned, asked no further questions of me. I told him once that Bonhomme was dead, and that was all. Except that Lorraine's men killed him.

Climène entertained me with Court gossip, frequently exclaiming how extraordinary it was that I did not know this, or already knew that. I heard of the Queen's death, a great deal about the state of the King's relationship with Madame de Maintenon, the latest fashion such as that hair was still being dressed á la Fontanges and lace from Guienne was in vogue. When we arrived at Versailles my apartment was besieged with all the friends of Ernst as well as Clement Cardinale and Climène and Francis, and for several hours I held court there – I, myself – in as merry a way as I possibly could, although I was still prone to sickness.

But it is hard to describe how utterly bereft I was when once I was alone. Without the familiar help and companionship of Bonhomme this place seemed almost as hostile as the country I had just left. I reflected miserably on the predicament of human mortality, and the callous enigma that makes us love our fellow men. I recalled the advice of Our

Lord, that we should love one another; and to tell the truth I thought that a man who could recommend such conduct to a species apt to be so over fond, and in circumstances so guaranteed to blight the heart – when disease and death are the preconditions of our existence – such a man, whether the son of God or not, deserved a good kicking.

When some time later I told Francis this, he said that he lost a servant once that he was very fond of. It was in the days when his father hunted him, and this man, whose employment was in the stables, gave up his position in order to accompany Francis when he first went to London, but was run over by a coach in the street.

"It was the first time, "Francis said, "that I learned that men are equal."

"What do you mean?" I asked "I thought you said he was your servant."

"I did. And does that mean he could not be my equal, as a man?"

I remember feeling almost annoyed. My senses were overburdened with the renewal of so many and such long lost riches from this life and I did not want to have new ideas thrust at me. The hierarchies of court were something I had always accepted, and those whom I most revered – Madame for example – were, for all their kindness, meticulous in the observance of correctness regarding a person's rank. What sort of an answer would Madame give to a fool who suggested that I, for example, could be her equal? If Francis had imbibed some new and unusual views on this matter from his own country, I did not want to hear them now.

"Did you never feel," he said, "that Bonhomme was your equal?"

"As a man... Oh, well! As a man..."

"I mean, as a man."

"But a servant is not a courtier."

"No. And a dog is not a cat. But they should both be treated with equal respect. Or none at all."

I thought just for a moment, and then I said, "I felt great respect for Bonhomme when he had learned to have confidence in me and showed himself in his true colours. I loved him."

"Ah!" said Francis. "Then you found out what I found out." And, to my relief I must say, he decided to go to bed, and left me.

It made no difference to my inner wretchedness. Once I had got over the relief of having escaped with my life, my homecoming was marred by Bonhomme's absence in so many ways. For example, do you imagine I did not think with extreme anxiety and impatience of my mistress? If Bonhomme had been with me I should have sent him at once to Fanette's lodgings with a message and an invitation to dine with me, and I should have had fresh clothes from the stores where he had laid them by and from which he knew how to extract the ones I liked. When night fell, I could not sleep. I remember how I lay there in my own room once more and how the darkness of the night and the flame of the candle until it went out seemed to feed my wretchedness. Exhaustion would have made me sleep if my heart had not been on fire, and the stamping of the young man whom Ernst had set to guard my door, and the clatter of his sword when he banged it against the skirting had not paid their part in keeping me awake.

If Bonhomme had still been with me I should have had great solace from talking to him, and when the dawn came he would have known how to make me comfortable with the proper food and clothes, attention to my wig, shaving and so on. He knew how to shave my lip, for example. When the morning did come, because I had not known how to send word to Fanette I experienced the most debilitating dread of doing so. Hesitation bedevilled me with all the uncertainties of a lover who has been untried, not merely absent, and while I still lay in bed my mind was tormented with anxiety and indecision. I felt almost as hopeless of being given the undeserved blessing of her favours as I had in the first place.

But fortunately Climène had no such scruples. She sent word to Fanette without asking any permission from me, and soon there came a noise outside of a whispered conversation and, as usual, the clumsy banging of that young gentleman's sword, followed by scratching at my door. I opened one eye but could not stir, being neither dressed nor attended upon. The door opened a crack, and through it came first Isabel, and then a young fellow who looked about him as if he had just been born.

"Monsieur de Brisse," murmured Isabel. "My mistress sent me. I hope you will forgive my intrusion."

I'm afraid I was speechless, which was not a good augury for the trial of strength that lay ahead of me to tell my tale at court. In fact, I tried to hide my face as much as I could, being still in my bed, but Isabel, as was her way, was quietly impervious to discouragement whether intended or otherwise, and said,

"Monsieur, this boy is called Gaudet. He wishes very much to serve you, since you have had the misfortune to lose Bonhomme. My mistress believes that, being intelligent, strong and honest, Gaudet may suit you well, although he is young. She has not come herself. Her heart is too full of joy because you have returned, and as soon as you are ready to see her she asks you to send Gaudet with a message. And in the meantime she has chosen for you this fruit which I have in my basket, and these flowers."

"Ah Isabel," I said at last, "I could not speak. Tell your mistress that my heart was near to breaking and she has mended it already. I will come to her as soon as I am fit."

When Isabel had gone, I began to rise. Gaudet attempted to help me. I was not sure about the boy, but for Fanette's sake I determined to like him. He could read and write. He was the sort who had got some kind of education for himself by paying 40 sous to gain admission to a reading room. But I told him to go and fetch food for me, and he did not know how to find his way to the kitchens.

CHAPTER FORTY

At that precise period Madame and Monsieur were staying in Paris, and after two days it was time that I should present myself to the Duchesse d'Orléans to pay court to her, before she should hear a rumour of my return and begin to measure my neglect. When eventually I stood in my room dressed and clean for the first time since my return, and took note of the various dents and gashes in my body – and my spirit – before setting out for Paris I began to recover my spirit. The thought of Lorraine, and the challenge before me, gave me again that sort of appetite for life which the chance of risking it arouses. I've mentioned the friends Ernst and Francis insisted should follow me everywhere with their swords clattering, on account of the possibility that Lorraine would be likely to do his best to have me murdered before I could get to Monsieur or the King with my story. But I counted on my wits and my knife as much as on them. As a gentleman I carried a sword, but I kept a knife, although I would not have admitted it to an equal at Court. Above all I had the confession and the poison I had procured from Morel, and these items imbued me with something of the sense of empowerment that weapons probably give to normal men.

On the open road, trotting towards Paris and mounted on Maud, with my new servant alternately running and walking beside me, the road was muddy and there was a sharp wind. According to Francis' views of equality, then, should I get down from my horse and let Gaudet ride it? He was certainly getting quite dirty, but when I caught sight of his face from time to time he was grinning from ear to ear. Then when we reached the Palais Royale, in spite of all that had happened elsewhere in the world the pavements, the stones, the very staircase and walls were exactly the same as before. I left Maud in the care of Gaudet, and went up to Madame's apartment.

The rooms there are much smaller than the palace of Versailles, and most of them very cold. Madame, however, had a good fire burning. Those of her ladies who I met in the ante room were very kind to me. Then I advanced to the open door and stood just inside it waiting for Madame to notice me.

From the entrance I glanced quickly around the room before advancing. My heart was beating fast. I felt less like a man returning home than like one brought from some distant star by magic with the sole purpose of taking revenge, and as soon as I stood on the threshold I felt the difference. It was not only my consciousness of the fact that I was armed in the way I mentioned just now. But it was also no longer Madame's safety and happiness alone, but also the murder of Bonhomme which was laid to the account of Lorraine, and by this addition the chemistry of my blood seemed to be changed.

As I rapidly surveyed the apartment, I singled out Lorraine immediately and two of his familiars in attendance on Monsieur; but despite the shock to my emotions the intensity of my increased hatred of the man and the knowledge that I was well armed to defeat him took away all fear. Lorraine did not fail to see me. He had just closed, with the tips of the fingers of his right hand, the golden lid of a little box he held in his left. Madame Gordon stood beside him.

I took two steps further into the room, and bowed to Monsieur, and Madame. The Princess noticed me. Madame de Vieuville was with her, and the Duchesse de Ventadour, the Chevalier Tilladet and others. As soon as she caught sight of me, she paused, completed the remark she was just making, and then did me the honour of welcoming me by name, and asking me to come and tell her about Italy.

"Monsieur de Brisse has been to Italy," she said, passing her eye over all the assembled courtiers. "To Italy," she repeated, with great significance, looking directly at Lorraine.

"Come closer, Monsieur de Brisse, and tell me what you found out!"

"Madame," I said, smiling, "I have done nothing more than satisfy the natural curiosity of a gentleman who travels for pleasure." And I told how I had sent Salamandre home and the bird had successfully found his way back to his nest in the hope that I could still confuse Lorraine and his friends enough to slow them down. Madame, realizing that this was not the place to make any revelation more significant, could not resist smiling at me and whispering "Did you get it?" when I was near.

"Ah, Madame," exclaimed d'Effiat, suddenly appearing on my other side, "Has Monsieur de Brisse accomplished a commission for you in Italy? A new medal perhaps; or some other treasure?"

It seemed to me as if all who were in the room were listening only to this one conversation, but I may have been wrong. A third lady who had joined Lorraine and Madame Gordon was about to speak at that moment, but the Chevalier silenced her, indicating that he also wished to listen to Madame. So that the room was suddenly made attentive. And since Madame had obviously meant to speak privately the insolence of such an initiative and the brazen style with which Lorraine controlled the company informed me, better than any other words, of how advanced their power had become in my absence.

But Madame had lost none of her courage or her dignity.

"Monsieur d'Effiat," she said, "perhaps in order to satisfy your curiosity you would like to put your question to my husband. I have no secrets from Monsieur, and it would be as well for you to remember that."

"Ah Madame," intervened Lorraine, "who is talking of secrets? I love a secret!"

There was a little discreet laughter which ran around the company, not excluding Monsieur himself, who had been studying an engraving under a magnifying glass held by Dou Dou.

But Madame, seeing that he would be able to make nothing of this unless she chose, simply turned to Monsieur Tilladet and asked him to read to her, and the moment passed.

D'Effiat was embarrassed. He lacked Lorraine's wit and resource, and turned almost clumsily to find a suitable prop among the company nearby on whom to bestow a remark and pave himself a way of retiring. But lo and behold, there was no one at hand except myself. For an instant he thought he might use even me, and he drew breath, but I stopped him. When last he saw me I would have been unable to avoid complying, and he was tempted to make an assumption based on the boy I was, until I met his eye.

"Alas, Monsieur," I remarked, "you find yourself at a disadvantage, I see, when wit, rather than knife or poison, is the only weapon."

An expression akin to shock lit his face, and I swear he would have struck me with the back of his hand if we had been anywhere but in Madame's drawing room. "Calm yourself Monsieur," I said in order to make it clear to him that his fury was visible and not only to myself. "I will give you an opportunity at a later date for a reunion with your weapons of choice."

I have never seen a man blush with rage before. And fear? Ernst said he was a coward. His colour became tinged with grey, and I thought I had better leave. I made my bow to Madame and she excused me.

Fortunately Ernst had come to join the other young man who guarded me, and together they escorted me from the Palais Royale to the house of the Maréchale de Clerembault in the Marais, where I was to make my next visit. Lorraine and his three friends would have to be left to themselves until I had made the evidence against them more secure.

I had brought with me into Paris all the money that remained from my journey, as well as the poison and Morel's confession. I had sent a message earlier, and so the Maréchale was expecting me. This time she did not keep me waiting, but if I expected any show of excitement, or joy at my safe return I was disappointed. She wore a gown of pale slightly gilded grey silk, and her lips were so pale and thin that she resembled a fine drawing of a woman, not one of flesh and blood. I looked in vain for a spark of friendship in her expression as I made my bow. She received me with that absence of any personal feeling which characterised her, and which tended to throw into such sharp and poignant relief those unforgettable instances of emotion or kindness. You would scarcely think, in this encounter, that I had been absent for six months, or risked my life in the service of an enterprise so close to her heart; and her purse. When I put the box containing the remaining gold and other coins on a table she took it at once and said, "How much is here? Have you got receipts for me, as I asked? "

The room was unpleasantly cold. I remember how I confused that with my reception.

I had all that she wanted in the way of figures. Bonhomme had taken care of it, and a roll of papers neatly made out rendered her an account of every sou. She took it all, and asked these questions without a smile and without greeting me with more than a direct look and a nod when I bowed to her, as I said. But then she turned from the table towards the window and said, "Come and let me look at you."

She had never wanted to do that before. I felt that I was old enough now to be excused this kind of scrutiny, and yet I could not think of how to make an objection. She got me in the light and looked at me down her nose, as if I were a cracked cup. At last there was a very slight softening of her eye, though by no means a smile, and she said, "I am glad that you have returned. Your sadness will go in a short while. He was only a servant."

She was referring, of course, to the murder of Bonhomme. I opened my mouth, but what could I say? This woman was a witch. And besides, I remembered what Francis had said about Bonhomme, and against my will I began to understand him. So that the Maréchale's remark, harping on a string that I would have plucked myself until but a short time ago, grated on me. I decided that I must not let it pass.

"Madame," I said, "he was my friend."

This time she made a little moue, tipped her mouth to one side, decided not to argue with me, and turned away.

"We are wasting time," she said. "I have friends also, and ones who will call for me soon, so please tell me without any further delay, has my investment prospered? Did you bring back the evidence you went to fetch."

"Yes, Madame," I said, and I proceeded to give her an account of it.

It is not a story I would ever tire of telling. When I set out I had not, truly, dared to believe that I would be able to discover the secrets of Lorraine's actions which he had been so careful to hide. Once something is done, a man has galloped along a certain piece of seashore, clattered the great hanging bell at the door of a monastery, met such and such a man, driven such and such a bargain, surely these events suffer the same fate as mortal man. These events fade faster than the thin weave of flags torn in battle; deeds, and parts of deeds are scattered like sheep wool on this thorn, that tuft of grass. And yet I had succeeded in gathering them all up. When Madame's happiness and safety had depended on it, it had been possible.

Standing there with the glittering eye of the old Maréchale fixed upon me, surrounded with the dark and dappled shadows of that great room, I felt fully, and perhaps for the first time, the complete triumph of having succeeded. The Maréchale also was triumphant. She gripped her hands together, and just for one moment, showed her teeth. A smile? Then she wanted to take the packet from me containing the poison and the letter immediately. She sat down, and as she did so held out her hand. But I held back. I was determined to strike a certain bargain with the Maréchale concerning the poison and the confession. In so far as they would be safer with her than in my apartment at Versailles I had every intention of agreeing to give her the confession (while keeping a copy myself) and most of the poison. But I also was determined to carry through the crucial denouement of this enterprise myself, and not leave it to any woman; or man, for that matter. Valuable evidence can get into the wrong hands and if she had invested her money in acquiring this, I had invested months of my life and Bonhomme all of his.

"Madame," I said. "I fear that you may be angry with me, but the fact is that I wish to retain some rights with regard to this evidence which it has nearly cost me my life to bring back to Paris."

She looked mightily surprised at my making conditions in such a way, and for a moment I was afraid that she would lose her temper. A little patch of red appeared in her cheek and she said, glaring at me, "Your travels, Monsieur, have made you forget the polite customs here in Paris. I demand that you give it to me at once." She was a great lady, and one who liked to hold all the cards herself, and not only at the gaming table.

I apologised; but I also said, "Madame, and you cannot expect me to give up this packet without any condition."

"Well, not without any condition," she said. "You may keep some of the money."

"I no longer need money," I said.

She was very annoyed at that, and looked at me with astonishment as well as anger.

"I presume that you do not contest the fact that His Majesty must be given this evidence!"

"Madame," I said, "That may be, but it must be accomplished in exactly the right way or the Chevalier will turn it to his own advantage. He is capable of anything,"

She was silent, considering what I had said. With some hesitation I crossed the room and handed the packet to her.

"Read the letter, Madame," I said. "But the poison is wrapped alongside, and it is best not to touch it."

She took the packet. I waited patiently while she first unwrapped and then unfolded the letter. I continued to wait while she read.

"How terrible," she said eventually, folding the letter with an expression of cold fury on her face. "A man of God!"

"Precisely," I said, remembering the relic of Ste. Catherine.

Then after a pause, "It's mine," she said. "I paid for it."

I held out my hand. You will remember that if she was sitting I could look her in the eye and if ever in my life I was utterly determined to have my own way, this was that moment. For fully sixty seconds the great lady looked at the goblin. Her gaze, cold and thoughtful, settled on me like a plague. But I had made up my mind not to submit. In the end she passed the packet back to me.

"Very well," she said, and stood up. "What are your terms?"

"Only these, Madame. That you keep our treasure locked. And that I hold the key."

For a moment I thought she was going to laugh – something that I had never in my life seen her do. She brought her head up high and the very thinness of her upper lip looked almost like it, but she was silent.

Then she took a few paces across the room away from me, half turned and beckoned. She led the way to a piece of panelling in the corner of the wall. Here she took a key from a number she possessed, and turned it in a lock set into the wood. A section very like a door opened. She peered inside. There was something that she took out, not letting me see what it was. The small cupboard was then empty. Into it I placed the packet, but not mentioning that I had retained a copy of the confession and a sample of the poisoned paper. She handed me the key. I locked it and put the key in my pocket. I should have liked to ask her if she had a duplicate, but I didn't dare.

"Now are you satisfied?" she demanded. "I want to be kept informed of everything that goes on. And for as long as you possess that key you may be sure the packet is in this place and no other."

I bowed, and thanked her. "Oh, don't thank me," she said. "I have not done this willingly. But things have come to a pretty pass when I can be bullied by a dwarf."

I simply bowed, and left her. Surprisingly enough, this lady had a great reputation for kindness in certain circumstances. And as I remarked once, before I set out on my travels, her smile, though rare, was very sweet. "Like the Summer," I thought to myself as I went out of that freezing great house into the Marais, "I daresay her smile will return in due season."

CHAPTER FORTY-ONE

Francis and Climène were waiting for me in my apartment when I returned to Versailles. My neck had started to bleed again, and stained the lace on my coat. Gaudet brought us wine and some delicacies to eat, but I was distracted at first, weaving in my mind too many alternative procedures by which to engineer the downfall of Lorraine and his friends. The question lay in how to set the trap in such a way that even Lorraine would not be able to spring it. In my mind I tried out different devices and then watched to see how this little band of friends would manage it. If I took my story to the King, and Lorraine succeeded in inventing some plausible counter story, as he showed himself to be so able to do, his lies coated with the sugar of his elegance and charm and his long association with the King and his brother, then we would be lost. Utterly. There could be no going back then. And His Majesty had shown himself to be – unpredictable? Very given to convenient solutions to keep the peace? The interior of my mind was like a lit stage on which the phantoms of the *cabale* and myself moved and spoke different words, and the fire of my blood would flare up at the thought of it.

"Berthon," Francis remonstrated. "Join us!"

"I am here," I said. But I knew what he meant.

"If you smile at me like that," he continued, "am I to assume that your scheme prospers? You will appreciate that we have shown kingly patience in doing without a full account of your adventures so far."

It was true. I had been carried on a sort of litter between two horses for most of the road back to Paris from the scene of my rescue. And when I entered the coach in order to arrive at Versailles in a less noticeable state, I fainted. But my recovery had been rapid enough, in all conscience.

"Well, I am not complaining of it," Francis said, mocking me. "I merely thought that you were too badly injured to be concerned with the worries of ordinary life or the confidence of your friends for a day or two, but here you have already found a new servant, and have been to Paris. Ernst says he is worn out keeping guard over you; is that not true, Ernst?"

"Yes," came a shout from the doorway.

"If I hear the sound of his spurs or his sword knock against the wainscot once more," I said quietly to Francis, "my head will split."

But of course, although it felt so strange to be back at court, I revelled in the company of my friends once more. I began to remember laughter, and good food, and books, and the theatre, and that Fanette awaited me, and I had been assured of it. I would be able to go to her soon. It is a most extraordinary thing that while one man struggles in his death agony and dimly hears his murderer run away through the darkness, or the clatter of the executioner's tools as he turns away, another tumbles laughing into bed with his mistress and thinks that the perfume of soft flesh and the crush of silks is all there is in the world.

"One foot on sea and one on shore," laughed Francis, quoting some English poet I had never heard of. "Save the rack for Lorraine, Berthon. Where's the fun in all this if you get onto it yourself."

His perceptiveness made me laugh. And his choice of words. I found the manuscript I had bought for Francis in Beaucaire and gave it to him, and I gave Climène a shawl that I had bought from the Persian in the same streets. I bought a very similar one for Fanette.

"Berthon," Climène exclaimed when she saw it, "We don't wear these in Paris!"

She was dressed in such a way that all her neck, her shoulders, and half her bosom, were all uncovered to the chill air of that early spring.

"Wear it when no one is looking at you then," I said.

"Don't be so impolite. There is no such occasion," she snapped. But in the meantime she had thrown it around her shoulders and as well as looking very charming, in no time at all she was warm. And then it was all 'what is it made of, and how can it be so light and yet so warm, and Berthon did you get two?'

Suddenly my desire to see Fanette overwhelmed me. I had already sent Gaudet to her lodgings, and she had asked me to dine with her at her house after the theatre the following evening.

The following morning Francis came and asked me to accompany him up onto the leads to see our birds, and the new chicks. I think he really wanted me to discuss my strategy for disclosing Lorraine's treachery to Monsieur and the King once more, and also to hear more tales of my travels, and this was a convenient device. Once up there, feeding the birds again, a feeling of peace began to take the place of the unbearable suspense that had overlain every moment since my return, and the feeling of grief that weighed on me for Bonhomme lessened.

And now at last I satisfied Francis' curiosity with more details of the encounter with Morel, and we discussed together the strategy that I was planning, to spring my trap on Lorraine. We talked about this for a long time, and when eventually the plan seemed complete, Francis pointed towards the road that I had travelled when I left for Italy, and there, by a clump of near trees, six birds included one that had been hatched by the mate of Salamandre soon after I had left. I remember looking at the birds, and at Francis' hand, that was large and rough, the bones and nails twice the size of my own; not a French aristocrat's hand at all, but one that I liked. Francis looked back at me, full of enthusiasm in describing the events that I had missed, and the details of the homing of Salamandre. He said he would like to take one of the birds to England, and the King had asked him – that is our own Louis XIV of France – whether or not a pigeon could fly home with a message if, for example, King Charles had some information of importance that he wished to send to him. I saw at once the political importance of such an idea. No doubt he thought this might be a far better way of negotiating with theKing of England than had been the case when he had used Minette as a go-between.

"And you have ridden a very long way on that saddle, now," Francis said with a smile.

"I shall be always in your debt for it. And other things," I said.

"Oh no."

"My life?"

"Please, Berthon."

You would have thought I was standing on his foot by accident from the expression on his face. I laughed. "And am I not allowed to thank you for choosing Maud for me? I only once rode any other horse for all the time that I was away, and that was in Italy when we had to cross an area so steep and mountainous that you would never have ventured to travel on horseback. But they have a breed there that climbs rock like a goat, and I know you will not believe me but if I had that horse in France I could go mounted up to bed in my apartment, and down again." And I don't think he did believe me.

In connection with Fanette, Francis, for a moment when we were talking together on the roof, had seemed on the brink of saying something but except for a moment of attention as if his eye was fixed on some fraction of the sky, it passed. If a Frenchman knew anything he would never have been able to resist a comment, but this man was different. When it came to it, the prospect of the renewal of my relationship with Fanette – the uncertainty of it – tested my courage more than Lorraine and all his spiteful ambitions, and ruthless cruelty. I might have succeeded in getting hold of the evidence that Madame needed in order to strike a bargain with her enemies and secure her own peace and happiness, but from the point of view of my own purely personal fortunes, I had risked something very precious to myself by going away from Paris at that time. This trial of either resuming my relationship with Fanette or losing her, was different from merely risking one's life. If in my long absence she had tired of me, or lost that extraordinary credulity that made her willing to consort with myself, where would I be? If I failed here, with Fanette, the *cabale* could eat me alive for all I cared. And when I reasoned with myself; when I considered for how long a time Fanette had been on her own without me, and how she, beautiful as she was, appeared on the stage almost every evening, when any man who saw her must desire her, and some of them would certainly have applied to her for her favours in my absence – well, when I thought of this, I hardly had the strength to prepare myself. I would go as she had asked on the morrow and watch her at the play. I could feel my blood beginning to leap and jump under my skin at the very thought of entering the theatre, leave alone seeing or speaking to Fanette. I was still with Francis on the roof of the palace when these thoughts invaded my mind again and my concentration was so shattered that the order of the objects around me disintegrated in sympathy, and my hectic eye took in half a chimney, stitched a piece of the parterre onto the leads, put sky up and earth down, and I remember a painfully accurate piece of Fanette's skirt, as I had last seen her wearing it, seemed to billow in the breeze as if it was caught on a piece of stone there, rather than snagged on the inside of my terrified mind.

In the end, Francis said to me, "Berthon! Courage. You will find everything that you care for as it was." So he could read my mind then.

But I dared not more than half believe him.

While Francis and I were still engaged in this conversation Gaudet came up with a message from Madame to say that she was returned to Versailles, and that I was to attend her. I went at once to my apartment to prepare myself. Simply moving again, and with haste, I was immediately aware of how my wretched body was exhausted when I needed all my strength.

Fortunately Gaudet was very adept with my clothes. I scarcely know how he did it, but he achieved a very sudden mastery of what I had, and perhaps he borrowed something because I certainly didn't remember the coat I wore. As soon as I was fine enough, I set out. Ernst himself was standing guard at my door and so when I emerged we were to go along together, but first he insisted on sending Gaudet to fetch Clement, to guard the door in his absence. He said that Lorraine might send some thieves to search my apartment, and although they would not find what they were looking for, it was as well to avoid the inconvenience their rummaging would cause.

Madame was alone when I entered her drawing room, except for her maids of honour who she dismissed to the other side of the room as soon as she saw me. Madame was engaged on her writing of letters, of which she made a daily feast sometimes five hours long. However, she put her pen aside, and called me to her with a face most expressive of suppressed excitement, anticipation, and anxiety. "You may sit, Monsieur de Brisse" she said with a smile as soon as I had made my bow, and pointing at Charmille's cushion. Although at court we either stood, or sat upon the floor when in the presence of the Royal family, except for princes of the blood and the premier dukes and their families who were permitted *tabourets*, Madame always tried to help me because of the difficulty I sometimes had. Charmille's cushion was filled with horsehair, and almost as high as a stool.

"It is good news that I bring you, Madame," I said. "My journey was not in vain. The Chevalier de Lorraine is precisely the man we thought he was, and I have brought back proof of it."

"Poison!"

"Yes!" I replied.

"And used to kill Minette?"

"Judge for yourself, Madame. From the monk in the monastery of Santo Stephano whose name was supplied by the friend of Ernst, Lorraine bought a poison which is used to saturate paper. When that paper is wiped on anything it leaves a residue which will kill anyone who touches it with their lips, or if the skin is cut."

Madame gasped, and looked at me with her eyes wide and round, and her lips parted. I remember it now. However majestic she was in circumstances which required it, she retained this connection with her girlhood, which was characterized by her round eye, the bright cheeks and naturally pink lips which she showed now, unable to suppress her shock, and then her excitement.

"They murdered her," she breathed with horror, as if she had only just thought of it. "It was the paper d'Effiat used to wipe the cup. Poisoned paper. They murdered poor Minette."

"Yes Madame," I said. "But let me tell you it all."

When I had given her a full account, she did not know, between one minute and the next, whether her horror of the crime, or her jubilation at the prospect of annihilating her enemies came first. She was utterly indignant at the fate of Monsieur's first wife, and if I had not insisted otherwise she would have gone straight to the King and demanded the execution of all four of them.

"I beg you not to act in haste, Madame," I said. "We must manage this cleverly." But I had very little faith in being able to persuade her and my heart beat unpleasantly fast as I looked up.

"True", she said impatiently, "but what can be more effective than showing this evidence to the King?"

"Perhaps some method which would not involve surrendering the whole of our proof, because if His Majesty asks for it we would have to give it into his keeping, Madame. Then the King would summon Lorraine. And knowing, as he now fairly does, what matter he would be charged with, do you not think that Lorraine would have concocted a credible explanation? The King might not give you or myself the opportunity to argue the case with him, and if he did, who do you think might win? The Chevalier is a man so adroit when it comes to dodging any attack, he might succeed in casting doubt on the evidence, or by some other lie evading judgment. And then having given the King the evidence, we could do no more. Remember the forged letter, and how he escaped from that."

Madame looked disappointed, and, for a moment, vexed.

"But I have a plan," I said, "and one which I think you may take great pleasure in. May I describe it, Madame? Because I do not think that Lorraine himself would have the rashness to disclose my evidence to the King, and dread of having to defend himself might be more effective than the desperate inventiveness of being forced to try."

And then I recounted the plan that Francis and I had discussed. I explained it to her, and although she said it terrified her, and she did not know how she could sit there to watch, knowing what she knew, she agreed to it because I convinced her that such a strategy gave me the best chance of surviving their murderous intentions towards myself, which I now made her aware of, as well as putting Lorraine in a position he could not escape from. We only had to wait a day, or two.

"But what of you in the meantime?" she asked with sudden anxiety, having become aware of the peril I was in. "They know that you have evidence against them. Lorraine will kill you. I don't know why he has not done it already."

"He has tried, Madame. But you see, first Lord Claydon saved me, and now Ernst and his friends follow me everywhere." And I told her again, and in greater detail, all the adventures that had befallen me, and exactly what the monk in the monastery had said, and how the poison had been prepared. When I once again described the poison she was very moved, and became quite agitated because as she said, she was so outraged that such wickedness should take place at court.

"Why then, Madame," I said, "I have Ernst and his friends as I said, who are both armed and guard me day and night, on the instructions of Lord Claydon. So until this trap is sprung and we have our enemies where we want them, I am safe I think. It is your safety, Madame, which depends so entirely on the evidence of the confession and the poison that these must be used to their maximum effect."

And so she allowed herself to be persuaded, and I left her after I had begged her not to tease the Chevalier with any warnings. I felt sorry that I had myself so threatened d'Effiat.

Just before I left Madame looked very strangely at me. I could see that in her lovely face there was a new thought – a remembrance of the past I fancied, and a faint air of speculation, as if she debated the wisdom of saying something more, but then refrained. It would be true to say there was sadness in her look just then, following on this thought, and this hesitation. I would have dearly liked to know what it was. I had a suspicion that she had Fanette in mind, but I could not tell.

CHAPTER FORTY-TWO

The next day it was time to prepare for my meeting with Fanette. I sent messages and gifts to her house, and fretted all day over my clothes and lack of strength in my scarce-recovered state. Gaudet waiting on me. In the afternoon I had to go through all the formalities of being shaved and dressed while my mind was tormented with the suspense of knowing that in an hour or so I might find myself lost in this world again, as I had been as a child, if my mistress was no longer mine. I have not mentined that while travelling along the sea shore on our return journey Bonhomme and I had encountered an extraordinary fellow who sewed up my lip. He offered because as a fisherman he knew very well how to ply a needle, and the problem intrigued him. I think he made me drunk first, by which I mean before getting my agreement to such a wild plan, and then again before doing it. I do not say that the result looked half as ordinary as I should have liked, but I grew the hair on my lip quite well and the underlying deformity was much less noticeable than before. Even so I still remember my own troubled reflection in the glass, and the thin young face of Gaudet above and behind me, the light of the candles lit early in the evening. The wind was so strong outside that and as it blew the windows it seemed to infect the mirrored images like the very wind of lost space full of depths and shadows, shards of light and uncertainties.

The play was to be Molière. I had decided to go alone, but Ernst insisted on accompanying me, armed to the teeth. I begged him to keep a little distance because of that business of him being so tall, but he would not. When Gaudet had made the best he could of my skin, my hair and my beard I wore my simplest wig and my lowest heels. I crept into the theatre very like the rat I had once thought myself, and I kept to the edge of the crowd and remained standing in the shadows. Every shred of my courage had left me. Lorraine would have been delighted to read my mind and my heart then.

As for the play, I had not seen it before. Others occupied the stage for ten minutes or more, apparently to the great delight of everyone except myself. I waited only to see Fanette. Have I perhaps been misleading in this account in praising her more than others did? Because she was not, and never became, an actress of the first rank. Her skills were excellent and her personality and appearance utterly charming and, to me, of an unequalled beauty. But others with more force of character, in the obvious sense, and, it must be said, more influential patrons, took precedence over her on the stage.

When she entered now, a pleasant murmur – no more – greeted her. The attention of the audience was on the other players. It was Molière, by the way, or did I mention that already?

I watched her as if she was the only person on the stage of the whole world. I cannot describe the intensity of my feeling when she was once more within my sight. I thought I saw her look among the faces, and I suddenly wanted to jump up on a chair and wave my hat! The passion that I had half feared lost from my own heart, and half dreaded encountering again, overwhelmed me. I had forgotten what a joy it was to look at the face and form of someone, and to find that their very skin was like a thin shade spread over the lamp of perfect bliss.

Then she turned.

She happened to have been standing facing the audience until that moment, and I think, if I remember correctly, that she had to pick up a fan from a table. I cannot really remember the details. Simply that she turned. And I saw that she was pregnant. I swear my heart stopped. And then when it had half choked me to death it started galloping around inside my chest like a mad horse. My first thought was that the child must be mine, and I was wild with joy. But my second was that Fanette must have had another lover. I had been away for how long? How many months? Suddenly I could not remember what month of the year it was when I went and what month it was now and how many lay between. She moved again. She was definitely pregnant. But not enough. Certainly not enough to have been pregnant since I left in November. When was it? December, January, February, March, April. But to conceal her pregnancy on stage she would have tied herself in. All actresses did so. Therefore, she could be – December, January, February, March

I think I stood there against the wall with my mouth open, my mind racing between despair and something else, until I was in danger of fainting. If I did, Ernst would have to pick me up. And I should be the laughing stock of the Court, because in this place gossip was honed to a fine art and what I thought secret was probably only ignored until some event like this one should make it worth a joke.

As soon as the performance was over I left the theatre to go to the dressing rooms. It was now pitch dark, and Ernst was joined by yet another young cadet as noisy as he was, but at least they were polite enough not to question me. Once in the passageway I saw Isabel standing with her hands clasped before a small green painted door, and I thought it a good augury that her face lit up with such a smile at the sight of me, and she curtsied very low.

"Oh Monsieur," she said, "may I tell my mistress you are here? She will be overjoyed."

Why – did she think I might not come at all? And why? I found it hard to breathe, but governed myself. I could feel the bone in my leg knocking about like a broken broom handle, but I stood as firm as I could, and said that I would go in. Isabel curtsied once more, the gracefully crumpled blue of her skirt rising briefly around her, then she was standing and slipped through the door.

Some men entered at the far end of the passage. They could not be well seen. There were four of them. Ernst drew his sword with a noise that was enough to deafen all of us. There was a sharp exclamation from one of the unknown men. Another door opened further down and at that moment, without seeing any more of what happened there, I found that Isabel reappeared and I followed her in.

Fanette was not, of course, alone. Even in the palace of Versailles the actors and actresses plied their trade in less comfort, or so it seemed to me, than the master of the King's hunt thought necessary for his stables. The corner occupied by Fanette was besieged by the frenzied activities of at least a dozen others, and there were gentlemen from the Court taking up as much space as they could to keep others at bay, and wig makers, seamstresses, messengers, servants, dressers, musicians and all their instruments, screens used adequately or otherwise, depending on their modesty or temper, by the actresses; there were dogs with ribbons on their necks, and china broken, food spilled. And yet there was order in all this. There was even a sort of calm; and besides, in such a crowded place it was not necessary for everyone to notice me, and I could approach Fanette without shame.

I did so. She was sitting with her back to the room, and saw me in the glass. She gently put down some colour she had had in her hand, and stood, and turned. There was on her face a smile of such radiance it brought tears to my eyes. She said nothing, and did not approach me, but let me come to her. I knew then that the child was mine and that nothing and no one had come between us in my absence. I didn't have time to feel ashamed of myself for my anxiety. It simply left me, like a bird that passes so quickly across a corner of the sky that the watcher cannot be sure that it was ever there. And in its place the quietest, the fiercest bliss took possession of my entire being, and I do believe perhaps hers also. She curtsied to me. I could have thrown myself on the ground at her feet, but of course I am a courtier and a gentleman, and I stood and watched her. I marvelled once again at her grace. I was aware of the scent of the air as her skirts brushed against it. I took her hand. It lay in mine as miraculously as the wild and exquisite body of one of my birds will consent to settle. I carried it to my face and laid it against my cheek. And then we went home.

CHAPTER FORTY-THREE

I wish I could have stayed away from Court for several days and let no one beyond Fanette see me, but it was too dangerous to leave Lorraine and his friends any peace in which to scheme an escape from the trap that they suspected was being set for them. But then again, in order to set that trap in the way it should be done according to my secret plan, it was necessary to have a morning when Monsieur and Madame were at court in the ordinary way so that events would resemble as closely as possible those on the day of the death of Minette. Only then, and in circumstances when the *cabale* could not show their hand in response, we would plant such dread in the heart of Lorraine and his friends that they would submit to the exaction of Madame's revenge.

Madame herself, having minutely attended to my own account and that of Francis, was eager to begin, but the day was set back first by Madame's unavoidable visit to Marly with the King, and then Monsieur caught a cold. The delay was dangerous, since Lorraine's best hope would be to kill me, whether he could also secure the confession of Morel and the poison or not, before Monsieur and the King could be approached. And of course, I now had what I could almost think of as a second body, and one more dear than my own, since I loved my mistress more than my own life. Lorraine must also know of that, and it was Climène who pointed out the danger to me.

"Berthon" she said to me, "you should not visit Fanette until this is over."

I was playing a game of cards with her. I put the Queen of Spades down on her hearts.

"Why not?"

"Do you not think that Lorraine might like to harm someone if he thought that you loved them? Myself for example. Monsieur d'Effiat looked as if he would have cut my throat when he came across me alone yesterday, but luckily Francis was nearer than he thought."

She was right however. My mind raced over the last few days. Who had seen me visit Fanette? Who knew any more than they had known last summer, when Madame had heard a rumour of my being in love with someone? The thought of Lorraine going near Fanette turned my heart to stone. She had her blackamoor to defend her. Did she ever walk alone without him? I would send a message to her at once never to do so. I rose to call Gaudet, but before I had taken a step there was a commotion outside, followed by the door being thrown open.

It was Francis who came suddenly in, but he had company. I thought at first it was a peasant woman with him, but as soon as she was safely behind the closed door the person took off first one covering, and then a huge cloak and hood, and revealed herself as Theobon.

I scarcely recognised her. She was very changed, and not just by the clothes she wore to conceal her identity and gain entrance to the Court. She was no longer a handsome woman. Not only did she look poor with regard to her dress and her shoes, but her face was altered almost beyond recognition. It was not just Time with his razor sharp sickle who had cut away the flesh from her face. Rage and disappointment and grief had clearly done it.

I greeted her with the greatest respect, and invited her to sit on the best chair. I would have said a great deal to her, but I was unprepared, whereas she was only too burdened with a weight of words which she started to throw off even before the formalities of meeting were over. She did not address one single word of polite enquiry towards myself nor even, at first, about Madame. Her one quality that seemed to have survived all others was that famous temper, because she cut me off with a sharp "Enough, Monsieur. I have business. I have business."

She sat, without allowing herself to be interrupted. "As you know perfectly well, they will treat me very harshly if it is discovered that I have set foot in this place. Set foot here! Here, where I was honoured, and where I served my dear Madame with the breath of my very soul!"

I was dismayed. Her eye, like a small burning coal, was directed at me but I wondered if she saw me. The anguish that her dismissal from court had caused her was evidently of the type that grows day by day instead of fading. I could hardly bear to look at someone who was so clearly being devoured from within by such a cruel flame.

I made a gesture to Gaudet for him to bring refreshments, but she spotted me. "What's that?" she demanded. "Play no tricks on me."

"Madame de Beauvron," I said, "you are my guest. I wish only to offer you something to eat and drink."

She shook her head at me. Typically of humanity, she had shed almost all the qualities which are capable of attracting compassion from others at the very time when she was most in need of it. She had always been inclined to sharpness, but she used to have grace, courtly manners, a quick mind and a very agreeable face. Now she only glared at me, twisting something in her hand under the cover of a fold in her skirt, her thinned lip slightly one sided in a way it never was before. I wondered if she was still entirely sane.

"This is what I have come for!" she now said, and suddenly thrust out the object she had been clutching. It was a fan.

Francis, whose capacity for restraint I have already mentioned, lowered his gaze and lightly touched his bottom lip with his hand. I recognized the signs of absolute astonishment and even disbelief at her lack of manners. For myself, of course, three quarters of the range of ordinary human responses are curtailed, and I simply stood there.

"Well, take it! Take it!" she almost shouted. So I advanced a step, bowed, and received the fan from her hand.

"Read it," she commanded. Not what I usually expect to do when taking up a fan, but in this case I quickly discovered that it was indeed written upon. It was a fan of plain silk, such as is used by ladies when they are alone in their bedchambers. It was painted on one side with a simple decoration of flowers, but on the other written all over. I have seen a fan used in this way, as a means of passing a message from one person to another.

"I got this from the servant of Madame de Grancy," hissed Theobon. "It cost me very dear. She has need of money for a special cause, so she came to me and made me an offer, and I took it. Oh, yes! I have no need to eat food if I can eat revenge, Monsieur de Brisse." She called me Monsieur throughout her visit. She seemed to have forgotten that she ever called me Berthon.

"Well, can you read it?" She could not contain her impatience, but ground the fingers of one hand with the nails of the other. I pitied her with all my heart.

"You see what it says there about the wicked scheme that led to my banishment from court? You see how she admits to the invention of it all. The malice!"

The language used on the fan was strangely playful for such a device, which must have been difficult to write. One sentence read, "Say she (Theobon) carries letters between Madame and the Chevalier de Sinsanet and he'll send her packing. Doesn't she look like a procuress after all! He'll believe you."

I closed the fan, and looked at Theobon. Now, suddenly, having delivered her main thrust, she seemed to recover herself a little. She sat back, laid her hands in her lap and looked about her. One could just about recognize, again, the great lady who had once been one of the foremost at Court, and who had been kind to me.

"I have come to you, Monsieur de Brisse," she said, "because I cannot do this for myself. This is what I want you to do. I will explain. You are to give it to Madame de Montausier."

"Who?" I said, in astonishment.

She wet her lip with her tongue, but mercifully said nothing. Then she spoke.

"You remember how several years ago, when the King was beginning to tire of the Montespan, Monsieur and Madame de Coetquen tried to promote Mme. de Grancy in her place. They thought they could make her the next mistress of the King. They were always arranging for her to be in the King's company, and it seemed at one point as if he was very attracted to her."

She paused, then looking sharply at me as if I had said something, repeated emphatically, "Pay attention! This has to do with my plan here."

She had spotted my incredulity when she said that the King had even considered taking Elizabeth de Grancy for his mistress, and she objected to it. Then, "Such a dirty woman!" Theobon conceded. "But when that ambition of hers came to nothing she blamed me for reminding the King of the scurrilous ballads written about her. It was true. I did do that. He could hardly want, for his official mistress, a woman whose bawdy adventures were sung of in the streets of Paris! And besides, I hated the woman, of course, for her unkindness to Madame."

She laughed very bitterly at this.

"But this was the beginning of their plan to ruin me. You see what is written there." I cannot tell you how sad it was to listen to Theobon as she recounted all this. Not so much the burden of what she said, but the way she said it grieved me beyond measure. She was displaying a form of slow death.

"Shall I show this fan to Monsieur, Madame de Beauvron?" I asked her. Because she obviously had something in mind, and my help must be involved, or why should she seek me here. She did not answer at once, but seemed to be agitated by indecision. She looked down into her lap, and plucked at her chin. I had forgotten about Francis, but he was still there, silent and politely waiting. Finally she looked up and repeated, "I want you to take this fan and give it to Julie de

Montausier."

I was startled into the repeating the name after her again.

"Yes!" she said. "I have very good reason for my choice. She will not be thought to be partial to my interests or those of Madame. But she will be interested in this opportunity to injure Mme. de Grancy for one reason only. She has always been – no doubt still is – utterly devoted to Madame de Montespan. She bitterly resented the Grancy's attempt to supplant her beloved lady in the affections of the King, and if I ever understood Julie de Montausier well, her animosity will not have subsided. And she is very clever also. She may be over sixty now, but remember, she was the leader of Les Precieuses in her day. Let her but show this fan to the King, and use her clever words, and we shall see who gets a thrashing!"

She began to stand up. "Will you do this exactly as I say, Monsieur de Brisse?" she almost shouted, between stumbling with her slippers and her skirt and beginning to look for her cloak and other coverings. I said I would, and called for Gaudet who came at once with all the draperies over his arm which she proceeded very impatiently and in considerable confusion, to try to put on. And now, to my surprise, Climène who had remained silent all this while, came suddenly forwards and in a tone of extraordinary softness and courtesy which I myself had never heard her use, said "Please allow me to help you, Madame la Comtesse." Then she handled the rags – they were scarcely anything else – with such skill that soon Theobon was swathed and hidden almost from view, like before. When she was finished, Theobon still had hold of Climène's arm, and my sister did not withdraw it. Then, for all her haste and impatience, our visitor, for the first time since she came through the door, was truly still a moment. In that interval, with her hand on Climène's arm, she stopped and looked right up into the young face of my sister, and her own softened, as if a lantern had suddenly diffused a calm light from within her skull. It was very brief, but she gave Climène a smile and before releasing her arm she jostled it briefly with an almost rough little shake. I remembered the long lost gesture, and how she had been wont at times to do the same to me, if we had shared a joke, or I had suffered some pain. Then with a return of all her severity and anxious irritation she put the fan in my hand without a word of kindness or farewell, and she left.

When she had gone I think for a moment I was not, in a certain sense, in that room myself. After a while I found that Francis had moved over to one of my tables without a word, and was about to sit down to read a book there. Climène was turned to look out of the window, to hide her sadness. Francis looked up, closed the book he had just opened, and said, "Well, Berthon, let me see that fan."

I gave it to him.

He said, reflectively, "I don't think this will help us."

"No," I agreed. "It would have. But now we have a better mechanism to attack him with. Nevertheless, I'll do as she asked."

"It won't help Theobon either, poor lady," remarked Climène.

"Too late."

"And malicious lying is just a little thing compared to murder." I held out my hand and Francis put the fan into it. Then he and Climène left, and I went straight off in search of Julie de Montausier.

Finding her was no small matter, but I felt that even my legs, for once, had wings of a sort. How many doors I scratched on, only to be told that she was there and not here, or not to be answered at all scarcely mattered. Eventually I found her playing cards with the wife of Monsieur Colbert and a few others.

I then had to prepare myself to wait, because for me to speak to anyone except a small number of friends it was necessary for me to catch the person I needed at a moment when they were detached from others. If just for a moment a man I wanted to speak to went to piss behind a pillar, then I had my opportunity. Or if a lady standing up to leave the room, found herself a few paces before or behind her companions, I could seize my chance to speak to her. I would pronounce her name and bow, and then very often there was time to exchange a few words. Unfortunately I scarcely knew Julie de Montausier.

I waited in the ante-room for upwards of two and a half hours until finally the game broke up and she rose from the table. Even then she stood talking for ten minutes. Apparently it was impossible to tire her; and by my estimate she must have been nearly seventy. Her voice was still high and lively, and she was witty enough to cause several outbursts of laughter. Occasionally she still indulged in those outmoded stresses on certain words and syllables which had characterized the speech of Les Précieuses, of whom she was the leader. As I stood there, my muscles aching and my fingers cramped around that wretched fan, I nevertheless thought the sound of her voice rather musical. For years, apparently, she pretended to be stupid in order to get over the ignominy of having been lampooned by Molière in his production of Les Femmes Savantes. In place of a pretentious display of knowledge she behaved for a while as if she could scarcely read at all. But she didn't keep it up.

At last at last there was a general move of three of the ladies towards the door. None of them noticed me. But I followed them, and in five minutes they separated, de Montausier making for the upper apartments, perhaps to visit the children of Madame de Montespan. I quickened my steps until I caught her up, put myself in her way, bowed and spoke her name. She stopped and drew herself up, as if in affront. She looked the very embodiment of pride and crossness, although she had been pleasant enough all the while when she had been playing cards. "Please excuse me, Madame," I said, "but I have a messages from the Countess de Beauvron."

"Who!" she exclaimed in tone intended to emphasise the extent to which she had dismissed the memory of this one-time friend.

"The Countess de Beauvron has asked me to approach you on a secret matter which might interest you," I said.

Being famously inquisitive and given to gossip, de Montausier could not resist this approach.

"Do you see her then? Often?" she demanded.

"No Madame. But once. Just now. She is very changed."

"Hm."

She continued to look at me, her head tipped, her mouth slightly open. Eventually she took a step or two to one side, where an alcove gave space for two chairs. She sat down with an expression as if her joints hurt her, and said, "Monsieur de Brisse, I think."

I was honoured that she knew my name, and bowed again.

"Well, what is it?" she said impatiently. "Don't be nervous, but please do not spend a great deal of time either. There are things I need to do."

Having said which, I must admit that she listened politely to the account I gave her of Madame de Grancy's role in the conspiracy of Monsieur's friends against his wife and Theobon, and she readily understood the importance of the fan as evidence of this. I could see at once that she liked the idea of being able to present something so damaging to the reputation of Mme. de Grancy for the attention of the King and Monsieur. The Grancy would be incriminated and punished, and no doubt in her imagination she anticipated that, and she smiled at the prospect and held out her hand. I gave it to her.

"By the way," she added, getting painfully to her feet. Once up, she composed herself very well. "Who retrieved this fan – this message – from Lorraine's keeping? Because I see that it is written to him. Did you steal it?"

This annoyed me. The assumption that the body and the spirit are so locked together that a bend in the one must be reciprocated by a twist in the other is infuriating to a cripple. I said that the Countess de Beauvron had bought it from a servant of Madame de Grancy in all honesty. I must have spoken in a tone which betrayed her offense, however slightly, because the old lady took the hint. With a tiny inclination of her head, which was, I suppose, all that someone of her age and eminence owed to a mere boy, she turned her back on me and walked away.

There was a lamentable sequel to this which came some while later, but I will mention it now. I left Julie de Montausier to get on with the business agreed for several days, after which I became restless. Besides, I received so many urgent letters from the Countess de Beauvron. I went back to Madame de Montausier again. That is to say, I had as much trouble finding her as before. When at last I ran her to ground she escaped me. Eventually, after having avoided me until well into the afternoon of the day I made it clear that I was seeking her, she sent word that I was to go to her apartment. I went. As soon as I scratched on the door it was opened. She was standing near the chimney-piece and turned to me with a mocking sort of air, and frowned. I could see that she had something unpleasant to say, and having bowed, I merely waited.

My apparent calm produced an impulse towards meanness in her. She looked at me as if I had transgressed in some way so as to thoroughly disappoint her. This is often a device used by those who intend to do the same themselves. She said, "Well, I am afraid I sold it."

Pausing an instant to see how I reacted, she went on, "It couldn't be helped. I had very bad luck at cards. Monsieur Chalumeau took five hundred livres off me. Five hundred!"

The pose she struck and the expression on her face would have been appropriate to a general announcing how many of his men had been killed in a battle which had nevertheless ended in victory; a mixture of vanity and ruthlessness. And so here came the coup de grace. "I pay my gambling debts," she said with an air of pride, as if laying claim to something honourable. "You would not think it right if I did anything else. And so I was obliged to sell that fan. I sold it to the Chevalier de

Lorraine. I certainly could not bring myself to bargain with that cheating woman. I dare say you are sorry."

But I must return to the sequence of my story. Having given the fan to Madame de Montaussier, I went back to my apartment. The passages were very dark, and of course I had avoided Ernst, who was getting tired of following me everywhere. I thought of calling for a servant to light me, paused, started at a shadow, saw no one and went on. My thoughts dwelt now on the assasin's knife and now on my regret, my pity for Theobon and that wretched fan. When at last I was nearing my own appartment I saw at once from a distance, that the door was not quite closed. I speeded my step as much as I could, and as I threw the door wide I found the room was strewn with papers, books, pictures thrown on the ground, furniture overturned. And in the midst of it, Gaudet lying in a pool of blood on the floor. Now, that was something to be sorry about.

CHAPTER FORTY-FOUR

The sight of Gaudet, of his hand lying in his own gore, his hair, which was normally a light brown colour, soaked in that disgusting blood that I had recently hated the very existence of when Bonhomme lay dying, had an extraordinary effect on me. I experienced a moment during which my senses dragged at my intestines, like a man trying to vomit from an empty stomach, and then I must have fallen on the ground. When, some time later, I recovered my senses, I thought at first that I had been asleep until I realized the floor boards were under my arm. Then I remembered very quickly what had happened, began to shout, and found Clement Cardinale gripping me by the arms. As soon as I was in any way upright I looked for Gaudet, but before I could ask after him Ernst strode in with that unmistakable clatter of steel which accompanied him everywhere, and said that my servant was already laid out on my own bed.

"Is he dead?" I demanded.

Apparently not. I went in there, and Gaudet tried to rise as soon as he saw me, apologizing for finding himself in my place, but I quieted him, and made him lie down again. He had one knife wound in the shoulder, and had hit his own head when he fell. And now at last I began to notice again the state of my furniture and hangings. All split, turned over, ransacked. I needed no explanation. I could see for myself what had happened. Lorraine had sent men to search for the treasure I had brought back from Italy.

You may wonder why Ernst had not been in his usual place, or Clement or any of the others. One of His Majesty's regular reviews had kept them all on parade. I knew it myself before ever I went in search of Julie de Montausier, but paid no particular attention, and had even relished the absence of a guard for myself. Now that I am older I can take the time to notice how extraordinary it is that a man, even one fashioned as I am, springs out of his mother's very womb with all the vanity so familiar to male creatures everywhere, so that I had even relished, to some extent, those incidents when I had had to use what physical strength I had to defend myself. But now I began to feel grateful for the protection of Ernst and his friends in a rather different way, since it was so obviously necessary. After this I was no longer impatient when the scabbard of Clement's sword hit the chair leg when he bent down to retrieve a couple of books from the floor. He had probably saved Gaudet's life, because Lorraine's messengers intended to force the truth out of him and not to stop until he had disclosed the hiding place. Neither did that surprise me when I thought more carefully about it. In Lorraine's shoes I would probably do the same myself.

Francis came in through the door at that moment with Climène. My sister seemed rather pleased with what she saw. She bared her teeth with a smile and said something rather rude about the Chevalier de Lorraine which was nevertheless admiring. As she was incapable of displeasing Francis he took no notice of the way she ended her sentence, but simply found, with admirable dexterity, where a bottle of wine had rolled against a chest, and he drew the cork and poured us all a glass. I was still sitting where Clement had put me. As soon as I had drunk some wine I felt extremely well, utterly comfortable in the companionship of my friends, and triumphant to be alive myself with Gaudet only slightly wounded. I decided to get up at once and go to attend upon Madame and tell her that it was too dangerous to wait any longer for Monsieur to recover from his cold; if he was still indisposed, we should manage without him. But when I stood up I nearly fell again. Francis sent Ernst to Madame, and with Clement's help made me walk to his own apartment where I lay down on his bed until I was sober again.

I woke to find Ernst sitting beside me. It was dark. A branch of candles on a table nearby flickered because Ernst was forever opening windows. He was sitting with his arms folded and his head dropped forward on his chest. I still remembered that straight blond hair lying on the pillow that he had wet with his tears as a small boy. I still remembered how grateful I had been because he wished to have me as a friend, and although as he grew up he showed such an unhealthy interest in sport and such an indifference towards poetry, I tolerated these defects in return for the way he had seemed so blind to my own. These were the thoughts I had squinting up at him, unwilling to move in case I woke him. I wondered what on earth I should do other than stay where I was. Gaudet, presumably, would be still in my bed.

I looked around as well as I could without moving too much. The room was a small one, opening off another. The scarlet and blue colours of tapestry showed muted by the shadows. Some silver glinted over by the chimney and, as my eyes became sharper, the woven straw sides of a well carved chair; or two. I was about to waken Ernst and say that I would go back to my own bed, but I must have fallen asleep again, because the next time I opened my eyes it was morning.

I told Ernst of my decision to wait upon Madame, and he sent his own servant to help me dress. Gaudet meanwhile had been attended to, and was asleep, so he could not be asked where any items of clothing were, or where the shoes with the kid frogging had been laid. It was a tedious business, but I was ready at last and set off with Ernst beside me.

Madame was busy writing letters. One of her ladies asked permission for me to approach, and when I came forward Madame finished a line with something of a flourish and said, "There now! That is the second time this week I have written to the Duchess of Hanover."

There was a huge bundle of paper beside her which was nearly upset by Charmille trying to stand up in Madame's lap, her paws slipping on the silk and her little excited snuffles and squeaks. Madame stifled her with one expert hand while holding the other out to me with a lovely smile, saying, "I hope you have some news for me. Marly was very dull, and our return being delayed by my poor husband's cold has made me mad with impatience, considering our business here. What has happened?"

I told her about the would-be thieves and murderers who had ransacked my apartment and come close to killing poor Gaudet. Madame was incensed, but also excited and even triumphant. "Lorraine!" she exclaimed. "Did I not tell you how ruthless he would be." She smiled delightedly, and said, "You see, he is afraid. You will have him, my clever goblin! But let us not give him any more time. He is too dangerous. I will persuade Monsieur that his cold is over now, and tomorrow we will follow our plan."

The next morning Monsieur was out of humour, but he no longer kept his room. There was some other cause for his mood. His close friends knew what it was, but Madame had no idea. I think some amour of an unmentionable sort was at the root of it. Towards mid day he walked in the garden and shortly came, accompanied by Madame and others, including Monsieur d'Effiat, Elizabeth de Grancy and Madame Gordon, into Madame's drawing room to take chocolate as usual. This was the occasion we had been waiting for. It was even a similar day to that other one when Monsieur had walked in the garden with Minette, and not Elizabeth Charlotte of the Palatine. The roses were not yet in full bloom, but the sun was shining. When the procession entered the drawing room I already stood motionless in my accustomed place and watched them. I saw Francis and Climène also in attendance, and Ernst in court dress by the door. I wonder, now, if their hearts were all beating as fast as mine. If so, they dissembled as well as I did.

At first the Chevalier de Lorraine was missing. I looked for him anxiously in vain. It would not do at all for him to be absent. Monsieur told the footman to bring chocolate at which point, to my relief, the Chevalier appeared late, with the lady who Madame called Dou Dou. This unfortunate individual had been tormented recently by her husband in a way that scandalised the whole Court and very much upset her. I was intrigued to notice how gentle and charming the Chevalier was to her. He seemed to feel sympathy for her, if such an emotion really found place in such a black heart, and his manner in expressing it was the height of grace. He took up a position in the room not far from her and, fortuitously, quite near myself, and was about to accept a cup from one footman which another was waiting to fill with chocolate.

At this point I, who was watching for my cue, stepped out and took hold of his cup before he had a chance to do so. I did this very calmly, but even so the unusual event of my appearing at all drew the attention of the company. I merely said, "Excuse me, Chevalier, but let me clean your cup. I see that there is a smudge on it."

I should say that like my arms, my voice was developed out of all proportion with the rest of me, so that I sounded like a normal man. Indeed, perhaps even a strong one. And since I managed to be very calm, no one stopped me getting the cup into my hand. I had a piece of ordinary paper ready, but of course a man who knew about the poisoned version would not have been sure of the difference, and with this, giving the business all the careful attention which might seem to be appropriate, I carefully wiped the cup and set it back in place. The footman then filled it and passed on.

Monsieur did not know what to make of this. I saw that Elizabeth de Grancy's face had gone red. And Monsieur d'Effiat had his hand on his sword. Monsieur was about to say something, but Madame de Vieuville chose that moment to compliment him on a new buckle, and Madame took up her part excellently by saying that it had been sent to her from Germany and if Monsieur wanted another, she had already told him that she could get a second to the same design, but with rubies instead of diamonds.

MALICE

This kind of debate was irresistible to Monsieur and he was led, by way of silk stockings and new patterns in brocade from Sicily, to a mention of myself as a recent traveller in Italy. Monsieur was so interested to hear about the latest fashions there that he condescended to question me, and I made sure to mention Genoa and Lucca. All this while the Chevalier de Lorraine was silent. He listened to the answers which I gave to Monsieur and I was sure that the mention of Lucca was not wasted on him. And he did not drink his chocolate.

When Monsieur stopped speaking to me and turned his attention elsewhere, I turned to face Lorraine. I said to him in a very quiet voice, "Chevalier, I observe you do not drink your chocolate and indeed I think that I might refrain myself if I knew that anyone in the room had recently returned from the monastery of Santo Stephano."

He said nothing.

"I will await you in my apartment at four this afternoon," I said, and with that I bowed and retired from the room. I think the Chevalier de Lorraine would have run after me on the spot, but Monsieur detained him.

In my apartment I had ready a copy of the letter which I had given to the Maréchale de Clerembault for safe keeping, and one piece of the poisoned paper, wrapped in oiled cloth. Ernst called the guard from the door and I gave him four letters. They were addressed to the Chevalier de Lorraine, Monsieur d'Effiat, Madame Gordon and Madame de Grancy, requesting in each case that they honour me with their presence. I guessed that the Chevalier would come anyway, but we wanted them all, and that they should know that they were expected.

It was now half an hour past midday and I had named the hour of four in the afternoon to the *cabale*. In the meantime there was one matter which pressed hard against my peace, and this was the safety of Fanette. I could not get the idea out of my head that Lorraine, suspecting that by the evening of that day I should have caught him and his accomplices like rats in a trap, might use the intervening time to harm my mistress. He was subtle enough to judge the feelings of someone like myself at their true value. He could strike the first blow while he was still free, and put a curse on my life which I would never get away from.

At first I thought I would go to her myself, taking Ernst with me. But Francis, when I sought him out, advised against it. He said that I would be followed, and my very attention to her safety would be the cause of her destruction. He begged me so earnestly to take another course that I agreed.

"But I must do something," I said, "and now, this minute. I am certain something is wrong. Believe me, I know it. There is no time to argue. "

The truth was that until the scene in Madame's drawing room had been played out, and I had dispatched the letters, the image of Fanette had been wiped clean from my mind. But the moment these things were done I encountered a sudden and appalling fear like a man who turns a corner on a narrow road and sees the way in front of him barred by an animal from hell. In fact I was in such obvious distress that Ernst left immediately to fetch two others and promised to be in Versailles village and knocking at Fanette's door within the hour. I wrote a message to my mistress begging her to stay at home and be guarded by them. And then I went with Francis and Climène to instruct his servant to fetch food from the kitchens, and have it prepared in my apartment. It took my mind off my anxiety to make these arrangements for our comfort. The disorder created by the would-be thieves and murderers of the day before had been set right again, and I had the table with a fine cloth on it, a picture in a carved frame by Veronese which I had brought back from Italy, my chair that I described to you, and several others, besides some fine rugs bought from Fanette's blackamoor.

I have not mentioned everything, of course, but I want to convey some idea of the degree of comfort and some elegance that my apartment had now, together with the fact that I felt, on looking at it, that it also had the air of a stage, set for an event; which it was.

The enemies of Madame would find me, when they came as I was sure they would, with my friends. They would find me supported and not appearing in such a way as to possibly tempt them into efforts of resistance. I thought there was a good chance that by the evening Lorraine and his infamous cronies would be like four serpents whose forked tongues had been removed.

Gaudet returned, and was well enough to help in serving the food and the wine, and Ernst, having left three armed men guarding Fanette, returned himself. The four of us had an excellent meal together, and passed the time in such a way that we could wait for our enemies in a way that increased our pride and strength instead of whittling it away.

To confront four rich and powerful members of the Court, and to successfully disarm them from the injuries that they constantly offered to Madame was a distinction we each coveted, although perhaps I more than any one.

The hour came and went when we could have expected their arrival. If I began to feel nervous in case they should not come, Francis said at once that, in truth, they had to come. They knew that I had found out about the poison used to kill the first Madame, and they knew that I had been in Italy. They would not dare to do nothing. However much they hated the thought of it, having failed to kill me on my road back to Paris they must bargain with me now.

The hour passed when they should have appeared. And another. The dishes had long been removed, and we played cards so that the time went without wearying us, and also without Ernst becoming too drunk. I should have known that Lorraine would wring the last drops of any opportunity to annoy and provoke his enemies out of the situation, and merely to keep us waiting was a simple enough trick.

At last there was a sound of laughter in the corridor, and then a scratch on the door which Gaudet instantly opened to admit all four of our missing guests. They appeared to be laughing among themselves as if they had no cares in the world, although this private joke of theirs was not to be shared. Lorraine even made some remark as he crossed the threshold of the room over his shoulder to d'Effiat referring to the King in some complimentary style *vis-a-vis* himself.

He then stopped and looked around him. The expression on his handsome face was open and as if at ease. As yet, only one rather sardonic line was etched on his face by the spiteful workings of his inner spirit, and that was even rather attractive. D'Effiat you could believe to be evil by looking at him, but not Lorraine. They noticed the presence of Lord and Lady Claydon, Ernst and Clément, with haughty bows and d'Effiat whispered something.

"Well, here we are," said Madame Gordon. "Must we stand, then?"

Gaudet immediately set a chair for her, and drew out another for Elizabeth de Grancy, who looked to be in a complete rage. The men all stood.

"Monsieur de Brisse," Lorraine said.

If you remember, he called me Thing when I was a boy, and it was a custom that he had never changed until now.

I bowed.

"Well then, speak up. What is this all about?"

"Chevalier," I said, "It is about the fact that you, probably with the help of these three friends but keeping the matter secret from Monsieur, murdered the first Madame d'Orléans, Henriette of England."

They were all prepared for it of course. Lorraine said nothing. He pursed his lips a little, raised his brows, looked to one side at nothing in particular and then, with his eyes contemptuously on the ground said,

"And what is that to you?"

The other three were silent, until Elizabeth de Grancy broke the spell by snapping at Gaudet, "Bring me some wine!"

"I have proof of it," I said. "But above all I and my friends resent the lies and the discourtesies and the slander with which you continually attempt to ruin the happiness of Monsieur's second wife as you did the first. We wish you to know that we will no longer tolerate any interference between her and her husband or other unkindness of any sort."

Madame Gordon let out a brief shrill laugh, but D'Effiat bit the inside of his cheek, and then suddenly, unable to repress it a moment longer, spat out the words, "You cur!"

The Gordon sprang up.

"You are indeed the most lamentable little dog of a man. How dare you call us here. Here! Look at it. You were brought to this Court dressed in rags. You smelled. I remember it." She laughed again. "Oh yes. Across the entire ball room. His Majesty called for pomade after you had gone." She felt Lorraine's restraining hand which he had settled, as if absent mindedly, on her arm. "I will not be silent," she protested. "I'd sooner die than bargain with this object." And she spat furiously on the floor. I swear I almost looked to see whether or not her spittle would burn a hole in the boards.

Her outburst made Lorraine even more elegant and thoughtful. She was in such a rage that when she had finished her tirade she spun round and stood with her back turned to the company; but she did not leave the room, and some time later she sat down again where she had been before.

"You had better tell us," Lorraine said. And he had the insolence to half turn and dismiss my servant and that of Francis, both of whom left the apartment. When the door was closed behind them he gave me my cue, as it were, with a look that was composed in a most deadly manner, but full of hatred.

"I have been to Italy," I said, "and I have spoken to Morel."

"Who is he, I should like to know," the Gordon interjected with rage. But she was ignored. Lorraine knew well enough.

"I have here a confession from Morel," I said. "Please read it. It is only a copy of the letter, the original of which is securely held elsewhere." I handed it to Lorraine. He set his teeth as he read it.

"You see how it describes your meeting with him, how much you paid, and what he provided. He gave you paper impregnated with a poison so deadly that if it was used to wipe over an object – for example, a chocolate cup – and someone then set their lips to that surface, they would die in great agony within two hours. There would be a number of symptoms that might mislead a doctor anxious to discount the use of poison; for example, the spleen would rupture."

Madame Gordon's face went very pale. She had been the lady in waiting to Minette, and was brought with her from her native land, which was Scotland. No unkindness from her mistress had provoked this attack. Only jealousy and ambition.

"M. d'Effiat was known to have been alone in Madame's room before she and Monsieur and other friends returned to drink chocolate there, and it is known that he wiped her cup with a piece of paper. But no one gave much importance to that fact because they did not know the paper was poisoned. They will know that now, if I choose to tell them."

"And how will you prove it?" said d'Effiat, his voice absolutely distorted with venom.

"Tell us that!"

"Very simply. Here is the confession from the monk. And here is a sample of the paper."

I indicated where I had laid it out on a small table. "And here is the confession which I desire you to sign."

"What!"

D'Effiat walked over to it. With one hand on the hilt of his sword he looked at all three. How could I ever have thought there was any resemblance between him and Bonhomme? The sneer so deeply etched on his cheek and under his eye was a parody of Bonhomme's uneasy look which for him time and friendship had in the end eliminated. This other man was cruel. And cowardly.

"Lorraine," he said, "who is to say that this is not simply a piece of paper. Look at it."

"Try it," I said. "Touch it, and then lick your finger."

He glared at me, his skin tinged with bile, but Lorraine saved him by saying, "Don't be a fool," as if only that command from a friend would have held him back.

There was a long interval of silence. Lorraine passed the copy of Morel's confession to Elizabeth de Grancy. Then he said,

"What will the King have to say when you accuse his brother?"

"I do not accuse his brother," I replied. "You did not take Monsieur into your confidence, and I know it. On the contrary, were he to know of your guilt even he would not attempt to save you."

Looks were exchanged between them. And silence. D'Effiat began to bite one of his nails. The Gordon got up and whispered something in Lorraine's ear. I and my friends merely waited.

At last Lorraine said in a contemptuous tone, "I presume you want money."

When I said no, he said, "How then, do you want us to – " and he paused, to give the bitterest emphasis to the word, "to buy your silence? I recognise that money is not the only currency that the vulgar sneak will deal in."

"Do not have the misfortune, Monsieur," I said, "to convince me that you positively lack the means of paying, since the currency as you call it, in this case is honour; and courteous behaviour to Madame, the present wife of the King's brother."

I had the satisfaction of registering a cut, because a small shock touched his face leaving a faint colour behind it.

Francis, who had said absolutely nothing throughout, smiled. Since Lorraine now waited for me to explain, I did, with the greatest care, draw a picture for him, and for d'Effiat and for Madame Gordon and for Mademoiselle de Grancy of what their behaviour had to be towards Madame in future. How they must refrain from discourtesy, from injuring her reputation, from urging Monsieur to dislike his wife. I explained that if any harm were to come to myself or any of my three friends who were present, or to my mistress, who I now named, the others would know who to blame and all four of us knew how to access the evidence that, once shown to the King and Monsieur, would be the end, for Lorraine himself and his friends, of any life at Court, and indeed probably life itself.

Lorraine knew this. It was not a matter of speculation. He knew very well his life would be at an end, and so did the others. Looking at him myself, I knew it. I think never since has my body, my spirit, so utterly mastered every shade of meaning, every trembling hair, every trace of moisture on a lip or suppressed fire of rage in the eye, as did mine as I stood between these vicious companions. When I spoke of the likely reaction of the King and the absolute certainty that a sentence of death would be enacted against Lorraine and at least imprisonment followed by exile for the other three, the two women at last began to look cowed, and mixed with the angry misery on de Grancy's face there was, I swear, a tear. She, who could not weep for anybody else, still had some pity left for herself.

"So these are your terms!" Lorraine said. D'Effiat merely bit his lip.

"Very well," turning on his heel to pass his eye over the two ladies, "we agree," said Lorraine.

"Monsieur," I said. "I also require you to sign this confession."

D'Effiat sprung forward and said, "Don't!" But Lorraine ignored him.

He signed the paper. I took it. I examined the signature that we had all watched him set to the confession. Francis and Ernst witnessed it, but so also was d'Effiat forced to do.

"I must remind you all," I said, "that we four will exact the highest standard of courtesy towards Madame. If we find that in the future we have a complaint, we will ask you to meet us again, and if you fail the result will be what it would have been this time, had you not come here in response to my request."

At that, Lorraine waited a moment and then he smiled at me. With an air of friendship, and indeed, sweetness. I was taken aback.

"Monsieur de Brisse," he said, "When I have to be pleasant, I know how to do it." And with that he bowed, and in succession his three friends followed him out of the room.

As soon as they were gone, Ernst said, "I'm not sure, Berthon, that you have made the right decision. Should you not have given this evidence to the King now, and got rid of these people altogether? A snake that is dead is surely safer than one that has promised not to bite any more."

I looked at the door that had closed behind our enemies. And fleetingly, I was aware of the awful power of vanity to tempt a man, even like myself. Why else had I not given this evidence to the King? I told Francis that we could not risk the possibility – however remote – that His Majesty might pardon Lorraine. But I had also wanted this moment for myself. This man had humiliated and tormented Madame time and again. Now with my own hand I had wiped the smile if not from his lips, then from his heart. Let him suffer, knowing that it was I who had defeated him, and that there was not one courtier at Versailles who would not laugh if they knew it. And there was no way he could escape from this with his life. So my heart sang.